"ONCE I STARTED READING GUS LEE'S BOOK, I COULDN'T PUT IT DOWN. I WAS SPELLBOUND.

As with Gus Lee's other books, this one has the kind of passion that can break your heart.... A fast-paced story with suspense, heart, and redemption."

—AMY TAN

"[A] provocative, disquieting look at the criminal justice system and the incubatory mean streets that feed it... Lee's characters sparkle; his dialogue is sharp, his observations tart.... Lee, a former district attorney, moves the narrative convincingly between the courtroom (where justice is possible) and the streets (where it barely rises to a theory). Jin's effort to coax speech from the mute Rachel is especially good, as is the courtroom sparring between Stacy August's well-heeled defense conglomerate and Jin's skeletal prosecution team.... What elevates the book to the next level is the out-of-court action.... If you like your investigations by the Sgt. Joe Friday book, or your courtroom endings Perry Mason tidy, *No Physical Evidence* isn't for you. With Gus Lee, convention is strictly for Shriners."

—*The Washington Post*

*Please turn the page
for more reviews....*

"A FAST-PACED LEGAL THRILLER THAT WILL KEEP READERS TENSE AND GUESSING."
—*Library Journal*

"[Lee] writes in touching detail about Jin's grief over the death of his daughter. Lee, who himself lost a young daughter to heart disease, captures the volatile array of emotions felt by surviving parents. His tone can be angry and cruel one moment, soft and introspective the next."
—*San Francisco Chronicle*

"The prose is passionate and jazzy, and the issue of sex crimes against children is chillingly framed."
—*Chicago Tribune*

"[Lee's] trial scenes, as one would expect, are convincing, and like Jin, he lost a young daughter to heart disease. He even broke down and cried in court once, which explains why *No Physical Evidence* is so moving—Lee makes it clear that he has lived his character's pain."
—*The Orlando Sentinel*

"POWERFUL . . . IRRESISTIBLE . . .
Lees' book is so well crafted, with so compelling a story, it's impossible to put it down for longer than it takes to check the mail or answer a phone call. . . . There's little predictable about the tale. Just when you think you know where this is going, it takes another turn. . . . Those who liked Lee's previous books—*China Boy*, *Honor and Duty*, and *Tiger's Tail*—will love this one. . . . It's his best-written and most approachable novel yet."
—*Colorado Springs Gazette*

"[*No Physical Evidence* is] set in a richly atmospheric Chinese-American Sacramento . . . Enriched by passionate pleading for the protection of children."
—*Kirkus Reviews*

"A rich premise here, mixing together Chinese life and American legal practice, political realities and private grief. He obviously knows his way around a courtroom: Jin's efforts to select, then romance, the jury read like a primer on trial practice."
—*Publishers Weekly*

By Gus Lee:

CHINA BOY
HONOR AND DUTY*
TIGER'S TAIL*
NO PHYSICAL EVIDENCE*

*Published by Ivy Books

Books published by The Ballantine Publishing Group
are available at quantity discounts on bulk purchases
for premium, educational, fund-raising, and special
sales use. For details, please call 1-800-733-3000.

NO PHYSICAL EVIDENCE

Gus Lee

IVY BOOKS • NEW YORK

To Jessica Michelle Lee, our firstborn, and to Rachel

A Ballantine Book
Published by The Ballantine Publishing Group
Copyright © 1998 by Gus Lee

All rights reserved under International and Pan-American Copyright Conventions. Published in the United States by The Ballantine Publishing Group, a division of Random House, Inc., New York, and simultaneously in Canada by Random House of Canada Limited, Toronto.

Ballantine and colophon are registered trademarks of Random House, Inc.

www.randomhouse.com/BB/

Library of Congress Catalog Card Number: 99-094420

ISBN 0-8041-1779-9

Manufactured in the United States of America

First Hardcover Edition: September 1998
First Mass Market Edition: March 2000

10 9 8 7 6 5 4 3 2 1

Acknowledgments

To Diane, for everything, and for happily remembering more about my trials than I did. To Jena and Eric, joy of our lives, for blessedly being who they are. To my sisters and the greater family for their warm support, and to Dad, who spent his American half-century as an ardent admirer of the Constitution and Perry Mason.

To all my former colleagues in the District Attorney's Office for Sacramento County. Special thanks to Deputy District Attorneys Robin Shakely and John Goldthorpe for their help and their keeping the faith. Appreciation to Deputy Attorney General Steve Perkins. To my former CDAA staff and faculty colleagues, with special thanks to the Sexual Assault Prosecution Committee, whose research, teaching, and writing have well served public safety, law enforcement competence, and victim recovery. To Steve Brown the storyteller, and to Janet Fletcher, for their help with the manuscript.

To Jane Dystel, friend and agent, and her brilliant VP, Miriam Goderich, my friends and allies. To my editor, Leona Nevler, for the pleasure of her company, the strength of her insights, and the benefits of her wisdom. To my publisher, Linda Grey, for her faith.

To Amy Tan, whose magical, literary voice opened all doors and made my present work possible, and to her mother, Daisy, for many kindnesses. To Charlie Murray, USMA '62, for years of good advice. To the USMA Class of '68 and my brethren and siblings of Company A, 3rd Regiment, USCC, past and present, and to Major General Robert "Moon" Beahm and William Joe "Meatball" Higgins, '68, who, with a grin, know why. With thanks to my other writing partner, Lee Mendelson.

To Herb Rosenthal, Diane Yu, and Mark Harris, for keeping the flame. To the American Heart Association and Parents with Heart, for selfless work.

With deep gratitude to my covenant brothers, Frank Ramirez, Barry Shiller, Rev. Paul Watermulder, Paul Benchener, Bob Laird, Tom Baker, and Ike Elliott, who know, as I, where all thanks are due.

F=FEMALE   M=MALE   sp=SPOUSE
7 females 5 males / 11 parents 3 divorced / 7 Democrats / 4 Republicans / 1 Independent

9	10	11	12
F Richards	**F Carlo**	**M Richeson**	**M Hendrix**
peds RN	sec'y	equip opertr	roofer
Divorced	Divorced	sp: UPS driver	sp: store clerk
dtr 12	sons 5, 7, 10	son 13	sons 16, 23
Republican	Democrat	Independent	Republican
MOTHER†*	MOTHER†	FATHER	FATHER
OK	PEREMPTRY	OK	OK

5	6	7	8
F Sobol	**F Wolstoncroft**	**F Takahashi**	**M Bukust**
Legis aide	homemaker	store clerk	truck driver
sp: lawyer	sp: engineer	sp: CPA	Divorced
son 14	dtr 8	dtr 6 son 2	sons 2, 4, 7, 9
Democrat	Democrat	Democrat	Republican
MOTHER	MOTHER*	MOTHER*	FATHER†
OK	OK	CHALLENGE	CHALLENGE

1	2	3	4
M Clayton	**M Goin**	**F Burda**	**F Becerril**
rad stn mgr	meter man	pic framer	dental tech
sp: minister	Single	sp: artist	Divorced
sons 4, 8, 9	0 kids	dtr 9	dtr 7
Democrat	Republican	Democrat	Democrat
FATHER	0 KIDS	MOTHER*	MOTHER†*
QUEST'BLE	PEREMPTRY	OK	OK

[RESERVE JURORS]

13	14		
M Machida	**F Ford**		
firefighter	teacher		
sp: broker	sp: dental tech		
son 20	dtr 26		
Republican	Democrat		
FATHER	MOTHER*		
OK	OK	***HAS A DAUGHTER / † DIVORCED**	

PROLOGUE

A sultry evening wind stirred trees and made old newspapers cavort down back alleys. Street dogs growled at shadows, and Metro cops knew that something was coming their way.

Sergeant William McManus trailed a tan Cutlass Supreme into brick-cobbled Old Town. Near Fat City Café, the Cutlass slowed, its four male, watch-capped passengers checking out dangling purses in the festive summer boardwalk crowds. The Cee Supreme was the most popular U.S. car for auto theft. McManus ran the plates, but they came back clean.

Sergeant McManus was a compact man with sharp eyes, good teeth, and a nose for trouble. He nodded; his partner unlocked the riot gun and called for backup. But the Cutlass accelerated past the overflowing bars and restaurants and headed for center city. McManus had no probable cause to turn on the lights. He followed, waiting to make a solid stop.

A mile away, in a modernist steel downtown café bar for lawyers and lobbyists called A Shot of Class, a svelte woman in red opened the door, admitting a warm night wind that made the air conditioner huff. Table candles flickered and the barman sensed something in the warning breeze. He retrieved a concealed Colt automatic and slipped it in his pocket.

The piano player was doing "Perfidia" while Thomas Andrew Conover III held night court for the faithful, the curious, and the thirsty. Conover casually checked out the woman in red. It had been a good press week for the District Attorney. Some columnists loved Tommy's rugged good looks, his history as a boxer, his robust optimism. But slam-dunk ballot box wins were news-killers and most journalists would welcome a

Conover disaster, something dark and insidious that would make the smug election a contest and drive citizens to their newspapers.

Her red dress slid on black leather, a trim hip touching Tommy with a soft, electric contact that made him think that somehow he knew her. But Tom was tiredly forgetful, dangerously unattached, and warm with drink.

"Yo!" he called. "Whatever she wants." He removed his coat and loosened his silk tie. In moments, she was considering him over an ice-cold Margarita. Tommy had been relating a long-ago bout. Now he rebegan his account of the fifth round, when he had knocked his opponent's mouthpiece into the cheap seats as the lubricated crowd roared and the enemy corner tossed a torn, pink-stained towel into the ring to a chorus of flash photography.

"Can you still fight?" Her question dilated his best capillaries. She was an advocate of blood sports, games of risk, and late-night shots at catastrophe. Hot lipstick broke the glass's salt rim. Sweet green eyes, heavy black hair, a good chest, a bumpy past.

The Cutlass's torn roof smoothed with the turn into the dead end of Eleventh and the K Street Mall. To the left of the four men was the looming Old Latin gravity of the Cathedral of the Holy Sacrament. Opposite was A Shot of Class, bright, warm, and rhythmic.

Billy McManus didn't like a four-pack of heavies this close to the DA's traditional Friday night watering hole. And Thomas Conover's bodyguard, a bald, spectacularly stupid ex-wrestler named Large Louis, was as useful in these matters as a dead cat in a pool game.

McManus kind of liked the DA, the way cops kind of liked all prosecutors. DAs were a necessary vice—they did the trials that put the bad guys away. But DAs were still lawyers who could bust good cops for overenthusiastic arrests, or publicly crap on the Blues to fatten a lead in the polls in a tight election year. Luckily, there was no sweat; this election was a done deal.

The Cutlass driver saw the trailing police cruiser and smoothly backed out. McManus turned to follow when a woman's bright, bloody cry of terror cut through the warm air. McManus braked, tires smoking toward the mall, giving up the Buick for the scream.

"I can still fight," said Tom with a sly Kevin Costner grin. He turned as a woman's eyewatering shriek jiggled ice cubes and made drinkers inhale mixed drinks. The piano player froze on the keys. Tom, his antenna alerted, looked toward the cathedral.

There, on the steps, an obese man bellowed violently at a woman in a short white dress, making her twist and scream crazily against his strong-armed grip.

With an oath, Tom was up. He knocked over jacketed waiters, small tables, and slow patrons, bulled through a fire door, setting off panic alarms. He stepped into the mall's warm night air, closed the distance, and rocked Obese Man with a huge right cross that induced a brain-rattling loss of memory and consciousness. Tom hauled Obese Man up for a combination encore, and now the woman screamed even louder, damaging local eardrums.

"Christ," assessed Sergeant McManus, exiting his car for the big man who was pounding the snot out of a fat, defenseless citizen. Billy sprinted up and put a hand on the big man's shoulder, tugging firmly. "That's enough, sir," said Billy. "Back off, right now!"

Thomas Andrew Conover III did not like to be touched. Not by men. He spun and punched ten thousand bucks of dental work into Billy McManus's rupturing teeth, following with a hard hook to the head. Billy's knees buckled and he went down. Street dogs scurried into shadows, chased by dismembered pages from yesterday's sports and business sections.

Panting but heavily inspired, Billy's partner blasted his nightstick into the skull of the Honorable Thomas A. Conover III, drawing a small, surprised sigh. The partner proceeded to industriously tenderize Tommy's face with his nightstick, rendering the District Attorney unusually cooperative, instantly unphotogenic, and politically bankrupt.

It was the svelte green-eyed woman in red who came from the bar and managed to stop the animated officer from playing pogo on the big, cop-batterer's head.

My political response time wasn't what it used to be. Assistant chiefs, gawkers, departmental flaks, and the press sensed a disaster and came in droves. Muted cop radios made it sound like a multiple murder scene. The café's panic alarm was still ringing. I felt the hot wind and adjusted my tie, looked into the glaring lights and said something banal about waiting for the results of the investigation. I was being recorded and filmed until the reporters screeched away in pursuit of fresher blood— four men in a tan Cutlass Supreme had hit an Arco station south of downtown, putting two shotgun blasts into a teenaged clerk, whose death was silently pinned on the intoxicated, double-fisted District Attorney.

Tom nursed his wounds silently. Without a public apology for the Incident, DA-cop relations worsened. Cops take disrespect poorly, and the surly edge in our often uneasy partnership soured like milk on a hot summer porch. The Incident angered cops on the street. The Incident had transformed DAs into a clutch of leeches with briefcases. The cops stopped inviting us to key arrests. Vital case data was slow to arrive or simply disappeared. Humor evaporated. The detectives and captains who used to tell me wince-inducing political jokes no longer schmoozed. Our cases suffered a blue fever of indifference or outright sabotage.

"Mr. Jin," asked a Chinese reporter, "you used to be a detective. Why's the Incident causing so much grief between cops and DAs? No one's talking to us. Off the record."

"Off the record, no one hits a cop—not like that. Not if you're the DA. Tom had a defense attorney plead Not Guilty in front of two hundred Blues who came to hear an apology. With that, Tom busted our partnership with the cops. Now we're a public enemy."

"This," she said, "will stir up Chinatown. You know, Mr. Jin, we never liked Tom Conover. The guy's big-time Republican white bread. Only one Chinese liked him. You."

The Incident on the mall was a tonic to Sethman Jergen. Jergen was a defense lawyer running against Conover in November. The Incident put the DA's reelection up for grabs. Gang bangers, meth cookers, child abusers, and Ponzi schemers sent cash to Jergen's coffers, joining in an unholy prayer that Sethman, a casual drug abuser and recreational, unreformed womanizer, would become the chief law enforcement officer in the upper state.

Papers pitching scandal would sell faster than Sno-Cones in

August. The Incident, as all bad news, elevated the media and fertilized the growth of offensive news reporting.

It became newsprint gospel—even between bitterly competitive papers—that the next big murder or rape case the DA tried would be the litmus test for Conover's political survival in November. If the DA lost the litmus test case, he'd lose the election.

Luckily, I wasn't doing trials.

And this time, people who distrusted government—everyone—would vote. Sergeant Billy McManus made the cultural U-turn from street cop to folk hero. Jergen took out commute-route billboard ads on Highway 80 and Interstate 5. Crime rates climbed and conviction rates fell, legal coverage boomed, and cynicism led the charge. Courtesy of our pugilistic DA, Sacramento was throwing a gangbuster political circus with Fellini-like restraint.

Tom shut his door, waiting for the media abuse to subside.

The salsa river wind grew hotter that spring, wafting under closed doors and through sealed windows, changing the political atmosphere in local government buildings. Metro cops tightened their equipment belts. The air carried a scent of rot and distant thunderstorms.

I knew that wind. Death had been on my trail, and I had begun to take it personally. I remember the Incident on the mall, and the events that pulled me into its wake.

It's not every season that your daughter dies, your wife leaves you, you get demoted, and your boss—the County's senior law enforcement officer and a front-runner for the Governor's office—punches out the teeth of a good cop. The DA had turned our work world upside down. You have to lose a child to know how unimportant that can be.

1.

INTAKE

Monday Morning, May 1

"I hate Mondays," said François Giggin, a grinning, aimlessly happy law intern with four earrings, a nose stud, pricey sandals, and Jesus-soft eyes.

Since my demotion, I liked Mondays. The sun was kind, coffee was strong, insults were amusing, broken furniture had been repaired, and police error was not without comedy. Work was my sanctuary. Everything that went wrong was long anticipated and probably deserved.

François Giggin and I ran Intake—the human filing Dumpster where all of the County's felony arrests come. On Mondays, I decided which of the weekend's killings, hackings, robberies, rapes, drug deals, and burglaries would be prosecuted by the DA, which ought to be reinvestigated by the cops, and which would be dumped. I processed crime, determining what morsels the great digestive apparatus of our criminal justice system could wisely consume.

The weekend had been hot, kindling open-window rapes, burgs, and beer-fueled DUIs. A husband, unremarkably, had killed his wife. A cop's nose had been busted by a feuding couple who learned karate from the Internet. A prowler-fearing citizen had accidentally shot a Jehovah's Witness through his *Watchtower* magazine and his chest, four times.

The radio played the Doors' "Light My Fire" with its circular, repetitive, Middle Eastern mantra. My cramped, downsized Intake office was in police HQ, filled with high cholesterol, low fiber, high-fat pastries, and endless processions of bleeding victims and scowling villains.

"Later, boss," sang François, bouncing to arraignment with

weekend felonies. He was brilliant, pleasant, and diligent, but he had trouble crossing the street.

"Careful," I said as he left.

Coffee mugs exploded on the hallway floor. "Goddamn clumsy asshole DAs!" cursed a detective. Once I thrived on friends and the laughter of cops. Now I was alone and enjoying it. Intake wasn't hard and I was almost done, ready for the void of the day. A knock.

"Hello," I lied. A mob invaded my office, absorbing the limited free space.

"Lunch," explained Isaac Krakow, my best friend. Isaac was a top trial lawyer with the gaze of a casual killer, six kids with expanding appetites and perpetually changing shoe sizes, and a horse that ate a bale of hay three times a week. "You're buying."

"Please, Joshie," said Diane Richardson, the DA's tall, humorous private secretary. For her hair, some women would murder a close friend.

"You've looked better," said Patti Kelly, who had made my earlier successes possible.

I endured her hug. They waited, as if I were about to rip off my shirt and sing an aria. "Let me take a rain check. Try the black-bean *chow fun*." Succulent noodles in a breathtakingly rich sauce that would soften the gallstones of a San Francisco food critic.

They left. I embraced the silence, but my e-mail dripped with social threats. Judge Thackery Niles, to talk me into becoming a judge. Jay Wendell Nobis, the former District Attorney, for reasons unstated. Reverend Joel Frost, for an overgenerous charitable contribution to his ex-con crusade. Colleagues, pitching guilt-driven invitations for lunch.

A bump: François. "Press wanted a sound bite on the DV and Jehovah Witness One-eighty-sevens. I said you were out and referred them to the Chief Deputy. Here's mail, and a confidential memo from De Hoyas. Boss, want some java? Research on that Hell's Angel's warrant quash? I got all the authorities from Lexis. How about tea?" He was chirping. I read.

TO: ALL FELONY TRIAL DEPUTIES
FR: GENEVA DE HOYAS, CHIEF DEPUTY

RE: **CONFIDENTIAL: AFFIDAVITING**
      COSTANZA & WALDO

<u>Judge Shelley Costanza, Department 34/Judge G. Wells Waldo, Department 29</u> have been openly sabotaging People's cases in felony jury trials.

You are therefore authorized, in any jury trial, to affidavit the above judges under §170.6 CCP without prior approval and until further notice. Trials are their new political venue for openly criticizing the District Attorney and his pending case with Sgt. Wm. McManus. As both judges face November reelections, it is presumed they are doing this for votes.

Public opinion was growing against our boss, Tommy Conover. It had spread to the courts. Some judges had decided that torpedoing DA cases would be a political plus. Mortal political cancers, initiated by a crisp right cross on a warm Friday night, were metastasizing.

Affidaviting a judge was a gutsy, last-minute courtroom maneuver in which a trial lawyer swore that his case couldn't be tried fairly by the judge to whom he had been assigned. This won a single change of court. But affidaviting a judge incurred bench resentment and enduring anger for future trials. It was like criticizing your fiancé's father at the rehearsal dinner.

Earrings jangled. I looked up. "So, François, why the self-mutilation?"

"Sick question!" He posed his brilliantly adorned nose. "My steel's metal poetry. Babes have to check it out. Not exactly being Mr. Male Body, it helps." He set down his coffee cup.

I moved it back from the edge. "François, you wearing them when you're a deputy DA?"

"Mr. Jin, you're funny. You wouldn't hire me with nose gear. Third-year law, they're gone." He sat in front of tall stacks of outstanding arrest files, tipping his chair. The legs slipped. "Oops," he decided as I picked up his coffee cup. He crashed heavily backward, flipping the table on himself, the table legs snapping as the room erupted in a sharp explosion of legal debris and randomized, shuffled, floating paper which steadily covered us.

I helped him up. When we restored order, he continued, "Soon, women'll run *it all*. Nose stud says, 'Hey, babes, I'm with *you*.' " He saw my face. "Sorry. I'm outa here."

I went to Rag's, an old fighters' gym. It used to draw lawyers and brokers when boxing had a brief Eighties cachet, but they had left for pricier establishments with lounge juice bars, pumped music, and leotarded women without deep nosebleeds or yellowed, cauliflower ears.

I dropped coins for the panhandlers at the door. I liked Rag's because it had no politics or reminders of my losses. The skip-ropers and speed-baggers stopped. The fighters in the ring backed off, blowing air through pursed lips, watching me warily.

Sal Ragusa stood in my path and motioned at the others. Slowly, with increasing speed, leather again smacked home, gym shoes danced, and men grunted with blows as they industriously sucked the sour air and punched each other with old leather.

"Hey," said Sal, "no more sparrin'. The guys don't get paid 'nuf for you to kill 'em."

I did the math. "They don't get paid anything." My heart was slugging. This was where I worked out my sickness.

An old, pink gummy smile in a leatherneck face, hooded eyes in a fixed long-distance squint. "Hit the bag. Just no ring work. Not a bad idea, *all* you DAs took a time-out on beatin' the crap outa people, am I right?" A chuckle. "Man, Gentleman Tommy sure fucked things up royal by beatin' up that poor cop." He waited, then frowned. "C'mon, man, I'm tryin' for a little grin here. Okay. Fine. Fuck your sensa humor." He grimaced, then dropped his voice.

"Josh, the wife run off? Yeah, I figgered. Aw, crap, it hurts like the burnin' shits at first, but it wears off. You get to like the peace." A crooked rictus on a face God had used for continuous and patient whittling with a sharp knife. Rag rubbed my trapezius, the shoulder muscle that supports high parries and drives deep lateral hooks to the opponent's head.

The two sparrers began to make contact. I flexed my neck, missing the ring.

"Hey, wanna do lunch? Bet the cops ain't takin' you out no more, am I right? I found a fancy-pants Chinese dive over by the Rusty Duck. You're the bigshot lawyer with the headlines and the bucks. And you got a badge that lets you park anywhere. I'll order. You buy."

2.

AVA PASCAL

The echoes of a grand piano. She brushed her hair or read a self-help book and my heart swelled as if she were rising from the bubble bath for me. I kissed her neck and she sighed, or moaned, or told me to go mow the lawn. She was a hard worker, a fabled kisser, a dreamer of happy children, and a firm believer in the kind God who eased the major pains.

We met at a smart party hosted by an acquaintance intent on marrying off strangers. It was when I was still a cop. A jazz quintet played as I headed for the kitchen and someone ran into me. She surveyed her empty plate. On the floor were a corn on the cob and the remains of a salad. On my white linen jacket was a thick red sludge of sliding ravioli.

"Color contrast," I said. "Soon to be the rage."

"I'm so sorry!" She brushed the mess onto her plate. "My fault." Her voice was of the Sirens without the cruel intent. Sometimes a voice can arrest a cop. I was staring.

"I should've seen you coming," I said. I cleaned the floor. She had intelligent eyes, a fine composure, and a no-nonsense body in a black dress. I had a girlfriend awaiting a marriage proposal and felt as if Chinese gods had dropped a stupidity packet in my brain and were adding the hot water. I felt stellar tides, wondering if it was merely hypoglycemia.

"I'll get it cleaned," she was saying, rinsing her hands.

"No need. I would've done it to myself. I'm a messy eater."

"There's messy, and then there's looking like a Cuisinart came after you. Take it off." I gave it to her, deftly removing the gun from my hip, placing it softly in an empty pot.

She was sponging my coat. She looked over a lovely shoulder. "You're Josh Jin. The homicide detective." She said it as if she hoped I were someone else, differently employed.

"And you are—?"

"A little hungry. I just drove here from Sacramento. Your coat's in trouble." She set it on a chair, poured water from a teakettle into the pot that innocently held my gun, turned the heat on high, and pulled out more corn. She put ravioli in the microwave. I recovered the gun, broke out the dripping rounds, and discreetly dried it. I liked her short hair.

"Two minutes." She set the timer, her smile breaking my unsuspecting heart. "I talk to myself. I'm sort of auditory." She listened to the oven.

"I'm visual," I said.

She caught me studying her. "I gather."

We tossed a salad. I optimistically set the table for two. The oven dinged. I delivered her plate and microwaved my ravioli, two minutes. She liked the salad and had no interest in me. My gun was moist and unloaded and the corn boiled in the pot.

My girlfriend and I had been off and on for years, spotted by breakups and other partners. For the first time, we were in synch. I had dropped by this party of strangers for a quick bite, unaware that reheated ravioli could cause the stars to shift.

I considered the woman in black. If I wanted to avoid pain and emotional hard work, I should leave. She was ringing deep and unknown bells in my psyche. The microwave dinged.

We ate like lumberjacks. I tried not to like her too much, but her words were bread crumbs to a deeper sense of self, or her, stimulating curiosity, interest, and focus.

It all became clear. She was smart and she was funny, a warm fire in a cold room. Beautiful eyes, brown, and deep. An oval face and sculpted cheekbones. A precise mouth that was a friend to laughter, competence, dear friends, fast meals, and verbal skills. I could listen to her forever, the sensations defeating memory. I wanted to turn on my field tape recorder, to capture the fleeting golden moments that ran through my mind with bewildering speed.

"What do you do?" I asked. The normal first question, coming, naturally, so late.

"I'm a public defender in the Capital." A smile. "I hate guns and I'm *very* careful with cops. Especially Homicide dicks." Whom she gutted in cross-exam, in trials against the People. She was a direct competitor in the remorseless legal justice food chain. For me, a bad answer.

I felt reckless and wise and a little stupid. "Would you like to bail the party?"

Patting fine lips with a napkin. "I don't date," she said.

Great jumping tea of China, she's married.

"I only see men who are looking for a committed relationship. I hear this is not one of your strengths."

My eyes spun like windows in a slot machine. "How could you know if you wanted a commitment, without dating first?"

"I couldn't possibly. But I wouldn't even *try* to find out, unless the man was also looking for a commitment. He'd be a great father, his career only a part of him. And I could know much of this by just pitching a thorough cross-exam." She looked up.

I felt the need for an accurate and comprehensive response.

She slipped a ten in my stained coat pocket. "Bye."

I didn't even get her name. I was just another slow, food-stained, tongue-tied cop.

She was sipping a San Pellegrino with her date. No, she didn't date, so he was a suitor. My life passed in waves of Taoist superstitions and hopes. Now or never. Never had never seemed so intolerable. Maneuvering by smaller men, I drew grunts.

She was aware of the mob but immune to it. She looked up. Open, unafraid, scary.

"The issue in the kitchen," I said, "can we talk about it?"

"No," said her suitor, "but thanks for asking."

She studied me. "Nice coat. Get in a food fight?"

"I was fiddling with a Cuisinart and it came after me."

She looked in my eyes. I free-fell into hers with her smile, the moment without gravity, greater than us, consuming the room's oxygen. She paused, then got her purse, turning to the suitor. "Thanks for inviting me. Forgive me, I won't need a ride home. And yes, I think it's best."

She retrieved her coat. We separately thanked the hosts.

"Where's Neal?" asked the hostess.

"I just broke up with him," she said.

Outside, I asked, "Are you always this indecisive?"

Her smile depreciated the Mona Lisa. "I'm Ava Pascal."

"Ava Pascal, how do you think we're going to do at this?"

"That depends on you. It's funny how my future could rest on your words."

"Funny like, ha-ha?"

She laughed. "Absolutely ha-ha. You're a cop." Her laugh was an elevator to a small heaven. We were on the Peninsula. I drove north toward the gaudy, green-roofed, Hong Kong–styled Flower Lounge on El Camino where crowds were thick and the food was genuine.

"What's the *worst* thing about you?" she asked happily.

"I have so many choices." I began mentally listing them.

She laughed. "Pick the big one."

"I may not be marriage material."

"Well, that's no revelation. Most men aren't."

"And you reject most men." I stopped for a light. "I have a girlfriend who's expecting me to propose. I'm feeling some pressure to figure out what I'm doing with you."

The Flower Lounge had valet parking and patrons too busy to care if your coat seemed to have been involved in a shooting. The Lounge was bursting with queues of waiting parties, but it was a Chinese restaurant and I was a detective, known in many Chinese establishments.

"Hey, hey, Detective Jin, *neh ho ma?* Window table, face Bay lights, okay?"

"*Dojieh,* Wong *singsong*," I said to the maitre d'.

"Police corruption," said Ava. "Lovely." I loved her refusal to accept anything less than truth. I poured tea. Like a canny cop, she grilled me, allowing breaks so I could gather my wits.

We shared politics and ideals but not faith. We talked as old friends, comfortable with the silences, as if we had time secured by a common future. She focused on my eyes. I told her about my girlfriend. I said I couldn't see two women at the same time.

I returned the ten she had offered to clean my coat. She paid half the tab. We stayed up and drove home separately. She had a two-hour drive on the Interstate back to the Capital.

I was the first Asian she had seen socially. She was the first woman who would not share a bed until I proposed. It was an old Chinese custom: marry me or leave. Ava knew no gray zones. She disliked the color blue, thinking police work too dangerous.

"How about law?" she asked.

"I guess DAs are okay, but I don't like lawyers very much," I said.

She kissed me. "We only have to like two of them."

I was accepted at King Hall School of Law, UC Davis. Davis is a small, charming college town with acres of trees and allergies where Ava had a small house on the west side.

To the shock of her parents and the extravagant relief of my worried mother, we exchanged troths in Chinatown's Methodist Church. Our oaths fell on my old, single, agnostic ways like leaden manna.

Ava was glory and God was nigh. The reception at the Empress was correctly above budget. There were champagne, yellow roses, weightlifting cops in JC Penney suits, sleek power-lunching lawyers with Vuittons, and silked, cheongsamed Chinatown matrons lamenting the loss of a son to the *gwailo*.

"She make beautiful baby," said Ma, clutching Ava with happy tears. I was the only survivor of five pregnancies. Babies, to the Chinese, are the purposes of life.

"I can't wait," I said.

"Umm." Stepfather Kwah feared his grandchildren would look foreign and distrusted Ava's skills in a Chinese kitchen.

I honored him without affection. BaBa, Father, had been a kind laundryman with big, water-soft hands. A heart attack had taken him when I was ten. Mother had remarried for me. Kwah was a bullying, unlucky third-son cook at Yet Wah, full of ginger, garlic, and quick fists. When I left for college, he gave me his benediction: "Keep eye open for damn white devil."

I became a boxer and a cop, quick to protect the small from the big. I had a tenderness for kids and was slow at the stove. I approached marriage as if it were a moody beast, silently blaming my stepfather's rages for any deficiencies in my character.

"Our grandchildren are going to speak Chinese?" hissed Andrew Pascal, partner in a medium-sized Chicago business law firm. Tall, handsome, and worried, sharing my stepfather's concerns. Children of mixed blood, fitting, perhaps, nowhere, cast into eccentric orbits around two separate American tribes with harshly different pasts.

"Hush," said his wife, Anne. She had given Ava her historic cheekbones and impeccable moral courage. "All the better if they do."

"Oh, Mom, yes. God loves us all," Ava caressed the party with her clear voice and bright faith, happiness permeating the sidebars, the side deals, the old family feuds, the gift disputes, the money comparisons, the quiet ethnic tension, the religious fears, the sad drinkers, the teakwood screens. "Our children will be wonderful," she whispered to me, a prayer, I thought, that worked its way through a green-tiled Chinese roof.

I was very happy that day, basking in good fortune, but I thought about *ji hui*, bad luck, the Chinese admonition about openly claiming happiness before its full bloom. It is only safe to speak of good fortune when it is a memory written in old stone. I passed red good-luck-money packets to the children. Anglo children looked at the envelopes in puzzlement. "Candy?"

I winked, the master of the day. "There's good-luck money inside."

Ma's face crinkled with worry for our bright, childish claims on an unknown future. She waved her hands, trying to brush away Ava's words before they reached listening gods. I hugged Ma, feeling her heart's investment in my life, passing to me a precious dividend of hope through her deep dislike of what she considered a dangerous profession.

I thought the strength and passion of our wedding pledge

were too pure to invite Heaven's retribution. They were strong enough to become an immediate and indelible memory, immune from bad fortune.

Later I recalled how Ava and I tempted fate that sunny day.

I should have remembered that death renders the final verdict.

3.

THE HONORABLE DA

Tom Conover was hiring deputies when I graduated from law school. But it was the District Attorney himself, the Honorable Jay Wendell Nobis, who held the last, determinative interview. A household name, he was overweight and reliant on the ancient virtue of muscular honesty. It was the old days, so he asked me an ethics question with but one correct answer.

On a cold November day in his crowded office, next to a tasseled American flag, Mr. Nobis swore me to a high oath. He gave me the seven-pointed gold badge and a fine, fat stogie. "I am genuinely honored," he said, "that you are a part of this honorable organization."

I thanked him, warmed by the wisdom in his old gray eyes. Cameras flashed. Mr. Nobis adjusted the desk photo of his daughter and Ava beamed.

Later, Tommy Conover closed my door and sat on the desk in my gray-steel office. "Jay Wendell's a beautiful guy, but way out of date. He still expects people to say 'sir' to him."

"This morning I said to him, 'Thank you, sir.' "

"Well, you're Chinese. You got that politeness thing."

"Get your damn butt the hell off my desk, right now."

Tommy recoiled into the chair.

"Just kidding," I said politely.

A laugh. "I deserved that. I'm going to run for his job. Nothing personal—I love the guy. But he's had five terms and—this is just you and me talking—he's slipping. A career prosecutor ought to be the DA, not some ACLU freak. I need the Asian vote. Will you campaign for me?"

I clenched. To him, I was five thousand votes in a close race. BaBa would have said, *Xing xing zhi huo ke yi liao yuan.*

A single spark starts a prairie fire.

"That why you hired me? To make political speeches?"

"No. But afterwards I saw the possibilities."

As a detective, I had sought facts, names, and small truths, and had grown accustomed to lies, dumb and flagrant. Tommy, unfortunately, was being honest with me.

"I hired you to be a trial lawyer. You're verbal and quick. You got fire in your gut. You're a boxer. Boxers take pain. They work for small purses. They think the next bout'll be their best. That's being a DA." In different times and towns, Tommy and I had been amateur fighters.

"Speeches scrape on the truth. And friction corrupts." I shook my head. "I hate politics."

"Hey, pal," said Conover, "no one more than me."

I sat back, tired in my new job. "Now, that's a lie."

"But you got to admit, it's hard to fight fate." He offered his hand.

That November, Jay Wendell Nobis lost his office. The Honorable Thomas Andrew Conover III went Upstairs to a sixty mil budget, a Fortunoff silver coffee service, a Sutter Club membership, and a bald pro wrestler bodyguard named Large Louis. He got a black town car with a radio and a riot gun, and a Chinese sidekick with old ears who spent eves as a criminal justice speechmaker on the friction circuit, where there's little justice, but plenty of crime.

Some Monday mornings, savoring the best coffee of the week, I opened my desk drawer and looked at Mr. Nobis's unlit cigar.

I was a rising star, the youngest bureau chief in the office and the object of my wife's admiration. I did well because I had a knack for trials, was careful about the law, and liked people.

But I was too ambitious to decline political patronage, and stupid enough to lose it.

A month ago, only a week after the Incident, I followed a warm rogue wind and asked Conover to do something he couldn't. Everyone knew better but me. Ava would've told me to not do it. But I was as animated as ten Chinese gods, relishing the pleasure of bad judgment and no longer capable of reflective analysis. Cops, my old brothers in blue, were dissing us.

"Don't do it, Josh," warned Patti Kelly, my admin assistant.

Large Louis had selected a comic book and was in the rest room. Tanya Churchill was not in sight. She was a prosecutor who made lean Cassius look chubby and overfed. She coveted my bureau with the drive of a lemming stampede for a cliff. Diane Richardson of the great hair sat at her desk as if at a funeral. "Josh, don't go in—he's not seeing anyone."

"It's okay." I opened his door. Tom's artwork lamp threw a cone of super white light on a newspaper. His face was hidden. I heard a pencil drop on a newspaper. I smelled rye.

"Get the hell out. Now." The words hurt his mouth.

"You mean, 'Come on in, Josh.' Tom, meet with the troops after court today. Apologize for punching out Billy McManus. We're in trouble and only an apology will work. Right now, only the cops hate us. You keep silent, the judges will be next."

Tom turned off the lamp. He had been struggling for a word, six letters down, starting with a d. My eyes adjusted; he was putting the cap on a diminishing bottle of bourbon.

The brooding, humid saloon silence felt like a prelude to violence.

"Apologizing isn't your style," I said. "Do it anyway."

"Fuck you." Tommy was tall with a boxer's bad hands and a squint that came from being hit too many times. Pin-dot shirt collar open, Brioni tie loose. Private coarseness had returned with his public calamity. He had strong, native-blue-collar looks and the rescue mentality that attracted women interested in hardship. Perhaps he regretted his choice of words. "Jesus, what the hell entitles you to be this goddamned stupid?"

"Personally, I blame the years of studying you."

"Once," said Tommy, "you were a funny guy. Hell, maybe we

both were. I'm not real amused. See you around campus. Get the hell out. Now."

"Tom. Tell McManus you're sorry. Get him the state's best oral surgeon. Buy him a subscription to *Novocaine News* and take him out for a Jell-O and cottage cheese dinner."

BAM! His gnarled hand slapped the desk. "HELL NO! An apology would be tantamount to an admission." He spoke slowly, as if to the endemically stupid. "I. Don't. Apologize."

"Tom, this isn't about pride. It's about our mission."

"Don't you *dare* give *me* that burnished bullshit! You bureau chiefs are more afraid of my losing the election than I am. I lose, you're on the street. Jergen'll bring in his own chiefs."

"Take my stinking badge. You're losing floor support."

"I oughta take it! What is this, a threat?"

"A weather forecast from a friend. You used to trust me."

"Yeah, I used to. Back when you could do a jury trial."

I knew that was coming but I still flinched. It had been four months since I'd seen the working end of a criminal jury. The results resembled sad butchery.

"I could be the worst trial lawyer in the shop—you'd *still* have to apologize. Thomas, you used to *hate* politicians. Take a good look, buddy—you've become one of them."

Tom Conover hit his intercom like it was a speed bag, banging off the receiver and driving the phone across the desk, snapping its wire to smash on the floor in the dark room.

Bright rectangled light flooded inward. Chief Deputy Geneva de Hoyas entered. She drew attention in a crowded court. Geneva possessed a superior legal mind, a caustic sense of humor, and an inner projection of raw power. The humor had gone south after Tommy battered the cop. The power remained. Her stylish purple suit matched Tom's beefy bruises.

"Hello, boys." She ran the office, freeing Tom to work media, voters, fund-raisers, and the government. No one questioned her or her judgment. Both were above suspicion.

"Geneva," said Conover, "Josh's bureau is killing him. Transfer him to Intake."

"Jesus, Tom." Geneva looked at him. Exhaling, "Okay."

Intake was a good rotation for a younger deputy. I had done

Intake when President Reagan released institutionalized mental patients into the streets, choking lower criminal courts with vagrants confused by acute psychotropic medication withdrawals. No—not that long ago; it just seemed that way. The Intake deputy was a liaison to the cops, who now would give me no credit for being a former detective. To them, I was working for Saddam Hussein.

I had just lost my bureau. Patti Kelly would now work for the next throat-grabbing ladder-climbing deputy DA. I had lost her, six trial teams, forty prosecutors, twelve investigators, twenty secretaries, fifteen interns, and an excellent parking place under a tall oak tree.

Intake had a staff of one, a court runner. A brilliant, accident-prone, second-year law computer geek with earrings, nosegear, and an innocent grin. Giggle or Giggis.

I could hear Ava. Josh, you *told* Tommy Conover to apologize?

"You okay with this, Josh?" asked Geneva.

"I'm the guy to go. I haven't hit a cop recently."

"You make me very happy," said Tom. "Now, leave. Please."

The Chinese detective who had given up chasing Bay killers to ascend the ivory tower of law was going back down to the cops. I went toward the elevators and sensed the approach of a pachyderm toting a comic book. Large Louis.

"Uh, Mr. Jin, ya didn't go in there ta talk ta da boss, didja?"

"Louis, what do you think I am, stupid?" I stood by the suddenly unresponsive elevator. I tried to not think about Ava. I tried to not think about anything.

Large Louis stuck his bald face into mine. He was chewing gum. "Uh, no, sir. Even if yur not real good no more, yur still Chinese. And all you Chinese guys, yur real smart."

I nodded and entered the elevator. "Stupid!" I shouted, making the walls ring. I punched the wall, cracking the paneling. "What an idiot!" To work that hard, to lose so much, so quickly.

I hadn't prepared the bureau, told Patti, assigned my duties, or packed my office. I pushed the third-floor button. The elevator kept descending. I pushed the second-floor. It continued, the DOWN light bright, gaining, it seemed, speed.

Sometimes it's hard to fight fate.

The door opened on the ground floor. Tanya Churchill, the one who coveted my job, stepped in, smiling falsely.

"Good morning, Joshie," she said, fooling no one.

4.

PLEASING CAPRI

Intake is located in the bowels of the Police Department so arresting officers can argue their cases to the Intake DA, a captive audience of one who decides what happens to police busts. It was a busy job that lately had grown stone quiet in the hush of malignant neglect.

Insulated from jury trials and shunned by cops since the Incident, I listened to oldies instead of jury instructions. I did paperwork on victims instead of preparing them for trial. I had not been banished to Siberia; I was hiding in Tibet with the donut eaters. "My Girl" played. It was bright and hot, but it was not a sunny day, and Saint Joel was at my door.

Reverend Joel Frost was angular, homely, full-bearded and wedded to tweed. He advocated for good ex-cons in rehab—a population group of perhaps five. Despite the odds, he tried to place despised cons in fair jobs. I liked his flawless, anti-intellectual optimism.

Years ago, he had brought a fresh ex-con into his home. The con promptly had an affair with his wife. She left him, taking cars and Giants memorabilia.

"Hey, Josh. You look better. Lots better."

"Reverend Joel. How goes it?"

"Hoping that you're still hopeful. I've been praying for you. Brother, can you tell? Are the wounds stitching for you? And are you sleeping better?"

"Like a man in a burning house."

"Josh, you still hoping Ava will come back?"

I took a breath. "You hoping *your* wife will return?"

"Oh, Heavens, no. But you're due some good luck. I pray for that." His look was warm and comforting. He paused, then left, greeting François Giggin while gracefully avoiding him.

François had a soft body, blond artichoked hair, a sly grin, limpid eyes, an endearing clumsiness, a high voice, and the mind of a mainframe. He bused files but hoped for Homeric chances in the field. "KO anyone, boss? You floor Sammy Lupo again?"

"Today I became a pacifist. Watch the furniture."

Giggin smiled, smashing into the door frame.

Once, I would've missed the DA mothership, the office of death penalty humor and murder-one anatomical jokes, the hotbed of our silly ambitions for minute raises and limited-view window offices. I gazed at greening maples and shuttling black and white cruisers. In the fields beyond, irrigation was slowing for the fruit orchards as they approached harvest. Flowering peaches in clouds of white, life repeating itself without reflection.

My associates, whom I had once cheered, were hard at work in court. I yawned. Before, I had depended on overachievement and collegiality. Now I fought the past and lost to insomnia. My head was down. I dreamed of Summer.

I was being shaken. I looked into the hostile gaze of Catherine Capri, a tough and sensitive DA investigator. Sensitive to kids. Tough on men. She released my bunched shirt and smoothed it, then kicked my door shut as if I were an insolent suspect.

The slam awakened me. Capri was with SACA, the DA's Sexual Assault and Child Abuse unit, the workers of the Dark World. When cops nailed pedophiles—infant-sodomists, child molesters, and kid rapists—the cases went through Intake to SACA for prosecution.

DA investigators like Capri did the final prepping of kid cases, working alongside SACA prosecutors before trial. Her victims were kids who had been raped and brutalized. The work took a special kind of DA and a special kind of investigator, a minority that did not include me.

She was a cop who didn't work for the police. She reported to us. But since the Incident, even our in-house cops had become distant and chilly.

"I have good news for you," she said insincerely.

I mumbled, "That's what Brutus said to Caesar."

"Pardon me?"

"I said, thank you very much for waking me."

"You now have a SACA case. Try pleasing me. Fake interest."

"Capri, I'd love to please you, but I'm trying to quit. SACA?" I produced a root canal expression. "Woof! Woof! No way."

"Shut up."

Capri's directness affronted lawyers. She looked too good for everyone who was aging that year. Capri had a prominent nose, fought a subtle weight problem, and had a knack for the neatness that is stressed at West Point. At a hot, fly-swarming rape-murder scene, she was as clean as an uptown Stanford grad arguing a complex, nine-figure product liability suit.

DA cops didn't have to look that good. DAs did. Jurors checked our zippers, hems, hairlines, guessing at private habits. If they could, they'd squeeze us like cantaloupes. They studied defense lawyers, looking for unrestricted Midean wealth and checking us for hints of moral imperfection. They were rarely disappointed.

We performed for them, our required audience, our necessary evil of twelve laypeople who were too honest or unimaginative to talk their way out of jury duty. In this odd business, a jury could hang because it was too hot or because the DA had experienced a bad-hair day.

Quietly, Capri cut random threads from our suits, adjusted crooked ties, smoothed unruly hair. Few enjoyed being schoolboys on picture day. We cooperated because she was observant, smart, and heavily armed.

Capri knew life. I knew law. Law school had cultivated in us an arrogance with which we could quickly offend major portions of the American public. But as DAs we were more modest;

we merely thought ourselves above drug lords, wife beaters, and serial killers.

Capri could sniff the rapist from a gaggle of sleazy suspects. I liked her nose when it wasn't aimed at me. Lately, my conduct had invited her analysis. I used to get that from Ava.

"A two-eighty-eight named *Moody*." California Penal Code section 288. Child sexual assault. The Dark World. From an oversized business purse she passed me a woefully thin, manila case file. "A personal gift from Geneva. SACA's way overloaded and the bullpen's empty. You're pitching relief today."

"Capri, I don't do kid sex cases. Even handoffs. Even undernourished handoffs."

"Yes, that's what everyone says. Imagine my pleasure, offering this kid to the incompetent. But SACA's drowning in overload and she needs help." Capri was composed, accustomed to people doing what she wanted. It was the best way to get rid of her. "It's a Chinatown case, and Geneva wants a dump." A dismissal. Capri waited silently.

A Chinatown case. My former specialty. I didn't say anything.

"The search was a wash. We hacked the case and Judge Niles dismissed. We don't have anything solid that says we got the right guy. An ex-con named Karl Moody."

I sat up. Any DA can convict the guilty; it was a special day when we pursued the innocent. If Niles said we were off base, we had problems. "Who did the prelim?"

Capri grimaced. "Gonzo Marx." Our Froot Loops prosecutor. Gonzo was a sexist lout, a saboteur of law, a diffident advocate, and an inspiration to guttersnipes the world over.

In a preliminary hearing, the DA put on the bare minimum evidence to show the court that the defendant did the crime, but without unduly exposing our witnesses to the defense. If we put on enough evidence, the court issued a holding order binding the defendant over to face a felony jury trial in Superior Court. If we had insufficent evidence, the case would be dismissed. The law gave us two bites of the apple—two chances to make the case in a prelim.

Gonzo's first bite had failed, leaving us with one last chance—a do-or-die.

"The girl hadn't said a word to anyone," she said. "Guess what he did?"

"Without a statement or a clue, Gonzo took her to prelim and blew up the kid?"

"You get a cigar." I still had the one Jay Wendell Nobis gave me on my first day of work. The same day I betrayed him.

"Conover," I said, "should have fired Gonzo four years ago."

"You got that right. Gonzo made the girl hysterical on the stand. Natch, no holding order. Judge Niles rebuked us; privately. Lucky for Conover, that SOB; no press. Not yet."

A child is raped, then humiliated by the DA. Gonzo was the only prosecutor less able to handle a girl victim than me. Now, the case awaited resolution. No. It awaited dumping.

"Was it a bad search?" I asked.

"You could say that. They didn't find anything."

That *was* a bad search. The attack was three months ago—if it even happened—by a doubtful attacker. A search now, in a rape, would be wasted motion.

"What do we have in physical evidence?"

"Nothing, Jin. I mean, NOTHING."

This was a staggering idea for a DA, who has the burden of proof. And damning in a rape, where prosecution is premised on physical evidence. Your Honor, in lieu of evidence, how about a lamp shade silhouette and some amusing birdcalls I learned in the Army?

Nothing? It was a dump. "This because of the Incident?"

"No, dammit, it's not because of the Incident." She sat. I relaxed marginally. "Jin, it's just a weak case that needs a lot of care from someone with half a brain." A forced smile.

"Come on, Capri, it's not 'weak.' It's a DOA. There's no irrefutable evidence linking Moody to the crime because there's no evidence at all. Not even a victim statement!"

Her eyes narrowed. "The girl hasn't said peep, but she was raped. I know it. So do the sex detail detectives. They gave her a photo lineup of local registered sex offenders, dropouts, classmates, neighbors, friends, and Fukien gang-bangers. I was there when she blanched—recoiled—at him." She snapped a photo onto my desk.

A booking photo of a square-jawed citizen. His nameplate: <u>Karl F. Moody</u>.

I put down the picture. "The cops popped him because she *blinked at a pic*?"

"They arrested him because I told them I believed he did it." Her unerring nose. "Jin, when a rape victim recoils at the rapist, it's not a cutesy little hip-hop. And I was *sure* I'd get her to open up, that she'd name him. I didn't want Moody taking down another kid, but she clammed up on me." She sat back. "Hey, it was my call. If it's worth my badge, so be it." She meant it. Unlike me, she liked her badge.

"And now, at the eleventh hour, you want me to fix it."

"I don't care about that. I want you to help a child victim. She needs a suit, a DA."

I rubbed my face. "Who has the defense?"

She named a midrange draft pick public defender, a barking canine at the heels of law. He'd object to sunlight at an outdoor wedding. He'd light a fire and blame us for coddling arsonists. He'd hit me with boilerplate pretrial motions, marginally coherent, largely well intended, reasonably well researched, and totally predictable. But pretrial motion law was not the problem. The problem was no victim statement and no evidence.

And SACA cases were blights on elections—a child rape not resulting in a quick conviction would lose votes by the horde. Worse, the media could label this the "litmus test" case that would determine who would be the next district attorney.

But dragging a kid rape victim through the second prelim was unthinkable until she agreed to speak. If I blindly subpoenaed her, she could remain silent on the stand, and we would be traumatizing her again. I'd be doing a Gonzo Marx. Except I didn't do trials anymore.

"Gonzo refiled on Moody after his flaming abort," she said. "The second-try prelim is set six weeks downstream. Plenty of time to dump. Or to resurrect." She looked at her watch.

Something sour made me ask, "The victim's age?"

"Her name is Rachel Farr. Thirteen. I'm sorry, Josh." She sat

straighter. "Look, Jin, if a kid's going to get better, she *has to
fight* the rapist in trial. That's gospel. And she *has* to be helped
by a DA who believes in her." Capri went on. "The pain to her,
by testifying about her rape, is *nothing* compared to her rolling
over for the rapist. She quits now, we stick her with chronic victim status for her whole life. A lot of male DAs don't know
that." Like Gonzo.

"The protocol says you should meet through a third party.
Rachel Farr will be at Rio Junior High day after tomorrow.
You'll be introduced by Kimberley Hong, her school counselor.
You meet Hong first, the Asian Community Center tomorrow at
ten. She's a political debutante who came out for the elections."
I had heard of Kimberley Hong, a rising butt-kicker.

Politics didn't determine the merit of the DA, but Tommy
Conover was old-money GOP. Rachel Farr's mishandled case
was a way for a heavily Democratic Chinatown to nail a highprofile Republican. A Chinese DA like me could go into Chinatown and dump *Moody* without hurting Tom; it'd be my neck
and not his. Ergo, Geneva gave me the case.

"This Hong woman asked for you. She thinks you're a
water-walker. She'll expect you not only to prosecute Moody,
but to *convict* him, even though you got squat."

Chinatown was pushing itself onto the city council with the
subtlety of an atomic bomb.

"Kimberley Hong came in to see Conover this morning. She
blamed him personally for Gonzo treating Rachel Farr like
trash. I hear Hong did pretty good. I'd wear a cup."

"Tommy behave himself?"

"He didn't hit her. The rest is up to you. Do something way
cool tomorrow, or Ms. Hong lights your underpants on fire in
front of the press."

I felt like cursing. "Capri, I'm not going to dump or keep a
bad case alive—for politics. With or without a Chinese face."

She smiled, liking me again. "Cool. *That* pleases me. You're
going to work the case." A warm smile. "Damn, I love a suit
busting some criminal ass."

"I'll check it out." I couldn't work it. Chinatown didn't care
about an Anglo girl; Rachel was just a way to zap Conover.

Tommy was a Republican cover boy and the Incident at the cathedral had pinned a neon-red bull's-eye on his political butt. Democratic Chinatown was going to hit it square with a white girl who, by zip code accident, lived with the Cantonese.

I hated politics. And that was before Tom hit the cop. I also hated SACA cases. Give me a clean murder without a child rape—I'm not strong enough for that.

No. I didn't want a clean murder case, either.

Capri came around my desk to brush unseen dust from my tie. "I talked to Rachel. Unfortunately, she didn't like me."

"Capri," I said, pulling away, "*no one* likes you." That was a lie. She was magical with children and men liked her the way dogs chase meat. But for her own reasons, she was a loner. "Let's sum up. Child rape cases are based on rapport with the victim. A million kids love you and trust you and confide in you and tell you the hardest secrets in the world. But this kid—"

"Rachel."

"—dislikes you, the Queen Mother of Child Interviews, so you give the case to *me*, the current Mr. Jinx who can't do a jury trial anymore." She said nothing. Snapping the folder open, I began reading Moody's rap sheets, the best part of the file. Moments passed.

"I like this, Jin. You're prepping. Like you were a DA again."

"Helpless in the grip of old reflexes. I'll try to stop."

"Don't. But you should at least have an investigator."

I missed the twelve investigators in my bureau. Capri watched while I phoned the Chief Deputy. She was in. "Thanks, Geneva, for a half-baked SACA case. I need a sex cop."

"Capri can answer questions, but she does absolutely no field work on *Moody*. You don't need a sex investigator. Dump it, Josh. It's junk. Go make Tom look good. Simon says."

Something kept me from consenting.

"Josh," said Geneva, "the girl stonewalled a good cop *and* Capri. And they're the best. Only Capri thinks Moody's the bad guy. This isn't rocket science. It's a dump. But it's a Chinatown case, so I want *you* to dump it. Do some damage control and get out."

"Geneva, there's no statement. Send me a cop first to confirm the bad news, then I dump it." Textbook prosecutorial procedure. I hung up.

Capri was detailing the thin case history. A fat man in a rumpled, ill-fitting brown suit with a once-handsome, hatchetlike face leaned in my door. He had a sports section open to the small-print "Transactions." He chewed gum generously. Capri groaned.

Harry O. Bilinski, the Backshooter from Vice. A lawsuit looking for a banana peel, a Nam vet who had done his last good deeds when Grace Slick played the Fillmore in the City. He had a legendary reputation for killing deer out of season and shooting young Asian suspects in the back. Harry's dream was to get fired from the department so he could sue for a big houseboat on Lake Tahoe. He was on admin leave after another Chinatown backshooting of a seventeen-year-old Hong Kong gang-banger. Harry wasn't happy unless he was killing someone. He had flat feet, chronic donut disease, and post-traumatic stress from the baby boomer virus of Vietnam, where he had traded young blood for medals he never wore.

"Jin, I really pissed off the geniuses big this time. I'm on fucking loan to you."

I sat back. "My bet says they're angrier at me than at you."

"Look at it from my foxhole. I gotta report to *you*. A political ass-wipe." He blew air.

"You're not on full status. Internal Affairs return your gun?" asked Capri warily.

"Hell, no," said Bilinski, sulking. He shrugged. "No sweat. I got another piece."

"Not around me, you don't." I stood.

A snicker. "Going to take it off me, Jin?" He dropped the paper and freed his hands.

I didn't much care if he shot me. Capri was tense but motionless. Harry squinted, openly checking the layout, his breath short and quick, eyes wild, uncaring, bullish, and red, signs without hope. He reached but I was ready. He pulled a heavy, blued Smith & Wesson .44 Magnum, then dropped it in my hand. It was symbolic; he had about two thousand other guns. I had to admit that getting shot by a .44 Magnum might make me care, if only for a moment. He exhaled, smelling of last month.

"Don't scratch it. I'm supposed to help you with some B.S. political two-eighty-eight. Shit, I'm no better at them damn cases than *you* are. I'm tellin' you up front. I don't like kids."

"I bet it's mutual. The case is *People v. Moody*. Here's our file. Make a copy and study it. Find the alibi witness. Then, we talk." I put his cannon in my desk drawer as he opened the thin SACA file. He shook it like a bear in a beehive, looking under the paltry case sheets.

"There's crap in here."

"Let's be honest," I said. "Or frank. You deserve it."

"Do some work. No guns. Time to start following the rules, Bilinski," said Capri.

"Yeah." His face corrugated. "Oughta do it like you. Wear makeup and cute clothes, show off my tits and carry a snub in a handbag. *That'll* scare the squirts outa the bad guys."

Capri leaned close to him. Quietly, a mother to a young child. "Harry, if they ever authorize human cloning, I'm going to have to kill you."

A Polaroid-moment grinch face. "Why the fuck pile-on *me*? *Jin's* the dead meat."

"Yeah, I'm dead meat. But I got a SACA case. Who knows. If you do a really good job, maybe I'll fire you." That could frame his houseboat lawsuit against the city.

He smiled. "Really? Jin, you wanna work with me on this?"

I disliked him enough to nod. He left to make copies. I asked Geneva for help and got a killer who favored fraudulent claims and was as welcome in Chinatown as a tubercular rash.

"Jin," said Capri, "this case'll take a *lot* of work. Back-to-school time. Before I sum up the facts, you need to know that kid victims require—" Her cell phone rang. Amusement became concern. She hung up.

"There's a girl running naked down Nineteenth." She closed her phone. "I got backup to SPD if it's close. It's close." The door banged open. In a whiff of soft perfume, she was gone.

I admired, even envied, Capri's focus, passion, energy, and commitment.

I thought so until she returned. She threw me my coat. I caught it.

"C'mon, Jin! Pretend you're a cop again! Back up any statements I get." She hit the desk the way adults draw the attention of newborn puppies and genetically slow men. "Let's save a girl!" She winced. Softer, "Sorry. Hey, if you crap out on me, you crap out. It won't be like you're the first guy to do it to me."

5.

TIFFANY PRUE

She was running far away, in heavy traffic. I couldn't hear her screams but felt them in the senses I had tried to numb. Capri hit the siren and accelerated. Trucks were doing fifty.

Our siren made the vehicles ahead speed up. A shadow near the girl. "Someone's chasing her," I said, and Capri showed her teeth. I reached to check my handgun; I had none.

The kid looked thirteen. Thin, brown-haired, unclothed. She took a lucky grip on a slowing red pickup and held on as the truck juked. She flipped into the bed. She was safe.

The pickup swerved and braked, making cars disperse; the driver was trying to toss the girl from his truck. He skidded, careening into a white Buick, driving it into a green freeway sign and a small stone and glass storefront. Glass erupted and bricks crushed the car's hood.

The girl was being bounced hard in the truck's metal bed.

"Bastard!" said Capri. A black Toyota, brakes screaming, glanced off the pickup and a Blazer crumpled into the black Toyota.

I called for emergency vehicles as cars swerved, skidded, and piled into the Blazer and Toyota. Brakes locked and a big GMC pickup banged into a minivan, rolling it to its side as it steadily plowed across lanes, spinning cars and smashing into vehicles parked on the east side of the street. Cars crunched in gathering ruin. Pedestrians scurried; some were transfixed. We blurred past drunks clutching bottles as cars between us and the pickup accordioned. Capri braked into a small space, leaving wide black skids and the scent of hot burning rubber.

Our bumper bounced in front of an elderly woman in a white dress with a frayed shopping bag and a scuffed cane. Capri was out and the woman clutched her chest. I killed the siren and sat her in our car. Capri was gone in black smoke and flickering, popping flames.

"Take slow breaths. Do you have a heart condition?"

She shook her head. "You were going to kill me."

"I'm sorry. Rest. I'll be back." I opened the trunk, grabbed blankets, and ran. Fire, smoke, wrecks, and a mediocre, quasi-fistfight. Capri was better than me in many things. Sprinting wasn't one of them. I passed her, looking for the shadowy figure. He was gone.

The debris would end up on my desk tomorrow morning as paperwork. Sirens howled from downtown. I hooked my badge and came out of the smoke. The red pickup was tipped at a high angle on the sidewalk and a motorcycle. The driver had the naked girl by her hair.

"Get outa my truck, ya stupid little fuckin' bitch!"

She screamed as he banged her against the bed, cursing her. She was pregnant. He had a hundred-pound advantage but she raked his face. He howled and punched her in the chest, making her sob and fall like a little doll while he called her vile names, all undeserved.

I threw a blanket over his head. "What?" he asked.

I hit him with a sharp right cross in the center of his face. His head snapped, arms dropping lifelessly as he went soft. I eased his fall, then threw the other blanket on her. She screamed. I ducked and weaved from her nails, the blanket falling. She called me names, but I didn't deserve them, either.

"I'm a good guy." I held up my badge to prove it.

She sought the clarity to weep. Capri came. I threw the blanket over the girl again. She shivered, bleeding everywhere.

Something had made her jump barebacked into a speeding truck in the middle of a fast inner city thoroughfare, precipitating a wreck waiting to happen.

"It's okay, sweetie," gasped Capri, offering a hand. "We're with the DA. You're safe now. Take my hand. Step down, baby."

Sirens wailed. Extinguishers hissed. Bad drivers argued hollowly and the homeless blinked at the disadvantages of owning cars. I didn't want anything to do with her but lifted her out of the truck. Fire trucks arrived, the slowing sirens a comfort. I needed to leave, but Supine Man wasn't moving. He might need air. I pulled the blanket from a violently bloody face. "Capri, he's been drinking. I'd get a Breathalyzer. I think I broke his nose."

She showed her teeth. "I think you broke his face. God, you Weedwacked him." She saw how I was looking at the girl. She pushed me. "Get out of here, Jin. Go. Go, now. Please."

The girl's fearful eyes expanded on me. "Don't go! Stay!"

I left to see the elderly woman we had nearly crushed.

Capri and the girl were waiting for me in the DA's office. Here, once, I had been a young metro prince endowed with political potions. Staff waved, smiled, focused on work or avoided contact. Some stowed photographs, as if they were contraband.

Capri had purchased her own furniture and pricey Southwestern art. A comfortable sofa, a paisley-patterned bed for Sagwa, her black cat, some countermale rose lampshades and pink easy chairs. Soft classical music from a CD went with the colors.

The girl was in Juvie Hall castoffs, small on the sofa, eating junk food like a young, cowering, wounded carnivore. She shivered in light shock, downing fat, soy lecithin, guar gum, partially hydrogenated soy oil, food coloring, maltodextrin, and other free carcinogens.

I looked at the file. The SANERs, rape nurses, had already seen her. The girl had been raped. She was now a SACA case that Capri was to investigate personally.

The girl struggled to swallow. Quavering, "How 'bout a cigarette?"

"Don't have the habit," said Capri. "The cigarette machine's busted 'til you're eighteen. It's bad for your baby. Jin, this is Tiffany Prue. Tiffany, you've already met Mr. Jin."

"You got any smokes?" asked Tiffany Prue of me.

"They turned my hair black, so I quit."

She looked at my hair. She was about to give a statement. It took one cop to ask and one to back up; I was backup because Tiffany had already met me, and she had to get used to testifying about horrible things in front of men, who typically infested the courts.

Capri had made a connection with her. My job would be not to interfere. No rapport, no case. Exhibit 1: my new file, *Moody,* featuring the twerp Gonzo Marx and the silent, process-abused victim Rachel Farr. Result: a dump. SACA was a relational business.

It was, in that way, Chinese. I tried to listen.

"You have," BaBa said when I was small and his heart was good, "*gahng,* bonds, to me and to all fathers before me. And you have *guanxi,* face relationship, with all workers in laundry shop. Where, someday, you *not* work. You go school, get smart, get good job. Make strong sons. These duties to other people define you. *Ni dung la?* Understand?"

"*Dung la, BaBa.*" I understand. I carry relational duties to my family. I always will. I was in the fullness of my thirties, and I missed my father with a deep and longing ache.

Unlike the silent victim Rachel Farr, Tiffany was talking, non-stop. She was from Corpus Christi, was fourteen, chronically malnourished on intermittent trans-fatty acids junk food, had been sexually abused by her father, was pregnant by a stranger, had a mild overbite, and needed braces, a hot bath, ten years of good therapy, and a cot in the Catholic Social Services Home for Girls.

She'd gone to Canada but changed her mind because it was cold. She tricked for bus fare to Sacramento; a kid said we had great beaches. "Are they cool?" she asked.

"Fair," I said, "but they're about a hundred miles away."

She expected surfers and rock bands looking for girls. Stiff, sore, grouchy, hungry, and needing a smoke, she had taken a few steps into the downtown bus station when a man asked if she was a model. She said, oh, yeah, sure I am. This was yesterday.

"What'd he do to you?" asked Capri.

She told us. It was easier to hear about murder.

"What's his name?" I asked.

"I called him Buttface."

"Describe him, please," I said.

"Real ugly. And old. Like, thirties." That old. He was a white male, five-ten, one-sixty, white slacks, white deck shoes, light blue short-sleeved collared shirt, hairy chest and body.

"Where'd he take you?" I asked.

"His place. It was nice. A new TV and a cool VCR. Two beds. A nice bathroom. Tub. A phone. Little teeny bars of soap."

"A motel?" asked Capri. "Remember the name?"

She was looking, seeing nothing. "He took pictures. Nasty." Her voice was flat.

"The name of the motel?" I asked.

She shook her head.

"Remember where it was, sweetheart?"

She looked vaguely at the window. Then, with a jerk, at the door, her small chest heaving. She blinked at us, panic subsiding. "It had two names. You know, like Ben and Jerry."

"Fred and Gary's River City Motel?" asked Capri. A West Sac shooting gallery and by-the-half-hour hooker hole on Jefferson.

"A nice place. Well." She teared. "He had a knife. That's when he did me, not all real good." She wept. I asked for the room number. Upstairs or downstairs. "Upstairs."

The manager said a man meeting Buttface's description was in Room 254. Ed Jones. Didn't have no car. Paid cash up front, Friday to Friday, a real gentleman. No, he wasn't quiet.

I said Jones was stiffing motels. Watch him for us?

Yes, sir, he would certainly watch that dirty bastard.

A cruiser was en route for Mr. Jones. I drafted a warrant.

"He said I could be a model, you know, like for magazines and I said, like, of course, how'd ya know?" She rubbed her legs. "I lied. I mean, like really, do I look like a model?"

"You could," said Capri. "After you finish high school."

"How'd you get the cuts?" I asked.

"His knife. Other men. And back home. And the bus stops. Buttface, he burned my clothes and then, like, cut me a lot. He liked me to squirm. Woulda done it without the knife."

Capri's microcassette turned. "How'd you get away?"

"I walked. But he saw me. I ran cuz he said he'd stab my eyes a hundred times if I split." She was trying not to cry. She cried. "Can you believe that beezo breath in the truck? Why'd he fuck with me? Didn't do nuthin' to him." A wet smile. "Oh, man, you hit him so hard! So way cool! You knocked him right off his fat ass! *So* twinky. Hey, you can sure hit people!"

I smiled painfully. Law school was paying off. I called in the warrant to search the motel room. Cops phoned from the motel: no answer at Jones's room. Tiffany was asleep.

Bilinski and I were underemployed, so I called him and told him about Ed Jones, aka Mr. Buttface, of Fred and Gary's River City Motel.

"That's Lost Kid Central," he said. "Where westside pedophiles hunt runaways. Pervs are into runaways they can pack into motel rooms that rent by the half hour."

"Why don't you shut it down?" I asked.

"Shit, Jin," said Bilinski, "like we got the manpower to do something like that? You talk like a goddamn politician."

I apologized profusely, awakening Tiffany.

"Don't go, okay?" she asked. "Will you, like, come see me? Mister—"

At court, I got a daytime warrant for Room 254, Fred and Gary's River City Motel, in case Jones had left part of his child rape kit—cameras, video, duct tape, rope, cuffs, kid porn.

Nineteenth Street was still a mess while CHP's Multi-disciplinary Accident Investigation Team worked the scene. I drove to the sea-level river wharfs and bent-back, scruff-barked palm trees of West Sacramento, parking at Fred and Gary's. Birds sang and flea-bitten homeless men sat under dusty shade trees. Heat radiated. Even when this was a new part of town, during the Gold Rush, it was probably old, dusty, flat, and ugly.

A very young hooker in a rusty Honda raced out of the

lot. Unattended, diaperless, sunburned toddlers sucked thumbs and stared. Hi, I said. Country, rock, and Mexican music battled without a victor. Adults yelled. Years of broken glass lay like fallen stars.

Inside, a counter, a round, center-pin bell, chipped, empty mint bowl, broken clock, a burning cigarette in an ashtray, and a dead plant. Cheap, hardened donuts.

I showed the badge and the warrant.

"Jones is out," he said. "Wanna see the room?"

"Not yet. I'm waiting for another man."

The manager nodded, relieved the Honda was gone.

"Why not give the leftover donuts to the homeless guys?"

"You ain't serious. They'll frickin' harass me to death."

"Give them the donuts and ask them to sit by the warehouse."

He shrugged. Bilinski arrived, hitching pants over ample hips, chewing gum. I introduced him to the manager, who jerked.

"Christ, it's him! The guy in two-five-four! Ed Jones!"

We looked out the tinted office window.

Male Caucasian, five-nine, one-sixty, balding, white slacks, white deck shoes, blue short-sleeved collared shirt, rough, stubby hands. Sipping a Big Gulp, no evidence of firearm or weapon if you didn't count the fresh racing form folded into the small of his back. He was facing away and I couldn't see chest hair, but I thought our chances were good.

I came from the left, Bilinski from the right.

"Hi," said Harry, taking the Big Gulp from Jones's hand, dumping it, spitting out his gum and holding up the badge.

"Detective Bilinski, Sacramento Police. You Mr. Buttface?"

6

AVA PASCAL JIN

I ate my sixth spaghetti dinner and salad of the week. Jodie ate with her mouth open, her tail wagging as if this were the first dinner of her life. ESPN flickered. If you watch SportsCenter for a while, you get replays of replays, and the beer commercials become news.

I washed plate, bowl, and fork, dried them and put them away. As if Ava were still here. I had been using the same items for a while. I thought about rotating the plate to the bottom of the stack and using a different one. The big issues of being alone.

I turned off the tube. In the silence of the great house, I opened the thin *Moody* 288 file. It was Gonzo Marx's trademark trash. Rap sheets, priors, and reports shuffled. No chrono log or legal research. Schlock warrant request. Spaghetti stains, which I could no longer scorn: Gonzo and I now had more in common than one might wish to acknowledge.

Joe Pelletier, Public Defender, a colleague of my ex-wife, Ava, had the case. Good it wasn't Stacy August, who'd kill me in papers and motions. She had beaten me a few years ago in a murder trial when I had been at the peak of my skills. Stacy. I turned the page.

The defendant was Karl Francis "Chico" Moody.

He had pulled four years in Soledad for 459, a residential burglary. Forty years old. Six feet. One-eighty. Single; no kids. Living in the Broadway on Tulip Lane with a candy-apple-red '67 Impala convertible. Employment: disabled. A work mishap had broken his neck and entitled him to fifteen hundred a month in Social Security. He had been paroled six years ago with no violations. In the judgment of the State, Karl Moody had rehabbed.

Moody had waived Miranda and denied abusing Rachel. His statement sounded unusually credible. His alibi was a John Quick, occupation unstated. No statement from Quick. No address. Of course, Gonzo Marx had not followed up. No investigative work.

The PX—preliminary hearing—transcript was short. Just as well; Gonzo had been so inept that Judge Niles had repeatedly called him to the bench for reprimands—resulting in Gonzo's asking worse questions. Transcripts don't reflect sound volume, but Gonzo must have been shouting because the bench ended the prelim.

"Do that again, Mr. Marx, at your peril," said Judge Niles, who was hell on crooks and very pro-DA. The case was not half-baked; it hadn't been walked past a cold kitchen. It should have been returned to the cops, FFI, for further investigation, before it was passed to Gonzo for butchering in court. Without work, it was a flamer, a lost cause, a smoking hole in the earth.

Why had the Intake deputy, the guy who preceded me, filed it? I couldn't find the Intake filing memo. Typical. I meant to make a note to call him.

The case was being considered for a jury trial but no one knew what had happened to Rachel Farr. Gonzo had killed any chances of recovery by harassing the child victim in court. The file was being kept alive by politics. A perfect case for me.

The house was an empty ache. The great, high-ceilinged living room was without music or the clack of dominoes, the kitchen without warming scents. A gut-stroke of self-pity. I put on gloves to punch the body bag in the backyard. Memories of Ava's voice stopped me. A fine silk, tearing through a crimson bolt.

She had been in the near chair with her dancer's posture, long legs tucked. Impeccable hair. A light jacket over a rose blouse and white slacks, silver necklace, prepared.

I was in gym gear, the bag gloves like dead man's hands on the rug. She was trying to limit her invasion of my space. Ava was beautiful, an impressionist composition in whites, softened by the sterile setting. She had the aspect of a stranger.

She had said, "You're not interested in me. You relax when I leave the room. You hit that punching bag in the yard, so *hard*. Josh, you're scaring me. And you're self-destructing at the office." She gulped. "You don't love me anymore. I'm not sure you even like me."

I had sat up. "Ava—"

"No—*this* is the time to let me talk. I should've let you stay a cop and not pushed you into law school. I always thought I forced you into marriage. I could make you do things. . . ."

"Not true." I wished I could change the channel.

"Well, it's funny. But not ha-ha. You joke with colleagues and ignore me. You're more loyal to your staff than to me. You argue to juries with that Chinese memory for details, knowing their foibles, strengths. Dreams—and you reject *mine*. You think in two worlds—American movies and Chinese aphorisms—but you can't even talk to me! We're not a couple. We're not even friends!" She looked at the vaulted ceiling where a white fan turned, tilling her words after tunneling through me. "Josh, you're getting worse. We don't agree on our lives.

"This happens—and you buy a Porsche?! I don't even know who you are!" She wept.

I could not stand, as if movement would shatter me and I would fall in a thousand pieces into the sofa.

"I'm not doing real well, either," she continued. "I'm tired of talking about this. To myself. Josh, I'm leaving you. I'm leaving the marriage. It's over, honey."

My stomach went sour with the memory. Other organs played catch, with hordes of fumbles and miscues. Fourteen years, to this.

"Think about therapy." She wiped her eyes. "I have an apartment. I can't be here." She sat taller. "This isn't just your fault. Things happen. I feel like I'm killing you. But I can't do that, can I, if you're already dead. The apartment won't take pets. Will you take care of Jodie?"

I nodded. Jodie was her idea but my dog.

Outside, Ava sighed as if I were the person I had been. "I wish it'd rain." She looked up.

"Rain. There's a word." I was making no sense.

She gathered words for a last pitch to her damaged husband. "I know you don't like to touch me. But I want you to give me a hug. And just once, I want you to call me by my name."

She could brave the emotional hurdles. She was a better trial lawyer than I because she was faster spatially, quicker with the resolution of puzzles, less angry, less brutish in the face of the bad people of our community. She feared no answer. She had loved God.

I had feared failure, to be a Chinese man trapped in an American laundry. Fear had made me dangerous in the ring and a killer in court. Ava and I had worked together well, strengthened by being on opposite legal sides. Her perceptions eased my angers.

We almost looked at the moon, where Chinese say that *yin*, the female spirit, and all emotion were born. I held her, feeling the heavy, injured slugging of her heart.

"Sorry you want rain," I said. "Wrong time of year."

"You used to be so optimistic." She held me tighter and tighter. Perhaps she said, "God, I still love you." Or I imagined it, as I had imagined so many things in our marriage.

I thought: God does not love us. We presumed our happiness, and our family. We exposed ourselves to Heaven, and I sinned.

Her face, her always-cool nose, pressing into my always-warm neck, as if she could coax and squeeze from me the man I had been. I had loved her body, a sweet song of the sea. I told myself to hold her closer, and did. Inside, a cold from distant and frigid steppes. The press of her no longer meant anything. It was like holding the body of a stranger.

Ava shut her eyes tighter, sadness in her arms.

I should call her by name. Sadly, she released me, her hands fine, eloquent, final. Ava Pascal Jin whispered like my mother in a Confucius temple, a Chinese woman hushed by the crowding of watching ancestors who judged every tone, every word, every look.

"Joshua, she's dead. Our daughter's dead."

Somewhere, to the sound of such bad luck words, small birds died. "Summer Nicole's not coming back. Except in memory. And when we hold each other. Oh, Josh, she loved you so much. Sum never would've wanted this awful sadness in you. We gave her a wonderful life—she was happy—and you were so much of that. It's as if you've forgotten who she was. You really ruin her memory with your depression."

I had no words. She stepped back. "Dammit! It's been almost a year! It wasn't like we didn't know it was coming. But you denied she was going to die. Honey. I'm not stronger than you—I just got ready for it. And I did therapy. It's your turn."

"With Dax Price?" A man who never stopped courting her. He had charm, Euro facial lines, a degree in medicine, and pedigrees in old money and cotillion dancing.

"That's not fair. I know you're not being malicious—it's that *damn* Chinese grief. Honoring her with pain." She exhaled. "Josh, there's a new guy at the Med Center. Teo Sandoval. He's good. You should call him. Or talk to Isaac. And return your mom's call. God, talk to *someone*." Unsaid: I wish it were me, your wife. Summer's mom.

She got in the van I no longer liked. Vans were for kids, trips to the lake, choir practice, and piano lessons, pizza parties at the end of brave soccer seasons. She turned the key.

"You can research my number and my address. Don't." She patted my hand, a mother's gesture, squeezing it.

I fought for words. I said, "You belong in this house."

"Oh, great! Be primeval!" Her face twisted, knives in my heart. "Not 'I love you and can't live without you'? Or 'I value you more than a goddamned sports car'? 'You belong in this house'? *You* wanted the BIG HOUSE to go with your BIG JOB. It's a mausoleum! You won't let me clean out her room and you're doing a deathwatch in it and you're not letting her death have any peace or her life have any beauty or meaning!"

Head down, she wept inconsolably. Slowly, I rubbed her back, making her cry harder. There was no beauty in Summer's death.

"Josh, you killed our marriage. God, don't you see that? I *hate* what you're doing! It makes me hate *you*!"

I stood under the stars on the silent, pastoral west side of Davis, loathing the empty house, the shell of my ambitions to be a successful American professional, just like a blue-eyed Anglo, watching her brake lights glow as she rounded the corner.

"I love you, Ava," I said, so softly even I could not hear.

Jodie sniffed hopefully for the reassuring scent of her people, whimpering as her mother drove away. Jodie yearned for the lovely girl with the sweet, lilting voice that was China, Scotland, and California. The girl with the smell of freshly mown grass, of flinty field chalk, worn soccer balls, and Skittles, of fresh shampoo and conditioner and skin cream and undying hope who was just figuring out female hygiene when she died. The girl who played Frisbee and tossed footballs and baseballs on this street. Who played Fetch with bright yellow tennis balls. And with her dad.

I opened my eyes. I was driving ninety miles an hour down County Road 96. I downshifted. I liked the Porsche's cold German steel, appreciated its engineering precision. Summer Nicole had been dead a year. Ava had left four months ago. Now I spoke to her divorce lawyer, not to her. Dissolution of marriage. Interlocutory. There were some words.

My daughter died and my wife left me. I've been relieved of management, I'm indifferent to sex, and my dog can't sleep. I have a SACA case with a stone-silent teenage victim—a lousy political Chinatown case where the kid and I are the pawns.

I drove back to the house and sat in my once-favorite chair. I played the tape with Summer swimming with a baby dolphin named Daniella on Isla Mujeres off Cancún, two years ago. Summer turning with the dolphin. Ava in a halter top and sun hat, her arm around me, leaning on my shoulder, tears in happy eyes.

She had loved me. Now, for a moment, I missed her, her ballet in which I loved to hum the tune. Her face. I wanted to hold her and carry her upstairs into a time when joy was your wife and love was in season and your girl loved you blindly and your

dog slept without whimpering, her legs twitching, trying to find
the missing girl.

The dolphin tape ended and automatically began its whirring
rewind to the beginning, leaving me in the present.

I yearned for time machines, miracle cardiac cures, and celestial transcendentalism—the grand, cosmic wishes of little
kids who see elves and fireflies and feel warm love and misun-
derstand everything related to work.

In the morning, I would be expected to dance a political lam-
bada in Chinatown, where an injured white girl and a wounded
Chinese DA would be used as small kindling in a growing election bonfire, fed by a warm summer rogue wind.

For me, it would be a relief. I felt sorry for the girl. But I had
trained myself, and it passed.

7.

CHINATOWN

Tuesday

Here, there were no trees. Black-silk-jacketed White Lotus gangsters, handguns sagging in pockets, promenaded the shops, reminding clerks that Friday payments were due. One saw me and
they dispersed. I gave them no honor, no face. Chinatown hard-
boys, flinty, arrogant, cold. If they got busted, they'd expertly
dump their pistols, turn stone silent, and bail.

We passed Celestial Bakery, inhaling *char siu bao*, sweet
barbecued pork buns, and *gai-lan*, hardy Chinese broccoli in
rich oyster sauce. Inside the shop, elders spoke without restraint, the sounds of dynamic Chinese rising like a surf of a
capella harmonics, carrying ten-thousand-year-old meanings
and intuitively obeying ancient relational accords.

If I apologized for Gonzo Marx's incompetence in the
Rachel Farr case, we'd get skewered. If I didn't apologize,

Chinatown would toss a press conference for Conover that would resemble Caesar's death.

Capri and I entered. Metal chair legs scraped sourly in the Asian Community Center's dark meeting hall as twelve suited men and women turned from a long teak table, fanning themselves with local Asian newspapers. Bright porcelain teapots marched in a wavering line down the center of the table. An old, chipped, blue box fan vibrated energetically in the corner, doing little good. These elders wore old suits to show humility.

In the shadows of the back wall sat five large, younger men in newer suits bulging from concealed firearms. Security to discourage the crazier gangs from making a mass raid.

"She called a party," whispered Capri.

"And we're the noise blowers," I said.

Kimberley Hong looked me in the eyes. "*Ne ho ma,* Joshua Jin." Cantonese, How are you? She smiled as we shook hands. Katherine Capri introduced herself. Hong's eyes were like thermal gun sights as she sized us up. Her hair was stacked, making her more dramatic.

"Jin *singsong*, Mr. Jin, come. You know everyone. Sit. Have tea." I inclined my head; the elders nodded, watchful.

We sat. Hong poured. The tea did not steam. She watched me.

"Jin *singsong*, you honor us by coming. The tea is hot?"

"*Ho, dojieh,* thank you for inviting us. Mr. Conover remains committed to the Asian community. He sends his warmest regards." I politely drank the cool liquid.

She smiled politely. "Your time is valuable, so forgive my directness. Your office did a terrible job with Rachel Farr."

With Chinese care, I said, "I apologize and I am ashamed."

"Ah," "Ah ha," "*Ho, ho,*" good, good, said the elders. Mr. Chew, a grocer of some seventy years in a white suit, clucked and accepted a roll of cash from Mr. Li, the travel agency owner.

Mr. Bao, a bookstore man, offered his palm. Mr. Tang, an herbalist, paid. One wager was on my apology; the other, on my shame.

Hong moved closer. "And Mr. Conover? Is *he* ashamed?"

"The chief law enforcement officer," I said, "is responsible for everything done right, and for everything done wrong."

"So. You admit he made a mistake?"

"I acknowledge his responsibility. My shame's not enough?"

"Jin *singsong-ah*, you hold back answers and make *me* look bad. Your office acted unprofessionally. You admit this! Now, you minimize its meaning and question me! You talk like a lawyer."

"I'm not paid enough to be a lawyer. I'm a prosecutor. Ms. Hong, what's important—assigning blame or helping this girl?"

She chided me with tongue clicks. "Clever words are why people hate lawyers."

"And many lawyers don't like me." This was a political lobster cookout, claws open and snapping. Did Hong care about the girl?

She laughed. "Jin-ah, maybe *you* should run for DA. This, I think, would make us happy. Will you?" She smiled wonderfully.

"Ms. Hong, my office made a sad mistake. Disloyalty to my boss will hardly cure that."

"Jin *singsong*, time for Chinese to be leaders. The *gwailo* do not like us. Only our money. Our food. Sometimes, the women." She touched a dangling gold earring. "Ask—what is my purpose? To help myself? Or help my community? We could give you the votes."

"I believe in helping the larger community. Helping everyone."

"Yes, help all, including those who hate us. An American answer. When were you in the sweatshops? You worked laundries as a boy in the City, but it is worse now. You are a Chinese leader, and give speeches about helping *everyone*. You have perfect English and education and you forget your own people. You share water but your clan's well is dry."

No one moved. Dark Chinese eyes fixed me like cannon muzzles.

"Our people are not the only ones who need meals and teachers. And I'm not the only one with English and education."

"Yes, but I do not have the male organ. Still, I do all I can." The heat in her eyes flared. "Sethman Jergen said to us, confidentially, if he becomes DA, he will appoint an Asian chief deputy and black, Latino, and Native American bureau chiefs. Hiring people who reflect the faces of today's California. You will be his chief deputy. Then you can run next time."

"Sacramento," I said, "is too conservative for that. That's why Jergen kept it confidential." I wouldn't be his chief deputy for all the Monday coffee in Colombia.

She sat back. "You're the minority bureau chief for Conover. His minority community fireman, his Uncle Tom, his Uncle Banana, yes?"

Banana: yellow on the outside, white on the inside. I ignored the insult. She didn't know I had lost my bureau. I opened my mouth to tell her, but politics made me shut it; it would make Tommy look worse. "Conover's pretty good at putting out his own fires."

"With his fists. And your face. I don't see him here, do you? How can an intelligent, educated Chinese man support a *gwailo* conservative who doesn't even like us?"

"Ms. Hong, he represents everyone. We came, offering *guanxi* to help a child." And to be political. "I apologized; you asked that I run against my boss. Mr. Conover is a good public servant. Seth isn't. Mr. Conover is a career DA; Seth's a lifelong criminal defense lawyer. Mr. Conover can run the office; Seth can't. It takes more than political speeches to be competent."

Mrs. Ida Jin owned five restaurants. She was my advocate by virtue of our common family name. She asked, "What will stop Conover from doing bad job with Farr girl, again?"

I said, "I am now personally responsible for the case."

"Ah ha," said Mr. Chew, flipping his hand with a flare of the wrist, taking a double roll of cash from a frowning Mr. Li.

"Good," said Mr. Wu to Ms. Hong. Pointing at me, "I trust *him*. Not Conover. A drunkard. When he drink, he forget us."

"I will not forget," I said. "Nor will he. Or Ms. Capri."

"Oh?" asked Mrs. Jin. She came penniless from Hong Kong and had more business wisdom in her small head than a boatload of MBAs. "You come, four year ago, when Conover need Democrat votes. You build *guanxi* with us. Eat here all time. Bring Americans to our tables. Celebrate New Year. Give cash to Benevolent Association. I tell you, we were proud, have Chinese man high in DA's trust! Yes! Is true! Made us feel safe at night! We brag on you!

"We say, *you* the man, save us from gangs and protection racket! This year, you stop come. *Never* see you. No come New Year banquet or Historical Society dinner or fund-raiser. Oh, checks, yes. Written by your wife, who is not Chinese." She pointed a finger. "*You* talk of *guanxi*! You do not live in our community! You do not even live in Sacramento! You live with the *gwailo laoshi*, white professors, in Davis! You think we not see?"

Davis was a college community filled with students and professors on bicycles.

"Jin *taitai*," I said, "I'm sorry—"

"You want bet?" asked Mr. Chew, slapping down his winnings. I smiled, too smart to accept.

"This year," said Capri, "Mr. Jin had health problems."

"I was fine—"

"Ai-ya," said Mrs. Jin. "He strongest Chinese man in valley!"

"Jin," said Hong, "are you an expert in child rape cases?"

"He is one of the top five lawyers in our office," said Capri. I looked to see if her nose was growing.

I wrote my home number on my card and gave it. "Ms. Hong, we have to go. Call whenever you want." I bowed; Capri bowed. Heads inclined. The bodyguards stood and stretched, joints cracking.

Outside, Capri said, "She looks at you like a wolf at a chicken."

"She can't help it. It's my manly chest."

"Not romantically. Politically."

My strength. "Cluck, cluck," I said.

8.

THE FACTS

We were in the car. "Don't pull that again." The trucks on the Interstate were flying in combat formation, wind-blasting Hondas and Harleys.

"What," she said, "telling them there's a reason for your moods?"

I spoke slowly, the words grinding. "Don't discuss my life."

"Fine." She crossed her arms to keep from strangling me. "The facts," she snapped. "Rachel Farr's thirteen, in seventh grade. She ought to be in the eighth. She flunked fourth.

"Monday, ten February, Rio Junior High calls the Farr home because Rachel's missed school. Stepmother says, So what. Rachel returns twelve February. Counselor Hong sees black eyes. Limp. Contusions. Inattentiveness. Depression, random weeping. Disassociation from kids, teachers.

"Hong takes her to ER. SANERs"—Sexual Assault Nurse Examiners—"try a colposcope." A high-tech fiber-optic pelvic exam camera, capable of finding minute tears.

"Rachel refuses. Not even an external visual of the pelvis. The RN smells rape, just like me and the sex detail detectives who followed. But no physical evidence."

None of the lab work that makes these ugly cases promising. No vaginal clefts or tears, no semen, saliva, blood, fingernail scrapings, hair, fibers, footprints, bite marks, fingerprints on buttons, handbag, stains on bedding, DNA, or bloody gloves—the scientific data that allowed skeptical juries to convict.

"No scope, no lamplight, no evidence," said Capri painfully.

Rapes, more than garden-variety murders, had become highly scientific. Jurors needed more proof before they'd convict. In the wounds of rape lay the spore of the enemy. Murder can be done at a distance, but rape requires personal invasion. Juries knew that a crime of such violence could not be undertaken without the assailant leaving a wealth of his highly individualized markers.

The sad equation: The greater the victim's pain and the deeper the trauma, the better our evidence. The greater the chance for conviction. The cruel ratio: The more he did, the more we had. This child had apparently been hurt, but we had zilch.

Unspoken was the fact that my trial skills had gone the way of Tom Conover's election chances—due south. I rubbed my chin.

"Rachel says zip. No statement to SANERs, cops, or me. Even the great Wilma Debbin struck out. Then I struck out."

And the world naturally turned to me. "You still think we got the right guy?" I asked.

She nodded. "But Rachel's the key to that question. And we're short on time."

"Wilma wrote the book on silent child victim cases. You're a trained sex cop. Smart, manipulative, observant, picky—"

"Geneva de Hoyas just needs you to look good for the evening news. Pitch a sound bite, dump the case, and save Conover the Chinatown vote. With Gonzo on it, it would've been Conover's fault. With you, if you win, Tom wins. You lose, he'll wrap the dead monkey around *your* neck. You're his Chinatown warranty." Chinatown would likely decide the election.

Politics. And kids weren't my strength; they were my weakness. But when tunes of disfavor were hummed, Upstairs thought of me. Back when Tommy and I were pals, votes were easy, temperance was in season, he was married, and Chinatown was ours. We pushed idealism. There were enough intact families and fathers to make law work. But demographics had changed. Families were passé, thugs had .40 caliber Glocks, summer heat had come early, and Thomas, without the civilizing effect of his marriage, had belted a cop.

"Jin, if you muff this case, in my book, you're scum." She looked away. "I can see you care. Look, Rachel was nine when her mother died. The stepmother's a Stephen King horror tale. No help at all with scooping residual evidence in her own home for us."

"What about the father?"

"He gave me the once-over. Pretended to care about Rachel. For show, he hugged her; she didn't flinch. He really doesn't like her. He's a turd, but he's not after her."

"But if her affect's flat, maybe she wouldn't flinch."

"Good point. But if an abuser goes to violence, a teen victim would recoil. She didn't. We eliminated the dad. Just a normal American family: indifferent parent, abusive stepparent. Kid got in the middle of their recreation time, so they chucked her into the street. Horrible narcissists. They want to play. The kid means work. They do that at the office."

I hated SACA cases. "Why do you think Rachel's silent?"

"Fear of reprisal by her attacker. Or love of the abuser."

"Your guess?"

"It ain't love. Hey, before you talk to Rachel, read Sandra Butler Smith's monograph on kids in court. And Ken Burr's outlines." Burr was a deputy DA and a statewide SACA trainer.

Capri talked as if I were the former Josh Jin, full of juice, a quick study who could nail a bad guy in a child rape without the training, a victim statement, or physical evidence.

I was too good a lawyer not to ask for help. "Help," I said.

She opened my briefcase and found my CDAA publications list. The California District Attorneys Association is the prosecutor's education consortium and general bookstore. She checked off fifteen items and called in the order for pickup. I drove toward CDAA, passing the shining white dome of the Capitol and its regal perimeter of immense redwoods.

"Capri, presuming the girl was raped, the last thing she needs, after Gonzo, is another male. She deserves a female DA."

"Shut up. You and Marx don't belong in the same category."

"Something change your mind?"

"I like that self-pitying attitude. Makes me want to puke."

"Gonzo's incompetent with kids. I am, too."

"Dammit! Then square yourself, 'cause you got a SACA case and you're all she's got."

"Hey, I didn't do these cases when I *was* squared away."

"Done sniveling?" she asked.

"I've only begun." I found a rare parking slot on J Street. I started to get out and Capri straightened my tie.

A CDAA training consultant named Ursula Donofrio had filled a box with texts, videos, audiotapes, and proceedings manuals. I loosened my tie and wrote a check. In the old days, the County helped defray the costs. Now, too many crooks, not enough books.

"Good luck with all this," said Ms. Donofrio warmly. Capri found *Forensic Psychiatry: Criminal Sexual Offender Profiles* by Dr. Teo Sandoval, and waved it emphatically in my face.

"Gonzo wouldn't use this to block a door. You'll take notes. He refused to go to Rio Junior High and thinks women are four-letter words. Bastard even ogles teenagers. He thinks rapes are the victims' fault. I've seen you romance a case." She tightened my tie.

In the elevator, she dropped the book in my box. "Jin, you were a great dad and a good DA. I loathe Gonzo. I merely hate your attitude. You know, you used to pick up my day. I'm counting on the guy I knew coming back again. Don't insult my judgment."

Holding the box with one hand, I loosened my tie. "As long as you know that Gonzo's been my role model ever since I wanted to be a lawyer." I took the box in both hands.

"You're not a lawyer. You're a prosecutor." She tightened it, rather sincerely.

"Who became a speechmaker."

She blew out air. "For a window office and a parking place."

"The stuff dreams are made of." I reloosened it.

She smiled wryly. I pointed my nose at the box of books. "I read all of this?"

Capri put them in order. "Get as far as you can. Come to my place at nine. You got to be ready to meet the victim tomorrow. Jin, your tie's crooked. You look like a cop."

Like a cop, I called François and asked him to gather all the meteorological data for the period January 15 to February 12, the likely time span of Rachel Farr's rape.

"You're taking this trial?" he asked.

"No. Just getting ready to corroborate a victim's statement."

* * *

It was dark and warm. Crickets chirped in stereo. Capri opened the door. I gave her Almond Roca candy and she let me in. Her house was compact, attractive, warm, welcoming, and spotless. The living room was made spacious by wise placement of comfortable furniture and the use of small-framed art. A semicircle of tan Asian fans arched above the stone fireplace. A small, elegant dining room with an immaculate glass étagère. Ample and well-stocked kitchen and a screened sunporch with a cat perch. Soft David Benoit. Sagwa rubbed against my leg and I scratched behind her ears. The smell of good coffee. I was in jeans and a polo shirt and my neck felt wonderful and free and she pulled a loose thread from my sleeve.

"Sit at the table." Capri handed me a cup. She wore a tee-shirt, black tights, and soft black shoes. "What's most important in a SACA case?" She sat facing me.

"The relationship between the DA and the victim."

Capri methodically stirred her coffee. "You have to care about her. Really care about her. What will Rachel think of you, the big, scary DA?"

"That I want to win more than help her. And that I'm a jerk."

A nod. "A bad adult. What are your major problems?"

"My fear of the child. My discomfort about a child being raped. My discomfort from talking about sex to a kid."

"Um-hm. Embarrassment. What must you project to her?"

"Confidence. Expertise. Objectivity. Self-assurance."

"That's right. Tell her you're the best. That you're *very* good at this. She has to believe in *you*. Like you've taught a hundred baby DAs. What questions will she have?"

"She'll want to know how long the trial will take. If he'll be convicted. His sentence. Who'll be in court. How long she'll be on the witness stand. She's going to think no one'll believe her. She'll worry that the rape was her fault, not stopping it."

"Good. Providing she talks. What's rape trauma syndrome?"

I closed my eyes. "Nightmares. Daymares. Flashbacks. Sleep deprivation. Emotional surfing. Eating disorders. Guilt. Ruminations. Chronic scrubbing to get him out of her skin."

"What do you tell her about that?"

"That the feelings are normal. She's not going crazy."

"You ought to remember that. What technique is good in direct testimony with her?"

Sagwa jumped in my lap. I petted her. "Echo-back."

Capri leaned over to pet her cat, taking time to do it right. "Jin, you like my place?"

I looked around. "Friendly and warm. Where you can take a bubble bath and get new."

"Thanks," she said, eyes narrowed, thinking. "Tell me one, Jin. Like the old days."

I brushed away some cat hairs before she could. "I don't tell jokes anymore."

"Yeah, you do." She rested her chin on her knee. "You're living one—Josh Jin doing Intake, making you a DA with free time during overload. That's funny. Tom Conover belting Sergeant Billy McManus and everything going to hell. Chinatown charging *us* with racism, using a white girl they don't care about. The *Moody* file's a laugher. Jin, you take things too seriously—all you lost was your daughter and your wife. At least you were married."

"Capri, you ought to have your own talk show."

"You'd be my first guest. Chronic mourning, it isn't good for you. It hurts your work."

She was a loner who busted bad men who scarred little girls. Here, I saw her. She had given up her life to chase the worst men in the zoo. She worked in the devil's playpen, where screams went beyond cinema. There was a price to fighting evil. It tended to rub off.

"Okay," I said. "I feel better already."

She stretched her legs. "There's something else. I want you to visit Tiffany Prue."

I grunted.

"Know what, Jin? I don't give a damn that it's hard for you. Go see her. She needs it."

Reasoning like that used to work in the old days. I felt old. "Okay," I said.

Capri smiled, satisfied. She closed her eyes. I thought she was asleep when she whispered, "When you busted Rostov, were you tempted to off him, to end it, right there?" Georgi Rostov had killed three neighbor children, drinking their blood.

I said I hadn't.

"Lately I've been thinking about giving pedophiles their rights and then shooting them."

We sat, listening to jazz and the crickets.

9.

RACHEL

Wednesday

. . .the initial meeting between victim and prosecutor should take place at the residence of the victim. . . . a feeling of security and trust must be built at the outset. . . . After the child has been greeted with a smile and pleasantries, the prosecutor should introduce herself and explain the purpose of the meeting. . . . The attorney must appear relaxed, friendly, and at ease. Children are much more attuned to physical signals than verbal ones. Child-victims are frequently . . . watchful and vigilant. They have had to learn to read adults by physical messages, and to distrust verbal ones . . . children who appear hard as nails will often soften if they are asked to protect another child.

—JUDGE SANDRA BUTLER SMITH,
CHILDREN'S STORY: SEXUALLY MOLESTED CHILDREN IN CRIMINAL COURT

Rio Junior High sprouted Chinese kids with an immigrant hunger for achievement and the machine-gun harmonics of fourteen-toned Cantonese. Some males smelled my badge and fled. I sat in the school office, trying not to think about children. A bell rang. In the relative silence came softly muted cud-chew, dental office radio music. Outside, tar melted in the heat.

Someone had to witness Rachel's statement: Kimberley Hong.

Establish rapport. Relaxed, friendly, and at ease. I practiced, "Hi, I'm Mr. Jin." Cough. Remember to smile like Bert Parks. "Hi, I'm Mr. Jin!" I shook my head, feeling sour.

A girl was outside the door, watching me from the thin shadows of sagging file cabinets. I would later be tempted to say that I appreciated her condition the moment we met, that her pain drew sympathy from me like water from a deep well.

When I saw Rachel for the first time, she made me ache, as if there were a cosmic, causational calculus that connected her to Summer's death. Rachel Farr had squandered her life, and my resentment was bilious. The death of your child kills charity at the root.

It didn't matter that I understood rape trauma syndrome or that I was paid to be compassionate. I had tried for a year to be insensate. I had succeeded.

She was coltish, emaciated and pale, bruised and defiant, rumpled and unclean, circles darkening eyes, radiating a Manhattan January disdain. A chronic victim, damaged, pierced, and tattooed on a wrist, fidgeting for comfort in a comfortless world.

I might have liked her had she been a different person. I felt a tug of empathy but resisted it. I could not help this sad, scornful teen who had run with cannibals to the demon. The beast had sniffed her and taken a big, bloody bite. Healing for months, but few repairs showed. Underneath, no one worth a chat was home.

She blanched. She had been tossed at me the way low-grade meat is flung at a toothless dog. I forced a ghastly smile and Kimberley Hong made a clucking sound, coaxing the girl forward. Rachel's pained eyes were cloaked by a dirty Raiders cap. She winced at my face, my crocodile smile, my body. She looked like dry kindling, ready to snap.

"Hi," I said, "I'm Mr. Jin."

"Rachel," said Hong softly, "Mr. Jin is a top district attorney.

This is Rachel Farr. Rachel, talk to this man. He can be your friend. We in Chinatown are very proud of him."

"I'm not important. You are." The reflexive words. I had made baby DAs recite them. We are the servants. Our power comes from the victims who are within our reach. Serve them. If you jerk victims' cases around for promotions or headlines, turn in your badge.

Rosy sunlight played through old windows on the stigmata of crime: fear gleaming like hot coals; quick, anxious breathing; old cuts simmering in the warmth of an angry sun. I ached for my daughter. Somewhere between us, our pains met and passed without speaking.

I had a silent girl's political case. I smelled her agonies rising from young flesh. A musty scent of old sheets and uncleaned wounds, of mindless years of absent care and disregard.

I was back, out of Intake's cocoon, no longer insulated by paperwork. The girl was thirteen and looked eleven. Haggard, defeated, insolent, unable to remember a good day, cloaked by bruising and the memory of haunting pain. I cleared my throat and she jumped. She was not going to say, How about those Giants? "Please," I said, "have a seat."

Fingers twisted. She waited for something bad to happen, almost writhing.

"It seems all our office does is make things worse for you. I'm sorry I'm making you uncomfortable. But I'm the lawyer now for your side." I took a breath. "I'm here to make sure that what happened to you won't happen again. I need your help to do that."

She sat awkwardly, crossing her legs tightly, pressing her hands beneath them. Her misery choked my words, begging tears, and I hated her for breaking my will. My voice cracked. "You're my only case. Will you talk when you're ready?" I looked away, eyes wet.

Kimberley Hong was staring, covering her mouth. I gave my card to Hong, who was looking sadly at her thin student and at me. Rachel leaned away, clenching her teeth. Unlike Chinese girls, Rachel cared nothing for ordered relationships. She was a child without the strength of a clan web, of people to trust, and had to bear her injuries alone.

I cleared my throat, clenching teeth. "Rachel, did the person who hurt you threaten you?" She twitched at my rising pains. "If we don't stop him, he can hurt someone else."

A slight blip in her face, and then she was gone again.

"Rachel," said Ms. Hong, "can you talk to Mr. Jin?"

Her chest moved, panting, no sound. She was shivering. She pointed at the radio.

Ms. Hong was puzzled. I turned off the dental office music. Rachel visibly relaxed.

"Rachel, have lunch with us. Same place. I'll meet you there." Ms. Hong left quietly.

I let some moments pass. "I don't blame you for not wanting to talk," I said tightly.

Rachel was gone. "That," I said to the empty room, "went well."

I joined Hong at a concrete area in the shade of tall and blighted elms. The oldest ones had been planted by the forty-niners who had struck it rich and could afford to plant shade trees to counter the murderous Valley heat. Now the trees were over a hundred years old; some were a hundred feet tall. Most kids were in the cafeteria, absorbing thin air-conditioning. A hawk circled the fields behind the school, waffling in the warm air with the thermal glider's oddly stiff grace. Boys played basketball. Anglos were the minority. The ones on the court saw the Chinese man, playing harder for him.

"Mr. Jin, I see a big Chinese prosecutor and say, Yes, *he* can be *the* DA! Help our people! I just heard you lost your daughter. Joshua Jin, I am sorry. You were going to cry in there, looking at Rachel. So I wondered—does he have a Chinese wife to comfort him? I hear she is white. Yes, I speak my mind. Like with Rachel. How many saw her and said nothing?"

"You think only Chinese women make good wives?"

"No. But Chinese women know men better. We've been helping you for thousands of years. You know, if I married a *gwailo*, he would make me feel *more* different. Is this true?"

I looked for Rachel. "Has Rachel been psych eval'd?" Psychologically evaluated.

"By a Dr. Sandoval. They say he's good. He is an author."

That would prove it. He was the doc Ava wanted me to see. "What's Rachel told you?"

"Joshua Jin, she says nothing to anyone. She only tolerates me. She doesn't eat. She used to. Now, no eye contact. Like you."

Looking far away, I asked who Rachel's friends were. Hong said she was friendless.

"How much weight has she lost?" Sign of clinical depression.

"About ten pounds."

"Do you have a Polaroid?" She nodded.

"Ms. Hong, I want you to take her picture every week. With the *Sacramento Bee* in the shot for the date." I gave her a twenty. "For film. I also want you to weigh her every Friday."

She didn't ask why. "Okay. You know, Rachel's very smart." Important to Chinese.

"But she cries and pushes away her former friends." Far away, a siren wailed.

I knew that feeling. "What do you suggest I do?"

"Be patient. Like me, waiting for you to take responsibility for your community. Time is the old Chinese ally, yes? See, you are *very* American—you could run and *win*. To help us. To be a son to your roots and loyal to your blood. Rachel is a Chinatown girl now, and needs your help, the help of a top DA. Are you coming back, to try to talk to her, again?"

"Ms. Hong, I'm not a bureau chief anymore. I was relieved of management duties."

The Catholic Home for Girls is four floors of old gray stone and mortar. I had never seen the Lowood Institution, which housed the orphan Jane Eyre, but this could have been it.

Ms. Bette Maddock was oddly welcoming, considering that the heavy doors, barred windows, and deadbolt locks were designed to keep out males, whose manifold sins had filled the home with abandoned and battered female children preparing to deliver babies of rape and abuse. Ms. Maddock wore a Lands' End shirt and slacks ensemble. I was disappointed in the absence of an English accent. It was almost painfully bright outside, but the halls were faded and poorly lit. Our footsteps echoed. Infants cried mightily from every corner. The building smelled of macaroni and cheese, drugstore juvenile perfumes, hard work, and Pampers. One baby wailed inconsolably. An upper door opened. "Shhh, baby, shhh," said a child's voice.

Tiffany Prue was in the quieter wing of expectant children, watching a soap opera in the overwarm TV lounge. A clutch of girls, stale castoff clothes reeking of cigarettes and stretching over bulging tummies, interacted with the cast.

"Forget you!" cried one at a male actor. "You tell 'im, girl!" encouraged another.

Tiffany waved at me. "Hi. You got any smokes?"

I watched for a while. When I left, Tiffany waved goodbye.

At my desk, I was listening to the Contours, "Do You Love Me?" I had an easy job and an ordered desk and too much free time. And my *Moody* file was missing. Someone had lifted it without leaving a file receipt. I was in the police station—I locked my office only at night.

Damn cops, taking vengeance for the Incident, preserving a sacred grudge for Conover by dropping sophomoric pranks on his local representative, the Intake deputy.

I called Bilinski. He swore he didn't do it.

"If I was gonna screw you, I wouldn't take the damn *Moody* file. Ain't nuthin' in it. Unless you're holdin' out on me, which you probably are. Hey, man, I'm just a dumb cop who didn't go to law school like some chumps I know. No. Fact is, I ain't made no progress on nuthin'."

10.

THE SAVING OF SUMMER JIN

I am from San Francisco, nexus of world cultures and scenic progeny of many bad habits. The City suffers from terminal tourism, lacks discernible seasons, and enjoys several cycles of soft fog that are neither winter nor summer. It endures systematic and macabre tectonic earthquakes and a thunderstorm every century.

I worked ninety miles up in Sacramento, a sprawl space for millions of refugees from the real estate oligarchies of the Bay Area and for drifters from the inbred, oversnowed communities of the High Sierras. As a railhead it draws from the great eastern stretch of mid-American wheat fields and their summers, winters, and tornadoes. Some come on parole from Soledad and Folsom state prisons; others are flushed from overcrowded local county jails.

Sacramento has the state capitol, a riverboat culture, as many lawyers and crooks per capita as Washington, and weather to spare. Julys can run exclusively in three digits and winter fogs can blind a driver feeling his way at five miles an hour.

River City's young roots are deep in the Wild West, making it an excellent town for prosecutors. Most citizens work too hard to free a felon with an acquittal, a book contract, and sleaze talk show appearances—the unhappy precedents in the greater cities to the south.

Capri drove. I loosened my tie. We were meeting Harry O. Bilinski.

"Rachel," said Capri as she handed me a Med Center photo. The girl was pressed against a wall, clutching a faded Miss Piggy doll. Stress circled frightened eyes. She looked like an injured doe on a freeway. I put it in my pocket, to keep her eyes from touching mine.

Had she been raped? I didn't know. But something had happened to her. A bad life.

We were in the Broadway with the Chinese and Indochinese, thrumming with gangs and *dai lo*, big brother, bosses. They were drawn to cash—the object of absent, overworking fathers—were better armed than we were and higher up the food chain than kids like Rachel. Her place was a mile south. Moody's house was closer.

"Tell me how Rachel took to you."

"Like your cat to a bath."

Bilinski was at the Tower Café counter, his gum in an ashtray. "Ed Jones, aka Buttface of Fred and Gary's River City Motel, is actually one Victor Petty, an L.A. pedophile with a long jacket. Tiffany Prue made him in the lineup. Petty's file'll be in Intake tomorrow."

"Good work, Harry," I said. "Thanks."

"That mean I'm fired?" He shook his head. "You know, the guys are sayin' I'm doin' too much for you assholes." He patted himself for more gum. "Conover ever gonna apologize?"

"I don't think so. Check out John Quick, Moody's alibi. Rachel's parents. Raps, priors, deep backgrounds." He didn't take notes. I asked him to step out. "What's the alibi's name?"

"Fuck you."

I said, "That's close. It's 'John Quick Fuck You.' "

"Back off. Don't you get it? They sent me to bung your case. It's got the hopes of a whore runnin' for Pope! Don't con me—you got canned, bigger 'n shit. They gave you a political crap case to dump. So dump it and unass my life, asshole! Or fire me," he added.

"Harry, it's true that I'm a little behind in the race for President, but we're going to try to save the case. If it's a dump, I'll dump it." We went back in. I paid for his pastries.

"Fuck no. I owe you nuthin'. And don't you fuckin' *dare* cry around me."

* * *

Early in trial work, I occasionally found, without volition, a momentum, an eloquence, an inevitable countdown to conviction. The jury would nod in accord and my heart would lift with the sense that a tiny corner of the world was going right.

DAs in the zone can shape history, creating a good from the overwhelmingly bad. Your dad was murdered, your child was shot—but here is legal recompense. A judgment, published and obeyed, that says evil was done and that someone will now pay. But you have to win.

Summer had asked about trial work as part of a school assignment. She, who accepted me and my ways as no one else.

"When you hum in trial," I said, "it's being in the ring when everything works. Your punches land, your timing's a gift. You're unstoppable and the bad guy's going down. The people who got hurt are getting a dose of hope. It's a big rush.

"Verdicts are forever. You can win things in the heart." DAs never fought for the purse.

I had smiled into her eyes with the words "Forever" and "Heart," sending a Chinese Taoist good-faith message into my daughter, creating ancient medical remedies with thoughts and words as my mother and BaBa had taught me on quiet, moonlit nights.

Her *foo chi*, good fortune, had not run its course. I would never tire, never slow, never be stopped. I would fight the good fight with Chinese patience and Mongolian ferocity, pouring all my skills, my soul, my learning, my good karma, into her pot. It was an effort never hurt by a single negative thought or a moment's consideration of losing. I would win. *We* would win.

Summer would live and to hell with all naysayers. This verdict would purchase things in the heart. If ever the concept of noble struggle had a purpose, it was the saving of Summer Jin, the girl I would not let die.

"That's what you do in court, Daddy?" she had asked.

"Sometimes. When I'm in the zone." It hadn't happened that often, and then I had been promoted out of trials, into the political lunch circuit, my words aiming not for reportable verdicts, but for elusive poll points. And Summer had died, seamlessly taking with her so many parts of me with which I conducted the simplest tasks. Working. Loving. Being. Arguing.

Rachel Farr was withdrawn, isolated, hypervigilant, sleepless, regressed, eating poorly, exuding fear, anxiety, and depression, and having trouble expressing herself. In my gut, I sensed her interest in suicide. I felt her fragility, induced by trauma. A jab of pain in my head.

I closed my eyes and knew she had been raped, and that prior to her trauma, she had been more whole, more viable, smoother with life. Now she was awash in her past, like her fragile prosecutor. We could sympathetically trigger new personal catastrophes with our mutual, sad harmonics of loss, like a poorly engineered bridge in a bitter narrows wind.

"Damn," I said.

11.

STACY AUGUST

BaBa had believed in hard labor, which was helpful since it was all he did. I was still at work, staring at an unsuspecting Taco Bell Burrito Supreme. The phone rang.

"Good evening, Joshua. This is Stacy August."

Her voice, a low sax in a dusky, candlelit room, crimped my breathing. Stacy Antoinette August was a celebrity attorney, a woman of diamonds and steel and one of the best trial lawyers in the business. She had won an acquittal in *People v. Hadrow*, a murder case where her advocacy beat me and freed a killer. She had once been the love of my life.

"Come, Josh. Talk to me about Tommy Conover's position in the polls."

"He's ahead with voters who secretly always wanted to beat up a cop."

She laughed. "It's more intricate than that. May I send a car?"

"Stacy, you can humiliate me perfectly well on the phone."

"But shark fin soup is being delivered from San Francisco." She hung up.

White & August is in the Double Quarter—a black glass monolith at 2525 Capitol Mall. It sits between the drawbridge and the Capitol; one straddles shipping, the other hosts lobbying.

Phillips T. Rittenhouse was a patrician White & August partner in an Armani with a loose Hermès tie, a fine shadow on a model's square jaw. Stacy's co-counsel in *Hadrow*. He greeted me politely. "I'm your driver tonight, Mr. Jin." A cordial handshake, a zing of ice.

Prosecutors do not visit law firms, particularly at night; there is something suggestive of corruption in a DA visiting the opposition's venue. DAs lean toward the Spartan and fear the seductions of wealth. For negotiations, we use the phone and neutral judges' chambers, where starkness encourages progress and appearances are cleanly preserved.

I had no caseload to compromise. White & August's kitchen had Chinese chefs with a global menu for its lawyers, while DAs ate tuna sandwiches, the lettuce wilted by noon.

A chrome and mirrored elevator without austerity. I was a bureau chief without a bureau, a DA without a caseload, a father without a daughter, and a man without a wife, sauntering deep into enemy territory on a Wednesday night. Rittenhouse loved Stacy August without success. He watched me from the corner of his eye.

Channing White and Stacy August had scored in the Eighties, the golden age of legal profits. Its lobby was cathedraled marble with a hushed infinity waterfall. It led to a reception area overladen in Ch'ing Dynasty chandeliers, ironwood screens, and heavy tapestries. An alabaster service center beneath a vaulted ceiling. The Ch'ing was the last dynasty of the fabled Chinese Empire; its art was not as pricey as T'ang or Ming, but it served as a smooth, dark patina for overreaching wealth. Beneath Manchu paint lay black Bismarckian iron and princely, Machiavellian ambition propelled by young legal blood and excess nouveau cash.

Stacy's brains exceeded her beauty, and the combination called for mental agility from those in her company. Rittenhouse spoke to the receptionist. We shook. He left.

Heels on marble. Stacy August was tall and tanned, a gentle, overwide mouth and startling blue eyes setting off heavy cherry hair around a model's face. Original physical gifts were maintained with a hard trainer. Her clothes that night could have required my monthly income. They highlighted sophistication, power, and raw beauty. A warm handshake, a familiar scent that crossed formal borders and instantly evoked the past.

Stacy August represented California lawmakers, electronic tech company CEOs, and venture capitalists, but her passion was trials, whose rewards included renewable triumphs and adrenal rushes not dissimilar to falling in love. She was a consummately prepared, technically brilliant, and precise advocate of immense intelligence who made me think of my own courtroom work as chopping wood in a hot sun.

"Good evening, Joshua. You look very fit."

Her office was Olympian marble without a hint of humility. Distinct executive, sitting, and conference areas. A step-down dining room framed in black Japanese teak screens and carpeted with an immense Persian rug. Soaring fauna, classical music, fine art, a great library. A spot to gather the multitudes for a reunion, or to park a Stoli beneath the gravity of success to await the offer, the deal, or the millennium. Deputy DAs had sat here and joined the firm. I was a fly in a soft, pliable web.

"Your first visit. It is a tad excessive, and I am at times embarrassed, but I recover."

"I question recovery, but admire the claim. How many forests and mountains did you kill to make this?"

"Charming. A trained prosecutor *and* an environmentalist." She gestured; I sat. "I know how you value food. Dinner first." With a gold Dunhill lighter she lit candles and sat opposite me as handsome high-cheekboned Chinese waiters in formal half-jackets poured wine and served shark fin soup, sliced pork and shiitake mushrooms, black-bean lobster, the aromas lifting and weakening me. Rice came last, as it does for proper Chinese gentry banquets.

We spoke of books, films, colleagues, and trial awards—she had just won a multimillion-dollar judgment in a premises liability case and was working a complex SEC case.

"Josh, what happens," she asked, "if you lose *Moody*?"

"Conover probably loses Chinatown by fifteen to twenty percent."

"I think," said Stacy, "Tommy has already lost the city."

"Well, so much for my political judgment."

A fleeting smile. "I am counsel of record now for Mr. Karl Francis Moody."

DAs hate surprises. Lately, I had been consuming a forced diet of them. Stacy was my opponent. In trial. I felt a flash of fear.

She had enormous legal resources. Superior trial strategies. Bright, winning ways. Unlimited jury pull. In court, she was smarter than me, a condition difficult to appreciate. And this was a SACA case. My mind spun: Stacy charged half a million for a non-celeb trial.

Moody had half a mil. "Really?" My taste buds were numb.

"Moody was the SACA case you could not bind at prelim."

"I know the name."

"I would hope. He is your only case. Where is my discovery?" Discovery was our investigative work which, by law, is copied to the defense. It meant we could never pull surprises or a surprise witness, the rabbit-trick of courtroom movies.

Joe Pelletier, PD, has it, I said. I'll send fresh. We made notes. She asked if I saw a constitutional problem in jailing Moody after the failed prelim without a rearrest. I saw an issue, not a problem.

No matter, she said. The judge will.

"Stacy, how does a fellow like Moody afford you?"

"Mr. Moody has assets." A smile, a monetary vanity, a vice. She had given something away. Moody, the ex-con, had assets. "What is your offer, Josh?"

"It's SACA." No bargains by law. "A plea, straight up."

"That's illogical. Your victim is silent. You have no physical evidence and you doubt Moody's guilt. You can dismiss or reduce on those grounds, even as we speak." Even as we speak. That was a companion to "Been there, done that," the Nineties mantra of the nondiligent. I had been a friend to hard labor, but I was not the worker I once was. If Conover lost the election, the childless, divorced Josh Jin would also be unemployed.

"You asked for the offer," I said. "You got it. Even as we sit." I smiled.

"Joshua." Stacy made my name sound like an address to Congress. "Gonzo Marx made an open offer of *twelve months' county jail* at the prelim. I can still take it."

"I revo—"

"We accept." A brilliant smile, a soft laugh. "I can't believe it. You had no clue! Gonzo and I beat you in a silent conspiracy." Her lovely hair shimmered. "I love his incompetence!"

I should have asked Gonzo. Not that he would've remembered. Or told me.

August sat back and crossed her legs. With time served, Moody'd be out of jail in four months. She had baited me, sucker-punched me, and ruined my meal. The possible rape of a teenager would be punished with some daytime TV and local broom-pushing in county jail. I didn't want to go to trial, but now I was part of an obscene wrist-slapping. I felt personal relief—no trial—mixed with professional nausea. And the evening was still young.

"I take it the girl hasn't spoken?" she asked. Something else was now about to happen. I wished I had a helmet. "Josh. Dismiss the case I-E and I will not sue you."

"I-E" was a dismissal for Insufficiency of Evidence. If I dismissed I-E, Moody would walk, his case dropped forever, without even a rotation at the county jail TV room.

"Stacy, you threatened a suit." I made a note.

"You waste time on Boy Scout points. Interested?"

There was no moral way I could accept. "You're joking."

From below came police sirens. Stacy August sipped from her Lalique goblet. "From anyone else, that would be a slur. Josh, you don't want the Moody trial. Or *any* trial. Worse, you bluff badly." The strengths in her face settled on the weaknesses in mine. Deep blue eyes, heavy with assessment, the face worthy of classical artists. She steepled perfectly manicured fingers. "You never did a child sex case."

"Your point?"

"Darling, I only make points in trial." A soft smile. "This is for fun." She sipped a Montrachet '59 from her private cellar in the goblet I had given her, long ago.

What made Stacy great was preparation. Stacy had just done me like Muhammad Ali did Joe Frazier. The smooth, blinding, lateral ring artist duncing the rough, linear field-worker. I had gone straight in for the knockout and found myself on the mat facing an acquittal.

"Rachel Farr is the worst victim in the history of law. She will not talk. And Harry Bilinski the Backshooter is the one cop in America who makes Mark Fuhrman look rather wonderful."

She sat in the chair next to me. Her perfume settled on my unfinished dinner, her eyes warming my cheeks. "I sent you and Ava condolences. But the bouquet will not excuse what I am about to say.

"Josh, I'm sorry, terribly sorry, that Summer died." Her chest rose. "You have no idea how much. But professionally, it is as if the person you are to race had his legs amputated. I will make you look bad and your case look worse. Worse than *Hadrow,* when you had forensics and only a cretin on heroin for an eyewitness."

Well-styled hair shifted softly. "Your victim! And you! Of all the prosecutors in California, you're the soft touch. You have a new vulnerability that is really quite charming."

I nodded. "I changed aftershaves."

"Don't quip while I'm nailing you." She came closer, eyes on my face. "Oh, Josh, you always had your lights on! You had humor, wit, strength. You had the love of friends and the fear of enemies. You overflowed with power, energy, vibration, *prana,* vitality. Joy of life. You made things happen." Her eyes, deep and soft and rather sad. "Now that is all gone."

She stood. "You know me. While you've been sucking donuts in Intake and beating up those poor fat boys in Ragusa's Gym, I've tried *Moody* in front of local focus groups. You don't even have a case-in-chief and I'm ready for oral argument before the Supreme Court.

"I am going to share something. Jurors do not like a big, broad-shouldered Chinese man prosecuting for a teenage white girl rape victim. There's too much cross-racial proximity. They do not like a stud of color knowing a little white girl's anatomy. Genitalia. Nudity. Men of color make white people prudes. For a child rape, they want a prosecutor who is an attractive Anglo woman. Or an asexual, intellectual, professorial Anglo man. Or a decent heterosexual Anglo male. And so forth, down the Anglo line. You know this is true."

Stacy moved, passing me something from her desk. A JurPro business envelope. JurPro was a jury selection consultancy firm. For six figures, they helped the defense pick juries to acquit killers, rapists, child abusers, and drug dealers. It was part of the White & August service package for civil cases, now apparently used for a criminal cause. Anything JurPro had to say would be expensive. Why would she show anything to me? To ace me.

"JurPro's extract on race, gender, and age of the DA, in a case where you have neither complaining victim nor physical evidence. But even if that poor, lost little girl names my client, they walk him. We put a shaky girl on the stand. We received three quick acquittals."

She sat. "Use this information, Joshua. I know you won't dismiss until you get a statement from the girl. She is not going to give one. Get out of the case. Conover gave this cheap case to you to save Chinatown votes. You have more friends than he. Give it to Isaac Krakow, who actually knows how to do a SACA case. He'll be smart enough to dismiss it, I-E.

"Sweetheart, get well. Then it would be my pleasure to tear you apart in court. Again." She sat and contemplated me as if I were an apple strudel she had prepared for the oven.

I preferred Stacy August's arrogance. Now she was slapping me with charity. DAs couldn't afford jury-selection consulting fees, even if we trusted them.

Stacy sipped wine, a *Vogue* model under cocktail-lounge-like museum lights that made artwork look pricier and women look more alluring. "Baby, tell me you'll get rid of this thing."

Tom Conover, Geneva de Hoyas, Harry Bilinski, and Stacy August wanted me to dump it. Capri, Kimberley Hong, and Chinatown wanted a conviction. Capri, for ethics. Chinatown, for politics. I wondered what Ava would want. What Summer would want. My stomach sank.

"Summer's death ended your trial career. You muck with the litmus test case, you will lose your last chance at a major law firm. Joshua, it is time for you to act. You look good, but you're not getting younger. Forget trials. Stretch your legal mind. Be transactional. Be a rainmaker. Do deals, own something. Make things *happen*." She opened a hand: join me.

I shook my head. International language for: no. There were a thousand reasons to decline, only one to say yes. To be with her. I had answered before that reason could vote.

She drew up tightly. "Don't be too full of yourself. You only know criminal law and you're not up-to-speed for a tough civil case. You are at the edge of economic viability. Two, three more years, no one will want you. And Moody is *innocent*. Do not look down at my office or my gains. I grew up poor, like you. I *made* this! Your office—*I* pay for that, too. My tax money. Someone has to pay for it. And someone has to suck at the public trough."

"That's beneath you." Even if what she had said about civil work was correct.

"It was no reach at all. Your life has changed. That which you had is no longer here. By all rights, you *should* be morally crushed, spiritually spent, legally indifferent. Losing Summer *defines* the great, acute wound. God, she was exquisite! Her loss is unbearable. Time to save yourself. I can help, a little. By reminding you that this case can only destroy you further."

She leaned forward. I expected sparks. "Look in my eyes and tell me if I'm wrong."

"It's just one case."

She snorted. "You're lucky that lying to me isn't actionable. Josh, Summer was your unapproachable accomplishment. She died. How could you not be disinterested in all else?"

"I'm indifferent to all but your next surprise. The JurPro stuff was great. How about a balloon lady and an elephant?"

She took an audible breath. "You can be quite a pain."

"Stace, you've been toying with me all night."

She had an unlovely anger, a heart-stopping profile, and looks that had distracted men for decades. She looked away. Her charisma made me look in the same direction.

"Joshua, did you ever look at Summer and think of me?"

A different voice. Stacy. Don't do this.

"Josh, don't tell me that you've never thought that Summer could have been *our* child, the girl we imagined coming from us. I saw her at Justice Kennedy's reception. God, she was flawless." She exhaled. "And, in a way, she was partly mine. . . ."

Stacy waited for me to speak. Then, "She's the daughter you lost. The girl I'll never have. This is no delusional, neurotic ramble. We talked about our daughter . . . her recitals while we held hands, everyone envying us. God, I loved how we drew stares."

Her voice, her message, were knives. "Stacy. Don't do this."

"'Don't do this?!'" Her features contorted. "Didn't I use those words, begging you? And God knows, I am *not* a beggar. 'Don't do this.' How long have I been the diplomatic counsel, nodding to you politely in master calendar, smiling at you at in elevators? Gunning you down in trial." She was breathing hard, arms crossed, body eloquent and beautiful. She was fire and wind, and I, dry, gnarled winter kindling from once bigger wood.

Stacy leaned against a bookshelf and licked her lips for a final argument she had long ago rehearsed.

"A Sunday in May. I smelled gardenias. We had a court at ten. I made you shrimp *chow fun* with a Beaulieu Petite Sirah, a '68. You called to say that you were chasing a woman you had met a couple hours earlier." A tightening of her jaw. "I said, 'Don't. Oh, baby, don't do this. I *beg* you!'" She looked out. "Your memory was always better, but I got the major chords." She sighed, too strong for tears. I wanted to go but it was time for atonement.

"I have gotten the things I set out to take. I make money. I own things. I have status and celebrity. I win big judgments. Men still pursue me, which is sometimes helpful in a small, egotistical way. It was not what I wanted." She straightened.

"I'd trade it in a heartbeat to have married you. To have had kids. Know why?" Her gaze burned. "Your *passion* for me. Your *loyalty* to me. Through all the men, my mad phases, our terrible ups and downs, when we were together, it was new and beguiling and I could give myself to you in a way I couldn't with anyone else. You always took me back. Whenever I saw my way clear to you, you were there. Forgiving me. Holding me, all night. Loving me, being one with me. Baby, you held me so close. You talked to me until I slept." Her eyes glittered.

"What a wonder, that the man I loved the most loved me." She held her head, hips slightly turned, a dramatic stance that inspired awe, memory, desire, and brainless action. "So don't you say, 'Don't do this' to me. I didn't cry when you phoned, fourteen years ago next week. I didn't intend to raise this tonight.

"But there you sat, infuriating me with that prosecutorial detachment, wearing Summer's death like a shield. As if we were just two lawyers with this case, and what books have you read recently, and isn't this food remarkable?" She took a breath.

"You need to acknowledge who I was to you. What I was to you. And what Summer was to me."

"I'm sorry—"

"Sorry? Sorry you married Ava? Sorry you came to dinner? That you have a stinking flamer of a dead SACA case publicly wrapped around your neck like a dead albatross with me as opposing counsel? Why didn't you marry me? I think I deserve an answer to that."

I stood, afraid to be too close, obligated by history not to stand in the hall. "I thought our past was settled. But here I am with you." Our old relationship tilled up all around us, unkind issues unearthed as if an enormous archeological land mine had detonated.

I faced her heat. "I loved you. I didn't marry you because I couldn't keep you. You were too beautiful, too sexy, too crazy with men. I saw a lifelong competition." I rubbed my face. "If there's one thing I won't do, it's embark on a lost cause. I like good odds." BaBa had taught me that. People wear clothes, so laundries work. DAs win eighty percent. I used to win ninety.

She sagged. I used to see her spent and gorgeous in bed. "God. You're telling me it was low self-esteem? No. . . ."

"I was Caucasian-challenged. You were the blond princess."

"And you loved blondes. Honey, you had me, completely."

"You left me too many times for me to believe that."

"Like you didn't?" She sat, her breath blowing her hair.

I looked at her and said very clearly, "No."

"Jesus." She touched her hair. "You remembered all the bad times. That's the Chinese in you." She took a slow breath. "The damn *DA* in you. Never forgiveness. Always the memory of injury." Her eyes narrowed. "Exacting a Chinese price, the max sentence. God, you have a blood lust. You *never* wonder if you have the wrong man. It's why people fear you. It's why I do defense." Her words, not all of them true, seemed to ring in her metallic artwork. Her fingers on her lips. "And then you met Ava."

"No. I had marrying you on my mind. I imagined the wedding, your men deployed around the church, ready to object with gunfire during the ceremony. Even without them, you were a reach. There was the guy who showed up our last night together. *Then* I met Ava."

"I've seen Ava. She's beautiful. She drew men. And does."

"She never played men in orchestrated mob scenes like you. You have a crazy streak that she doesn't have."

"You liked that streak," she whispered, looking up at me.

I looked out her window. God help me, I loved that streak. The part I hid from my father, long after his death. BaBa, I like dangerous women. I like to beat the hell out of men I hate. I do not respect my stepfather, even though the Master K'ung says I must. I am not virtuous.

"That was then," I said. There was no now. Her silence had hushed the music. Time to go, but I owed her more courtesy.

"Okay, Joshua. I gave you jury selection data, dinner, and music. And once again, you've slam-dunked me. But you ought to know that I wouldn't represent a child molester."

For an instant, I wondered if she was correct, and I wrong.

"You'd represent Joseph Stalin if he could cover the fee."

"Stalin, no way. Khrushchev, sure. Yeltsin, certainly. Josh, the girl is a false accuser, without the courage to admit that Moody is innocent." She shook her head. "She is an insult to everything Summer Jin was. She is a cheap, unintelligent, low-class, immoral—"

"That's enough."

"Oh, get off it! She's tattooed, body-studded, with no—"

"I said, that's enough."

"No. You have NO moral right to silence me. It is quite the opposite. You can't move your manhood in and suddenly have the right answers. Why no physical evidence? Because she's a hateful liar, a little self-impressed bitch, and there was no rape." Her words cut.

I touched Rachel's stricken photo in my pocket, to stop her wounds, as if she heard and felt Stacy's puncturing words. I sensed Rachel's shock in the picture. In that moment in the black glass tower, I sensed her pain from the collage of my own. She had been raped by Moody. I felt I had been raped by God. Rachel was coping better.

Stacy had not seen Rachel as I had seen her. Unsatisfied angers coalesced around Stacy August. Too bad there'd be no trial. I could use this outrage to overcome my hesitancy to face a jury. It gave me a purpose. Prosecutors are supposed to remain coolly objective, and neither rant nor rave. But I had lost my will to fight, and needed anger to do battle.

I stood close. "I'm sorry I hurt you. A shame you didn't have kids. You'd be a great mom. If that's my fault, I'm sorry."

Her eyes were wet. "You're so magnanimous, dispensing papal apologies, years too late, the martyrs long dead. I used to think you didn't apologize because I didn't matter to you. Now, I know the truth. You're *afraid* of me! I think you still want me. Still think of me."

I shook my head. There had only been Summer and her heart. Perhaps only someone with a dying child could understand that. Now didn't matter.

"Josh, would you convict an ex-con to save your office from a Seth Jergen election? If the ex-con was innocent?"

"I must look real bad to deserve that question."

"You look wonderful. But other things have changed." Her eyes touched me. "Except, some things." She was close. The armor of my marriage and the comfort of passing time had evaporated. The old fogs of confusion and desire, our former colognes, persisted.

"I better go."

"Yes." A word like a portcullis in a great, deep castle. Her eyes sank softly into me.

Once, her eyes were the path to the only world I wanted. She was close, touching my neck, softly kissing my cheek. The touch of her lips crossed the years and made old nerves surge. She grazed my lips. Beneath the warm hazy wonder of her was the warm sweet breath of an epic disaster. I backed away.

"At night," she whispered, "I remember your mouth."

I was remembering too much. Her eyes were cloudy and blue. "I'm the DA on the case," I said, backing away.

She blinked, stepping back in a hurtful retreat reminiscent of other times.

" 'The DA on the case.' Oh, that's really beautiful. What are you doing, carrying a wire in your pants, speaking for an audience of bishops?" She shook her head. "Okay, Josh, we'll play by your rules. Next time it's all business. You poke your head out, I'll cut it off."

"I'll try to remember that," I said.

"You won't be able to forget." Her eyes, passing through various levels of me: a sorceress, hot with knowledge, hurt, and anger. Her muscular legal memory had kept the past alive. A breath, studying me. "I decline Gonzo's offer. Mr. Joshua Lawrence Jin, son of Jin Tse-hsu, a noble laundryman who brought his family to America, this case needs to be tried."

There was no hiding it: Stacy Antoinette August wanted this trial. Had always wanted it. For the money, for the fight, for the publicity, for a triumph over me, for a thousand harshly competitive, jugular-driven, Rambo-rhythm causes. The calls I no longer heard.

"Why are you doing this?"

"Josh, you should know better than to ask a 'why' question

of a hostile witness when you don't know the answer." A pause. "I get to dance with you in public. And I get to save the life of a man who's being hosed by a baby tramp and a politically damaged DA's office." The trial was on. Defense lawyers could tease about plea bargains; DAs could not.

I gathered words from the wool in my head. "Rachel Farr's going to have her day. You're free to call it what you want. Don't be so sure you've figured out this case."

She laughed bitterly. "You don't have a case and Tommy Conover's in deep trouble and the press is up. I draw media. I will confer with them daily after court. You, your badly needed Guilty verdict, and your office will be hung on a high line.

"You won't serve the girl, aid Tom, serve justice, or win. By doing this trial with me, you'll give the Upstairs keys to Jergen. Every lawyer you disrespect for weak ethics will become a deputy DA with a badge and license to carry a concealed weapon.

"And why? Because you lost Summer, and you think she's come back to you in some strange, cosmic Chinese way, in the body of Rachel Farr, a cheap, dishonest street urchin. No, no, don't look at me like that. I can't stand that. Look inside yourself."

I looked at her. She shook out her hair, making me close my eyes. "Deep down, you know it. The girl's a liar, playing you for a fool. God, I'm sorry for you." She touched my face.

I opened my eyes. She was gone, but it didn't help. I smelled her, felt her, remembered her. I had loved three females, and lost them all.

12.

THREE LITTLE BOOKS

I told Gonzo Marx that when he put Moody back in custody after the failed prelim, he had forgotten to rearrest him. "Gonzo, at jail, flag him, so if Moody bails, the jail commander notifies me and the victim first." A logical way to avoid a tragedy. "And Bilinski's helping out. I want you to brief him on what's not in the file. On anything you remember."

"Oxymoron," said Gonzo. "'Bilinski helping.'"

"Then we'll need more of your help than usual."

"That's what I like about you, Jin. You're a rule freak."

"Hey, if DAs don't follow the rules, who will? And I love you, too, Gonzo."

Isaac Krakow phoned, inviting me to a late meeting. "Bring François Giggin. I got gourmet pizza from Biba's." I told him I had already eaten shark fin soup.

François's car had broken down. Over objections, I picked him up in a southside Sacramento trailer park, rich in waste and dog feces.

François introduced me to a tall, overweight woman in a tee-shirt and shorts whose age and grace had been lost in a mud slide of Hamm's Land of Sky Blue Waters and Pabst Blue Ribbon. Hollowly, he coughed. "This is my mother. Mom, this is Mr. Jin, my boss."

"Good evening," I said, shaking her trembling hand. I knew her. Gabriela Tomasina. I had put her husband in state prison for attempted murder. Of her.

She squinted at me. "I seen you before. Wanna drink? Wanna tip one with me?"

I turned onto Florin Road. "François, I put Albert Tomasina in state prison."

He was looking out the window. "I know."

"Albert Tomasina your mother's second husband?"

"No. He's my dad. I changed my name. Mrs. Giggin was my high school English teacher. She taught me a lot. I always liked her."

Unspoken was the fact that François had concealed his father's status from us.

"God, I'm sorry," he said. "Boss, do I have to resign?"

Isaac Krakow welcomed us. I had never seen him without a starched shirt and strictly disciplined hair. A hurricane could flatten the city and Isaac could pose for a *GQ* hairspray ad.

"Our runaway population is way up," said Wilma Debbin, the cop who arrested Moody. She was six feet tall and had a smooth complexion you can't buy at Nordstrom's.

"Jin," said Capri, looking up from a PC, "in Intake you see every felony that goes down. Got a question for you. You see a spike in runaway-related crimes?"

"No. But I'll watch for it."

"I hear," said Isaac, "that Mr. Giggin here is a young Jedi programming master."

Wilma Debbin slid a photo to François, of a man and a boy together. It was in bright color and they were nude. It was not Norman Rockwell. François dropped his pizza on his lap.

"God!" he said.

I shook my head. "I hate these cases."

"I hear that," said Wilma. "Pedophiles are working the Internet. That's where this photo's from. Pedophiles are super-secretive. We can't get past their gatekeeper. Help us?"

François told her what he needed. She took notes. "I'll get this for you. Mr. Giggin, these are absolutely the worst criminals we'll ever chase. Keep working the screen."

"Wilma," I said, "tell me about Moody."

We went in the hall, leaving François to contemplate the problem.

"Silent girl. Rachel Farr, right? I didn't do the search. It was

Gonzo Marx's case. God, what an idiot. He ought to be shot."
Wilma was the worst marksman in the department.

"Funny, coming from you. You going to qualify this year?"

"You're a clown. Heck, I got no pride—*you* shoot Gonzo.
Pico did the *Moody* search. It was a rush, my fault. The girl
hadn't made a statement. But I think Pico'll help you."

A big concession since the Incident. "Tell me exactly why
you popped Moody."

"I had a feeling. Pico'll be here at nine. Ask him."

"I'm asking you. Give it to me, Wilma."

"Off the record?" Even Debbin was talking politically.

"Off the record."

"Geneva de Hoyas called. Told me to drop the case and
didn't say why and didn't say Pretty Please. No DA's ever
pulled my chain like that, telling me to dump an active case on
a guy that looks, in the gut, to be very good for this crime. Excuse my mouth, but fuck her! You better believe I filed it, that
damn minute. I used to like de Hoyas. Hell, I liked all of you."

I hated domestic disputes. "And now, because she ticked you
off, we got a case at last-bite, do-or-die prelim with no victim
statement and no idea of what happened."

"And if you dump it, Chinatown screams and votes for Sethman Jergen. And Tommy Conover loses." She shook her head
and snapped her fingers. "Bummer, huh?"

I set the house alarms and avoided Summer's bedroom and her
box of memories. I had an image of Ava, her sadness and anger
on a cool pillow. I went downstairs and looked at the phone. I
had no idea what her new number was and had nothing useful
to say if I did.

I studied Stacy's former, high-grade, uptown, migraine-
inducing motions against me, pulled from our automated brief
bank. Later, despite what I read, I slept, better than Jodie.

Next morning, after running around Stonegate Lake, I show-
ered and headed for a Saturday meeting with Pico Larry.

Pico was fit at 125 pounds and five feet four. He used to be a
narc, but he got chronic lung infections from being the first in
the meth lab raids, inhaling toxic chemical precursors. He

transferred to Gangs, worked Vice, and ended up in Sex. He had steadily burning bright blue eyes, as if someone were driving nails in his legs. To shake, Pico offered his hand from the floor, where he was doing abdominal crunches while chomping unpeeled carrots.

"Counselor. Moody's place on Tulip Lane—I found it Lysol-soaked—wiping out traces of sex, drugs, and rock and roll. Not many latents. Upstairs was fresh-painted and wallpapered."

"Consciousness of guilt. Or a hung-up housecleaner."

"Well, Counselor, it was way too clean."

"Search extract shows you didn't seize anything."

"That's bull. I took three schoolbooks. Math, social studies, science. I was looking for hints of girls—clothes, barrettes, *Seventeen* magazine. Books were hidden, and Moody had cleaned up. Don't mean he's the man. Could've had drugs and stashed everything."

"What's your guess?"

He shrugged in mid-stroke. "I don't think it was a major narc thing. I'd be surprised if he didn't have weed. Beyond that, I don't know."

"Where are the books?"

"They're in evidence." Stored. "But it's a Gonzo Marx. Who knows?"

"Think Moody did it?"

Another shrug. "The books were no big deal. His *hiding* them—that was a big deal."

He speeded the crunches, popping a sweat.

"Maybe he was distancing himself from her case, from a bust he could smell coming."

"Sure, could be. What *you* think, Mr. Jin?" He paused in mid-crunch. "You here to back up Wilma or bust me in the chops for a bad search?"

"I'm just trying to work the case. For the girl."

He nodded; we were cool. He finished and stood, looking at the wall clock, which displayed the logo of the Sacramento Kings basketball team. Pico was an optimist.

"Pico, if you went back there, what would you look for?"

"I wouldn't go back. Not 'til the girl says what the hell we're lookin' for. Rachel Farr's so stale, she's moldy green. Hell, even she makes a statement now, you got no physical evidence. It's a her-word-against-his and she's not real likable. Not her fault. She's had a shit life. But the jury won't be thinking that. They'll want to slap her. Problem is, Moody's likable."

"Sounds all uphill."

"It's Chinatown and you're Conover's political deputy, tryin' to pull votes. And you're not so hot at trials no more, are you? It don't matter. Your man's gonna lose big. Every cop in the state and his uncle gonna vote in Sacramento this year against Conover." He aimed an index finger upward. I didn't want his digit in my chest. He stopped.

"Don't waste Wilma's time. Me, you can screw with; I'm nobody. But Wilma's our spark plug and Moody's a flamer, a bad sinkhole for good cop hours. We got us a bad rash a pervs, worse I ever seen. It's like a fucking molester convention. Mr. Jin, you're slowing us down. Wilma, she likes you, even though, right now, all you DAs look like turds in the cornflakes.

"Jin, you lost your kid. That has to hurt. But it'd be *real* nice to nail some a these SOBs. Now shake my hand like an old cop who remembers the Brotherhood and tell me you copied me in the clear."

We shook. "Pico, I'm gonna follow Rachel. Any advice?"

A shrug. "She's a street kid with no prospects." He looked down, sad. "You and I know that all she's got comin' is a long string a shitheads who'll beat her, cut her, and burn out her little heart. Ain't no doubt in my mind that she got raped bad. Hurt her permanent. And left no calling cards, no evidence." He looked up at me. "That's cool, you putting in hours on her. I wish you good luck, partner, even though every cop in the Valley's pullin' for you to lose this case big. Conover, he deserves a BIG fuckin' fall. And you look like the man to do it for us."

I went to the Evidence Locker, thinking about François. He had fabricated data on his background. The law said he had to be fired and then reported to the State Bar. If DAs didn't follow the rules, who would? And someone had snitched my *Moody* file, thin as it was.

I found Pico's log entry, but no textbooks from Moody's house. The locker custodian and I searched the metal shelves, without luck. The custodian was sweating; he'd no idea that the three books were snitched. He called the other custodians—no info, no clues, no luck.

I called the Crime Lab—there was no record of any analysis on a case called *Moody*.

Was Pico pulling my chain? I didn't think so.

What about Wilma Debbin? She, a cop, had gone ballistic after the Chief Deputy District Attorney illegitimately ordered her to dump an ongoing police investigation in the wake of the Incident. Wilma was willing to have a child undergo a questionable court process to plink Tommy Conover between his peepers. Would she dump evidence? No. She'd just applaud as Conover went under on a case doomed to fail from the start.

And something had made Geneva de Hoyas desperate and undiplomatic. Geneva was never rude, but she had dissed Debbin. She had only one person above her: Tommy Conover.

13.

FOLLOWED HER FROM
SCHOOL ONE DAY

Thursday

Victor Petty/Mr. Buttface was arraigned at the top of the Department C Arraignment calendar. Arraignment comes from the Latin, *adrationare*, to account. Petty didn't wish to account; he wished to bail. Low bail was successfully resisted by our C Deputy.

Rachel did not escape the heat and return home, but drifted by the Broadway's brightly sunlit shops and stores. She quickly passed Wendy's and Denny's, crowded after-school hangouts.

The sun dulled the signage for Wing's Laundry, where a young boy inventoried dirty shirts and soiled dresses, working hard to form English letters on the tags. He looked up to study the wan white girl as she unsteadily marched past his father's shop.

Rachel entered the Chinese Methodist Church on Twentieth, and lay on a front pew, her head on the Miss Piggy doll, her fist pressed to her lips. Rape causes regression. She could sleep in daylight in a church; nighttime was for wide-eyed vigilance.

The custodian was a small southern Chinese man with a mustache and a big push broom. He said she came every day to the same pew, had for a month. He'd wake her at six-thirty before the committee meetings, choir practice, and the Confident Kids program.

"She not pray. Minister, they pray for her. Jin *singsong*, this girl, she in trouble with the law?" I said she wasn't.

"She Christian girl?"

"I don't know." I thanked him for watching over her.

He smiled. "Maybe, you her angel, yes?"

I said, "I think you are." He laughed, covering his teeth, then grew somber.

"She very sad girl, cry all time. I pray for her. Every night." He looked down.

I sat, swamped by memories of Summer's funeral, images interrupted by station breaks as I was transported back to my last trial. I was cross-examining a defense forensic mercenary when I remembered, with startling clarity, Summer, looking at me from surgery, and the tears flowed. I tried to stop them, making a sound that resembled the death of a gut-blown horse.

The judge had said, "Mr. Jin, when you cry, the jurors cry. So does my clerk and the reporter. I'm losing control of my court. See a doctor. Get some pills. Please."

Ava crying on my shoulder, reciting, "The Lord is my shepherd, I shall not want. He maketh me to lie down in green pastures, he leadeth me beside still waters, he restoreth my soul . . . yea, though I walk through the valley of the shadow of death. . . ." I left.

Rachel emerged with Miss Piggy, flinching from loud street noises, afraid and alone.

* * *

Dr. Teo Sandoval had clear gray eyes in a narrow, photogenic face. For someone who worked intimately with the psychotically ill, he was composed. He studied me with a professional gaze that reflected forensic collegiality and psychiatric curiosity.

"Rachel's oriented but depressed. No history of mental illness. I estimate a trauma-induced withdrawal. Numbness, lack of appetite, sleep deprivation. But her silence is willful. You know. If she *was* attacked, she probably knows her assailant, whom she yet fears."

"You trust the rape model?"

Sandoval was surprised. "Am I to infer that you're not a SACA attorney?"

"It's a Chinatown case in an election year." Unsaid: and I'm Chinese.

"Hm. So you need her to talk. But she may be killed or hurt again if she does."

"She may be killed or hurt if she doesn't."

"Fair enough. You know how difficult this case is?"

"I have some clues. I have no physical evidence."

Sandoval sat back. "I didn't know that. I'm sorry. I was thinking that people like children but dislike teens, who are insolent, outlandish, rude, poorly attired, defiant, wild, lacking judgment. Most adults regard them as nonpeople. Get surrounded by them—you feel threatened. The mob from *Lord of the Flies*, grown tall. No, no one likes these kids."

"Really," I said.

"A twelve-year-old blossoms. Rachel's thirteen—chaotic, hormonal, from an abysmal home with a dead mother, booze, and abuse. You are familiar with the rapist categories?"

I nodded. Anger Rapist, Power Rapist, Sadistic Rapist.

"Rachel's symptomatology suggests an encounter with a combination Power Rapist and Sadistic Rapist. Sadly, the same symptomatology makes her unappealing to a jury. I explain that in my book. But it's academic until she speaks. If she speaks."

I had read his book.

"Could she be protecting a rapist father?"

"She is too silent for me to form an opinion. My professional guess is no."

"We need her to talk. To someone." I wanted to pace.

Sandoval stood and walked about. "She is strong-willed. I could not get her to open up, and I am not unskilled in these matters. She won't talk until she trusts someone, and she trusts no one. It does not help that I am a male, or that her resentments spark antagonism in others.

"You have to consider the possibility that, with her off-putting ways, she might have inadvertently invited her own beating from an emotionally stunted male adult. Intermediately, she needs sanctuary, a sense of safety, a place to heal. I sense her home does not offer this." He considered his nails. "Her counselor says she hates a deputy DA. Is it you?"

"She merely detests me. She hates someone else."

Dr. Sandoval leaned against the wall, smoothing a trim mustache. Most shrinks I knew had facial hair, perhaps to appear opaque to patients. DAs, obligated to present cases without obstructions, had to let our faces hang out so the jury could read them.

"Mr. Jin, I have met Ava. I extend my deepest condolences for your loss. Your daughter—a patent ductus, mitral stenosis, a missing ventricle. How many times you came to the edge. Three valve replacements and countless cardiac caths. You must be exhausted."

"Dr. Sandoval, what can you testify to regarding Rachel?"

"Nothing, really. Sir, have you considered therapy?"

"No help in trial, but therapy for me." I stood. "There's a deal."

"People here say that Summer wanted to help everyone. She was a year younger than Rachel." He was talking fast, trying to keep me. "You see how deeply they're connected. One was your daughter, one is your case. You loved Summer but lost her. Kismet has given you another girl with whom to work. Mr. Jin, may I presume that your wife wants another child?"

I opened the door. "You may not." I stepped out. He followed me.

"I am sorry and I withdraw the presumption. Eighty-five

percent of marriages fail when a child dies. Often, because the husband is reluctant to risk losing another child, and almost universally because he cannot cope with the *feelings* attached to unbearable loss. This is innately understandable to therapists, but not to wives, nearly all of whom are desperate to fill the void of the lost child. Yet lightning seldom strikes twice in these matters." A tight mouth. "You face hard work, none of it pretty. It's internal dredging in areas you have long defended."

I said nothing. Capri was rushing down the hall. "Now!" she called.

"Fax me your eval and send a hard copy," I said. "Thank you for your time."

"Done," said Sandoval. "I'm available if you want to discuss—"

Capri was running. I caught up with her. She was crying. I didn't like that, so I ignored it. In the crowded elevator with a patient on a gurney, orderlies, docs, RNs, and visitors, she ground her teeth together and put on her cop face.

She exited, running. "Billy McManus is downstairs, DOA. Shot by a chickenhawk named Flute." Chickenhawks—pedophiles—were absolute hell on kids but invariably cordial to cops. McManus was the good cop Tommy Conover had beaten up in the Incident.

Chickenhawks never fight cops. "McManus got two shots in the creep, who's in ER with a punctured lung and a rash of out-of-state warrants. The creep wants to deal Karl Moody, and you're the DA on the case." She wiped her eyes. "McManus took six rounds. A quick death."

A pedophile wanted to trade info on Moody for a deal. Not in this state—bargains for pedophiles and cop killers were barred by statute and conscience. But it was a break. It was no break for McManus. And no favor to Conover; the press would revive his battering of Billy McManus. Bad news had become adhesive and deadly.

Capri's mascara was ruined, so she hit me. "God, Jin!"

"Capri, pedophiles don't kill cops."

"That's what Bill McManus thought. Ah, shit." He had a

wife and three sons. I had done Metro cases with him. He had
been a strong, resourceful cop with a good nose.

We pulled our recorders. In the hall were downtown cops.
We grabbed gowns and masks.

"Don't waste your time, Mr. Jin," said one.

"You do surgery," said Capri. "I'll take our boys."

The surgeon looked at the wall as I entered. "Declaring him.
Nine-eleven a.m." An RN covered the body. The team was serious but not somber. No one liked the deceased.

I turned on the recorder, stated date, place, and time. "I'm
recording. He say anything? ID yourself, please."

A scrub nurse gave her name. "He said 'moody man.' "

"Try to use his tone of voice, his pace."

"He was all torn up. Before we trached, he said 'moody
man.' He was trying to get out a word. We couldn't wait."
Pause. "Cops brought him. They were slower than an
ambulance."

The cops had questioned Flute in the squad car, driving
slowly. This wouldn't have happened before the Incident, when
the DA had moral influence on cop behavior. If I were still a
cop, I would've wanted Flute to die. But I was a DA and
wanted him alive.

"A *g* sound," said another woman in scrubs. "Lips like this."
She gently pursed them. "Like kissing, but not serious. I'm
Donna Delgado, peds intern, doing a surgery rotation."

"Can you imitate what you heard?"

" 'Give you moody. The man . . . moody, the man-ghhh. . . .' "

Capri was still talking to one cop while others clustered
solemnly by the bay in which McManus lay. The other cop was
in the lot. "Did Capri take your statement about Flute?"

He looked at me. He didn't like DAs anymore.

"What'd Flute say on the way in?"

No answer.

"I'm sorry, officer. *No habla inglés?*"

Slowly, with clenched teeth, he said, "Mr. Jin, I thought you
had Intake."

"I do. This is to keep me fully employed and out of trouble."

"Isn't Intake kind of a shit detail for a top guy?" He loosened his shoulders.

"Well, I'm not a top guy anymore. I have to work for a living." He wasn't laughing. I affably got ready. "Come on, brother. What'd Flute say?"

He put his breath on me, uncaring about my DA badge, law degree, size, or readiness. Blackish-blue uniform wet with blood, smelling of downtown and brotherly fear, he had been with Billy McManus as his sergeant bled out. He was ready for Fist City.

"Tell me, Mr. Jin," he said tightly, "was Conover outta bounds when he knocked Billy's teeth down his throat? A little shitty on the integrity side, by *never* apologizing to the force?"

"Just between you and me?"

"No, sir, between *your* office and *my* department. No chickenshit, Mr. Jin. Unless you forgot, you were a cop. I'll quote your ass all over town." His eyes were watering with anger.

"Be real. I can't say anything official."

The cop showed teeth. "Hey, Mr. DA, I can't either. Want to know what the hawk said? Bash *his* fucking teeth out. Maybe he'll come to and tell you." He pressed a finger in my chest. I thought about letting it stay there out of fraternity, but I removed it and gave it back to him.

"I got a SACA case that relates to Flute. You want to flush that, for Conover?"

He snorted in my face. "Tell the DA if he comes to McManus's funeral, I'll knock him out on the steps." His partner arrived to pull him back. Red-faced, fighting his pal, he pointed at me. "Sir, you excuse us. We got work to do, citizens to protect. Tell Conover not to send flowers and to keep his sorry ass the fuck away." They slammed doors and drove away mad.

Conover, once a prince in the capitol, the city of camellias, would be in the poorhouse if he had to send flowers to all his detractors. That cop had been close to swinging on me.

McManus had blown away his own killer and then died of six bullet holes. So no DA was needed to adjudicate his death. Prosecutorial integrity was shot and street justice was on the rise. The city looked normal, but it wasn't. The sun seemed hotter. I took off my tie.

What was the link between Wayne Flute, chickenhawk of boys, and Karl Moody, rapist of girls? They weren't in the same corner of the perversion galaxy. What had Flute said? How'd he know Moody? What was the *g* sound? Man-ghh. Manga. Mannguh. Mangah.

Capri was in the car, weeping, and I couldn't take that. I needed a ride. The psych ward was on the ground floor of the Med Center. That was so patients couldn't jump. I could tell Sandoval, who was on the second floor, I'd do therapy if he gave me his car keys.

Before, I could have called Ava. She had taken the part-time training lawyer position for the Public Defender so she could always be available for Summer. I could call her, ask her out to lunch. But I had no effective way to deal with my wife— ex-wife—to persuade her into a different stance, to make her smile. That which she needed—another child—I could not give.

I heard Ava's voice. "You *could,* Josh. You *won't.*"

Later, riding an ambulance on a downtown call, I was reminded that life was transient and unreliable, as if homicides, rather than being in the margins of life, had become the thesis.

Do something. You can't chat with Moody because he's represented and you'd have to through his lawyer, and you don't want to do that. Check out the lesser evils.

Interrogate Harry Bilinski about the missing *Moody* file.

Interview Rachel's family.

Eat a donut. I had just gotten two dozen Old Fashioneds, Glazes, and Chocolates to clog the department's coronary arteries like cement in a pipe. The world was looking up.

14.

I'LL BE BACK

Harry snored amidst the incriminating crumbs. No pastries had survived. "My donuts," I announced with more sadness than I intended. A chair crashed. François jerked up.

"Hey, boss! Got Harry's report." He searched for it, found it, and read. There had been no luck finding Moody's alibi, Mr. John Quick. There were seven hundred John Quicks in the National Agency Check printout in California. One of the drawbacks to having thirty-five million citizens in the hard-drive memory of possible statewide perps, fugitives, and doubtful alibis.

And, according to Gonzo Marx, nothing was missing from the *Moody* file. It was the fox saying there were no chickens when he got there. And then someone had snitched the file.

To his credit, Harry had gone to see the Farrs, but there had been no contact. Ray Farr had two DUIs on his record and probably hated cops when he was asleep. Dierdre, Rachel's evil stepmom, had unpaid speeding tickets and had intimately witnessed two bar fights in the Broadway, a comment on her habits and her influence. DMV photos make movie stars look bad. Ray looked like something that would leave the dog pound with four paws straight up.

I wrote: *Sorry: Sgt McManus shot dead by Wayne Flute, LA chickenhawk. Flute wanted to deal Moody but died: Check him out. Find John Quick, Moody's alibi, now. I'm at the Farrs. Return your .44 to my desk. Where're my donuts?* I taped it to Harry's right sleeve cuff.

* * *

Coriander Lane is a leg of Chinatown's recent sprawl. A few Anglo and Hispanic families had been caught in the migration. Asian vegetable patches were replacing lawns.

Isaac had said that in a SACA case, rapport with the parents, like everything else, was crucial. "Unless they're the offenders."

"What if they're just bad parents?" I had asked. He had said, "Pray."

The foliage was the result of long neglect and good weather. Over the roar of the window air conditioner came lowbrow TV noise. I watched the window and rang the bell. The blinds moved and the TV switched off. I waited in the silent heat, listening for the sound of a hammer cocking. Homes should have southern solar exposure; this had northern, which was bad *feng shui*, wind and water geomancy. A cracked window, a door needing paint and a new seal. Someone with a small right foot who stood about five-one had tried to kick it in. Persistent, amateur, almost animal-like tool scratches around the dead bolt.

She looked older than the thirty-four years and shorter than the five-eight reported on her license. Chartreuse tank top, white shorts, makeup, perfume over Scotch, red, discouraged eyes. Blond hair that would crack an egg. She checked my face, body, and shoes. Old habits, as if life were a honky-tonk and Mr. Farr were fungible.

"Good morning, Mrs. Farr. Josh Jin, deputy DA." I showed my ID.

"Jesus, did Ray screw up? This ain't 'bout me, is it?"

"No." Reassuring. "But if you like, I can come back when it's even more inconvenient."

Long eyelashes blinked. "Was that a joke?"

"No, certainly not."

"Jay Leno with a badge and a Porsche. Come on in. I was fixin' to make one." She guarded a limp. The apartment was overdecorated and knickknack-cluttered. The air-conditioning was glacial. Mr. Farr's lounger was black with use. She'd been watching the tube during early cocktails. A fireplace mantel, perhaps for a dream home, sat lonely in a corner.

"Water's fine for me, thanks. Attractive home. You put work into it."

"Just an apartment. Never heard a man talk about it before." She reassessed me, the limp more apparent. She gave me a dirty glass of water and sat down hard, raising mite dust as she crossed her legs. "Ray lacks ambition. Forces me to make do." She ogled my clothes.

"You do well. Mrs. Farr, I have Rachel's case. May I ask you a few questions? I appreciate it. Was Rachel a happy person before she was attacked?" I leaned forward.

Dierdre Farr waved dismissively. "She's a pain, know what I mean? God knows I try, but she's not a good kid. Not by a damn mile."

"It must be very hard, raising a teenager. Before, did she have a lot of friends?"

Lips curled. Who cares. "Her?" A flat chuckle. "I plainly doubt it."

"Which of her friends used to visit? Just a name or two."

"Hell, you know what those kids could do? Black Nikes and damn crap *everywhere*." She looked away, taking a deep breath, offering me the chance to look, to say something good. Her body said: Change the subject quick or you're out of here.

"Mrs. Farr, what do you think of Karl Moody?"

She frowned. "He that bastard ringin' the bell last night?"

"Dark ponytail, square face?"

"Oh, hell no. Big, fat man, face like an old wood axe. Looked like a cop."

"He is a cop. Moody is the man charged with raping Rachel."

She wrinkled her nose. "Don't use that shitty talk here! Hell, that stinking little bitch *always* lies! I told that lady lawyer, what was her name—"

"Ms. August. And Mr. Rittenhouse."

"Yeah. Damn, *he* was cute. Brought me some Scotch and I'm savin' it." She looked about me: Where's my gift? "Rachel, she lies, constant-like." She rolled her eyes. "Little bitch."

On the stand, Mrs. Farr could try to hurt Rachel, but she'd only hurt the defense. She was no threat to the victim in trial, only in life.

"What did Rachel tell you about her being attacked?"

She looked away, bored, sipped Scotch and relaxed her chest. The interview was over but for the slamming of the door.

"Mrs. Farr, in February, she came home hurt, after being gone for a while. Please describe how she looked." Silence. "You know, Mrs. Farr, Rachel really needs your help."

She stood. "This is my home and it's time for you to go, okay?"

I stood. "Mrs. Farr, I used to be a cop. I see you punch someone who's short."

She colored under the makeup, crossing arms, hiding her knuckles under her chest.

"Someone who kicks the door when she discovers the lock to her own home's been changed. It happens a lot. It's someone you kick, busting your big right toe. It's someone who fell and knocked that lamp into the wall. It's someone you've thrown into that window."

Her eyes narrowed. She got ready to kick, changed her mind and flexed her fingers, the nails sharp. She backed up, scared, tense, her voice higher. "You get the hell out."

She beat Rachel. Had she caused bruising? She was a short-fused bully and a happy face wouldn't work, even if I could conjure one. And a deputy DA can't threaten. We fulfill idealistic promises on an untidy, violent, bloody battlefield. We're advocates, not cops.

"Mrs. Farr, if you hit Rachel one more time, I'll be back for you. As much as you hate her, you want me in your life a lot less. Someone hurt Rachel. You didn't protect or help her. But she has people now who will stand up for her. Mrs. Farr, when you get ready to hit her, remember me." I softened my gaze and voice, as if I had Summer's gentle eyes, abating my heat. "Open your fist. Take a deep breath. Back off. Let her be. I'm not saying don't be her caring parent. That's your job, a job you can start any day. But don't hit or kick her, or I'll put you behind bars. That's a place where your very good looks will not help you, at all."

She was looking away, blinking, furious, face red and hot, blood boiling.

"Mrs. Farr, I don't want to lock you up. You deserve a nice summer. And Rachel, bad or not, deserves not to get hit. Okay? I don't want to be your enemy."

She exhaled bitter air. "It gives you a big charge, to hassle me, don't it?"

"A little," I said.

"I used to like men like you." Her color returned. "Smart guys. Less hassle with sex, but they wore me out. Ray's a chump, but he does what I say. I kinda like that, know what I mean?"

"Yes, ma'am. You have a real nice day. I mean that."

"Hey, mister," she said. I stopped. "You live in a house, a nice house?"

I nodded.

"Lawyers. They live in the places the roofers build, know what I mean?"

Outside, women argued in Cantonese, loud but friendly, pausing to study me as they worked their garden patches of *bok choy* and *gai lan*, shrinking their useless brown lawns.

In the car, the cell phone rang. "Josh, Thackery Niles. How are you?"

"Hello, Judge Niles. Sorry for not returning your call. I quit the lunch circuit."

Thack Niles was soft-spoken, florid of face, politically greased, and pure hell on crooks. I knew him distantly, having done only one trial in his court, but Summer's death had brought condolences and offers of lunches from many in the legal community. I used to be political, for votes. Now I was political for a case. I would listen.

"The Governor's appointment secretary has asked me for recommendations to the bench. Let's do dinner and work it out."

"My name's not in for nomination. I'm not interested in the job."

"Don't argue. The Thirty-third Street Bistro, six sharp. I'm buying."

15.

MOODY'S CRIB

Tulip Lane is a truncated street with graying homes and no children outdoors. It once was an exclusive, turn-of-the-century alcove of elegance shielded by enormous sycamores. But the drought of 1938 killed half of the treasured trees, driving landed aristocrats across the American River toward surviving shade and the new California ranch estates. I stared at the pair of side-by-side, faded-rose, two-story Victorians, flanked by younger, postwar shade trees that would rustle and bend in a warm, rogue wind.

Moody's had double gables, dirty windows, and flapping roof shingles. Someone who knew how to care for a house lived next door to Moody. Make a note to check out the neighbor, I said to myself.

In front of Moody's was a candy-apple-red '67 Impala convertible. His shiny wheels. The house had a rooster weather vane so encrusted with rust that it reflected no sunlight.

My senses came to attention the way they do when you hear a noise when everyone's in bed. I had slept like that for over a decade, as if I could hear death trudging up the stairs for my daughter. As if I could confront it, form a convincing argument, or pummel it in a fury of crowding blows, knocking it down the spiral staircase, killing death.

The day was in the low nineties, the hot air hinting at what would come in two months—the sensation of having lighted matches pressed down your throat. I shivered as something crawled into my Chinese guts. Every Taoist animistic sensor from childhood was alerting my bioelectrical system, hitting fire alarms and intruder alerts. I could see no reason for it.

The house had old, neglected steps and a weathered screened

porch. There was nothing particularly sinister about the high, long-legged iron bench or the darkened windows, or the doors that could have been used to secure Notre Dame. But in sum, it made me feel ill and in jeopardy. I looked around, but it mattered not if no one else felt it—this house meant something to a prosecutor. I would figure out the why of it later.

One of the double front doors was open. I moved closer. From it came youthful music on tweeter. Incense. Aroma of carcinogenic hot dogs and fat-sizzling fries.

Karl Francis Moody lived here with unknown assets. The place was the Overlook Hotel, Scream 5, Halloween frights for kids, and flypaper for free-floating teens. All that was missing was the offer of body piercing, Pepsi, and some free CDs. The heavy scents, the loud music, made me thinly nauseous. Youths would say, Hey, way cool!

Rachel deliberately avoided Moody's place on her daily way home. Or she enjoyed window shopping and I was using heatstroke as a basis for inductive reasoning. I wanted to knock on the door and ask for a glass of lemonade and consent to a full search, but the only way I could speak to a criminal defendant was via cross-exam in open court—with Stacy August guarding him.

I imagined ripping into Moody on the stand. Frontal attack to the face, flurrying hard questions, driving him deep into the ropes, into the back of the witness stand, crowding and sweating him with his contradictions, his hesitations, his fictions, his lies.

I stood on Tulip, letting the house work its sorcery on me, using the jangles of mystic apprehension as an accelerant to motivation. I was light-headed when I thought of Summer, and I had one of those unpredictable seizures which, in the days after her death, had made shaving impossible.

I put my head down and cried horribly, as if I were Chang-o, the distant and saddened lady of the moon, swept away by the forces of females, of *yin* and blind feelings, helpless before the cruelty of cold, cadaverous, frigid lunar gravities, seized by emotion, against which culture, learning, training, education, reasoning, logic, and testosterone meant nothing.

16.

GIRL IN THE SHADOWS

Harry Bilinski was on the phone. "Some perv called the girl. He breathed hard. The girl freaked, the guy laughed, then he hung up."

"Rachel call you with this?"

"That damn kid ain't gonna talk. It was a line tap."

"We don't have a line tap. Harry—you got a warrant?"

"Sure I do, Jin, I got a personal green light from the U.S. Supremes and a box a Tootsie Rolls. Be real. This stupid case don't have a Chinaman's chance. Who gives a crap about a warrant? You told me to work it. I worked it."

"Did you interview John Quick? And Gonzo? What'd you get on Flute?"

"Who the hell are they?"

"It was on a note I taped to your sleeve. . . . Harry, I'll do a wiretap request. Until then, disconnect it. Write this up and discover it to Stacy August."

"Jesus, you ain't serious. She'll fry our ass."

"That's what happens when you break the law. Do it. I'll back you up. Send copies to Wilma Debbin and Capri. They might have heard the voice before. By the way, you're fired."

He gasped. He could touch the Tahoe houseboat, his name on the bow, white fluffy clouds on a blue horizon. "No shit? You serious?" He laughed and laughed. "Damn! The wire got you! Or blowin' it with the alibi? Or sayin' 'Chinaman's chance'? Damn! That was it, wasn't it? Hello? Hello? Jin, you there? Goddamit!"

I had library work to do in preparation for Stacy's paper on-slaught, but delayed it for more SACA homework. I read manuals and watched past seminar program videos until it was all Urdu, a beautiful, difficult tongue of limited value in an American criminal court.

The training faculty said to avoid our regular "law-and-order" jurors. With 288 cases, we simply needed good parents who knew and liked and believed in children. A major switch.

I noted the best voir dire queries. I understood them, but they weren't natural to me.

Do you feel children are more likely to lie in court than adults? Can you convict someone based solely on the word of one person? What if it's a child? What if the crime's a sex crime? Can you think of a reason for a child to not report being raped?

August would dismiss my best jury candidates—the good parents. I would dismiss people who hated teens, cops, and the law. She wanted W. C. Fields. I wanted Mary Poppins.

I reviewed the rapist profile. They were Fixated or Regressed. Moody could be either. Fixated Rapists included Preferentials, who could try to groom a girl into deviancy; and Sadistics, who eroticized power or anger.

With power, they did bondage. With anger, they tortured.

The Sadistic was the most sexual of the profiles, having eroticized his aggression; the Angry and Power Rapists tended to not enjoy the sex, which was but an irreversible means of expressing repulsive violence. The Progressive Sadist sought higher thrills.

Preferentials could stalk former victims. Their pleasure was heightened by imparting fear before the new attack. They could leave hints. Phoning, taking items, killing pets.

Someone had phoned Rachel, creating panic. Jodie sat up as I petted her.

Progressives imagined more grandiose assaults. They played out heavier fantasies with greater pain and stricter controls and more screaming, more evidence of their work.

Doing that, they could exert the ultimate control—killing.

Dr. Sandoval described the child prey of Preferential Sadists as "girls in the shadows," pushed away from life by fear, self-loathing, anxiety, depression, shame, helplessness, problems in school, verbal expression delays, anger, hostility, delinquency, and flight. If a Preferential Sadist had attacked Rachel, she would be hoarding horrendous psychic and physical injuries. And the Progressive would be prone to attacking her again. I read on.

Preferentials were often smart and devious, devoting years to crafting their tortures. They were men who should never be paroled, but often were. My clock alarm sounded.

Time for dinner with Thack Niles, the politico judge. A judgeship would pay fifteen thou more—which was inadequate inducement to sit immobile all day in a robe, watching others and thinking law school thoughts. But I couldn't do trials, and Niles was offering me a job. I reminded myself that my job was getting Rachel's story. She needed someone to work for her.

Showering, I was glad that Moody was in custody. I was happier that he hadn't killed Rachel. Was she masking marks of torture under her clothing? I thought about Moody.

To bail, Moody would have to pop the ten percent premium—five thousand. I jerked: the guy owned a house. Few defendants were homeowners, but Moody could pull five grand out of a second mortgage. That he hadn't the first time he was arrested meant little.

He could have bailed. It was Gonzo's case. I banged out of the shower.

17.

VIGIL

The news was bad.

I told SPD to Code a patrol car to the Farr apartment, then called Bilinski, and was forced to leave a message. I rang the non-burned-out staffer, the intern François Giggin.

"This is Jin. I need your help in Chinatown. Turn down the music."

Hootie and the Blowfish took a breath. "Too cool, boss! That's sick, you asking me! You're gonna force me to deal on the street!" *Sick* was a new, positive, transient adjective.

"You're on an open stakeout." I gave him the Coriander address. "You're watching over the two-eighty-eight victim, Rachel Farr. Moody's loose. Be obvious, but be very cool."

"Menthol! I'm yours. Uh, boss, can I have a gun?" His plea rang on my car speaker.

"No. Stop asking." I merged on the Causeway. "Moody made bail and has been on the street three days. We were supposed to have been warned." Gonzo hadn't asked the jail commander to flag Moody's release. "Moody could've made the crank call to Rachel."

I gave physical descriptions of bodies and cars.

"You sure I shouldn't have a gun?" asked François.

"You have a mobile phone? Your car working yet?"

"Sure, boss. And I got a mistress in Paris and an apartment in San Francisco. I'm stinkin' prelaw. Lucky to have pants. But we're in luck—the Corolla's running."

"Cops are waiting. They'll give you a camera, mobile phone, and raid jacket."

"Uh, boss, isn't that a little *too* obvious? For a stakeout?"

"You *want* to be obvious. I want you to scare Moody off."

"Boss, I'm *de novo* here, but wouldn't it be cooler to *catch* him? Like wouldn't it strengthen the case if we got him?"

"François, I don't have a complaining victim, a witness, or physical evidence. Crim Law 101: I have no case. I want the girl protected. You're not a cop. Moody's bad news from the SHU at the Q." Security Housing Unit at San Quentin, the crap cells for hard-time cons. "You catch him, he'd take *you* down. That'd leave Rachel uncovered and me without a clerk to break my furniture and trigger the metal detectors with his nose-ware." I slowed for traffic.

"I relieve you at two a.m. You have my mobile. I'm going to a political meal. Call the cops if you need any kind of help, which includes an Asian gang deciding it wants your cheesy law school wheels. Phone me if you have a question. Park at their door. No music so you can hear. If someone makes a play, call for help, lean on your horn. Yell. Raise hell. Break windows. But François, you fall asleep on this girl, I'll tear your lips off. So stay awake.

"Tomorrow, find out how Moody bailed. He used Socks & Sons Bonds. I want to know whose money was spent and what property secured it. Any questions?"

I rang his bell. Gonzo was still short, barrel-chested, and rude. "What?" he asked.

"Great how you see everything egocentrically. Get dressed."

Gonzo squinted. "You gotta be kidding."

"I look like I'm kidding?"

He didn't back down. "Listen, you're not a bureau chief anymore, and your ass is grass. And I don't work for you." He kept thinking. "And it's late."

"Think of it as being early. You're working for a kid named Rachel Farr. She needs your badge. Get dressed or come as you are, but you're coming."

Stupidly, he hoped I'd leave. "What pissed *you* off?"

"I'm feeling fine. Best in months. You got five minutes."

I drove him downtown.

"Listen up. You didn't flag Moody and you didn't refile on him. Moody bailed and is on the street and the kid was uncovered. You offered Moody twelve months' county jail, but made no record of it, which sort of crimped my negotiations with the defense. I can't read your search warrant and there was no clue that Pico Larry found anything, much less that it was analyzed by the lab, which also has no record. Now the books are gone. What else did you mess up?"

He thought about it for a while. "Screw you, Jin."

"And some say you can't think on your feet." I tossed a notepad in his lap. "One: Refile on Moody. Two: Go with the cops at rearrest. Three: Memo Geneva on your errors—"

"You trying to get me fired?"

"Four: Write P&As"—points and authorities—"to Stacy August's Nine-nine-five motion to dismiss. She'll file for jurisdiction, insufficient evidence, and malicious prosecution. Maybe for idiotic prosecution. You got the facts, research the law. Five: Draft a civil rights memo to Writs and Appeals on detention without arrest. Call when you're done and I'll drive you home."

It was one-thirty when I got there. François had observed the midnight parade of Chinese restaurant workers returning to diaspora. He had jumped when a man came toward him with a flashlight, but he was merely watering new shoots in his vegetable patch. A neighbor was cooking fragrant onions and ginger mushrooms. François had seen nothing beyond a few teenaged drinkers, prowling cats, and loose dogs, one of which had urinated on his car. At night, Rachel's apartment building looked like a pink, soulless fragment of Stonehenge that served as cause to live in the woods.

"That light's been on all night. Doesn't that girl sleep? Hey, I gotta crash, boss." I took the phone, camera, and raid jacket. He drove away while stretching, swerving to cartwheel innocent garbage cans across dead lawns. Dogs howled.

The moon was full and National Public Radio's "All Things Considered" was being replayed for the sleepless. I could have stayed all night with Sylvia Paggoli, but I turned it off. By moon and car light, I studied the intricate motions Stacy had filed against other DAs in past cases.

Dinner at the Thirty-third Street Bistro had featured Thackery Niles pressing me to submit nomination papers to the bench. I had said I had no interest. He argued with me.

I would never permit a judge to buy my meal any more than I would pay for his. This avoided the appearance of evil and the establishment of debts, however small.

"I'll pick up the tab," said Niles. "I make more than you."

"That'd be inappropriate. Let's split it."

"No. I want you to owe me." A strange smile. "And no one'll know."

"I'd know." We split it.

With a start, I awoke. A dog was prowling Coriander Lane, checking garbage cans and checking out the car, skittering away when I rolled down the window. Sirens wailed through the night. I yawned. No way we can pull day shifts and do this. We couldn't keep this up. A gang cruiser—a dented Subaru—with five slender and intense occupants glided down the street to sniff the Porsche. I turned on my interior light and they sped off.

Bilinski called. I told him that we were on a three-man stake-out on six-hour shifts for the 288 victim. He had next shift.

"You fired me, asshole," he said petulantly. He hung up.

Sacramento dawns are cool, the horizon a red eastern rim that promised a hard and smoggy day. I said, I wish it'd rain.

Gonzo called. His work was good. I thanked him. "Take a cab home—I'll pay for it. In two hours, bust Moody but don't ask Pico Larry or Wilma Debbin to do it. Get some other cop."

"Yeah," said Gonzo. "Like who? If a cop punches me out, I'm blaming you."

"And flag Moody, for real, this time. Please, Gonzo, no more surprises. Good luck."

It was six. I needed a shower.

Ray Farr, short with a gut, spat as he approached. I got out of the car, stretching legs and discreetly showing the badge. Beyond basic biped physiology, I could see no resemblance between father and daughter.

"What the fuck?" Gruff, pores sour with alcohol and old tobacco, thinning hair matted. He had slept in his jeans, the probable consequence of having angered his warm wife.

"Mr. Farr, the person who attacked your daughter might try it again. He won't if someone's out here."

Ray Farr scratched himself. "Don't talk to my wife. She—she needs her rest. I mean, like . . ." He stopped himself. "Look, don't park so close. The wife don't like it. You really pissed her off. And, I mean, me too. And I don't want you here, either."

"Tell her I'm sorry she had to roust you from your BarcaLounger to come out here."

"Okay." He looked at me, then frowned.

"What'd Rachel look like in February, when she was attacked?"

He shook his head. He didn't know what I was talking about.

I didn't say: you're a lousy pencil-necked chump for ditching your kid. I didn't strangle him as he stumbled back to his apartment to have breakfast with Lady Macbeth.

Half an hour later, the apartment entry door cracked; I was being watched. Rachel moved fast with her Wal-Mart sack. She ran skittishly and unevenly toward the corner, heading into the painfully bright sun, anxious, jumpy, and hesitant, hastened by memory.

She moved as if her fleetness could win her something. I liked that. It suggested a spark of self-preservation. With an instinct for survival, she could support hope.

Make a fist, Rachel. Fight your damn demons. Be strong, like me. I dried my eyes.

18.

LUNCHTIME

I was fifty feet from Rachel. She had the shade. Kids kept away from her and my coplike presence. Her thinning body daunted my weak appetite; her withdrawal was completing itself. Kids played basketball and others looked slovenly. I read François's report:

Moody had only chump change in the bank. Stacy August had paid the five grand premium and signed the forty-five thousand bond, due in full if Karl "Chico" Moody jumped bail. It could be anyone's money. No second deed had been filed at the County Recorder on Moody's house. So his assets, beyond the house, were a secret, or not even his.

Lamont Socks of Socks & Sons Bonds asked Moody why, if he had the scratch, he hadn't bailed the first time he got busted.

Moody said that he missed jail food, but not enough to suck it down twice. Now Moody had been rearrested under Gonzo's casual eye. And rebonded with unaudited assistance.

Rachel wasn't eating. Next day I left a Quarter Pounder at her shade tree. Sacramento has a fine assortment of bad food appealing to the young. I liked my chances, but she didn't eat. I improved my pitch with Biba's *pasta frolla*, China Moon's long bean, Fuji's pork *tonkatsu*, Luis's chicken chimichangas. There were no nibbles, except from Kimberley Hong, who ate the food with gusto, smacking her lips comfortably as Chinese will do in each other's company.

"How's Rachel doing?" I asked.

"Failing everything. She comes to school to hide. Hmm. Good burritos!"

I returned to the people's choice—Quarter Pounder, fries, and a Pepsi. Squirrels were mobilizing at the tree. I baked as May and the desert heat of the Valley gained momentum. Sum had loved the hot Valley sun and let it play on her face without fear of long-term melanomas. I recited her last poem:

I am a sensitive girl who wants to understand life.
I wonder how long forever really is
I hear the cry from every suffering heart
I see my hopes and dreams in millions of stars
I want everything to be okay
I am a sensitive girl who wants to understand life.

The first of three stanzas, composed with a calligrapher's flair.

Kimberley Hong sat. A touch, a presence intruding. I thought of my mother, singing in our old City church for her dead granddaughter, her absent daughter-in-law, her silent son. For a moment, I missed her, her smile, her superstitions, her belief in a pantheon of flighty gods.

"You should run for office," said Ms. Hong.

"I would if I didn't hate politics."

"Jin-ah, you're a tough guy, aren't you?"

"I'm so weak it's been in the papers. I'm just not interested in formalized corruption."

"Why didn't you marry a Chinese girl? Forgive my curiosity."

Ma never asked that question aloud, but I had heard it. Questions had ended with Summer's birth. Ava forgave my mother's bigotry, but now Ma would not forgive herself. "I wanted Summer too much for myself. The gods took her back for an old grandmother's greed."

Rachel was up. You have a heart, I thought: use it. I hated her ghostlike mannerisms, her physical cowardice, her bending to the bully. Fight. Not like me. Like Summer.

Rachel slunk away. A kid bumped her and she fell, fragile and light. No one noticed. She rose, crying, holding Miss Piggy tight.

19.

THE VOICE AT THE LAKE

I took Jodie to Stonegate Lake to chase ducks and get drenched. She liked the lake because it was where Summer had taught her to catch a Frisbee. Summer liked it because here I told stories of her Chinese family, tales passed down by BaBa when I was little. Stories of my mother when I yearned to know anything about my dead father, the man who would never again smile at me or run his strong hand through the brush of my youthful crew cut.

I never knew why Summer's Chinese roots pulled on her with greater strength than her more popular European heritage. I thought it was the humanist in her, her natural cleaving to the sense of difference and alienation. She had possessed the strongest of hearts.

I remembered Ava's happinesses in those days. "She shouldn't be thought of as perfect," Ava had said once, laughing.

"Why not?" asked Ma. I was the good, strong Only Child, giving Ma a grandchild with a beautiful international face and the wisdom of two worlds. I recited the poem's second stanza:

I pretend that everyone has to overcome differences
I feel like a grain of sand on the beach
I touch the door to my soul and open it
I worry about the future of this world
I cry when I see others in pain
I am a sensitive girl who wants to understand life.

Summer had ended our mirth, becoming our glue. She had given us an unshakable purpose, a bond that surpassed mere true love. In the combatlike intensity of managing her chronic illness, we were no longer a couple. We were a committed survival team, fighting for her life. Our marriage centered on a wonderful girl. Our future, on a faulty heart.

Now we were divorced. With Summer dead, I had no battles to fight, no war to win. I did not know how to navigate the gap to Ava, because she wanted another child. I could not do it. Another child to love. Impossible. Sum was my girl and always would be. Ava and I had not been intimate since Sum's final crisis. I felt many things, but no urge. Ava did, with a fury.

Having another child would be a living insult to Summer, an artifice to her memory. Loving another child would be hollow, an imitation of a truer love. A second child would be only Sum's shadow. Chinese are blessed with long memories and loyalties to undying pains.

Summer, I said, is not dead.

I could have spent my life here, sitting by the lake, taking the warm sun, licking wounds, loving my absent, delicate girl. We had fished here for unhungry trout, her head on my shoulder. "Dad, it's really okay if we don't catch anything. I'm so lame at this. You know, if we're patient, they'll find a cure. A real cool surgery. A real cool anesthetic."

I had been blindly optimistic; she will not die. Not Summer. I awoke with a start and checked the time.

Summer's voice crossed the still lake. Geese honked.

"If you're patient, Daddy, Rachel will talk to you."

I sat breathlessly. I disbelieved, waiting for more.

I stood. "What, baby?" I asked of the lake. Sunlight shimmered blindingly. I asked louder and a sudden flight of ducks shook me into the unwanted present. I had stopped breathing, trying to will my daughter back into my life, and she had spoken to me.

20.

PROFESSOR SACHS

Friday Night

Davis is the oasis of the hot Central Valley. The Ag College had imported floral exotica for its study, turning the community into a colorful paradise of thick vegetation and booming allergies. Along curving Putah Creek is the crown jewel: the campus arboretum with its lush white and pink blossoming fruit trees, immense, ancient walnut trees, and congregations of aquatic avian life. The King Hall School of Law sits above the jewel and the creek. It was fitting that its law library avoided full computerization, honoring books the old-fashioned way.

I sat where I could see the thick, leafy plant life and the tall redwoods as I worked the heavy tomes by hand, sensing their noble histories, the fine, legal sweat embedded by generations of scholarly searches. I set each book at a precise angle to the others.

I prepared motions in limine for the day of trial—defensive maneuvers to slow Stacy's direct assault on my case. Protect Rachel on the stand from Stacy. Make her sexual history irrelevant. Stop Stacy's deceptive definition of reasonable doubt in voir dire and final argument.

Stacy liked to bust DAs with 995 motions to dismiss, well-structured and impeccably prepared. Phillips Rittenhouse, no less a slouch in the law library than his boss, had five attorneys with law clerks. As I sat, they were churning mountains of motions against me.

Her second-favorite weapon, 1538.5 Evidence Code motions—

motions to suppress evidence—would be no problem. I didn't have any evidence to suppress.

No need to sweat a new quash by her on Gonzo and Pico Larry's search warrant—the evidence was missing. What I had was the fact that Moody had cleaned his house. That would warm the hearts of the Martha Stewart fans, but would win no verdicts.

I was seven hours into my response to her first anticipated 995 when the librarian asked me to leave. It was closing time.

Rather than face unbeatable insomnia, I forced myself toward Fanny Ann's in Old Town, a saloon decorated with a cascade of arcane knickknacks suspended from the ceiling. Prospectors' picks, pans, stuffed animals, weapons. Vehicles and clothing. The patrons produced a warm roar of cheer while recorded bands played contrary music. Younger DAs circumspectly watched me—the office's cautionary tale—as I absorbed the noise and the cheer of good Scotch. In the din, I remembered that Sergeant Billy McManus had picked up the scent of four armed hoods here in Old Town, on a trail that led to A Shot of Class, where the District Attorney would knock out his teeth and change the course of local politics.

"God, it's you," said the Reverend Joel Frost. He was dressed up, an old blazer over older jeans, a brave laugh over old pains. "Welcome, pilgrim, to your old haunt."

I shouted, "What's your secret of enduring optimism?"

"Hope, youth, love." He sat. Laughter erupted nearby. I saw his ex-cons.

"How many are here? Any of them mine?"

Joel pointed. "Big Foot Silas. You got him for a two-eleven about four years ago. He got early parole on the work program. He bears you no grudge. He was sentenced by Judge Niles the Fascist, not you." He shrugged. "I like Fridays. You can forgive everyone."

I hated Fridays. The offices were closed. "You forgive the con who took your wife?"

"I like to think my wife's love helped him. And, in some good way, me."

"You're a leaping marvel," I said.

"And you're a hard case. Working a sow's ear with a lost, silent street kid. They're the worst, on everyone. Any way I can help you?" Energy radiated from him. He was a nocturnal who worked the bar crowds and saved souls. I was diurnal but it did me no good.

In the morning, I drove up College Street, an enchanted, arboreal lane of Oxfordian faculty homes shaded with sycamores, flowering crabapples, and almond and peach trees.

"Professor." We shook as he jostled four case reports, spatulate fingers, and a broad thumb marking important pages. He read law for fun.

Clifton McFadden Sachs was an iconoclast who railed against academe. He was an ethicist who championed the lost nobility of the practice of law. His posture was rigid, his beard gray, and his glasses small and round. He was the most ardent legal researcher I knew. He smelled of book dust. I had drifted away from him and his wife, Maggie.

His house was a library. Sitting on his patio under a kind shade, he asked about Ava. I said we were divorced, depressing him, his sad eyes reminding me of the weight of my loss.

"I have a sow's ear." A sow's ear was a notoriously weak case which, hopefully by dint of epic, Darrowinian trial work, could become a silk purse.

"It's a two-eight-eight with no physical evidence. The girl's too withdrawn and distrusting to speak. And she's still under the shade of trauma. We don't have a statement."

"Not even to name the rapist? And it's going to trial with no physical evidence? All this in the wake of the Incident, with intentionally poor police support? Oh, my. That *is* bad. Well, losing it would be no dishonor." He was showing time's passage. Sachs was a fierce competitor who didn't like losing a parking slot to a pregnant mother of five in a flaming car.

"Clifton, it's the litmus test case for the election."

"No! That case is *yours*? Next, you'll say you have Bilinski the Backshooter!"

"I do." He roared, his head back, whooping, slapping knees. I laughed, almost crying.

He removed his glasses and wiped his eyes. "Oh, too much. So who's the opposition?"

"Your favorite student, Stacy Antoinette August."

Sachs straightened his back. "Egad."

"And she wants to castrate me." A squirrel shook branches. White blossoms fell.

He crossed his legs. "I knew, the moment I saw her, that there was a woman inside whom you never wished to anger."

"Now you tell me."

"Never guessed she'd fall for you. How many of my learned colleagues made asses of themselves for her? How big's your caseload? You have Intake? What the bloody hell are you doing in Intake? Ah, don't tell me—office politics. Well, for you, it's nothing. Want my help?"

"I'd love your help. I need your help."

"Alongside the great Josh Jin. Sit at the counsel table again." He had a random thought, pulling a scrap of paper from a pocket, scribbling. "For what other compensation?"

"The good fight and hope and glory."

"Josh, that's one of the worst offers any lawyer's ever heard. Stacy'll beat us like old rugs. She'll feed on your fractures and crushed nuts. She drowns you in paper so you come to court like a bloody shipwreck. Then she dances seven veils—or eight—for the jury. Gad, how they love her! Well," his eyebrows lifted, "you know her magic better than most men."

He was remembering her performances. "Her voice is from the clouds. Makes men vote for tobacco killers and killer heiresses. And women say, 'Aww, she reminds me of my pretty daughter.' Stacy is Astraea with that great face, that honed, irresistible stage presence, not to mention her sparkling brains, her drop-dead body, and her big, beautiful—well, you know."

Astraea was the blindfolded Greek goddess with the scales of justice who stood by the courthouse steps. This Astraea wanted me to sing very high.

"Glad I stopped by for the jolt of blooming confidence."

He stretched in the sun. "The jury will love you, too. It always does."

"My victim's a lost teenager."

"Oh." He reconsidered. "One of those little miserable ones?"

"Mother's dead. Father and stepmother abuse her."

"Impossible! Ah, I envy you. Look at my silly job. We teach thinkers to become angel counters, prepping the elite to serve the corporations and the superelite. We don't prepare them to serve *people*. To *care*. We prep them to get *rich*. Although, thank God and thanks to some of this faculty, many of our graduates help wonderfully, despite the damned culture."

"Law of averages," I said.

He laughed. "You know we laud the grads who earn millions. We write ponderous, obscure treatises which no one reads or uses. Like I said. I envy you."

"You envy *me*? Court's the most dysfunctional human system since mob rule. It thrives on greed, ambition, and raw power. It permits manipulations of truth, facts, law, opinion, precedent, and legislative intent. It exploits misery, fear, and ignorance. It *depends* on misery. No misery, no lawyers. It's fathered by politics, the great Satan of all communal living."

"Aye, but you can *fight*! I tussle with windmills and look like an old gaseous fool. Hell, boy, you're *paid* to do combat! Tell me you believe in what you're doing!"

I looked for the squirrel. "It's junk, one step above the courts of Robespierre."

He kicked my foot as if I were a dozing pupil. "It's a bloody good step. Ah, I've missed the sting of a good battle. Josh, you're a godsend, you are. We can put up a bloody good show before Astraea's knife takes to our knippers. Let me try talking to the girl?"

"Of course." I looked at him and smiled. "I bet you could get her to talk." I wrote down her phone number, address, and directions to Rio Junior High.

He offered his book-dust hand, his deep, wise look. We shook. In the high gamble of the coming trial, I had drawn an ace.

21.

SNIFFING MOODY

Monday

Nighttime surveillance slides you into barking iguana land. You need a sarcastic, bantering partner. Even then, Morpheus, god of sleep, can slip in. We were grinding down.

Then I thought: Hire someone to do this. It wouldn't be cheap, but it'd be great for your back. I stretched, groaning. I had Summer's college fund, diminished by surgeries.

Rachel left for school. Time to go to work.

Oaks and fairyland-pink rhododendron shaded the Firehouse from husky noonday heat and filtered searing spears of light on the brick courtyard, casting a soft Parisian glow on diners who had purchased the ambience.

We were here because Stacy knew I preferred cheap cafés and because I was buying. She was bringing Moody to lunch with us.

DAs and cops tend to be early; defense counsels and clients are the opposite. If dogs and cats ate together, the cats would be late. I was twenty minutes early and Capri was sipping iced tea. A waiter enjoyed hovering, looking at her legs.

Capri brushed my sleeve. "Let me get this straight—Stacy August thinks we'll just look at Moody and dismiss? I've heard of her doing that, but never seen it. Well, as The Stacy Herself says, the moon can fall through the roof. How do we play it?"

Capri wore a pink blouse over a taupe skirt. She brushed me. I moved away.

"Stacy does her dog and pony show. I look fascinated. You sniff Moody and tell me if he's our guy."

114

She stirred the iced tea to ensure a perfect dissolve of artificial sweetener. "Your opinion's not exactly chopped liver."

"But you got the gift." Discerning lies was not easy. But most ex-cons were proven liars. Capri got a suspect's gestalt: eyes, quadrants of gaze, neurolinguistics, gestures, respiration, speech, mannerisms, tone, quaver, anxiety—in the context of a verbal, visual, kinetic, auditory or contact sensory personality. And drew a conclusion: he's honest, he's lying, or he's good.

She sipped: just right. "And Stacy said no to the box?" The VSA, voice stress analyzer, had replaced the lie detector as a reliable but inadmissible gauge of truth. Capri and I liked the old lie detector, but most cops loved the analyzer. I nodded.

"What will The Stacy wear? Gucci? Chanel? And how much?" A game played by female staff. I didn't know labels. The softer side of Sears? JC Penney? Army surplus?

Stacy August entered. Cleopatra, or a Claudian empress with no heralds but her appearance, no praetorian guard but her apparel, adequate to create a parting of attention and a pausing of lifted forks, a widening of pupils to appreciate what they saw. "Roderick St. John's," said Capri. "Two grand." I saw a black Mandarin-collared blouse, jacket, and skirt.

Moody had a square face, cool gray eyes under black brows; he was in a collarless white shirt, a new camel sport coat, faded jeans, and boots. My heart sank; he looked really good. He would've been told not to shake hands: no free forensic clues for the DA.

I made introductions. I offered and Moody shook without thinking. His hands said that he didn't do manual labor or enjoy contact with men. He was flop-sweaty with anxiety. Why not? I was the prosecutor, the lawyer who was trying to put his life in a steel box.

Stacy was angry at the handshake but said nothing. She ordered the fish special and raspberry iced tea and asked if the waiter could rush the order; she had to make a court appearance. The waiter, bending from the waist, assured her instantaneous service.

Moody ordered a burger, fries, and a Coke; Capri, a salad;

and me, a veggie burger, drawing a Moody eyebrow. He was a scrubbed con. He looked up at me, eyes quickly darting.

The crowd knew Stacy August from the papers and the evening news; she had gained notoriety by winning the acquittal of a U.S. senator in a vehicular manslaughter case in which a child had died, and in suing a landlord for a rat-trap fire hazard that killed sixteen residents.

Stacy said, "My client will speak. You are not to ask him *any* questions. Not even of a harmless, social nature. Agreed?" She was radiantly intense and focused. I agreed. I focused.

Moody eyed my bread knife. Child molesters, as a stereotyped group, had poor social skills and were uncomfortable with adults.

He flexed his jaw. "Okay. Rachel," he said easily, "was one lost kid. I met her about a year ago." A splash of Virginia Baywater, his "about" coming out "aboot."

"She was bein' tussled by the Namese. I ended it. Let her clean up in the latrine. I saw she didn't call her folks." He shook his head solemnly. "She was a messed-up kid, ran with *bad* people. I'm not exactly upper class. I got a record. But I been clean. The girl needed help."

He took a breath. "I gave it." He looked down and right. His voice belonged to a guy who chopped dawn wood, tracked elk, and made fair coffee from old grounds. A good voice for Sacramento jurors. They wouldn't get to shake his cold, sweaty palm.

His eyes narrowed. "Not in a hundred years did I think the *one good thing* I did in my life was gonna be stuck up my ass." He raised an ironic eyebrow, stopped, looked away.

The food arrived. Stacy snapped her napkin to her lap. Moody licked a broad upper lip, dropping his napkin with the left hand as he studied his plate and the server. With the right, he lifted his burger for a big bite, avoiding eye contact with August. Still chewing, he said, "Truth is, I don't like lawyers much. Cops less." A glance at Capri. Left hand placing a fry in his mouth.

"Least favorite are DAs." He chewed my way. "You enjoy puttin' people down. We're notches to you." He sipped Coke. "You take freedom for granted. But *you* get the pigs on you. The lawyers play with your mind, the damn DA with the big

college words. Live with bulls and red punks. You'll do a *lot* of
damn shit, to avoid it again." Bulls were prison guards. Punks
were hard gays. "Avoiding it" was the high claim of every lying
con on his way to perpetual recidivism. A con got better when
his $C_{19}H_{28}O_2$, testosterone, burned out in about twenty years
and he found books and God, putting his name in for a Shaw-
shank Redemption.

He looked down, angry. "I didn't hurt Rachel. All I did was
teach her. I confess, right here, I studied her books so's I looked
smart. Funny. Didn't do books in school. I did it for her."

His eyes shifted. "Know what the real question is? It's why's
she burnin' *me*? I thought I knew the girl. I don't. And I'll tell
you this—"

"No," said Stacy. "Getting angry at her will not help."

Moody nodded, kicking back, breathing hard, eating fries
with the left, remembering, occasionally, to close his mouth.

Three of us had ignored August, which was not normal. She
had finished eating.

I had no idea if Moody was the guy. The lunch had clarified
nothing and cost me a hundred and twenty bucks. I had expected to be able to read Moody, but he was Stealth Man.
Cloaked, sharp angles hidden, radar returns foiled.

I thanked him and Stacy. So did Capri. Stacy thanked us.

"The car," said Stacy. Moody's summertime prison yard
strut, shoulders in heavy motion to slow, unheard music, the
arms ready, butt downplayed, a ponytail bounce.

"I expect a dismissal on tomorrow's eight-thirty master calendar." Her look was enigmatic. The sun played with her hair
as she left, the crowd enthralled.

"You're not sleeping with her, are you?" asked Capri softly.

I frowned. "I don't sleep at all." She looked at me hard. "We
were together a long time ago. When dinosaurs ruled the cool
places and the earth was molten lava. It was just before Moses
brought the Law. But you probably knew that." I paid the bill.
"What about him?"

"Not a standard-issue pedophile. Too skilled, too confident.
Too sexy." She brushed her hair. "He could push the buttons for

most women. He'd be hell on a hormonal girl without a good and attentive father, an affectionate dad. Girls hunger for that."

"Under all that, did you smell a pedophile?"

"Neurolinguistically, he was all over the map. He gave kinetics, auditory, visual. His eyes played with the upper right quadrant, which is lying, but not at all the right times." She scratched her arm. "He kind of confused me."

"You're telling me he could be factually innocent."

"Maybe. I got clearer signals from your opposing counsel. She wanted to watch you more than her client. Pupils dilated, lips parted, breathing with a hiccup. Jin, this isn't history. It's current events. The kind *The National Enquirer* reports on page one. She wants you or your blood. We don't need that. Conover belts a good cop, a father of three, who then gets blown away by a perv. Then Jin, his Chinatown DA, has an affair with his opposing counsel in a child rape case—a woman the press follows like she was Elvis reborn. It gets reported, and you offically become a royal putz."

22.

Foo Chi

We had dreaded a ringing phone. I had denied Summer's terminal condition, but a jangling phone could bring news of a heart attack. Or that she was already dead.

The cell phone rang while I was in a drive-up line. "Hello," said Ava. "How are you?"

Her voice stopped my breath. "Okay. How about you?"

"I'm okay, too. It sounds like you're at a truck stop."

"Burger King. Trying to buy the girl's statement with Chicken Tenders. Say hello to your dog." I put the phone to

Jodie's ear. Ava's voice made her whine and madly whap her tail.

"I miss her," said Ava. "What's she doing in the car?"

"She's lonely." I didn't say: Some bad guys I may now know kill pets.

"And you're not."

"What's up?"

"Call my lawyer." A problem with mutual funds, an old wedding present from the Jin Family Association. She said I sounded tired. I explained our surveillance. I asked what she thought of using Summer's college fund on a PI to watch over Rachel Farr.

She thought for a moment. "It's a good idea. Tell me more about this girl."

I did, and for a moment, it was the old days.

"So besides the girl saying nothing, and having Harry Bilinski and no physical evidence or corroboration and the animosity of the DA and his chief deputy, how goes the case?"

"If you don't think of the politics, not so great."

"She loosening up with you?"

"Like a nun on *The Howard Stern Show*."

"Don't be angry at her for having a good heart. She had few chances, and now she's been raped. Spend the money on her."

I saw Ava, sitting with great posture, long legs crossed, and against original intention, I said that Summer had spoken to me at the lake.

Her sigh stirred old pains. "Not surprising, Josh. *Everything* reminds me of her. I keep turning, expecting to see her. You know, I'm rested now. I'm ready to fight for her again. But she's gone." Her voice faltered for a moment. "Well, Josh, good *foo chi* with her."

"The girl?" I asked.

"Is there someone else?"

"That's more a question for you."

"I'm getting on with my life."

"That's understandable."

"Not to you, it isn't."

"Don't do this," I said.

" 'Don't do this' is one of your worst expressions."

"Your worst is 'Goodbye.' "

"I only used the words. You used the behavior. Anyway, it feels good to have someone interested in me."

The remote speaker said, "One twelve-piece Chicken Tenders with barbecue sauce. . . ."

"I have to go," I said.

Clifton McFadden Sachs called. "Laddie, the girl's hopeless. The sickness from the rape has spread to blood, brain, and soul. There's no girl left."

"She's in there. Just suppressed by rape trauma syndrome."

"In spades. Without her, there's no case. Josh, there's no *her* there." A thoughtful, scholarly pause, and I was again his student, in the great, tiered, second-floor Trial Advocacy classroom, uneasy with the watchful silence, hoping he wouldn't ask me to recite Facts, Holding, and Dicta, and knowing that he would. He broke the silence.

"You're running a felony prosecution on your instinct—against an ex-con, making it smack of prejudicial prosecution. Josh, this is beneath you. I can understand the breach in judgment—the victim is a girl of Summer's age. But I can't participate in it. It's insane to press this far without a witness statement. If I'm wrong, Mr. Jin, cite your authority."

"Professor, my authority's the fumes of instinct. My precedent is a cop's good nose."

"Uh-huh. That's fine for a homicide detective, working probable cause on the street. You know it's insufficient for a DA with the burden of proof at the high standard."

"If I'm wrong, Clifton, I'll pay with my badge. But if I'm right. . . ."

"You'll never know, lad. The case is dead. Sure, you love the good fight, but it makes no sense to join battle against a prepared enemy bearing a frayed jockstrap and short hairs."

"Those are the best battles. We have a good cause here."

"You don't even know if anything happened! Lad, I can't do this, and you shouldn't. *You don't have a case!* Conover will lose fewer votes if you dismiss now than if you lose the litmus case in trial due to an uncomplaining child victim. You'll get dismissed. No, I'm out."

"Then I'll miss you."

"No, you won't. You'll wake up with your brains in order and dump this sad, ugly beast. Spare you and this broken girl a great deal of unmitigated grief. Let go of her. Move on."

I hung up and the phone rang. It was a junior associate at White & August. Ten new motions were en route on *People v. Karl Francis Moody*. Would I personally accept service?

23.

OBSTAIN

"The man who attacked you might come back." Birds moved lazily in the elms. "Three of us take turns watching your house at night." A warm wind played with my words. Rachel did not move. I couldn't tell if her immobility came from fear, discipline, or emotional inertia.

"We're getting a private detective to help watch your house. After school, you could help us select the agency."

She shook her head and my heart skipped—she had communicated.

I smiled. "Is this okay with you?"

She picked up her books. Summer had loved stories about her grandmother, her *na-bu*. "My grandparents," I said, "were Chinese farmers in Argentina. Mother was born in Buenos Aires. When she was ten, the Río Matanza flooded, drowning her parents. Clutching a cutting of her mother's hair, Ma was sent down the Río de la Plata. She sailed on a tramp steamer across the Atlantic to an aunt in America. They zigzagged to avoid German submarines. She landed, quite seasick, in New Orleans. She took a train to San Francisco's Chinatown."

Rachel was blinking. Hesitantly, she put down her books. I licked my lips.

"Ma worked as a cook's assistant at Johnny Kan's to earn out the four-hundred-dollar passage to America. She spoke Chinese and Spanish but had no time to attend school. At eighteen, as a rare woman chief cook, she hired a private eye to find her a husband.

"She said, 'Please, sir, find me a kind man.' The detective found Jin Tse-hsu, a big, smiling laundryman. My father." Paper rustled and Rachel jerked—a squirrel was scoring the Quarter Pounder. Limping slightly, hugging Miss Piggy, Rachel walked away, favoring the shade. Her high tops were torn, as if by teeth and force. "They lived happily ever after," I said.

Time to visit Tiffany Prue. She'd ask if I had any smokes. Then the PI.

Kenny G played the sound. I smelled roses. David Obstain had been a Sacto homicide dick with a habit of unsmiling hard work, a weekend jazz band, and a private flower garden in black Oak Park. When his father, Willis Sampson Obstain, the famous private eye, died, David had to choose between remaining a cop or firing his relatives who worked the agency. A sentimentalist who kept plants going in winter, he turned in his badge and took the business.

Thick forearms rested on a lemon-fresh ebony desk as wide latissimus dorsi stretched the threads of a stylish charcoal blazer. He was very tall, very dark, and very handsome. Hard cheekbones in which you could hide light. The prominent, knowing nose of knowlege, of judgment. A lean body bursting with hard muscle. A fine face that saved smiling for weekends.

I told my story in a dark office that would put a mole at ease. Serene African wall art merged softly with Italian sepia shadowing. The sax was at home. It was a place of mood, to relax a client into the quick truth, to comfort the meter and pay the low light bills.

Clients often select detective agencies on the likelihood of privacy. Here the lighting said: We're discreet, while the photos proclaimed success, showing Obstain with an ample lineup of lowlife, high-risk celebrity bookies, and legislators. Many wore cheap white suits that made the palm-sprinkled southside tracks of Sacramento look like Biscayne Bay.

Obstain's was in a refurbished railroad warehouse, five doors from the Fox & Goose, where I used to take Ava and Summer for Sunday brunch to celebrate my surviving another church service. Jazz in the background, ice tea on the desk, he had stopped crunching revenue data, his ledgers and HP calculator quiet. He spoke, his body stilled.

"Want to do it right, gonna need a man on the girl, but *another* on the defendant. Save you money by usin' a camera van, rotate it between Tulip and Coriander. It'll give Harry O. some beauty sleep. The man could use it." David Obstain's mouth moved thinly, quickly, and politely for a visiting DA, reflecting belief in speedy, full payment.

I wondered what it would take to put a full smile on his face. "Obstain, you tricky devil. Why are you interested in saving me money? And helping out Harry Bilinski?"

"Me, a church elder and a baritone in the choir, a devil." He said flatly, "Jin, you a funny man. The political cat from the DA's office, askin' why I ain't gonna retire off his wallet. Hey, business is business, but politics be politics. I save you, some-day you save me."

"I'm bringing you business, not politics."

He flared a finger. "I don't hardly think so. I don't truck with the DA. You rub against the grain. You want my private practice on a police case. That mean my troops don't do right, I catch a virus downtown with Consumer Affairs licensin'." He held up two fingers.

"And you doin' this with private funds. What happens when you run dry and we ain't done?" He canted his head, the leather chair flexing silently with his big frame. "Word'll be I'm more cop than private practice. I'll feel *that* pressure. In *my* damn wallet."

Three fingers rolled my way. "There's also *political* down-side. Conover goin' to lose big. Dig it. Anyone helpin' you now, come the election, be singing the outa-customer blues to the new man, Mr. Sethman Jergen, 'bout fifteen minutes after he take his oath a office."

"I'm not exactly free of risk." The saxophone riffed.

"Wrong, Mr. Jin. You in the breeze. Ya'll don't gotta sweat. It's even money on the street—you keepin' *your* badge. Jergen, he runnin' a minority ticket. He can't exactly fire a colored man, the only Third World bureau chief he got. Or ex-bureau chief." He softened, as if the words might hurt. "An' your girl dyin', well, hell, man. He ain't gonna fire you."

"Maybe. But you run the only minority detective agency in town."

"Hey." A shake of the head. "*Big* damn difference, Chink with a badge and a nigger with a business." He shrugged. "But a payin' customer today always take precedence over politics tomorrow. I'm sayin' I ain't seen nuthin' so hinky since the mayor got caught with that exotic dancer and said to the papers she was my sister doin' work for the firm."

"That bad?"

"Yeah, that bad! This case smells to the Causeway and the floodplain. When it dies on you—and that's the likely result—and with the election goin' south and the press sniffin' and blame start kickin' in doors, I be the first damn fool they think of." He sipped tea, liking it.

"Get real. This case goes down—and it sinkin'—with *my* name on it—Downtown gonna blame a poor, private black dick in a heartbeat over a Uncle Tom–Chinese deputy DA."

"Uncle Tom? What are you saying?"

"C'mon, Jin, we sittin' here, bein' polite? How'd you get to be a Frisco homicide dick in two years? Man, you out-whited the Anglos. I don't mean just nailin' the board exam. Hell, you affirmative-actioned your way to the damn top! You got a *good* white-man voice. And you did it again with Tommy Conover. Tommy, who needed the Asian vote to become The Man. Shit, he *bought* you! Dude, you far from Chinatown now. Yo' face so light, it gonna raise a utility bill.

"You did the white-man jive so good they think they got Tom Cruise with a haircut and gave you a bureau and a budget. But, hey, that's cool. Got nuthin' but *fine* admiration for a man who can climb the white man's ladder without havin to sue 'im.

"Jin, you was a homicide cop in the Big City. That's worth a discount. But you got bad hassles comin' outa your pants an' now you sittin' in my furniture."

"I'll clean up before I leave."

"Uh-huh. That's five thousand down, no credit, a thousand weekly when you get the surveillance reports and you pay all incidental expenses includin' meals, gas, and parkin' violations and don't give me no shit about a Brotherhood discount. Cool with you?"

I nodded. He smiled broadly. I had replaced the ace I had lost.

On the way to lunch at Rio Junior High, I parked in the Broadway and walked to Tulip, opening my collar against the oppressive heat. Chinese and Vietnamese women ignored me as they gardened while children stared. I found shade and an angle and watched.

The bum was doing a languorous Sunday strut across the street from the old Victorian.

The bum worked for Obstain and was probably a cousin. He walked as if on a beach, toes yearning for white sand. He had a small gut and hair down his back. The rhythm of an unseen surf timed his stride and the high hot sun and concrete were his friends. His job and the water bottle he held were both kind gifts. Tulip was his racetrack, the Moody crib was his focus, and anyone who showed was his baby to watch and understand. Obstain's bum sat, low and tired, looking sleepy and being anything but.

It took him two minutes to see me, figure my identity, and ignore me.

24.

FANNY ANN'S

"I said, 'Want another beer?' "

I think those were her words in the great resounding din of the saloon. I held my place in the book and shook my head. I like Sam Adams, but I support small businesses, ordering local microbrews. The book came from The Avid Reader, an independent bookstore. This was Fanny Ann's, as independent a business as I'd ever seen.

One band slowed. "Like being alone?" She was young, educated, and Gothic. Black fingerless lace gloves, ebony hair, black lipstick, black nail polish, a black bra, cut-off black jeans, and fishnet hose of the black persuasion. "What. Don't like people?"

I shrugged.

"Are you, like, famous? Those lawyers are checking you out. But no one talks to you."

"I'm a bank robber."

"For real? Are you rich and dangerous, or something like that?"

"I'm thirsty," I said. And I have to work tomorrow. "Lemonade, please."

"Two, please," said Stacy August, materializing from the crowd. The waitress left. Stacy's Forties, off-white, open-necked, high-waisted dress with a leg slit flashed. Men noticed.

"Hello, counselor," she said, her voice clear. "Trying to relive callow youth?"

"I'm studying the jury pool. What brings you here? Am I yelling?"

"I was brought here by a warm wind. And a desire to make peace. Yes, you're yelling."

The waitress delivered tall drinks. I thanked her and paid. Stacy watched her leave, then stood and walked up the stairs with the grace of a First Lady ascending. Eyes followed.

I sat. It was quieter up here.

"Josh, I have a problem. I'm having trouble fighting an unarmed man."

I checked. "Not me. I have two arms. What's up?"

"I didn't feel very good after our last visit."

"The food was excellent."

"I threatened you. I slurred your victim. I'm sorry. I think I came across rather hard. I'm not in the habit of being a pain." Her eyes were large and there was nothing to doubt and much to believe. The lemonade was flat. Stacy had a way of diverting ambient senses her way. She had been a smooth companion, brilliant, sweet, and only modestly demanding, letting my passion for her serve as the engine for our romance. As a trial lawyer, she exuded a supreme, incisive control, a death grip on the law, a confidence at many levels and the mastery of a skilled stage actor, playing nuance on demand for her jury. Not my jury. Hers.

I sat back, trying to relax. "That night was about my apologies. Not yours."

"Do you ever wish, Josh, that you could start over again?"

I shook my head. "Do you?"

"Sometimes, yes. DAs use the past to dictate the present while defense lawyers dwell on regrets. What if Hadrow hadn't seen the gun in the desk? What if I had been more focused on you, on us? What if that crazy guy hadn't come to the door our last night together?"

" 'What if the moon fell through the roof?' " Her favorite saying.

She laughed. "Your memory. Can we be friends, Josh?" Her eyes burned. "Please. I can't stand this uneasiness. The tension. There's too much between us for that. It doesn't mean that I won't wax your behind in front of the jury." She offered her hand.

Reflexively, I shook it, just as Moody had shaken mine.

Stacy held on. "Remember how you used to tell me stories?" She leaned on her elbows. "This time, I have one for you. It's about a little girl from the Midwest." Stacy's eyes were bright, teasing memories. She held my hand, caressing it, studying it.

"Her name was Susie. She was a HUGE tomboy. She was chubby like a gumball and had dimples in her knees and short hair that fit under a Detroit Tigers baseball cap. She loved baseball, but her *life* was on Sandman's Creek in hot Julys and Augusts, building forts, fighting with the boys who didn't want her near their sacred pissing grounds, snatching brown frogs and catfish, swinging on ropes over the muddy water.

"The other girls were learning to bake brownies. They hated the creek boys, the mosquitoes, and the scratching reeds. Susie didn't care. She loved being free, and that creek was nothing if it wasn't freedom. What's a bump on your head from a boy's rock or a branch scratch or a little mosquito bite—for your *liberty*?"

She smiled. Her hand felt silken, snug, and warm.

"Susie was twelve when her body changed. And her dad said she couldn't go to Sandman's Creek anymore. He said she had outgrown it. Her dad—there was no arguing with him. He was a very controlling man.

"Josh, she snuck back one last time. Built a fort. Got in a fistfight. Caught a frog and freed it. Swung on the rope and dropped into the creek. Dripping wet, on the bank by the reeds, she promised that she'd find another place like this. When she grew up."

Stacy smiled happily. "You know where Susie found it?"

I nodded. "The law."

She shook her head, returning my hand. "Trials."

25.

BREAK

A week passed. I was watching Rachel at school when the cell phone rang. "Get here, now," said Obstain. "I'm at Tulip."

I was there in four risky minutes. The van was hot, filled with gear and the smell of men. Obstain's big arms flexed from a white tank top. His cams turned. He played a tape for me.

He looked at the recording clock. "This was seven minutes ago." The black and white image cleared of video static. "Watch the tape. I'll watch the house."

Rock warbled tinnily from Moody's opened front door.

"You need a universal high-gain mike," I said.

"Not for what you're payin'," he said over his shoulder.

At 1201 hours on the tape, a sunburned, redheaded girl in faded jeans and a halter top slowed. She passed out of the camera. A minute later, she returned and walked up the steps.

The door opened. Mr. Moody appeared in a leather vest, black jeans, and butt-kick boots. He looked good, square and smooth, cool in the hot day.

The girl said something unintelligible.

"Not good sound quality," I said. He shrugged.

"This *is* cool music," said Moody, the sound track full of audio snow. He was nodding. Couple beats. The song ran, "If you believed in magic the way I believed. . . ." Jefferson Starship's great tribute to Motown sound.

". . . want something to eat?" asked Moody.

"Cool," said the girl.

Moody was hawking a girl Rachel's age. My pulse went up. The girl spoke. Unclear. I grunted unhappily.

"Sorry, man," said Obstain. "Audio'll be fixed tonight. It's the heat."

The girl stepped inside. The door closed. Half past. She had been inside ten minutes. Obstain stopped the tape; now we were seeing real-time video of the Moody home. It would take five to ten minutes to get a cop here. But a cop would chase Moody into the rabbit hole, and a girl entering his home for a snack was not against the law.

"Get her out now," I said.

"Jin, we ain't heard nuthin' bogus in there. Not yet."

"Obstain, get her out."

"I could do a truant officer call. Cost you extra."

"Truancy? It's not enforced anymore."

"Maybe Moody don't know that."

"Do it. Talk to her with a witness. You know the drill."

His African face was more anonymous than my Asian one. But whoever went in was making an automatic bad police search as a surrogate of the government.

"Flushin' a fine search opportunity. Cousin," he said to the radio, "east side. I'm chasin' out the kid. You stop whoever come and cover my flank. Copy, bro?"

"My man," came the reply.

Obstain put on a half-buttoned shirt with a loose knotted tie already in place. He tucked, tightened the knot, put on a jacket and crossed the street, picking an identification card from a thick stack which he returned to a breast pocket. He rang the bell, then rang again, longer. On the third, the door opened.

On the right of the house was the street bum. He would be the interview witness as David slowly drove the girl to school, pitching quick questions in the correct, random order.

Obstain showed ID and stepped inside, rendering everything he now saw or seized inadmissible. Proxies of the police can't search without a warrant any more than the cops themselves could, and David Obstain was my proxy, paid in full.

I didn't care. My heart was pounding, my blood pressure was up, and I felt like shooting Moody and crying. The risk of another girl's getting hurt was driving me crazy and it brought back parental panic—the mad illness when you lose a child in a crowded mall.

My phone rang.

"Josh," said Geneva de Hoyas, "you dump that sinkhole two-eighty-eight yet? Tom wanted it dismissed last month. Tell me you understand."

"I hear you."

She considered that. Moments passed, then she hung up.

I needed time. The *Moody* case had just spiked the biggest life sign of its sad and marginal existence on a teenage waif who dug Sixties rock and would unwittingly trade her life for a midday snack.

"Got her," said Obstain. "What's your name, girl?"

"Belinda," came a small voice over the radio. "Belinda Howell."

"Copy that?" asked Obstain.

"Got it," I said, writing it down.

Time to talk to Rachel.

26.

RACHEL

Rachel sat in a hard, straight-backed chair, her head down.

"You and Belinda," Kimberley Hong said, "were friends."

I said, "Moody offered Belinda help with her homework." The light in the room seemed to dim as Rachel covered her ears and ran blindly to the door, desperately raising her hands in defense as I moved toward her. I backed off and she whimpered as she fought the doorknob, breathlessly banging the door open and running out into a warm, rogue breeze.

I stopped. We had pushed too hard.

* * *

Wind rattled the Cyclone fences and the sky darkened. The storm came low and fast, leaking ozone. California kids, strangers to summer storms, looked up at clouds blacker than any they had seen. Lightning flashed and thunder broke the stillness. El Niño had come.

Everyone stopped breathing in a collective moment of tribal shock, and then the rains came. The deluge evaporated the cumulative, ponderous heat of the early Valley summer. The cooling cloudburst fell on my scorched face, my hot neck and warm arms. Thank you, I said, hot skin absorbing the downpour. Lightning sizzled in bright arcs. I counted to the rumble and divided by five. Two miles. More bolts and reports.

One mile, coming fast.

Summer would have loved this. Kids screamed and rejoiced in the cleansing downpour. Getting totally zapped by lightning was better than being cooked by a desert sun. The world burst into sheer white and hail bounced as I quickly herded students indoors. Teachers grabbed paralyzed kids, moving them, and they were safe.

The flooded yard was empty. The rain was a curative, bringing a sea change and geomantically easing losses of a sad earth with the chance of floods. In sheets of pleasantly hard, blinding rain, Summer could materialize, and she and I could dance to the Indigo Girls. It was better than a Disneyland ride. I closed my eyes, sensing her aura, her keen warmth.

A girl's voice. Diminutive, plaintive against a retreating storm. I dropped my arms. A voice I didn't know, made small by erosions I could not understand. I turned.

Rachel, thin arms around herself, blue bracelet tattoo unnaturally bright around a small wrist, red-hot brown eyes glowing, hair matted close to the skull, her small face revealed, cleansed, and framed by the streaming rain, her needs powerful and unclear and shouting.

Thunder rumbled distantly. Her hair was sienna, her young features aged by an undeserved past. Lightning flashed brilliantly, illuminating her, exposing delicate skin, as if I could discern skeleton and viscera and soul. She was a young

Catholic Madonna made of dark, bleeding wood and pale white paint, cleansed by ancient storms.

Thunder cracked as she spoke, her words indiscernible. I wanted to take her to safety, away from the refreshed storm. Her words were more important.

She looked up like a small Chinese woman, weeping, jerking as thunder rolled metallically across an aluminum sky.

"he can't do it again." Her face was intent, her words weak, indiscernible. She fought for air as the wind gusted, making fences rattle and her hair whip wildly. She blinked as it lashed her eyes, tears thick and almost gelatinous, her fears touching me, grating inward.

Through the thunder and wind came small, pained words.

"can't do it again. . . . you have to stop him . . . you *have* to . . . he's gonna kill someone. . . ."

27.

RAGUSA'S GYM

Ragusa's Gym at the P Street tracks is a Fifties throwback. Even now, old managers can squint and recall the details of a silk-robed welterweight with his entourage buying Rag's to train for a Saturday night bout at the arena.

Rachel had refused to speak to Wilma Debbin, Capri, and the irresistible Gonzo Marx at the police station and in court. Ergo, the gym.

Rag's hadn't produced a contender in ten years or a positive smell since it opened, but Rachel looked at the gym with cautious curiosity. It was early. Rain fell softly.

Two guys in the ring. Lupo and Nate Collins. I put towels over her narrow shoulders and asked her to wait. She stood, a tiny person, rainwater puddling at her feet.

"Rag, I need your place," I said. "How much?"

Salvatore Ragusa looked up at Lupo, a thick-torsoed heavy with a mule kick in his slow right hook, pale flanks slick with sweat, face still puffy from our last and final sparring. He leaned ponderously on the ropes, breathing hard, looking at me warily. "Cop business?"

"Yes."

"A hundred bucks," said Lupo. "Each."

Few DAs carry hundreds in cash, but I used to be a homicide cop. I counted out the bills. "Thank you very much," I said.

"You're fuckin' welcome," said Lupo, counting the bills.

I rolled eyes toward Rachel. "Be nice."

"Hey, I'm sorry," said Lupo. Looking at her, "Really."

Rachel's face closed in on itself. She wasn't accustomed to apologies.

Rag gave a flyweight sweatsuit to Rachel.

She went to the locker room. I changed to sweats.

I needed a witness to back up Rachel's statement. I called Capri, who was en route to testify in court. "Josh, that's great! How'd you do it?"

"I didn't. She's doing this to protect the Howell girl."

"That's not true. She's doing it because she *trusts* you. Think: how many men have cared that much for her? The way you have?"

I made more calls. Braxton, DA Chief of Investigations, said Geneva had ordered a total resource embargo on *Moody*. I tried all female associates. Everyone was putting out their own fires. I tried women lawyers in private firms and state agencies. Bust.

I needed a woman. I looked around the gym. No women.

"Sal, how much to buy your time? I need a witness." I looked at his hard, thick-veined arms, hands that had passed the point of readable pain decades before. The head that had taken ten thousand shots, becoming leather. "It'll be hard stuff. The girl was raped."

"Jesus, that little girl?" The thought saddened him. "Tell me what to do."

I did, giving him a notepad and a pen. He flourished a blunt pencil; it was his writing tool. From the car I got the gear, wishing I had an investigator. I set out chairs and Gatorade.

Rachel came out dressed and smelling clean. She held wet clothes and a Raiders cap, faded gray sweats swallowing her form, sweatshirt hood framing brownish hair of a pretty girl. Miss Piggy was also wet. Rachel flinched as thunder burst overhead.

I used to like victims with voices; it meant they could testify, singing the unique, *sui generis,* painful lyrics to the prosecutor's hard, one-note song. Convict, convict, convict.

The sun faded from cracked skylights as the rain drummed harder.

She smelled of Irish Spring soap. Abrasions of post-rape scrubbing, the victim trying to expunge the screams from the epidermis.

I spoke softly. "Is it okay if Mr. Ragusa, the man over there, sits in while you tell me what happened?" I explained why; that if something happened later, we'd have two people who heard the statement. That as the DA, I couldn't testify in my own case as to what I heard.

She looked down, blinking. "you mean, like, if i die? or run away?"

"That's right. Mr. Rag looks tough, doesn't he? But he's a softie. He already likes you." Rachel peeked around my shoulder at him. She refocused on my chest, a child before getting a shot at the doctor's, trying to shrink the big world. She wasn't used to making decisions.

"Lotion," said Rag, passing her a bottle. His harsh New York accent made her look up.

"Rachel, Mr. Sal Ragusa, a friend. A famous boxer and a very good man. I've asked him to listen in while we talk. Okay?"

Rachel looked at Rag's dented face and badly broken, re-shaped nose. Avocado-shell skin. Aging, farsighted eyes. Hard, square body. She took the lotion bottle, holding it tightly, saw the desk, tape recorder, camcorder on a tripod, the sign on the door that said *Open* to us and *Closed* to the world.

Rag took her wet clothes and hung them on the ropes.

"can't do this." A small voice beneath a cricket call.

"Yes, you can," I said. "You can help me stop him."

"this'll stop him?"

No promises, no guarantees. "I think so. I hope so."

She shut her eyes tightly, a precious child with a tiny voice.

Rag sat. I turned on the equipment and Rachel jumped. I was a goat trying to capture a butterfly. "Close your eyes and think of a safe place. Now take a breath and relax. Then let it out, slowly. We have all kinds of time."

Rachel raised thin shoulders, took a breath, sagging but still tense.

"Describe this safe place you see, for us."

". . . families . . . kids . . . a playground . . . lots of people . . . fruit stands . . . a park. . . ."

"That's like the Farmer's Market in Davis. A great place. Rachel, pretend we're there. It's easy and gentle and dry and you're totally safe. You can rest. You can relax."

"don't look at me." Swallowing pain. "it freaks me."

I focused on the ring. Rag looked away from it. The leaky roof pinged water in dented spit buckets. My clothes dripped monotonously next to Rachel's on frayed ring ropes. Sunlight warmed and faded, grew intensely bright and then ominously dark with the shifting of clouds as the city stirred after the spectacular storm. A box of pink Kleenex was near her.

A train whistle blew from the tracks and the old phone rang. I stopped Sal from answering it. I had waited a long time for this girl's statement. Thunder pealed.

I opened with direct questions, spoken softly. Nothing. She was stuck. A lot of people who get raped think they should have stopped it. Or feel they caused the attack.

"Rachel, this wasn't your fault. There are a lot of adult women who don't report rapes because they think it was *their* fault. It wasn't. You're not alone and you are not going crazy. Rachel, talk to us. Let it out. It's like a poison inside you. Don't hold on to it."

Time passed, but not by the clock. This was the moral march of time. For this, cops wait with infinite patience in a space without statutes of limitation.

Rachel began in a small, self-conscious, fragile voice that was absorbed by the old floor and the frayed apparatus.

We listened. Her voice strained, as if it alone had absorbed all the injury. She touched Miss Piggy's small patent leather shoes, cleaning them of prints.

Salvatore Ragusa looked at her softly and made a soft noise in his mouth, an older hummingbird whispering to its young during a storm.

28.

_____

RACHEL'S STORY

"ohmygosh Momma she laughed and she was so pretty and she was so happy 'til Dad, he killed her after we come up from Texas."

A vomit of words under long, pent-up pressures. An alien voice, unaccustomed to the world, tremulous, tentative, and small, the exploratory steps of a newborn foal.

Rag and I looked at Rachel. She tolerated it, studying her doll.

"Momma she liked *Sesame Street*. i kinda liked Elmo and Big Bird. Momma, she liked Miss Piggy, even though Miss Piggy wasn't a real Christian, bein' mean and sassy and eatin' too much." She added. "for a pig. Momma she was always strict for God." I released my breath and Rachel kept talking. The story unfolded: Rachel's mother, Debbie Murphy Farr, had stood bravely by her young daughter against the father's unpredictable anger.

"Momma said that for me when i grew up, there'd be no drugs, no sex, no booze. Dad he offered Momma a hit from an eight ball of crystal meth. he said it was to save the marriage, but the meth killed her. i never, ever, liked Dad's trash. Dierdre moved in Momma's room that night, and they stayed up late, laughing." She swallowed painfully. "in the morning, Dierdre kicked me upside my head, sayin' this was her home now, and did i have any questions."

Rachel flunked the fourth grade and ruminated about suicide.

Rachel stopped talking. "Still think about it?" I asked.

She was withdrawing, circles into circles, leaving us.

"Rachel, what's your dad do for a living?" The rainfall became heavier.

"he's a roofer now. but he's always been a prick. he slaps you for a word, his breath like glue. sweet with people around, bad to you later." Her words were too small to echo in the gym, but they reprised in the mind. In the silence, she added, for affirmation, "i know i am just a dumb little bitch, okay?" Her voice was anorexic, weak, marginal, full of depletion.

"That is not true. When do you think about suicide?" No answer. I repeated myself.

"sometimes. not too often."

I pressed her.

"Momma said it was a sin to do that to yourself. don't you worry." She resumed.

Rachel had been pulled to Moody's crib by big Bose speakers, Guns n' Roses, junk food, and curiosity about a haunted house. He had not rescued her from Namese toughs. He invited her in. *Bose speakers,* I wrote. *Where's he get his $?*

She could hang out, scarf snacks, tube on MTV and E! or play Nintendo or bond with the Moody dog, or just be left alone. Rachel did it for the alone part. She needed a place.

Moody was fairly weird. But Chee-tos, Fruitopias, tattooing and body piercing, and Spango the spaniel, with him never hitting on her, and Rachel made him as decidedly cool. Chico didn't cuss. He was gentle. "he called you sweetheart. he used way nice words." I wrote: *She calls him 'Chico.'* A long pause, sliding toward permanence.

"Describe being there," I said. "You ever go during school?"

She cut class to nacho at Chico's with Nine Inch Nails on MTV. She and five runaway girls. "hitchhikers they bail in Sacramento from I-5. some, who are into it, trick for Greyhound fares. Chico put the runaways in some motel and let 'em hang at Tulip during the day."

He had rules which she recited as scripture. " 'touch my PC or go up the stairs, i'll dish you to the street. live and let live. no cursing or you're not righteous. no boys in the house. follow the code or hit the road.' he was a big word mack daddy."

July Fourth, the runaways split with Chico's funds. Rachel said Chico should look for them. Chico didn't even know their last names. And last summer, Rachel became the sole member of Chico's abandoned children's organization.

In the fall, he went through some changes. I don't want you cutting classes anymore, he said. Do your homework. I'll help.

Rachel had shared the opinion that the idea sucked.

You need to grow your brain, he said. How do you think I made it?

She said, You broke your neck and got Social Security for life.

He laughed. No, sweetheart—I got myself educated. That's how I found my life. C'mon, you can do it, bit by bit. Go with the flow. Do it cuz it'll make me feel good.

"i said, 'well, you know i'm just a stupid little bitch,' and he slapped me. but i deserved it, cussing in his house against the rules when he was feeding me and all." A garbage truck hydroplaned outside, drowning her voice, but I knew what she had said.

Ten minutes of algebra followed by an hour of MTV. Some history that became two hours of hard work. Chico eased it with snacks and music. He knew how to make a girl happy.

She was quiet. Lightning flashed. "What are you remembering?" I asked.

Leaves falling like little drunk men on a Saturday night while she wrote a paper on the original Stephen King dude— Edgar Allan Poe. Chico not looking at her—looking *through* her—head somewhere else. She asked what he wanted for Christmas and he got choked up. He smoked pot, so she gave him a ceramic ashtray she made at Rio.

"no, i didn't smoke weed with him."

He gave her perfume and a watch. "i was always late. so stupid, you know?" She became good at school. Teachers paid attention to her. They liked her. New friends, and a Chinese kid named Art Chen had a crush on her. She knew she couldn't bring them to Tulip.

"Why not?"

"they, like, have families."

"So they wouldn't fit?"

" 'course not." She shook her small head.

February, she went to Chico's. Moody was going on a trip. Rachel would take care of Spango the spaniel for twenty bucks.

She wanted to do it for free. The door was open.

It was six on her Timex on a Saturday night. She thought it was the beginning of February. I checked the almanac François has assembled for me. Saturday was the first of the month. It had been unseasonably warm—sixty-six in the day, fifty-three degrees at six in the evening. A quarter moon in a partially cloudy sky. Winds from the south at twelve miles an hour. I stirred, remembering that disturbing rogue wind.

"It was February," I said. "How cold was it?"

She shook her head, frowning. "i don't think it was cold."

"Was there a moon?"

She tightly shut her eyes and almost turned away. "a little one. with clouds."

Rachel had looked at her watch. She was on time.

"Hey, sweetheart," he called from the kitchen.

Rachel had sung back, "Hi, Chico!" He was wearing a suit. Rachel was in cords and a pink Nike sweatshirt, ready for nachos, embarrassed, underdressed, staring at handsome Chico in a tie and wondering where Spango was. She kept calling him, but no dog to bond.

And I was there with her. Rag was nodding. The ring tested guts and muscle. It dug out the verities in a man and revealed all falsehoods. Ragusa was, in that way, an old judge of truth. I thought of Moody at the Firehouse. That boy from Virginia was lying to us.

Rachel looked at me, her lips bloodless as lightning illuminated the gym and thunder rattled the windows. Now comes the pain. She looked like a big-eyed corpse. Rag sighed.

Chico made dinner. Salad with a yuck dressing. Filet mignon

steak and potato, a beer—her first with him—and apple pie. A special night—he lit candles. He was so quiet and sad, like when he thought about being in prison. She liked him—his ups and downs didn't come out in fists or boots. The steak was the best, the beer was sour, and she got sleepy before dessert.

Now she wanted to cry.

"It's okay," I said. She cried hard while Rag and I frowned with all our might.

Then, "see, he gave me something. I like crashed out, real hard."

Half an hour after the beer, she was falling asleep. I thought: Rohypnol, or "R-2," "roach," "roafie," "rib," and "rape." Ten times more potent than Valium with a half-life of three days. The drug of choice for date rape, smoothed with beer and who knew what else in the reckless pharmacology of an uncaring child molester. I blinked; I was presuming Moody guilty.

Rachel's voice had been in the rain too long and had shrunk. I strained to hear it, and what crept into my ear aged me.

A cramp, growing worse into a real bad hurt.

She was in dim light.

For a moment, she thought Momma was helping her into bed to take care of the owie, the pain. To sing to her and hold her hand.

A thing stabbed her, inside. She cried out, hurt, terrified, knowing what it was, not believing it. She heard her own screams. She had this thought that she was an orangutan in the zoo down the Broadway, swinging in the Monkey House. She couldn't stop thinking of monkeys in pain, her mind floating from the zoo to Momma. Momma's a pretty woman. *Pretty Woman* was Julia Roberts. How tall's Leo DiCaprio? How old's Harrison Ford?

"It's okay, sweetheart," said Chico, but it wasn't. Nothing was okay or could be again, ever, ever. She wailed and he gasped as he did her. In the dark, she smelled Akami, his perfume gift, now on her ears and neck. She said it twice before I heard her.

"now it makes me puke so bad."

"Were you on your stomach or on your back?"

"my stomach. i felt sick . . . oh, man, i *was* sick . . . so sick. . . ."

"Were you wearing anything?" We needed clothes. Evidence. Washed or stale.

She shuddered. "panties," she said.

He pulled them aside and was on top and inside her, ruining her. Her tears were the commas, the semicolons, the periods, the paragraphs, the blood.

"he was killing me. i begged him to stop. you're my friend, my gentle man. my tummy was on fire but he'd put it out. he'd end the burning. it was so awful. you don't know. can't know. i was gonna die and i was crazy and couldn't wait for it. i just wanted to die."

The wasting inside her. Her mind slowed and thickened, pain growing, almost visibly. Rag was wringing his hands, making a desert sound on a wet day.

The head pain went away as her body hurt more. Pinned and trapped, helpless, a thing for Chico to use.

She cried. Handcuffs cut her wrists and spread her, a blind, pinned little monkey on a bed in the zoo in the Broadway. Now she had unmarked wrists. "Were there cuts back then?"

"maybe. yeah. i think so."

"Go on," I said.

Chico was holding her, grunting. She needed to be free, and nothing mattered. Teachers liked her knowing Odysseus and Toltecs, and the Miwok, pharaohs and improper fractions, declaratives, pluperfects, and infinitives, all of it now meaning nothing at all.

Later, when she was done crying, she asked him why? "oh, Chico, why? why, Chico?"

Her tiny voice pierced the gym. Summer's cry with her last heart attack—Daddy! And in that moment, as she recounted her words, Rachel was again being raped and Summer was failing and the sand in her clock, the short time of her life, fell through my dead fingers.

Rag blew his nose. My head was light, balance gone, legs made of rubber and I was forgetting something; I was getting decked in Rag's without taking a punch. Rachel looked at the

Gatorade. I drank, spilling down my chin. Rag rubbed his leathery face, watching me out of the corner of an eye. He punched my arm. Rachel was talking.

She thought Moody was crying as he wiped her down with a warm washcloth, tending her as if she were his daughter and she had gotten dirty. He covered her and stroked her hair, wet with loss. He turned on KCTC, the old people's music station, and left her.

Trembling, she tried to touch her injury, but couldn't. Her muscles were torn from the spastic efforts to escape.

"i can't listen to that shitty music, not ever. never again. never. it makes me so sick."

Her throat was raw from screaming. Her eyes and hair hurt. No windows. The room was strange. No sounds. Rachel thought she was upstairs. He had drugged her and she couldn't move or breathe deeply. Wheezing, bleeding, she listened to that old music, smelling the perfume. She cried so hard she threw up on herself. She called for help. For her momma. She asked God to kill her. She tried to cover her ears.

"i was gonna die like momma died, ugly and old and pasty with vomit. i cussed God for not killin' me and takin' me outa there. i talked so bad. i didn't care. it was so mis."

"Mis?" I asked.

She flicked small fingers at me. "miserable."

After two or three, or five or six hours' sleep, she awoke, gagging—milk in her mouth and a pill stuck in her raw throat. She swallowed it. The bed was clean and she was tied up, on her back. She slept. When she awoke after a long time—no idea how long—she knew he had done it in her mouth and inside her. She was ill, asking never to be awake again.

"i barfed. i barfed so bad it hurt my back."

"At this point, where were the underpants?" I asked.

She narrowed her eyes. "still on me." She shuddered, panting. She sipped Gatorade, covered her mouth, spat it out, and moaned as she became violently ill. It was a boxing gym, accustomed to spillage. Rag cleaned the floor while I helped her to the bathroom.

Rain dripped faster from roof leaks.

This had not been a simple rape. She had been snatched by a person she liked and trusted. She had been violently, sexually blitzed and wrecked. Eradicated, soul and being flagellated. The sounds of her retching filled the gym, making me shut my eyes.

"Jesus H. Christ," said Rag. "The poor kid."

Moody seduced kids with kindness and Chee-tos and drugged a girl who would've broken the law for him. I added up the prison terms, taking comfort in an arcane formula contorted by prison overcrowding. Techno-blather New Math that was music to my ears.

Moody would get eight years—upper term—on the first rape because it was forcible. The sum would later double under the California Three Strikes law for an ex-con.

Another eight, upper term, for using a stupefying drug on a child. Plus one-third the midterm of six years for the second injection, and once again, for the pill with milk.

One-third the midterm of six—two—for kidnapping a child for rape. There was technically too little asportation, movement. But distance wasn't everything. If he had moved her out of the house, I'd get a 207 kidnap. In the house was normally not a 207. This wasn't normal. I'd prosecute Moody for late library books.

But I don't prosecute anyone. I just do the math. Someone else would do the trial. Now we had evidence—moral evidence—a victim's statement. Robin could do it. Isaac could do it. Any SACA DA could do it. I took comfort in that, knowing there was a flaw in my thinking.

I resumed. Eight years for forced oral copulation, full force consecutive because it was a 288. Eight for the second rape. Add five years for an ex-con, then doubled under Three Strikes law for a qualifying ex-con. Moody's prior felony qualified him.

If we could nail Moody over Stacy's zealous defense, he'd do eighty-six years in state prison and die of old age in the black hole in Soledad or the SHU in the Q. Not another breath of free air. I thought of Tree Frog Johnson, who kidnapped a child and kept him in a van for eighteen months. He got 480 years.

She unsteadily returned.

"Rachel," I said, "you're a brave and wonderful girl. I'm proud of you."

"You're real strong, kid," said Rag. "Got iron in yur guts."

No reaction. I reminded her where she had stopped. She said that Moody blindfolded and uncuffed her and took her to the bathroom. There was a warm tub. She soaked.

"You're sure that's what happened next?"

"it happened. then he took the blindfold off. so gross. the water was all pink."

"Did you know that bathroom? Had you been in it before?"

She shook her head. "no. i got a Pepsi. he drugged me again. and did it again. it hurt."

"Upstairs?"

"Yes."

I undid the math; Moody was still attacking her. Grimly I added a second kidnap using stupefying drugs for sexual assault to the undoubled forty-three years.

"Rachel, what attacks did he repeat? Please, be real specific."

Maybe there were three more. Dark room. On her stomach. Shackled. *Maybe three.* The sums grew like sadistic usury.

Moody gave her another bathroom trip and massage while she begged him to not touch her, to let her go. She wouldn't tell anyone, and she meant it so all-the-way, swearing to it.

"Rache," he said, "relax. Relax, sweetheart. Go with the flow."

"Were the underpants left in the bathroom?" I asked. I needed physical evidence.

She shook her head. "he put them back on me. . . ." She shuddered as she had before.

"How do you remember this so well?" I asked.

She licked dry lips. "i tell Momma, most every night. Momma, she knows."

I wrote: *She tells her dead momma.* "What happened next?"

She was strapped facedown on clean sheets in the black room. More Akami on her neck and body. She threw up. He cleaned her. She felt everything and felt like dying. No drugs. He liked her struggle, her efforts to escape. He liked her on her tummy, facedown.

He was rough with her. And then, in her mouth.

"but he didn't, you know—he didn't let it out. wasn't so bad that way. not anymore."

"It's okay," I said. "It's still so wrong." Eight more years.

I flexed my arms against the demon in our presence. In her narrative, he was gaining momentum into cruelty. The angry sadist, sliding into abuse and torture, alternating with assurances. Incredible pain followed by soft assurances. She was hit with a medley of blows while she begged him to stop. There were six more sexual assaults.

Then he sodomized her anally. While he did that, he was at the apex of his rage. Holding her by her hair, pulling her entire scalp upward, he hit and choked her. She was bleeding inside and out, screaming and screaming until he choked her.

"he hated me then. he was tryin' to kill me. or break me, like I was an old stick. i think i blacked out. i woke up and i was alone. i didn't feel very good."

No colposcope had been taken—vaginal or rectal. Rachel's resistance had failed with Chico, but had worked with the SANER nurses' exam protocol. It had been nearly four months since the attack. No, not the attack: the ravaging. The savaging. The wasting.

I wondered if she'd take a colposcope now. I didn't know if it'd do any good. But there had been so much trauma—there had to be scar tissue.

"Would you let a nurse examine you now?" I asked.

Violently, she shook her head, crying painfully, her body closing. "he used me like toilet paper. no one's ever gonna touch me again. not him. not a nurse. not you. not nobody."

I said, You're right, but no sound came. My voice could only form prosecutorial questions, racing an anonymous clock. "Do you bleed when you go to the bathroom?" *i don't know. i don't look. don't wanna look.* "What side did he hit you on?" *Right side.*

"How hard did he hit you?"

"he like to choke me to death. why didn't he just kill me?" Her accent was stronger.

"You were supposed to live so you can testify against him," I said, writing: *"2 counts Attempt 187."* Attempted murder during a 288 could bring two consecutive life terms.

When she woke, she thought Chico had done more to her, but wasn't sure. After the choking, she didn't care. "two more times at least. maybe more." She was wearing down.

I assumed two more assaults. Moody was facing an exposure of 360 years. In penal terms, fourteen lifetimes. Maybe, for a molester, worse. "Take a break, Rachel," I said.

Light played in the boxing ring, lessening the purples of old stains. I would show the video to Stacy August and she would know Moody was guilty. I had the high ground. I looked at the clock; we had been at it for ten minutes. That was wrong. I looked at my watch. Three hours had passed. I checked the camcorder and audiotapes; they hadn't moved. They were dead-fried by a lightning strike. It meant I had no electronic record of this interview. I had nothing to show Stacy but my own personal opinions. They were worth something when I used to do trials.

I did low, slow breathing. My mind hurt. I exhaled, cursing silently. Okay. Bash on.

"What is it," I said easily, "that you haven't told us?"

She squirmed, a child's frown. "what do you mean? God, i told you everything. everything."

I smiled. "Hey, no one ever tells me everything. Tell me. It's okay."

Rachel wept softly and blew her nose. "leave me alone." Rag glanced at me.

"I think you really cared for him," I said softly.

"i hated him! he beat me! he—" She covered her face and muffled, wept, her thin form racked with horrible sobs. "oh. oh, why'd he do that? what'd i do to make him do that?"

"Nothing. It wasn't your fault. It's his. But you're holding back. Rachel. Don't stop now."

She wept bitterly. One day it was hot. She had worn clothes that were sort of sexy.

"you know. halter top. cut-off jeans. i don't know why. it felt cool at first but it was so retarded, so stupid. look what happened. God, i'm such a dumb *stupid* little bitch!"

"Rachel, it is not your fault," I said. "It's okay to be sexy. Part of growing up. Guys do it, too. It's just a thing. You don't invite rape. Rape's not about sex." I took a breath. "It's about men's anger. Their power." We were quiet for a while. Rainwater dripped. Salvatore Ragusa scratched his head. His breath whistled through the broken gristle of his old nose.

I thanked her for telling me everything. "The part you were holding back. It shows you were wrong to blame yourself." I asked her to replay the beating. She had been hit mostly on the right, same as when he sodomized her. I remembered Moody's ambidextrous way of eating at the Firehouse. Fries with the left, hamburger with the right.

"How'd you get out of there?" I asked.

Moody drove her home. He didn't apologize to her. She apologized to him.

Why?

"i threw up in his car. sort of dry heaving." She said it matter-of-factly. I remembered Stacy August's unkind words about Rachel. Geneva telling me to dump *Moody* before it did real harm. The girl, apologizing to her attacker, for being sick after he ruined her.

"Sorry to keep asking about the underpants," I said, "but I need physical evidence. Were they left in the house?"

She nodded. "he took them." She didn't know when. "i just don't have them anymore."

No physical evidence. But I had Rachel Farr. I had her story. It will open the hearts of a good jury. Ragusa believed her. He was crying.

The girl looked at me, her eyes asking, *You believe me?*

"Rachel, I believe you. I believe in you. I'm sorry he did this. It must hurt more than I can imagine. It's not your fault. It *wasn't* your fault. You tell the court, they'll believe, too."

She made a sharp dismissive sound. "oh, yeah, fer sure. it'll be like O. J. Simpson. he'll look good in a suit. big and so cool. he'll look at me. i'm just a stupid little. . . ."

I opened my mouth and she said, "i need to take a bath." She rocked, hearing herself, hating her voice and, I think, hating us for bringing it all back into the surface of her skin.

"You're not stupid. Rachel, you're so cool, so strong. You didn't deserve this."

She sat with the stillness of a cop on an exposed stakeout, as if her eyes were dead agates, her lungs sealed in formaldehyde, pores closed, fingerprints fading, and the need for oxygen erased. Sal Ragusa moved a glass of water toward her. She didn't move.

"Go ahead," he said. "Good for you."

She winced as if Sal had punched her in her floating ribs. "i don't like to put stuff in my mouth anymore." Her shoulders jerked as if she were hiccupping. She sobbed and fell. I caught her, crying, weightless and spineless, her small, thin arms lifelessly around me. Sum when she was eleven and had hit her first home run, high-fiving teammates at the plate and jumping into my arms, spent. My pains rose and met Rachel's as they spread, looking for safe harbor, a living, crawling thing that came out of her. I shut my eyes. I missed my girl so much.

I blinked, realizing that she had been speaking. ". . . i couldn't tell you . . . just couldn't. so dirty. so gross. so dirty. . . ."

"Oh, honey, you're not. You're clean, you're pure. There are precious parts of you he could never touch. Never." She cried and I stopped myself from saying, Don't cry, baby, please don't cry, and the pins came out of my disguise and I wept for her.

Later, in a miserable, inattentive mood, I said, "Did he threaten you?"

She was hiccupping, holding me with a blind and childish need, with tiny fingers and a weak, sad breath. "he said he'd kill me if i talked. . . . he'd stab me in my eyes a hundred times. . . ."

The sleep deprivation, the lost days, the lack of motivation, the loss of purpose, dissipated in the face of a cresting violence. I embraced the rage, emotions beyond category, blind, volcanic, bloody, wrong for the law, so good for my crooked soul.

There was no handing-off of this case. I couldn't pass her to anyone else in the office. If I did, she'd have to start over again with another DA, another interview, another relationship founded on her rape, her agonies, her thin, tragic trust. I couldn't let that happen.

Because she had told me, I had to do her trial.

Hot anger subsided into sadness. Rachel was blinking against my wet neck. She pulled back and looked into my wet face the way little girls do at their fathers, my eyes in that moment slipping into her small, unguarded, dying soul. What I saw—a sad, weeping void—broke my heart. There was not much girl left. Too much had died, beyond the reach of medicine and nurses, doctors, and horses and all the king's men. I sobbed, an animal-like wrenching.

"why you crying?" she asked with a hiccup in the middle.

"For you," I said. "Baby, for you."

29.

GENEVA DE HOYAS

I don't go to Chinese cafés for the décor. But Frank Fat's served the Capitol, where cuisine is subordinated to politics and atmosphere is acknowledged as the primary spice.

Fat's merged a velvet Twenties speakeasy with a vermillion Shanghai wailing cathouse. It was a slick sublit forum that lubricated deals. Lobbyists, senators, members of the assembly, lawyers, and other despised power lunchers were at work with forks and tongues. Our office lobbyist waved. Geneva nodded. We got a backroom booth. I waited until we were alone.

"Geneva, I've been a good boy. I've flossed, said my prayers, and have three hundred years in state prison waiting for Moody. What's behind the move to dump the case?"

She leaned under red lights. "No physical evidence and she's the worst victim, ever."

"She's never contradicted herself, which puts her ahead of a lot of lawyers and judges. And DAs. Since when did we take only slam dunks to trial, and dump the sow's ears?"

"Josh, enough. Just disappear it tomorrow on the eight-thirty calendar."

"I'll ignore that. You gave me *Moody*, putting it under *my* DA discretion. And my discretion says a guy who drugs, rapes, sodomizes, and strangles little girls gets a jury trial of his peers. Go ahead, question my judgment. Postmortem my legal analysis. Drown me in good advice. But don't interefere with my case. You better pull my badge first."

"Dammit!" she hissed. "Don't play games! It's the needs of the many versus the need of the one!" She gathered herself. "You try this turkey, you make Tommy into an idiot with a suit-case. The press has this stupid *Moody* case as the litmus test for the election! You're giving it to Jergen and busting our balls here."

"Negative. Tom did that when he punched out a cop and didn't say he was sorry. *You* were supposed to keep him out of bars." I was being petty. And she thought I was busting her balls. Women, like Chinese and others who had to sprint for the *Walk* sign, had learned the Anglo male argot of law enforcement, heavy on machismo, scatology, and personal anatomy.

The night Tommy was at A Shot of Class to rescue a damsel and beat up a cop, Large Louis was in the rest room, perusing a comic book. He should've been on the floor, guarding the boss from himself and the demons of the night, blocking the door for Conover's folly.

"If you dismiss," she said, "there'll be grumbling in China-town. A Chinese DA can do damage repair. Unlike me, they still like you. You try *Moody*, it gives Stacy a bully pulpit. Go figure why she wants Jergen to be DA, but she's doing it. Let's just win this damn election."

"Even, unethically."

"No. By being smart. Use the brains God in His wisdom gave you. Josh, you're not the lawyer you were before Summer died. If you were, we could take the chance. But you're not."

"Funny. We're in a Chinese restaurant, but we're not eating. You're a DA, maybe the best in the state, and you're using a rubber hose on me, and calling it deduction."

"Okay, Josh, *don't* dump it. Just change your prelim date to *after* the election. The statute on two-eighty-eights is six years. After November, *I'll* help you take Moody down."

I sat back. "If one of our guys even *suggested* doing that to a *misdemeanor* case, we'd pull his badge, report him, and hold him down on the Astroturf while State Bar Discipline kicked him through the crossbars. Your advice is a reportable violation. It's worth *your* badge."

"Damn, you're turning stupid on me!" Her eyes flashed, then looked away. "There's no justice—it's *all* politics! And if Jergen becomes DA, politics'll turn to *crap*—of the brown, drizzly variety. The man's a coke fiend—he'll give the County to the gangs. My advice, *as a friend,* is to think strategically. Summer's death screwed all of us. Now you're confusing this girl with *her*. *Compadre,* you can't save her. This girl's life is over. Yes, *Moody* has political overtones. But the facts are that you're damaged goods and the girl is old roadkill selling herself as a rose.

"I know you believe her. You think you got a chance to make chicken salad out of chicken crap. Listen, friend, *I* don't believe her. And where's the beef? The science? The phosphoglucomutase readouts, DNA pellets, and ABO blood typing? You need semen and all you got is thin air, a stale report, and Harry O. Bilinski and a recipe for a five-minute acquittal."

"Geneva, don't believe your own B.S. Your job is not to re-elect Tommy. It's to be a People's advocate, whatever the cost. You taught me that. Our office is the last resort for victims. We're not a local 7-Eleven to pick up a quick vote. You're not supposed to screw with me—you're supposed to back me up. You're supposed to back up Rachel Farr."

She shook her head.

I folded my napkin. "*People versus Karl Francis Moody* is a weak case but I got a victim and I got a defendant. I got a case to try."

"You try that case, Josh, I'll move to dismiss it myself."

"And I'll fight your motion and the press will come running."

"And I'll flat-out fire you."

I was fighting for Rachel's day in court. "Your prerogative." It was just a job. I opened my wallet to expose the badge. I tossed it on her unused plate. "Eat up. It's okay. I could go back to SFPD Homicide. Or train some amateur fighters. Coach kids' soccer. But that's all mouse crap. Know what matters? The girl." I leaned toward her, my voice low.

"You want me to dump an active case of child sexual assault to help Tommy's reelection. That's what you told Wilma Debbin. She filed this weak case to retaliate. Geneva, when the TV evening news asks why I got fired, what's your advice, as a *friend*? What if I recounted this conversation? Or should I lie for you?"

"God, you give me brain scurvy."

"That's what I get paid for. How'd you know Gonzo offered Moody county jail when it was his case? *I* didn't know that until Stacy August told me."

"We've always had a deathwatch on this case. So does Jergen." And I knew that Geneva de Hoyas hated me and hated my dead daughter for the evil contagion of lost hope we had worked on the office. I knew she hated Thomas Conover's reelection and what it was doing to her. She had grown up wanting to be a DA. No one was better. Now she probably hated her job. Politics had soured her, put extraterrestrial words in her mouth, obscured her shining virtues. She and I had climbed the political staircase and found at the top, politics.

"Geneva, you think I'm a stubborn SOB? Imagine what kind of a bastard *you'd* be if Carinita, your daughter, died." I sipped cold tea. "Now, I only got one case. Maybe I'll screw it up. Maybe I won't. But either way, no child torturer gets a free pass or a wrist slap or a delay for an election. I'm taking *Moody* to trial. Trust me, Geneva, as if I were someone worthy of your respect. Stay out of my road. Now either take the badge or give me my wallet back."

She folded it. "You push too hard, Josh. Under *Bishop* I could, as the ranking rep of the district attorney, enter your court and move to dismiss your case against Mr. Moody. Over your objections." She smiled. "My badge is bigger." She returned my wallet, stood, and walked out.

30.

PRELIM PREP

I turned on the lights. The empty court was antiseptic and full of foreboding. Without warm defendants in flop sweat, it was as cool as a morgue. Here, acute human failing was resolved by reluctant amateurs drawn from a lottery. Here, I tended to openly weep.

"The hardest part will be facing Chico again."

"The hardest part," growled Bilinski, "is life."

Rachel stayed by the doors, holding Miss Piggy. I felt her answer: the hardest part is being so alone. Harry and I entered the court. I sat at the table in the defendant's chair.

"Chico's here, like last time." First name only.

Rachel wore a black shirt and purple pants. Her hair was brushed and clean. She looked good and didn't know it.

"This time he'll glare and use his face because he'll be afraid. He's scared of you. He'll feel like running around in circles like his pants are on fire." She grinned nervously.

I asked Harry Bilinski to sit on the bench. He did, and the door banged open: François Giggin, the door hitting him, knocking him into a seat. "I'm late!" He struggled up.

"François," I said, "you're Moody today. Take the defendant's chair."

I moved left into the DA seat, closest to the jury and the flag. An advantage of being the prosecutor. Giggin, blond hair bright, sat. Clean jeans, Tevas, bright earrings, no socks.

"Look at Rachel and cross your eyes," I said. François complied. "Moody'll be here, looking goofy." Rachel made a tense near-smile and rolled her eyes at François. "Between Moody

154

and me will be his lawyer, Ms. August, who, remember, asks only good questions.

"The jury box'll be empty for the prelim.

"Later, during trial, twelve jurors sit here. Two reserve jurors, there."

I pointed at Bilinski on the bench. "You get one judge for the prelim, a different one for the trial. The judge's job is to run the court fairly. My job is to convict Moody. Your job is . . ."

"to tell the truth."

"Excellent." Rachel trembled as I escorted her to the stand. "It makes sense that you'll be afraid. He's a bad guy. When he stares at you, pretend his eyes are crossed." François crossed his eyes again, sticking out his tongue. "The clerk comes from her desk to swear you. Like we practiced." We did it again. I smiled. "Rachel, who's Chico afraid of?"

"me," she said.

I comically puffed out my chest. "Here, in court, who has the power?"

"i do."

"Who admires you for your guts?"

"you. François. Capri. my Momma. God."

"And Harry. Rachel, what happened when you begged Chico to stop hurting you?"

She licked thin lips. "he didn't listen to me."

"In this court, does he have to listen to you?"

A nod. "yes."

"Absolutely! In this court, can he touch you? Say it big."

"No!"

"*All right,* honey!" boomed Bilinski, his voice making Rachel jump.

"In this court, what *can* he do to you?"

"make faces, run in circles, scream and shout."

François pulled at the corners of his mouth, crossed his eyes, yipped like a small hairless dog, and ran in circles in the common conduct of second-year law students.

"And, really, he can't even do that. Rachel, what do you do here?"

"tell the truth. say what happened."

"And then?"

"the judge sends Chico to a bigger court. for trial." She gulped. "i get some time off. i come back to court, with a different judge. and a jury. i tell you, all over again."

And Chico Moody will go to prison forever.

"All right, Rachel!" François, Harry, and I applauded. Rachel bounced a little, cheeks coloring. I said she could get up, but she didn't move. The chair had power and she liked it.

"can he hurt me again?"

"No fucking way," said Bilinski from the bench. "Honey, not while I'm alive. I'm your bodyguard." He stood, flicking away my raised eyebrows with the toss of a meaty hand. He shook his head, speaking softly. "No one hurts this girl. No one, goddammit." He looked down at me, a hulk on the bench, eyes small, menacing and red.

"You know, it'd be so menthol to get a gun," said François.

Rachel's eyes were down, her legs bouncing to help absorb her emotions.

"Where do you want me to be when I ask the questions?" I asked.

A tiny quiver. A pause. "can you be close?"

"Yes." I edged closer. "Later, Ms. August will question you. She may be rude. I'll try to make her behave. But they're just words. You've survived much worse."

"if they're just words, why are mine such a big deal?"

"Because your words are more important than a lawyer's."

She looked around, nodding, one eye small. "they keep this place so neat? but people who sit right here, they've been beat up, shot or cut up, or, raped, right?"

"Yes. Girls who sit here get to deal out justice to the men who hurt them. So they can't hurt anyone else."

She nodded. I had used that one already. "yeah, i know. wish my friends could come." I started to say something, but she added quickly, "but i don't have any, no more."

"Your friends are here," I said. "A deep breath, let it out slowly." I asked the questions.

Rachel, instead of sleeping at night, had been thinking about those February days for four months. I asked her the questions.

She did not do very well. Self-conscious, hesitant, unsure, un-clear, mumbling, voice fading, sliding, disappearing, the power of the witness stand now remote from her reoffended wounds, the words bringing the acts, the acid, the memories.

"You're doing fine, Rachel."

"i can now but not when he looks at me and i'm all alone up here!"

I spoke clearly. "He can look. Don't look at him. Watch me. Keep your eyes on my handsome, movie-star, Leonardo Di-Caprio face."

A spontaneous grin. "that was pretty funny," she said.

My heart lifted. "Let's try again."

She did better, and then it wore off.

"Let's take a break. Have any questions?"

She shook her head. More practice would lend the aspect of a trained witness. No more practice, and it could lower confi-dence. Rachel was tired. She hated this. Time to stop.

At the bench, Bilinski was bent over, his face in his hands.

"am I bad at this because I'm a girl?"

I laughed. "No. You're doing fine because you're being hon-est. Men are a lot worse. Stand and stretch. You can get away from the witness stand. You okay?" I asked Bilinski. He was sweating profusely. Old malarial fevers from a distant triple-canopied jungle.

"Fuck off. Just make sure you do your job." He left, canted, heavy, and angry.

Capri drove us to Rachel's apartment.

"Harry looks bad. Want me to drive Rachel in the morning?"

"Let's trust him. But back him up, just in case."

"Okay. Let's beat traffic—seven-thirty a.m. Baby, want to get a bite?"

Rachel shook her head.

"Your dad or Dierdre hitting you?" I asked.

She sat up. "you know, it's so weird. they stopped."

"Remember to lock up at night. Chain and deadbolt, outside door. Lock your own door. But with Obstain watching your place, I'm more worried about what happens in your home than

I am about Chico. We can move you if you want, if your father agrees."

"i have to stay with my dad." She turned up the radio for a song by Babyface. "Momma says i have to take care of him." Traffic thickened in the Broadway. She was looking at me, her eye contact making me somehow sad. "you have kids?"

"No," I said.

Capri parked on Coriander. "Mr. Jin had a daughter. She died of heart disease, a year ago. She was about your age."

Rachel was quiet as she played with her seat belt. "that's why the 'tude."

"I have an attitude?"

"uh, like, yeah."

Sunlight highlighted her apartment building's flaws.

"Jin, you're not messed up," said Capri, "you're just a man. You're not as strong as we are." She turned to Rachel.

"Honey, let's talk about what you're going to wear. I think a pretty spring dress. Not too short and not at all low-cut. What colors do you like? You'd look great in blue or pink."

31.

PRELIMINARY HEARING

Rachel was about to have her wounds reopened, by me. Humor was medicine. I put some of *The New Yorker*'s best cartoons in my suit pocket, hoping they would make her smile.

Five suits were needed to do a short-cause jury trial but you need only one for a prelim. I picked a charcoal suit over a striped Oxford French dress shirt and a gray and burgundy tie.

"This okay?" I asked. Jodie canted her head in wild approval.

Harry Bilinski was Rachel's driver and Capri was backup. I

looked at my watch; time to go. I hit the freeway, headed to a prelim with a briefcase, just like a real trial lawyer.

I parked by the front door of the Catholic Home for Girls. Tiffany Prue was one of the sixteen girls at the long breakfast table, eating scrambled eggs in a bathrobe, puffy with sleep.

"I don't wanna go," she said. "I don't even know that girl."

"It'd help her, having you there. And I could sure use your help."

Tiffany threw back her hair. "Nice suit. Got a smoke?"

I pulled into the parking lot, where Gonzo Marx in a shiny blue pin-striped suit leaned on the concrete parapet. I got out. Gonzo said, "I'm now your co-counsel for *Moody*."

"Geneva's orders?" I asked. I was early, but I walked smartly.

A scrunched lemony face. "No, Jin, I volunteered." Running. "Yeah, she sent me."

"Rachel Farr won't be happy to see you, and victims rule. As of this moment, I'm relieving you of all *Moody* duties. But thanks for the offer."

"Geneva said I had to."

I put my hand up and he stopped. "It's not her case, Gonzo. Good-bye."

Sacramento County's courthouse occupies a square block. To the south are downtown and the police and sheriff's departments and the public defender; to the north are the slums of Alkali Flats and Emiliano Zapata Park. East is the district attorney. The courthouse is approached via stairs to a pre-Columbian-like mesa sprouting stone sculptures that could serve as guerrilla-war barricades. A bank of glass doors leads to a wide lobby with overburdened center-core elevators to reach the hierarchical courts. Traffic, ground floor. Prelims and misdemeanors, lower. Felonies, above.

Witnesses, jurors, divorcing couples, angry, Technicolor spike-haired teens with dirty vests and bright chains, unjailed defendants, briefcased lawyers, burned-out cops, DAs, investigators, gum-chewing process servers, tobacco-stained bail bondsmen, kids in strollers, beat reporters, clerks, interns, and professional voyeurs maintained our delicate legal system.

"Welcome back," said a prelim deputy.

"Thanks, Scott. How are the boys?"

Master Muni Calendar assigned me to Department 14. Judge Grace Hays, a strong jurist who looked too young to be robed. She demanded punctuality. Rachel would be early.

Lights. Department 14. Camera crews had illuminated Stacy August and Karl Moody. Emerald Yeh, a Bay Area reporter. I heard, ". . . using circumstantial evidence . . . unreliable child."

I avoided them and knocked next door at Department 12's staff entry. "Peggy, Josh Jin." Peggy Bakarich opened and I passed through her office to their security door. This opened into the backside transit hall through which secured prisoners were escorted to court from basement holding cells. I walked down the sunlit corridor to Department 14's security door and knocked. Bob Laird, Fourteen's bailiff, checked me through the door window and opened it. "Hey, Josh. Got your victim?"

I alerted. "She's not here?"

"Bilinski neither. Only your intern."

François was waiting. "Boss, they're not here."

Thirty minutes to court. Rachel was twenty minutes behind her planned early arrival. Bilinski chewed gum with his mouth open, carried too many guns, and scored low on the Calvinist work scale, but no one in our biz was late.

I dialed Bilinski. "The cellular customer you called," said the recording, "may have reached their destination or traveled beyond the service area. Please try your call later." The grammar needed correction and Bilinski's phone should have been on. I called Capri.

"Jin, I saw Bilinski pick up Rachel forty-five minutes ago. They're not there? Oh, man. I'll start looking, right now. This crazy weather could've knocked out some traffic lights."

Giggin, Deputy Laird, and the court reporter, Earline Klein, watched me. Judge Grace Hays came out of chambers.

"Good morning, Josh," she said pleasantly. "If your victim's a no-show and Stacy August asks for a dismissal—this being the second bite of the apple—your case is toast."

"Judge, whatever's making them late is bona fide. And you're mixing metaphors more creatively than even I do."

A grin. "I'm not questioning your sincerity, or inviting comment on my verbal images. I only note the absence of your victim in a case where appearing early would seem normal. Mr. Bilinski is not a favorite of this court, and I find it curious that he would be the transportation in a SACA case. The man likes to murder Asian people. Well. Find your victim, Josh." She looked at her watch. "You have twenty-eight minutes."

Outside, thunder rumbled.

32.

BILINSKI

Lightning flashed. The sky exploded. Some cars slowed and others accelerated. Many drivers reacted poorly to the rare electrical storm and the spewing of pebblelike hail.

I think Rachel looked up when the cars began to honk. Bilinski was weaving erratically on Fair Oaks, a fast city thoroughfare thick with splashing semis and speeding buses.

Bilinski was probably sweating and struggling for breath.

"what's wrong?" Rachel would have asked in a high voice. Maybe she tried to say, What are you doing? But her voice was the first victim of fear. All that would result was small panting. "god, are you like having a heart attack?"

The thunder rolled and Bilinski pulled a .44 Magnum from his shoulder holster as he crossed two lanes against a blaring of horns. He fought for air in a cold sweat, his rasps the musical lead to Rachel's rasping harmony, backed up by thunder.

"don't do this," pleaded Rachel.

He wiped sweat, dragging the muzzle sight on his forehead, drawing blood that trickled into his eyes. He blinked as tics raged and the girl was yelling at him and he tried to orient himself in the artillerylike thunder, cursing, making noises she could not comprehend.

"Fucking monsoon," he said. "Fucking Nam." Detonations made him cock the piece, searching for the mortars. An explosion clapped so hard it shook the car and his heart clenched as a pickup, in an unsafe cut-off move, slammed into Bilinski's door, driving Harry's forehead into the steering wheel as he braked and yanked to the right. A truck's air horn blasted. Brakes squealed as he rammed a small white Honda, triggering the beeping of an unending horn. The Honda driver unbelted and jumped from his car as tires screeched. Hammer blows, smoke, rounds thunking. A jolt. A girl's scream froze his blood and his muscles tensed, then released.

A Jeep skidded toward the smoking blue Ford as a girl in a pretty pink dress got out. The crunch of metal concussed the air. In four-tenths of a second, the Jeep bumper, grillwork, lights, hood, and windshield disintegrated into Harry's Ford. Two-tenths of a second later, Harry was violently rammed and air bags deployed. The Jeep drove Harry's Ford into the empty Honda and all three cars jumped the curb and pile-drove into a Western Auto store as the big pickup truck sped away, blue paint streaking the red body.

Eight-tenths of a second into the collision, the Jeep's front end came to rest and the accordioned front seat forced Bilinski into the air bag, breaking ribs and wrenching every muscle in back and buttocks. The Jeep's seat belt held its driver.

Twelve-tenths of a second passed and the Jeep's rear fell to earth, its wheels chucking debris like a bone-hunting dog, driving the remains of the Jeep into Bilinski's Ford. A spark jumped at a growing puddle of gasoline. The Ford, the Honda, and the remains of the Jeep were warped like a kid's face during a roller-coaster turn. The mass struck load-bearing walls and Harry's spine was jerked violently upward as the building stopped the ride. The Jeep driver, fingers barely cooperative, unbuckled, busted his window, and crawled out, falling to the street without the air to make a complaint as a Camry slid into the wreck.

Lightning flashed. Hail rang metallically off the hood and then everything jumped forward. Bilinski groaned, hurting broken ribs and a traumatized back.

"Assholes!" cried Bilinski. "When I get stateside, I'm movin' to Sacramento where there *ain't no goddamn thunder-storms!*" Pain consumed him. Someone was screaming. It was him. He had to move. For a girl. He couldn't remember her name and tears ran down his face and he knew the dinks were going to get her. He had the gun. Fuckin' gooks aren't taking *me* alive. Fire licked at his face.

François and I reached the accident scene as the EMTs decided to follow police advice by clustering behind their vehicle. Uniformed cops, out of respect for the injured driver of the Ford, kept hardware in their holsters. The storm was retreating but the sergeant wasn't happy.

"We don't need any fucking DAs, here. Unless you want to punch a cop."

"Bilinski's my investigator. You find a girl with him?"

He ignored me. I grabbed François. "Find Rachel—she's got to be close. Call me." I pushed him and he flew halfway across the street and skidded into the wet asphalt.

I approached the crumpled, burning Ford. Side-crushed and rear-ended, the bright fuel fires slowing. Beneath it was a white Honda. Next to it was a Camry. Behind were the remains of a Jeep. "It's your funeral," called the cop. "He's armed."

I stopped. "Sergeant, please call Department 14 for me. Tell them my investigator was in a wreck and the juvenile victim's missing and I need a continuance for *Moody*."

"Mr. Jin, you're one cocky bastard. You better say 'pretty please.' "

"Pretty please, Sergeant." Lightning flashed to the east and thunder cleared its throat.

A pause. "Department 14, continuance for *Moody*," said the sergeant. He left.

Fire crackled. "Harry. It's Jin. Put down the gun."

Harry had the bright, thick muzzle pressed against his right temple. His face was caked in soot and dripping in extinguisher foam. He was wheezing, bleeding from a forehead cut. His face sallow, black and wet, ample cheeks mashed on the steering wheel. The dusty white safety bag was red with blood. No

Rachel. The car stank of burned polymers, hot metal, gasoline, and feces. Rain sizzled on the cooling metal.

"Harry, you're okay. Put down the gun."

He pointed it at me. "Fuck you, Vee See," he snarled at my Chinese face.

"Harry, it's Josh Jin. DA's Office. You're in downtown Sacramento, California. You had a car wreck on Fair Oaks. And I'm Chinese, not Vietnamese. It's just a thunderstorm." Thunder clapped, louder.

Bilinski tried to say something: Incoming.

"Harry, where's the girl? Where's Rachel? The girl."

A quick, nervous blink. Soundlessly, he said, Rachel.

"Harry, EMTs are here and will patch you up when you put down the gun. Harry, we have to find the girl. Where is she?"

He looked at me, tics around his eyes, trying not to cry. It took a while for him to find a whispering voice, "Dunno." He looked down. "Jesus, I shit myself."

"We'll get you cleaned up. Harry? Bilinski," I said, loud and slow, "pass me the sidearm, handle first. Good man." I safetied the Magnum on the half-cock and stuck it in my belt at the hip.

Slowly I put my hand on Bilinski's shoulder and rubbed. Harry's face crunched in hot tears and his head fell sloppily against me, face stretched in pain. On the floor on the passenger side, lying in a bunch with a shoe missing, was Miss Piggy.

"Harry, Vietnam stretched thirty years to bite you on your butt. It happens. I think the trick is to be good to yourself. You survived for a reason. Okay?"

"Okay, guys," he whispered, not to me, but to others not present.

I waved on the EMTs and they came, running. It was as if the sun had flared. I saw Bilinski's misery, a billowing, expanding gas of toxins that poisoned his every breath. It was huge and horrible, an infestation of spine-biting grief that rose above the steam and rain.

The passenger-side door was yawed wildly by the side-crunching Camry. Fresh blood on the lower door, hints of small pools on the ground. Harry couldn't have thrown blood that far. The red drops weren't heavy, which was encouraging. Unless it was a head wound. The splatters that would have told me more were washed away.

Through a crowd of worried bystanders, riveted and horrified, I followed hints of an infinitesimal blood trail. Rachel had headed downtown, as if to court. Two blocks away, it ended. I imagined the injured, frightened girl with her thumb out. A car stopping. Let it be a woman driver. A kind person. Please, God.

"I saw her, go hospital," said the custodian, mopping up the wet, narthex, yellow plastic WET FLOOR signs sprouting like spring blooms. "No go. I fix leg. Bad cut. Should go hospital."

She was on the pew, right leg bleeding. Holding herself, humming a tune. The cut was clotting under a bandage. The tune was old Shaker, "Lord of the Dance." I sat behind her. Wet worshippers were sprinkled through the sanctuary. Some sat with eyes opened.

Her humming stopped. "stupid little bitch . . . like that asshole would help. girl, you're so retarded. girl, God hates you and just wants you to die so just do it . . ."

"Hello." I didn't say, Twenty minutes ago, our case got dismissed, Moody's on the street, and I don't know if I can put Humpty Dumpty together again. I put Miss Piggy next to her.

"go away," she hissed.

"I can't do that." We listened to the custodian's mop. I looked up at the chandeliers and told her about Harry and the war that haunted people his age. "He's going to be okay."

"yeah. sure he is. and it's gonna happen to me. gonna be a test dummy. . . ."

"If you try to stuff the feelings." How many victims had heard my litany? Bring your pain to court and get the cure. How could she buy that? I hadn't done it myself.

Rachel curled tighter, brown eyes glancing. "my fault."

"No," I said. "It's not your fault that Harry went to war. You don't get to decide which of us lives or dies. There are a lot of things you're responsible for. It doesn't include that."

"but Momma died cuz I didn't help her."

"Your momma died because she chose to live with a man

who killed her. And she did that for herself, not you. Doesn't mean she didn't love you. It means it wasn't your fault."

The custodian finished mopping. "bull," she hissed.

"Rachel, if you marry a man like your father, and you have a little girl together, and then he kills you, will it be your daughter's fault?"

She twisted on the pew, disliking to be wrong.

"Baby," I said, "your momma loved you. That's the only part that counts."

She nodded as hot tears splashed down her cheeks. my momma loved me.

"With all her heart. Mothers do that. Even after they die."

She touched her chest. "you know," she whispered, "i trusted you so much, it made my stomach sick down to the pit. it was gettin' real extreme."

"I'll try not to let you down."

She shook her head, looking momentarily into my eyes. "that's what God does. like you know. he let your daughter die. just like momma. he made my dad the way he is."

Summer would not have agreed. "I don't think God does that. Man does that."

She sat up, shivering, face wet. "you think they're in a better place?"

"I hope so."

"gotta be better 'n this." Somewhere a door slammed.

"Rachel, you know, I was feeling sorry for myself, thinking no one could be hurting more than me. I was wrong." Summer in the choir, singing "Lord of the Dance." *I danced in the morning when the world was begun . . . I danced in the moon and the stars and the sun . . .*

It echoed in the rafters, sweet and heavenly, and now unattainable. My Chinese memory was too strong. I was losing control. "I'll be back," I said tightly.

I found myself in the prayer garden, wet and making fists against God. The God of Compassion and Love. I closed my eyes and tried not to cry. God of rain and God of fire.

"WHY'D YOU TAKE HER?! WHY'D YOU DO THAT? She was good she was everything you wanted in a child you asshole come down here and fight ME and take ME you dirty sonofabitch! Give Summer back to her mother!" I was on my knees, weeping out my will and my life, utterly feeble, my masculinity gone with my daughter, beyond the reach of gods, the stars and the sun, unable to move, barely able to think about moving, crying from the gut.

Rachel was at the door, bleeding on the bricks. She looked at me, weeping as if I had hit her, her small shoulders jinking from inner pains. Awkwardly I stood and took a step forward and she ran away blindly on long coltish legs, and I had no strength to follow.

33.

COURT

"Name the three prelim proofs," I said to François in the hallway.

"One, jurisdiction. Two, elements of the prima facie offense. Three, ID."

"I love it when you guys talk like that," said Capri. "Absolute blood rush."

"How's Rachel?" I asked, happy that my tie was perfectly knotted and straight.

Capri adjusted it. "I think she'll do okay." The court emptied. We were next.

Judge Grace Hays said good afternoon, inviting us into chambers. The court reporter calmly sat. Hays said she would not tolerate theatrics that might upset a child witness.

"I'm granting the People's 765b motion to protect a child from harassment during testimony, and the 1346 motion to videotape the prelim, to preserve testimony should the child witness be unable to testify at trial. Ms. August, there's no jury to sway—only a judge with sensitive ears and zero tolerance for child abuse in her court. Stacy, violate my order and I'll remand you for contempt. You're an excellent lawyer. I expect the best of you.

"When we're done, neither of you will hold a press conference outside my court or even on this floor." She spoke into the intercom. "Bob." Bailiff Laird entered.

"Bob, if an attorney in this case clears a throat in front of the media on this floor, arrest and hold that lawyer."

"Judge," said Stacy, "you should have retained the prejudice in your earlier dismissal." Meaning, I could not have refiled. "Mr. Jin has refiled on my client—for a *third* time."

"This has been litigated," said Hays. "By motion, in writing. I dismissed the case but removed the prejudice when I learned the victim was in a car accident not of her doing. I compensated you with a short-set prelim on the date of your choosing. That's all you get from a car wreck." She rubbed the tip of her pen against an eyebrow. "I'll give the girl every chance to testify, but I won't be surprised if our severe formality and the presence of the defendant undo her. I'm not worried about your client; you're here to represent him. I'm concerned for the victim and her mental status. Josh?"

"May the victim bring a Miss Piggy doll to the stand?"

"I let Bilinski in. I have nothing personal against pigs in my court, as long as they're appropriately dressed. Well. We may not get full justice today, but let's do our best."

The video operator switched on lights. Chico Moody appeared relaxed. Stacy sat as if it were her courtroom.

Rachel took the oath and assumed the stand. I gave her the first of my cartoons. She looked at it without reaction. She had trouble not watching Stacy with undisguised awe, as if she were an icon, symbolic of the unreachable.

Rachel answered every question. But her fear of Moody, her awareness of Stacy, and of being on stage occasionally made her answers appear illogical or incomprehensible. Anxiety made her miss the question or omit a word that changed the character of her answer. My heart slugged, but I was patient, rehabilitating her incorrect responses.

I stood close. Rachel had averted her gaze from Chico Moody and Stacy August, glancing at Capri and François Giggin and squeezing Miss Piggy while she answered earnestly, nervously. Harry was at the Menlo Park VA center. We didn't know if he'd return.

For the past hour in the cool courtroom, Moody's presence and Stacy August's constant gaze had made Rachel shiver.

"i'm cold," she blurted while recounting how Moody wiped her with a warm washcloth. I gave her my suit jacket, which she clutched and squeezed. Capri tried to get the air-conditioning turned down. I wasn't optimistic; outside was a heat wave which was creating a Mississippi-like sludge of mosquito-breeding humidity from the season's heavy rainfall.

Stacy August and Judge Hays were taking notes, tracking the sixty-eight counts ranging from kidnap and use of a stupefying drug to child sexual assault and attempted murder.

"What happened next?" I asked calmly, quietly.

Rachel watched her hands fret as if they were someone else's, as if amazed that they could move and flex and touch the doll with only one shoe. She described Moody beating her.

Stacy had contained her projective personality. She studied Rachel and moderated her interaction with the court and with me. She made few objections and voiced those politely. She would throw her crashing thunderbolts at Rachel in trial.

"We're almost done, Rachel. Do you see the man who attacked you, in court today?" Rachel was tired and weak; I should have asked her to identify Moody at the very beginning.

She nodded. The flexible metal microphone hose was coiled, aimed at her mouth. Judge Hays leaned closer.

"Let the record reflect," I said, "that the witness nodded her head in the affirmative."

"The record will so reflect," the judge said.

"Rachel, please point to the man who attacked you."

Rachel looked at me, unmoving. I smiled and nodded. She bit her lip and moved her entire head to the right. Slowly, phantomlike, she pointed at Chico Moody.

"Your Honor, let the record reflect that the witness has identified the defendant, Karl Francis Moody."

"The record will so reflect," the judge said. The victim had stated that the acts occurred in Sacramento County, establishing our jurisdiction. She had named the offenses and she had identified her attacker. Time to pass Go and collect two hundred dollars.

"Your Honor, no further questions. People rest. Rachel, Ms. August will now ask you some questions, very politely."

I smiled assuringly. Rachel squirmed, taking short breaths.

Stacy respectfully remained in her chair. Her clear voice filled the courtroom.

"You stated that the defendant attacked you sexually eight times after he gave you a massage. Is that correct?"

Rachel shook her head. Stacy was going to attack Rachel's math.

"You'll have to speak," the judge said.

"how come I didn't have to talk when I was pointing at him but I have to talk now?"

"Because I say so," the judge said.

Rachel was very tired. "no."

"Please speak in the microphone," the judge said.

"What, then, is the correct answer?" asked Stacy.

"six times," Rachel said.

"But didn't you say, Ms. Farr, that he forced you to orally copulate him after the massage?"

Rachel nodded, coloring. She coughed. For something to do, she took a sip of water, her hand shaking, spilling down her wrist. I made the talking gesture with my hand.

"yes," she said. The glass dropped from the witness stand to the floor. Rachel winced, covering her eyes in embarrassment.

"Did you not then say that Mr. Moody assaulted you six times?"

She looked up, mortified. "i'm so sorry. uh. seven."

"And then he sodomized you?"

She closed her eyes. "eight," she said softly.

Stacy was also letting Rachel know what might come at trial. A taste of poison.

"Rachel, did you try to escape Mr. Moody's attacks?"

"Objection. Irrelevant. Minors need not show resistance."

"Your Honor," Stacy said, "this was covered in direct."

"Restate your question," the judge said.

"Rachel," Stacy said, "you were handcuffed and cuffed at the ankles, correct? You struggled against those cuffs?"

"yes."

"Rachel, hold your wrists up so the court can see them."

"Objection. Four months've passed. It's irrelevant."

"Sustained. Not probative, Ms. August. Present ecchymosis could be caused by any number of subsequent events."

"Rachel, who is Aleta Meers?"

Rachel frowned. "Aleta was a runaway. a friend of Chico's. don't know her last name."

"Do you recall telling her that you were going to really mess up Chico Moody's life by falsely claiming that he raped you?"

"No!" Rachel said.

Stacy looked at her hard and long. Rachel averted her eyes. "No further questions," said Stacy lightly.

"Any redirect, Mr. Jin?" asked the judge.

"Please, Your Honor." I returned to my station near her.

"Rachel, Ms. August's questions can be pretty confusing. Do you understand that she didn't catch you in a contradiction— she was just using some New Math on us and trying out some imaginary evidence."

"Objection, argumentative," said Stacy.

"We have a young witness," said Hays. "And senior trial lawyers. I'll allow it. Do you understand Mr. Jin's question?"

Rachel nodded. "yes," she said. "and my answer's yes."

"Thank you. You told the court," I said, "that the defendant let you use the bathroom and gave you a massage. Is that right?"

"yes."

"Then you smelled Akami perfume and became ill, and the defendant cleaned you up?"

"yes."

"He then forced you to orally copulate him. Correct?"

Smaller voice. "yes."

"Then he attacked you six more times. Correct?"

"yes."

"He then sodomized you. Correct?"

"yes. and then he beat me."

"Judge, may the record reflect the witness did not contradict herself. That defense did not impeach her testimony."

"I understand your reasoning," the judge said. It was now on the record.

"Rachel, describe your wrists immediately after Mr. Moody's attacks in February."

"they were all red. and sorta tore up. . . ."

"Thank you. No further questions."

"Re-cross? Ms. Farr, you may stand down." Stacy studied Rachel as, sad and barely breathing, she left the stand. Moody squirmed. I nodded grimly. It was a cardinal sin to personalize a case, but I was beyond trying to separate *People v. Moody* from my life.

"I must determine," the judge said, "if the prosecution established probable cause to hold the defendant to answer sixty-eight felony counts contained in the aforementioned Complaint. Defendant will rise." Stacy August, Karl Moody, and I stood.

The judge leaned toward the defendant. "This court finds probable cause except for counts fifteen and sixteen, alleging kidnap. Mr. Moody, you are bound over for felony jury trial to answer all other counts recited by the Complaint."

Capri whispered, "Thank you, God."

"Your Honor," I said. "May we reevaluate bail?"

"My client," said Stacy, "is a long-term member of the community with attachments to—"

"Vulnerable minor female children," I said.

Hays froze me with a glance. "Uncalled for, Mr. Jin."

"I apologize. People's bail position is recited in Points and Authorities. I submit on that."

"In view of the severity of the charges," the judge said, "and defendant's lack of current employment and family, bail is set in the amount of one hundred thousand dollars. Defendant is remanded to custody following this hearing. I want this defendant in restraints, now."

Deputy Laird motioned. Moody the ex-con, brows furrowed, stood in the old drill, hands behind, wrists flared for tight cuffs. Stacy spoke. Moody wasn't listening. He started to leave, but the deputy pointed at the chair; he had to remain for calendaring.

I thought: Rachel's testimony had surprised him.

"Does defense waive speedy trial?" The constitutional right to trial in sixty days. A perfunctory question; there wasn't a defense counsel in the County who would want a jury trial so soon. Delay helped the defense and hurt the prosecution. Delay wore out its anxious witnesses and frightened victims and gave the defense time to find creative areas to attack.

"No waiver, Your Honor," said Stacy, "we want a quick-set."

My job included never showing surprise, disappointment, or dismay. Normally, a speedy trial would be fine for us. This wasn't a normal case; it was historically weak, needing time for workup. I wouldn't have enough time to get ready for the jury trial.

"Monday, July fourteenth," the judge said.

"That is acceptable, Your Honor," she said.

I could have my Bar Mitzvah that day but it wouldn't matter; the rights accrued to the criminal defendant, the rightful focus of the Bill of Rights. All the prosecution could do was try to win the case at a time of convenience for the defendant. It was okay; we were in the right.

"Mr. Jin, this is not a long case. How many days?"

"One week, Your Honor."

"You'll need more for physical evidence." Hays knew SACA cases.

"He has no physical evidence, Judge," said Stacy. "One week is optimistic."

Hays nodded. No physical evidence. She then set the pretrial conference forty-five days downrange. We were done. Moody was escorted away.

"He is innocent," Stacy said.

"Thank you for your decent treatment of the victim."

"She is not the victim. The victim is my client." She leaned on the table. "You know, Josh, next time, I'm going to have to burn her." Her eyes were eloquent. She looked down at her chest and then at me, as if her gaze had been captured for transfer into my eyes.

34.

SHE USES MY VOICE

"What happened to her knockout punch?" asked François.

"Saving it for the bout. This was just the weigh-in."

"Rachel did great," said Capri. She touched my cheek. "Warm."

"Heat of battle. I haven't done this for a while."

"Heat of something else." A fine eyebrow rising. "Ms. August tweaking you?"

"Capri, thanks. You made all of this happen."

"You resurrected a dump. Really, a great job. It'd be dumb to lose it to hormones."

"You have a low opinion of male self-control."

"Those words don't even go together. You better keep Biff in his box."

Biff? The doors opened. The bailiff said that Ms. August would speak on the courthouse steps. Reporters erupted with questions, creating discordant noise. News never sounded pretty. Bailiff Laird silenced them and ordered them downstairs.

Rachel was slumped in the security transit hall through which, minutes before, a shackled Chico Moody had been escorted for transportation to county jail. She was breathing hard, eyes shut. "Rachel, you did great. I'm very proud of you. You have guts."

She jerked with my voice, quickly tracing a finger along the pale-blue tattooed bracelet on her wrist. We had been the last item on the afternoon calendar; courts were done, and there would be no prisoner processions to interrupt us. Lights began turning off.

She stretched like Summer when Jodie's cold nose awakened her in the hammock from an afternoon nap. Rachel's eyes were old and tired. She whispered, "everything's dead," or something like that. "Chico, he was just into the world. and the world, it's all like changed."

"It has," I said. "The trick's finding the good in a lot of bad."

She asked me if I thought this courtroom stuff was good.

"It's the right thing. Moody deserves to hear your testimony. The truth needs to come out. That's how you fight evil. You call it what it is. You don't run from it."

She didn't nod. We sat quietly. "you having trouble, you know, at work? like my dad?"

"I kind of am."

She sighed in a small way. "that's why you got me, isn't it? someone who was doing good wouldn't get me. you have to be in trouble. like Gonzo Marx."

"There's nothing wrong with your reasoning, but I got you because this is a Chinatown case. Chinatown says your case was mishandled, and they're right. But it's politics. They're sort of using both of us as an exercise in power. It's not really about you or me."

She was thirteen and understood perfectly. She curled up on the floor. I rolled up my jacket and put it under her head. I looked at my watch.

"what was she like? i bet she was real smart."

I took a deep breath. "She was a very good kid. A great kid."

"you going to cry? they say crying's good for you."

"The people who always say that aren't crying."

A near-smile.

"Rachel, you ever talk with this Aleta Meers?"

She shook her head. "she didn't like me, at all. what's her name?"

At first I didn't know what she meant. She re-asked. I said, "Summer Nicole."

"do you really miss her?"

"God, I do." My voice choked.

"Momma likes me to miss her. i keep the lights on so she comes and talks."

I cleared my throat. "How does she come to you?"

"i feel her. it's not like I can see her. she's just there."

"What does she say?"

Rachel exhaled. "you think i'm crazy, don't you?"

"No. But I know crazy things happen. What does she say?"

"sassy things. 'Turn off that radio. Do your homework, girl!' stuff like that." Rachel used an adult woman's voice to quote her mother. "that was Momma. Chico taught me how. We smoked weed. He told me, she uses my voice, from inside."

Slowly I said, "How often you smoke with him?"

She snorted. "yeah, I lied. you know, Mr. Rag, i didn't want to edge him. she's tough."

"And I'm not?"

"not to me. you're weak with me." She hugged her knees. "but you can turn. like Chico."

"Are you afraid of me?"

A shrug. "you're a man."

"Yeah. How many times you smoke with Chico?"

"all the time. like, every day."

"How much you smoke now?"

"i quit, cold. Chico kinda took the fun out."

I took notes. "When she speaks, is your momma really there?"

"uh-huh. you hate me now, don't you?"

"No, baby, I'll never hate you. Never."

"words," she said, "are, like, so easy." She turned away from me, moving my coat.

"Rachel, I'll always care for you. And wish you well." We were quiet and she cried, a little girl, her head far away from me. She whispered that she didn't want to go back there.

"Court?" I asked.

"home."

"Are they hitting you again?"

She somewhat shook her head. The movement said: but they could anytime.

I wanted her to protect herself. "I want you to stand. Now, make a fist, like this." I modeled it and she looked up, wiping her face. I gave her a Kleenex. She blew her nose.

I held up the fist and cocked it. It took a while, but she did it.

"Make a fist with your left. No, keep your right closed. That's it. Now hold them up, like this. The left higher, eye level. The right one, close to your chin. Now lower the chin, keeping the eyes up. See how they cover your face?" I smiled. "We'll make a fighter out of you yet."

"i don't want to fight."

"Yes, honey, you do."

35.

I LOVE MY WIFE

I sat in the chair opposite her desk.

Ava looked up. "God. What are YOU doing here?"

"And some say courtesy is a lost art. Nice seeing you." I stood to leave.

"No, stay." Her voice was kind, killing me. "You look good."

"Two can play this," I said. "You're beautiful."

She touched her hair. "Is something wrong? Why are you here?"

"I was wondering. Do you think of me anymore?"

"Only in small bursts, but I'm getting over it. You know, you can't do this. It's not fair."

I knew better than to ask about her personal life, if she was seeing him. It'd be dumb *and* lame. "So, you seeing him?"

The breath through the nose. She nodded.

"I hope it's going badly. Terribly. Awful."

"Thank you. Want to make some kids with me?"

I looked out her window. I wondered if she was sleeping

with him. I killed the thought. "Ava, I love you." She was trying not to cry. I did not say what was in my heart. That God had punished me for my resentment of my stepfather, for my knowing too many women, for thinking myself big and important, for being happy. For loving my daughter, far too much.

I pulled her from her chair. "What's your best quality?" I whispered in her warm ear, holding her. A deep breath as she looked in my eyes. A faint voice.

"I only see men who are looking for a committed relationship. I hear that's not one of your strengths."

"I love my wife." I liked her cool nose and beautiful eyes. Softly, I kissed her nose, grazed her lips. We kissed, a broken gold band healing. Her finely formed lips, a remembrance, an acceptance, a forgiveness, a door no longer locked, a river border offering a ford. I kissed her, held her, the fit good and strong and only ours. She was warmth and heat. "I missed you," I said. I kissed her neck, her, again, forever. "I love you," I breathed, and there was no monotony to the poetry, said to her a thousand times across the span of marriage. She kissed me hotly and I had never left her, her open mouth a gift beyond ribbon and silk.

She was beautiful, a delight, saying my name, restoring me.

"Yes," she said, a speech, an oration, a ballad of the Scottish Highlands whose lyrics I knew. "I need another baby . . . once you see her and hold her . . . and love her, your heart will heal. I—"

"No! We can't just *replace* her! It's wrong and unfaithful to her and there's no guarantee the next kid wouldn't also have a heart problem and die on us, too." I had released her.

Ava bent over. She held her face, sobbing. It took little to make either of us cry.

I held her. She was trembling.

"I love you. I want you. I want to live with you forever. But only you. Say yes."

"No! Leave!" she cried. "Just go!" She pushed me away.

I exhaled. At the door, with all my courage, I spoke. "I need a favor. A big one. Move in with me first. Just for show."

"What?"

"I want you to move in with me until the end of July. The victim in my case, the thirteen-year-old, lives in an abusive home. She won't accept out-placement with a temp family. I think she'd live with me, but it's not right, a kid living with a man not her father, without you there. You could have the master. I'll sleep in the guest room."

Slowly, "You're doing the trial. To save the girl."

I nodded.

"Help a strange girl, but won't give us a baby. Create the appearance of a family. But not make a real one." She took a deep breath. "You drive me crazy," she added.

"So," I said, encouraged, "you *do* think of me?"

She began to cry. "God, there's no way I'll do this. Not now. Not the way you are. How can you ask such a stupid thing?! Do you think I'm completely crazy?"

She looked up. "I bet you told Conover to apologize for beating up Billy McManus. That's how you lost the bureau, isn't it? God, you're an idiot. Don't you get it? Conover doesn't apologize! And it's *over* for us. Completely done. Poof! History! No way am I going to move in with you to play house!"

36.

A GIRL IN HER ROOM

Dierdre Farr wouldn't look at me as Ava and I sat in her living room. Mrs. Farr held a pillow that hid her chest. On the TV was a talk show with hairy men in black leather tutus. Mrs. Farr turned down the volume. I smiled as if we had just watched *Wuthering Heights*.

Ava warmly complimented her apartment. "You know that my husband is prosecuting Mr. Moody for attacking Rachel. He and I would like to move Rachel into our place until the trial's over. There have been some threats against her. We'd make sure she got to school and back every day. We'd sign her up for summer school."

Mrs. Farr frowned, wondering what the trick was.

Ava smiled winningly. "Mrs. Farr, you can think of it as a vacation. No cooking or cleaning or waking up or waiting up for a teenager, who, I know, can be a *lot* of work."

Mrs. Farr licked her lips, glancing at me. "There any money in this, for me. And Ray? You know, like some sorta payment."

"No, ma'am," said Ava. "Only the money you save by not having to feed her or pay for her utility costs and transportation and laundry while she's gone."

"Is this normal?" she asked, squeezing the pillow.

"No," said Ava. "It's not. Not even nearly."

"Cat got your tongue?" asked Mrs. Farr of me.

"I'm just the driver," I said.

"RACHEL!" shouted Dierdre Farr. "GET YOUR BUTT DOWN HERE NOW!" Silence. "THE DA'S HERE! FOR *YOU*!"

After a pause, a door opened.

Rachel emerged in old, baggy sweats. Sleep marks marred her face. Ava and I stood. I said hello. She halfway waved, looking at Dierdre Farr, ready to back up, her eyes large.

Ava waited for Mrs. Farr to speak.

"These people want you to stay with them," she said flatly.

"Rachel," I said, "this is Ava Pascal Jin, my wife."

Smiling, Ava approached and offered her hand. Rachel looked down, shrinking, as she briefly touched.

"you're divorced," said Rachel. "Capri said." She looked at us suspiciously.

"We are," I said. "But we're under the same roof, living in separate rooms, for one reason. We'd like you to stay with us in Davis until the trial is done. We have a great dog who'd love you. We'll drive you to school and pick you up after school. We think it'll be tougher for anyone on Moody's side to bother you in Davis. You'd also be doing summer school."

"If it's all right," said Ava, "with you, Mrs. Farr."

Dierdre Farr was nodding. "Hell, I don't care. What do you say to these nice people?"

Rachel was licking her upper lip, eyes down, saying nothing.

"Do you want to pack some clothes and cosmetics and get your schoolbooks and backpack?" asked Ava.

"Dumbie lost her good green backpack," said Mrs. Farr. "Wasn't cheap, neither. Get your clothes, girl. Use those Wal-Mart sacks."

Rachel was breathing fast, looking at me and Ava again and again, weighing disbelief against retreat. And then she left. We heard her packing and she came out with a handful of sagging plastic sacks, Miss Piggy under her arm, her arms straining. I took the bags.

Ava sat in the middle bucket seat, talking with Rachel while I drove. Rachel said little, listening while Ava told her about what she liked about Davis, the idyllic campus community that sat on the other side of the Yolo floodplain from Sacramento. I heard the voice of a caring mother and had to concentrate on the road. She asked Rachel what she liked to eat.

"fries," she said.

"How about for breakfast?"

She shrugged.

"waffles, omelette, French toast, fried eggs, bacon?"

I looked at Ava: I didn't get to eat fried eggs and bacon.

Ava made a dismissive motion: Drive. You have hypertension.

"waffles," said Rachel.

I pulled into the garage and carried in Rachel's clothes while Ava showed Rachel to Summer's room. Jodie whined in excitement, trying to not jump on Rachel as she sniffed her, hoping that she might replace the one who had not returned.

Rachel played with Jodie in the backyard until she saw the boxing bag that hung from the upper deck framing. I think it reminded her of Rag's gym and that day of thunderstorms and storytelling, of remembered bloodletting, of her nightmare. She stared at it.

That night I unbolted the body bag from its frame and stored it.

37

THEME OF PROOF

Saturday

"How'd you sleep?" Ethically, I didn't kiss her. She wore a sleeveless blouse and white shorts and her hair was perfect; she had the master bath.

"Not bad. How about you? I forgot about the neighbor's barking dog."

"It's Davis." And it was wonderful, seeing her in the house.

"Josh, what's your theme of proof?" She was making strawberry waffles as sparrows sang and I forced myself to not gaze at her. I ran the water filter for orange juice.

"Moody violated a position of trust. He was her mentor. She, the trusting child."

"That's the premise. I mean *theme of proof.* The argument that makes the jury say, 'Oh, yeah! SNAP!' " She snapped her fingers. " 'This *happened*!' " She finished the batter, poured a waffle, and pointed at the strawberries. I began washing them.

My heart skipped—it was Summer—Rachel in her bathrobe.

"Good morning, Rachel," said Ava. "How'd you sleep?"

Rachel blinked suspiciously, sullen in the morning's exuberant light. She wasn't good at sleep and was inexperienced in morning conversation. No answer. Summer had blossomed to fill all available space with courage and humor; Rachel had been in retreat for years.

"Juice or milk or both? Have a seat." I pulled out a chair. Bright morning sun filled the breakfast room. Outside, white Japanese wisteria and pink flowering almond trees decorated the yard. "If you're not hungry, we can give the waffles to Jodie."

Rachel sat, eyes scrinched. She sipped as if the juice might be poison, watching us, waiting for the hammer to drop. In ten minutes, she had eaten part of one waffle. Now she was watching the Cartoon Channel, sitting in my once-favorite chair, legs curled under like Summer, elbow on the armrest, hand supporting her head. Miss Piggy on her lap and Jodie at her feet.

In my study, we looked at my witness list on the flip chart.

1. **Kimberley Hong,** Rio Jr. High counselor: EMOTIONALLY OVERINVOLVED
   Observed Rachel's injuries, demeanor, weight, social decline.
2. **Killian Boyce,** UCDMC Sex Assault Nurse Examiner/ SANER: EXPERT
   Observes signs of rape. Explains why no physical evidence.
3. **Dr. Amy Karenga,** psychiatrist, rape trauma expert: EXPERT
   Explains rape trauma syndrome. Rachel's reluctance, silence, guilt, awkwardness
4. **Ray Farr,** Rachel's father: HOSTILE
   Reveals indifference to Rachel. No parent present to watch over her.
5. **Rachel Farr,** victim: SMALL VOICE. FRIGHTENED
   Explains relationship with Chico. Events on 1 February. Crimes.
6. **Wilma Debbin/Pico Larry,** cops: HOSTILE TO CONOVER
   Only if we find the missing textbooks.

It was short, shaky, and weak. On another sheet was Stacy's.

1. *John Quick,* neighbor: Interview request denied. Investigate after testimony.
   [Δ's alibi; we were out together: WHERE IS HE?]
2. *Priscilla Anna Jost,* pvt criminalist: EXPERT
   former criminalist supervisor. Helped bust FBI lab.
3. *?* [re: Rachel's honesty?]
4. *?* [re: Rachel's hatred of Moody?]
5. *?* [re: Rachel's alleged sexual promiscuity?]

* * *

"We know what Stacy's going to do to your witnesses on cross. Confuse, dismay, disarm, discredit, and impeach. What's the theme? Rachel's word against Moody's.

"And the JurPro data"—pointing at one wall display—"says a jury will believe Moody and won't believe an uncertain girl victim." She sighed. "If only you had some physical evidence. A pinch of DNA and serum, narrowing it down to one in every five hundred million men. A pubic hair. The smallest piece of clothing!"

"But I haven't. I got a victim who sounds like a pipsqueak. I need to turn that little, subdued voice into a strength."

Ava nodded. "Her fear, her small voice, because of Moody. If Moody takes the stand, your tactic would be to agitate him, get him to uncork, to vent his feelings on Rachel. And then, as you'd say, rip his head off. I just can't believe Stacy'll let Moody testify. It's too big a risk."

"Ava, there's a tension between them. And Moody's testimony is my *only* chance to make up for no physical evidence." Under the law, it was Moody's decision whether he'd testify or not. Not Stacy's. All she could do was advise him to not take the stand.

"All defense lawyers have problems with client management. Even the Stacy Augusts."

"Ava, I have to let the jury see Moody's face while Rachel testifies." I looked at Rachel through the French doors. "I have to let Moody stare her down. I have to invite *his* anger by how I question *her*. Even if it unglues her."

"Unless it *totally* unglues her."

A tightrope with no net. I remembered how Gonzo Marx had treated Rachel. I rubbed my face. "There has to be something else. Something we're missing."

"I know. What is it?" She rummaged through the thickening folder until she found the time-dated Polaroids that Kimberley Hong had taken of Rachel. She taped them to a flip-chart sheet. On another, she drew a Cartesian graph. The vertical axis was weight; the horizontal, the date, beginning with January and ending in May. On the graph, she drew a steadily declining line.

"See it?"

"Tell me."

Ava looked; Rachel was asleep. "Josh, she lost *every-thing*."

On a clean sheet, she drew five graphs. She labeled them, reading off the headings. "Grades. Attendance. Teacher contacts. This one, her contacts with friends. Sleeping in the Methodist Church."

"And," I said, standing and drawing another, "for her eating lunch. Or not eating lunch. Yeah, that's it. You got it. You're very good."

She looked at her nails. "It's true. What's your third-least-favorite expression?"

"You owe me?"

"And so you do. I kind of like that. By the way, I won't be here for dinner. I'll be late coming back. Don't wait up."

I smiled hollowly, my insides bitter.

In the study, I went through the steps of trial, rehearsing my motions, my words, my arguments, my hopes, haunted, at the worst moments, by thoughts of Ava with another man. I had no appetite. After four hours, I had memorized nothing.

I wanted to hit the bag, but it was stored. I ran hard down Lake to the university campus, unaware of whether I was fleeing or chasing, Jodie happy to have the exercise.

38.

THACKERY NILES

Monday, July 21

In Chinatown dawns, I would toss the Anglo *Chronicle* as other boys delivered the *Chinese World*. I watched the men leave the Ping Ah apartments and the dark tenements to march through the morning fog while dogs still slept. In ten minutes, they'd be cleaning and chopping food for the restaurants and ten thousand tourists. We pitched papers under the calls of mournful foghorns. Hours would pass before cable car bells would ring brightly on California Street, toward Grace Cathedral, the Union Pacific Club, Huntington Park, the luxury hotels and apartments of Nob Hill, bringing us curious and hungry tourists, who stared at us the way pigtailed Chinese farmers had once stared at bewigged, stockinged European traders.

Prosecutors go to court with individual strides. Many are preoccupied, reworking logical, legal arguments. Some are jaunty, eager for combat. Younger misdemeanor deputies shake off stage fright and unruly stomachs, grimacing, blood pressure rising. We all feel anticipation.

I brushed teeth, gargled, and warmed up the vocal chords. I loaded up with Ricola drops; like drill sergeants, trial lawyers live on the durability of a convincing voice. I got my trial binder and briefcase and went to court. Most lawyers do not do trials. Those who do gird themselves for the emotional demands of a jury trial, of a public performance to win or lose.

In court, a thin blow of bluster rose from a clutch of inexperienced civil litigators who secretly hoped no courts would be available. They'd use the delay for further negotiations.

Civil cases have secondary priority to criminal cases. Most civil litigators are lucky if they try a few cases a year. DAs and public defenders try several cases a month and have no more misgivings about trials than sharks possess regrets about their eating habits.

I was in the minority. Anxiety was making me ill. I rehearsed my opening voir dire questions as six deputies sat next to me in the conventional DA pews. Soft speech was permitted, and they asked about *Moody*. I asked about their cases. Once I had been a mighty bureaucrat, elevated above their work. My being here cast a shadow on the wages of ambition. And *Moody*, the election's litmus test, made them nervous. If I lost, they'd be working for Seth Jergen. "Good luck," they chorused. If I hadn't once been a bureau chief, they would've clapped my back, high-fived, or punched a shoulder as folks will before a physical contest.

Stacy entered. Only the most preoccupied failed to notice.

Many looked at me for a reaction. In an echoing voice, the bailiff called us to order. We stood for the PJ, the Presiding Judge of the Superior Court for the County of Sacramento.

The PJ sat and handled admin, advising civil litigators that, as usual, no courts were going to be available for them. Torts tomorrow, crimes today. He called *People v. Moody*.

Stacy and I retired to chambers for a pretrial conference browbeating. The PJ wanted deals—quick, approvable, and politically digestible. His habit was to adroitly impose sentencing variations on *The Price Is Right* with feuding lawyers, creating accord between savages in suits. He employed unimpeachable judicial demeanor, a theatrically low and commanding voice, occasional wry humor, and an elevated, scholastic syntax.

"Josh, Mr. Conover avers that your case was destined, from birth, for a generous offer. I am short on courts. You are shorter on evidence. Let us be precise: your case sucks."

"Don't try to build me up, Your Honor. Fortunately, all I need is one court."

"You may be asking too much. Bend just a bit, Josh. The initial offer was twelve months county jail for a misdemeanor. I want you to revive that. No? Stacy, it is your turn."

"Two misdemeanors, consecutive county jail, credit for time served."

"Okay, I'll bend," I said, "for any plea that puts Moody in state prison for life."

Stacy smiled. "Wonderful. Give us a court, judge."

The PJ closed the court file, looking at me. "You have no physical evidence and have overcharged like a special prosecutor on speed. In an earlier hearing, Josh, Stacy suppressed a videotape that showed a teenager named Belinda Howell being lured into the defendant's home. This would have shown common pattern and explain why the Farr girl suddenly decided to cooperate—to save the other child. Without it, you have chaff and low victim credibility.

"Meanwhile, Stacy, you have an ex-con facing two million years with an alibi witness the DA has never seen. I recommend one count, attempted rape, no deal on sentencing."

"Unacceptable," said Stacy and I simultaneously.

The PJ sighed. Flatly, "Josh, someone wants to talk to you. I'm retaking the bench. Then we'll see where we are. I'm disappointed we couldn't work this out." He and Stacy left.

The door opened. Judge Thackery Niles. It was unusual to see a judge during calendar, away from his court. I stood. He swept robes and sat next to me. A smile, a florid face.

"Josh, I'm committed openly to your judgeship. Sit down."

"I've never understood why. For me, it'd be a bad job." I looked at my watch.

"I know good judicial material. The bench would be good for you—you can *dispense* justice instead of just *argue* for it. Josh, you're not happy. In your office, people have taken down their children's photos, to not remind you of your daughter in case you visit from Intake. Which brings me to *Moody*." A pause. "My boy, you're not ready to do a trial which depends on advocacy. Nor one which centers on a teenage girl victim the age of Summer. Not now. You shouldn't be carrying the future of the legal community. You lose, and Jergen becomes DA."

Thack Niles was going to pat my leg. He stopped and stood. "Dump it, Josh. Dump it now. And don't say no to a judgeship while you're recklessly endangering your legal career."

Then I was back in court. At the tail of the line instead of its head, waiting for an assignment as the available trial courts were given to other cases. *Moody* was finally called.

"Your Honor," I said to the PJ, "Josh Jin for the People. I have a short-cause two-eighty-eight and attempted murder jury trial. I need four days for my case-in-chief."

"Ms. August, you agree, one week?" asked the PJ.

An opaque look at me as she slowly said, "I do."

Judge Shelley Costanza, Department 34, and Judge G. Wells Waldo, Department 29, were already assigned out. They were the ones we could automatically affidavit for their zealous opposition to the People's cases. But Departments 42 and 47, Judges Candy Duluth and Mark Nash, the system's weakest jurists, notorious for poor judgment and a dislike of child victims, were still in reserve. The PJ assigned heavy cases to them only as last resorts. My heart lifted: Finley Maxwell's Department 49 was also still available.

The clerk seemed apologetic as he handed me the court file.

Let it be 49. Judge Finley Maxwell. Old Fin. I had done trials in his court before. He was quirky, pompous, and irritable, but mostly fair, as likely to hurt the defense as the prosecution.

"Department 49, *People v. Moody,*" said the clerk for the record.

Happy, I kept a poker face. The clerk muttered, "Sorry."

"Why?" I asked. The clerk looked at Stacy and imperceptibly shook his head.

"Who's left?" I asked.

"Forty-two and Forty-seven." Duluth and Nash, the dregs. Compared to them, Fin Maxwell was worth a year of standing ovations and a free ice cream.

"Thanks. Department 49 it is."

39.

TRIAL COURT,
DEPARTMENT 49

Liz Heck was Judge Maxwell's court clerk. She was short, she dressed simply, and, like many abused people, was hugely codependent.

"Oh, Josh, how are you?" She came to hug me, patting me. "Can I get you something? You have a trial? Oh, dear, are you ready for this? So soon? You poor man! Coffee? Tea?"

"Hi, Liz." I passed her the court file, giving my case to Judge Maxwell. "In custody. One week, two reserves, multiple two-eighty-eight and attempt murder. No coffee."

"Okay, dear. Ms. August, how are you this morning? You are absolutely gorgeous. Oh, that suit! I believe your client is in the holding cell and will probably be here in minutes. Coffee for you, even if the DA is going cold turkey? Well, the judge is waiting. Let's bustle."

A longer counsel table had replaced the normal one.

Judge Finley Maxwell was a pudgy, short-limbed wheezer who could wield judicial authority like a bully with a baseball bat. He had a drinker's nose, an oddly thin neck, and the longish comma haircut of Spanky and Our Gang's Alfalfa. In election years, he spoke artificially, with a hint of an English accent, in the belief that it was worth votes.

"Stacy August, my dear, how are you?" he asked. She said she was fine.

"A gracious pleasure as always." Coldly, "Mr. Jin, be seated. Any preliminary matters?" As if I were going to affidavit him under the Code of Civil Procedure, charging him with bias against the People. Maxwell was a different duck, but not a foe of the People.

"No, Your Honor."

"Good. I sense pigheaded thinking, related, I fear, to the loss of your late daughter?"

I took a breath. "No, Your Honor. To quote Ms. August, the case needs to be tried."

"Yet you have an obstinate, hallucinating child witness—"

I held up a hand. "Victim, Your Honor. And quite courageous."

"Courage in a child is not necessarily a blessing. You have no physical evidence. You had some books, but lost them. I pray you will not—as did your boss, Mr. Conover—lose composure and unleash emotional outbursts in my court? I won't tolerate that."

I smiled good-heartedly. "I wouldn't think of it."

"Yet you weep in open court in a blatant cry for sympathy. No offer to settle this, Mr. Jin? No?" A disappointed shake of the head. "Stacy, what have you for me?"

"Motions in limine." Late motions at the edge of trial.

"As do I, Your Honor," I said, quietly studying the judge. Anger wafted from him.

Judge Maxwell buzzed. In came Rebecca Coggins, the precise court reporter with her machine. She set up. Stacy pitched her motions and I responded.

He ruled. "Ms. August's jury selection consultant may sit for voir dire. Co-counsel, Mr. Rittenhouse, can be seated for the trial. Mr. Jin, that leaves no room for Investigator Capri.

"Ms. August, your nine-nine-five motion to dismiss is granted; there's no attempted murder. Some choking, if we are to believe a teenager." Loudly, he crossed out a page and two consecutive life terms. Gone. "And I see nothing of a scientific nature to indicate that the alleged marijuana was cannabis. No lab report, Mr. Jin! No search finding cannabis!" Gone. He crossed out page after page. Fifty counts. Seventy-eight years, state prison, gone.

"And stupefying drugs, without a lab report or blood. No search finding drugs! This," slapping the Information, "premised on the word of a *child*!" He leaned forward, eyes angry and small. He crossed them out. Maxwell had become anti-DA. No. Antichild.

"Judge," I said, "these are issues of fact for the jury to determine."

"Not in *my* court, they're not!" He flipped the thin, transparent, hundred and two pages of the Information. "How much *waste* we endure due to the accusations of a teenager!"

"Judge, rape is a crime of violence. She was beaten and choked during the rapes. Moody's attack was pathologically that of a Sadistic Preferential Rapist, focused on anger. Third parties saw *injuries*—that's what led to the arrest of the defendant. You dismiss the choking and beating, and witnesses will end up testifying to uncharged misconduct, and we'll mistry. You want a mistrial, Stacy?" I asked. I needed her help.

Mistrial meant lost hours and no clear victory. "I wouldn't oppose," she said, "an amendment with misdemeanor battery. Then he can bring in his evidence, without mistrial."

"For," I said, "months in jail compared to two consecutive life terms in state prison."

"Counselors, open your files." Like pupils, we turned to the Information.

On short legs and puffing redly, he reached across his great desk to cross out felony counts with red feral rips as we turned the fragile pages. He inserted PC 242, misdemeanor battery. I closed my file to staunch the bleeding. The most significant charges survived.

I renewed my motion requesting relief for failed discovery; the defense had not offered any assistance in allowing the People to interview John Quick, the alibi witness. It was denied.

Taking a shallow breath, I made the routine Evidence Code 765b motion to protect a child under age fourteen from harassment on the stand.

"Denied," said Maxwell. "This coddling of children has gone too far. I will permit fair cross-examination of this victim."

"Your Honor, 765b is statutory. It's not discretionary to the court."

He nodded. "Anything else? Let's be snappy."

"Judge, why have kids suddenly turned into cow pies in the middle of your chambers?"

"Evidence Code section 352, Mr. Jin, provides wide judicial interpretation of the admissibility of relevant evidence. Perhaps even members of our illustrious, model-setting district attorney's office know that."

"I'm aware of my faults and regret our shortcomings. Judge, don't take it out on a kid."

"Are you done?"

"No, sir. The People have a right to know what's in the bench's mind, and not get ambushed in open court in front of the jury. You're being openly hostile to my case."

"Here's what's in my mind, Mr. Jin: a fair trial. Proceed."

"Judge, may I speak off the record?"

Maxwell looked at the reporter. "No, you may not."

"Judge, your behavior toward my case gives me the feeling this isn't the day to try a two-eighty-eight in your court. Rather than threaten our relationship, let's explore options." I was thinking about a Section 170.6 Code of Civil Procedure affidavit of Judge Maxwell.

Finley Maxwell reclined in the great leather chair. "You 'get the feeling.' How sweet. Mr. Conover, the chief of law enforcement, gets the *feeling* that he wants to belt someone, so he beats the brains out of an innocent citizen and a police sergeant. *You* get the feeling that trial is too stressful and you cry like a baby, in front of bench and jury and opposing counsel. Feelings? No, sir. No more decisions based on *feelings*. Mr. Jin, make your motions."

If I affidavited him late, he'd deny the motion and I'd be at sea without an appellate chance. I nodded, "Okay, Your Honor, fair enough. No more feelings. They were wearing me out, anyway." I made an EC 11032(b)(1) motion prohibiting exploration of Rachel's sexual experience. "Sexual history goes to consent. And children, as a matter of law, cannot consent."

"That's the traditional reading. But I'll allow some."

"Under what circumstances, Your Honor?" I asked easily.

"Those I deem appropriate."

I gave them copies of my voir dire questions to the panel.

"Not necessary," said Judge Maxwell. "You are both professionals." In other words, he would let August ask any question she wished. I was facing a disaster in the making.

"Dr. Karenga," I said, "is my expert on rape trauma syndrome. Any problem there?"

"Mr. Jin, good you asked. I've researched these so-called experts. Ironically it turns out that they are *very* antifamily. Odd that when a toxicologist testifies, it's never with feelings. But these so-called child advocates come in with their angers and outrages, mostly against men, as if men were the cause of all evil in the world. These witnesses are invariably Professionally Unhappy Females. No, no such 'expert' will testify in my court."

"Judge, let's rethink this. Dr. Karenga has testified hundreds of times in this courthouse as a qualified expert. Disqualifying her would be oppositional to the holdings of—"

Maxwell jumped up. "That's *exactly* the manner of unprofessional slander I expected of you. You and Mr. Conover, *boxers,* crude bullying men. It isn't enough that you have the vast power of the State—you threaten any who stand in your way and you have found a weak codependent female who'll spout abstractions that would confuse Einstein. She is out."

I had vexed him for no benefit, and he was dispensing a

judicial venom I had never witnessed in any jurist. I decided to slip his punches; normally, I'd never stipulate—agree—to the credentials of my own expert. It's best for each side to trumpet its expert's credentials openly to the jury by asking the expert to list Ph.D.s, publications, awards, recognitions, citations, and past forensic triumphs. Logically, this information meant a great deal to jurors.

Unless I were in Department 49 in the Twilight Zone. Judge Maxwell sat.

"May we stipulate," I said, "that Killian Boyce, the Sexual Assault Nurse Examiner from UC, is an expert witness? This would save time establishing her as an expert." And save me getting my head snapped off.

"You got it, Josh," said Stacy, happy to have a stipulated prosecution expert whose bona fides would not be brightly advertised to the jury. It was a compromise to avoid having Maxwell quash the nurse.

"Thank you," I said. We signed the stipulation. I gave it to Maxwell and waited for his signature. He asked if Ray Farr was related to the NRA lobbyist. I said I didn't know.

"My motion, Your Honor, to exclude Mrs. Dierdre Farr from court on the day that Rachel Farr testifies. We have the victim's statement that her stepmother beats her. The stepmother's presence will intimidate an already anxious child victim. If the court's serious about pro—"

"Mrs. Farr has rights, too. Denied."

I submitted my most important motion: to restrict Stacy from using the defense's deliberately deceptive version of the standard of proof—beyond a reasonable doubt. The defense's pitch would sound like the legal standard was "beyond a *shadow* of a doubt." That wasn't a legal standard—it was an excellent 1943 Hitchcock movie. The title *Shadow of a Doubt* still plagued prosecutors, who went to law school and not film school.

"Denied, Mr. Jin. Let's call the venire, the sooner to end this charade." He pronounced the last word "sha-rod." We stood.

"Judge, may I have my stipulation?" I asked.

"You'll have it," he said. Stacy August touched his arm. He smiled, coloring, and they entered court. I brushed myself for lint, impressed that my pants weren't aflame.

Les Goss, the bailiff, put a cup of coffee on Maxwell's bench. Rebecca Coggins set up her ten-thousand-dollar dictating machine to face the witness stand, adjusted the seat pillow for a long campaign at three hundred words a minute, and sat. If murder occurred in the court—say, the DA throttling the judge—she would continue recording events, sounds, and words. In the middle of a courtroom shooting or a counsel table brawl—no strange events in River City—she would keep typing as bullets whizzed overhead and chairs were broken on thick heads.

Liz Heck, the clerk, phoned downstairs for a jury panel.

Phillips Rittenhouse, Stacy's elegant co-counsel, and Mr. Karl Francis Moody in a suit stood as the judge took the bench. On the defense table before Phillips lay an array of binders with color-coded indices and a rack of pre-flagged, tan, California case reports, ordered like good and able mercenaries. I would argue some of the same cases they had marked, for opposite effect.

Mrs. Aldo, the curious octogenarian, court observer, and needlepointer in her usual flower-print dress and lime-green shawl, sat next to her best friend, a postal service retiree named Mrs. Idora Afreem. They had been watching felony trials for the better part of twenty years. I thought of them as the Knothole Kids, peering through the walls of a construction site.

Geneva de Hoyas entered and sat solemnly in the back row, wearing a severe black dress, the one she had worn to Sergeant Billy McManus's funeral. A gaggle of reporters sat near, mikes offered, hoping for a sound bite. François Giggin and Dierdre Farr were apparently late. Capri, inundated by work, would appear later.

Stacy looked like a pre-inflationary million bucks; the judge gave me an ugly glance; the defendant Moody seemed pleased with himself; and Rebecca Coggins smiled at me from her ready position at the dictation machine. In the old days, I would've smiled back. I was too busy gritting my teeth and feeling weak.

It was show time.

40.

VOIR DIRE

The spiked, purple-haired woman from the jury commission delivered black jury venire binders to Maxwell, August, and me. In Anglo-Saxon law, the venire was the order that authorized the levying of a jury from the community. It now referred to the daily draft of prospective jurors to fill the needs of trial courts, all of which, today, were criminal cases.

Four floors below, sixty innocent prospectives were being called from the jury room. Many had already tried energetically to be excused; these sixty were the stalwarts, some of them suspecting that the large number of their party meant a murder or a rape trial.

I read the binder, noting good prospects and bad. They were mostly bad—an amazing collection of drifting, childless adults. Finley Maxwell glanced at his copy. Stacy and her team pointedly ignored it; their data were far better than the jury commission's.

Les Goss pointed. I went to Geneva, who was at the barrier. I shook her hand. "Thanks for coming to wish us good luck."

"Dismiss it, Josh. We might have other options on Moody."

"Tell me about that."

"All I know is—"

The door opened and the prospective jurors filed in. Geneva squeezed my arm. "Tell Fin Maxwell now. Dismiss."

"Madame Chief Deputy with the Bigger Badge, what's this *really* about?"

The jurors began taking seats. Phillips Rittenhouse was leaning back in his chair, eavesdropping.

"Brains 101," said Geneva. "You were out that day."

"Yeah, I was taking a tougher class. Ethics 101."

"May we help you, Ms. de Hoyas?" asked Judge Maxwell.

"No, Judge." She ignored him. "Do what I say," she said softly.

I returned to my seat as she pushed through the entering crowd into the hallway; reporters followed. No overriding dismissal from the chief deputy. Not today.

"Domestic problems?" asked Stacy August.

"Same old stuff. She wants me to cook tonight," I said.

Stacy nodded. "Cooking like that caused the Vietnam War."

I looked at the people who would decide the case as they basked in the sharp coolness of the courtroom—an intentional design feature to discourage sleep. They wouldn't miss the close discomfort of the jury call room. Some huffed from the walk. Most were wary, studying the lawyers who had dislocated them, as if we were going to line them up and shoot them.

The judge said, "The Court calls the case of People of the State of California versus Karl Francis Moody, Number 983422. The record will reflect the personal appearance of the defendant with attorney Ms. Stacy Antoinette August. The People are represented by Deputy District Attorney Joshua Lawrence Jin. Ready for the defense, Ms. August?"

"Ready for the defense, Your Honor." Her voice a song.

"Ready for the People," the judge said flatly.

"Ready for the People, Your Honor."

The reporters returned unhappily; Geneva had said nothing.

Mrs. Dierdre Farr appeared in a modest top over white bicycle shorts. The reporters, none of them veterans of Broadway bars or child abuse in Chinatown, were unaware of her identity or her lethality.

Judge Finley Maxwell instructed the clerk to call the roll and to swear the panel to the oath. They stood and swore.

Educated by bad television, the panel knew that criminal cases were the personal fault of a stiff-necked DA. He would be a relentless and ambitious pencil-necked bastard with a

corncob up his rear who would readily convict the slow and innocent to make himself look good on the way to the governor's
office. Judge Maxwell did nothing to dispel this notion. We
stood for introductions. I noticed that the defense team was
color-coordinated.

The judge stated his rules: no Walkmans, gum, talking, reading, or case discussion until the case was given to the jury.
Twelve would be called by lottery of the court clerk to enter the
jury box. He would ask questions regarding fitness to serve.
Economic hardship would not be an excuse, even for the self-
employed. Two reserve jurors would later be called.

"Then the lawyers will question you. I expect brevity in my
court, but we know how they are, don't we?" Laughter. He explained the peremptory challenge.

"The lawyers," as if he had never been one, "may excuse you
without a reason. Don't take that personally. After all, if
a lawyer doesn't like you, can that be all bad?" Smiles and
giggles. Moody guffawed. Stacy touched his arm and he faced
front like a good con.

Maxwell said the press had an interest in this case, and
that henceforth they were not permitted to speak to the media
about it.

He told them the nature of the case, establishing an air of
quiet shock.

He delivered a necessary monologue about the DA having
the burden of proof, to prove Mr. Moody was guilty beyond a
reasonable doubt. For this, we needed an impartial jury.

Liz Heck spun her lottery wheel and called twelve names. In
a few minutes, we had seven women and five men, including
homemakers, engineers, and a truck driver.

Our black binders contained the standard County data on
each member of the venire: name, date of birth, marital status,
number of children, employment, political party, years at
present address, prior jury experience. Most jurors didn't
know that.

DAs prefer people with long-term employment, with responsibility for others, with clear links to the community. We sel-

dom keep psychologists and never retain priests—people
sworn to saving, rather than convicting.

Disliking stereotypes, I picked juries based on them. I
needed twelve parents who loved their kids and would care
about Rachel. I'd dismiss anyone who hated teens. Because
conviction requires a unanimous vote of all twelve, I couldn't
afford one bad juror.

Stacy needed only one negative vote to hang the jury. She
would seek the oddball, the misfit, the repulsive, domineering
male with a big voice who'd throw babies from a lifeboat for a
better seat. She'd look for a codependent woman who'd bed
Dracula while trying to get him to find a day job. Someone who
thought rape was the victim's fault, asking for it with a short
skirt; who'd believe an ex-con over a teenager. A woman who
liked Moody. A man who disliked me.

One hanging vote and Stacy could expect that we would
dismiss. She knew the fragility of Rachel Farr and the improba-
bility of her—or even me—surviving a retrial.

This trial was it.

The judge finished asking his routine questions of the jurors.
He had challenged no one, looking like a good guy. It was
Stacy's turn.

The men tried not to stare openly. Women studied her great
hair, understated designer suit, modulated jewelry, sculpted
body. They applauded rather than envied, feeling intrigue rather
than competition. They looked forward to Wonder Woman, full
of grace, blowing the socks off Charlie Chan, the ambitious,
stiff, corncobbed Chinese DA who would convict the innocent.
The man who was unloved by the judge.

It was good Rachel wasn't here to see Stacy charm the room.
The girl from the woods of northern Michigan was making the
citizens of California salute the diva. As witness for the prosecution, Rachel would appear later. To be scorned by the judge,
to be questioned by me, to be weighed by the jury, to be
watched by her abusive stepmother, to be cross-examined by
Stacy, master of the interrogational scalpel.

Stacy spoke from a notebook with more juror data than I
could have acquired with two full-time cops. JurPro had state-

ments from juror coworkers, bosses, ex-spouses, neighbors, teachers of their children, ministers. It had each juror's opinion of law enforcement and child sexual assault, kidnap and providing narcotics, most of which was no longer part of my case.

Without a word, Stacy had set the tone: I would not represent a guilty man. I never lose. I look good, speak well, and have a smile for which you'd market illicit drugs. Why? Because I *am* good. She instructed on law, knowing that Maxwell should, but would not, remind her that this was his job. She said that the government was prone to error. The problems with the FBI Lab. Ruby Ridge. Waco. IRS's notorious errors. Jurors nodded.

Stacy and I each had ten peremptory challenges to spend on panelists who disliked us or our cause, without having to state a reason.

Regardless of how badly the jurors might like to escape the duty, a change occurred once they were in the box. Then they resented being judged as unfit. Particularly if the one doing the judging was the DA—the paternalistic, easily resented authority figure. I had to use my challenges sparingly to avoid looking like Robespierre. Or, worse, a bad parent.

The first twelve loved Stacy not wisely but too well. Stacy made men desire her special company while drawing the common admiration of women. Mesmerized, they nodded if she asked them to. They trusted her as they marveled at her beauty, her eloquence and easy use of conversation in a formal setting, her command of the law, her brilliant reasoning, her svelte voice that carried a hint of the solid, trustworthy Midwest. This wasn't manipulation; it was the strength of her will, the glory of her preparation, the common seduction of the beautiful.

"We're all reasonable people, our minds open, ready to follow the law. To hear the reasonable argument. Aren't we?" Eyes looked brightly at her as heads nodded, and her monster of a defendant suddenly looked better, sat taller, breathed easier.

Stacy's exacting voir dire revealed that an L.A. cop and a truck driver knew some of the lesser witnesses. That an Asian store clerk, after a bad traffic stop, resented cops. Stacy knew I'd dismiss her, but she kept asking questions, again and again, to impress the store clerk's negative experience on the panel. A good tactic, smoothly performed as I sat silently.

She'd soon discuss the standard of proof—"beyond a reasonable doubt." Lawyers can't use voir dire to argue their case. Stacy, as many lawyers, already had. An ugly pragmatism.

Judge Maxwell had earlier defined what doubt was *not*: "It is not a mere possible doubt, because everything relating to human affairs is open to some possible or imaginary doubt."

Stacy was about to define it by the theology of the defense: that "beyond a reasonable doubt" meant I had to prove *more than* reasonable doubt—that I had to *exceed* it. This was contrary to law and a long lineage of unfettered appellate decisions.

I took a breath as she began framing the question to Juror Eight, the truck driver.

"Objection, Your Honor," I said. "Counsel knows her definition of 'beyond a reasonable doubt' is not stated in law. The People do not need to *exceed* reasonable doubt. We simply need to present evidence that *excludes* reasonable doubt."

Maxwell nodded. "That's too esoteric. Let's move on."

Stacy repeated her question. I renewed my objection.

"Ms. August, our DA is suddenly feeling vigorous. Let's be nice and use the California Jury Instruction language." He looked sternly at me. "Your objection is noted. Now, sit."

Stacy smiled and asked her question without changing a word.

A bad moment. The judge was telling the jury that even if the DA was correct in law, it didn't matter. Its corollary could be: Even if the defendant's guilty, it doesn't matter either.

Better to get rebuked than to roll over and lose by forfeit before the opening bell. I stood. "Your Honor, I'm sorry, but it's unsupportable that the defense is spouting a totally incorrect definition of the standard of proof. A definition that would earn an F in first-year criminal law in any accredited law school in this state."

Judge Maxwell rested his chin on an index finger. "You fatigue me with puny arguments. You underestimate this jury. I do not believe as readily as you that they can be misled." He smiled, trying to work on votes. "Ms. August, please continue."

I sat. Stacy nodded at Maxwell. She continued.

"Mr. Bukust, do you understand it is the DA's job to prove my client guilty *beyond a reasonable doubt*—a world-class-difficult standard. A high-jump bar ten feet off the ground!"

"Objection. World record is eight feet, one-half inch. Heck, if we believed counsel, no jury could convict anyone. People in this County and in the U.S. have been convicting the guilty for years. I've seen *that* high-jump bar." A gesture. "It's about a foot off the ground."

"Mr. Jin, you're arguing like a lawyer. Ms. August was using a metaphor, not a standard. You are overruled."

Stacy smiled graciously at me, winning more points; Wonder Woman, with the etiquette of Melanie Wilkes. "Mr. Bukust," she said, "the DA has to jump *over* that and clear it, without a doubt, without even the slightest shiver on the bar. Do you understand that, sir?"

He nodded eagerly, making me dizzy. "Yes, ma'am, I sure do."

In the afternoon, Stacy left the counsel table to romance the panel. Not all lawyers can enter the jurors' space by touching the box. These jurors would have spread palm branches.

She looked better up close, confirming the judgment of longer vision. Her voice and eyes caressed, guided, held. The way she touched and then held the rail brushed the consciousness of the jury. No one worked a crowd like Stacy August. Judge Maxwell mooned. Jurors listened, nodded, lips parted, breathing shortened by her drama.

Juror Six, the engineer, remained composed. He was my ideal jury foreman, but August was going to kick him out of the box.

Each of us possesses a finite ration of intelligence, judgment, attentiveness, patience, memory, and reason. Each of us bears prejudices, good, bad, and indifferent. Stacy sensed those of the jury, remembering. Staying close, working artfully, she extracted most of their attentiveness, patience, and reason. She inspired their sympathy for a poor, solitary patriot named Karl Moody, besieged by a government made evil not by a malignant heart, but by a bloated budget, an oversize, overmuscled, broad-shouldered staff, a tradition of not knowing trees from forest, good from bad, hopeful from stupid.

"Imagine," she said, "the district attorney, *helping* us."

Comedy-hour laughter. Jurors were looking at me. I felt the stares from the remainder of the panel behind me. In Stacy's voir dire, identification with the flag was becoming a negative. If I weren't careful, I'd end up hating the DA, too.

I objected to the more flagrant questions, losing points. My best tactic was to seem bemused. Stacy's methodical and patient voir dire took the rest of the day.

The judge admonished the jury not to discuss the case with anyone, including each other, and not to fraternize with lawyers or witnesses. "You can say hello, but nothing more. Have a good evening. Be here tomorrow morning at nine sharp." He hit his gavel.

The jury box emptied, its occupants smiling at Stacy.

The press crowded her and I escaped. I was stopped by the lean Tanya Churchill in an elegant blue suit. She was the prosecutor who had taken my bureau.

"This is for you," she said, handing me a note.

Friday

Josh—

I'm under a direct order to avoid all contact with you and the Moody case. If I violate it, it's *Braxton's* neck. Also: Judge Finley Maxwell's on the DA's Authorized Affidavit List. If you happen to get assigned to his court, challenge him and get out of there, pronto.

Seems Maxwell's committed to Seth Jergen's candidacy for DA, and thinks a friend of drug dealers is better than a drunken brawler. Go figure. Maxwell just tubed two of our cases in pretrial and another before a jury—we had good evidence in each. I saw the memo distribution list—someone removed your name. You're being set up.

So whatever you do on Monday, don't take Rachel to Maxwell's court. Call me at home if you need anything. Maxwell's gone weird and anti-DA. Stay close to Rachel now. Romance the case, Jin.

CAPRI

It was a thoughtful tactical warning, delivered one day too late.

41.

THINKING LIKE A WOMAN

Ava and Rachel picked me up at the police station.

"Hello," said Ava. I waved and sat in the back.

"How was The Stacy dressed?" asked Ava.

I buckled up. "Pink suit. White blouse. Pink shoes. Klieg lights. Light perfume and lots of press. Standard modest jewelry. Low heels. Hem at the center of her knee. Here it is the turn of the century and I still don't dress anything like her."

Rachel laughed, a delicious sound. Ava smiled at her. In the Eighties, women wore dark suits like the guys, to be serious. With high FM heels and big jewelry. FM: Fornicate Me.

Now dark was out. Women for the defense wore warm, kind, compassionate colors—taupe, mauve, light pink, rose, soft reds, pastels, cream. Short heels to avoid sending the wrong message to male jurors. Stacy was the It woman, brainy and dressed smart.

Rachel was dozing, like a younger child in a moving car. Ava lowered her voice. "Stacy's client is a man from hell. She wears soft colors to offset him. She'll hint to the jury that she's shapely. Nothing overt. Small earrings, never dangly ones. No bracelets or jewelry that jangles or catches the eye. A Seiko. She probably has three Mercedes, but she'll drive a minivan or an SUV. Nineties modesty versus Eighties flaunt."

I drove a Porsche to court. I tried to imagine taking a bus—an act that was against all California religious beliefs. Traffic on I-80 was heavy, choking toward the Causeway.

"You *also* have to go with softer colors. Only for Closing Argument will it be your traditional dark navy, white shirt, and high-contrast tie."

"I'm getting a headache. And for Rebuttal?"

"A lighter suit. It's a different world."

Closing Argument. The trial lawyer's shot at oratory—to sway opinion with words, to wax eloquent, to imitate the Bard. We summarized the case and tried to win votes. I had been running the argument through my mind constantly. I needed twelve votes out of twelve.

Stacy needed one. And she'd be practicing, too.

The customary DA doctrine was to be prepared and earnest, remind them of their duty. Wear navy blue and stand by the flag.

Ava parked at Nordstrom's.

"Aha," I said slowly, "we're going shopping."

"Women dress for men *and* for women. Stacy dresses for the jury. DAs tend to dress merely to avoid being naked. You have to do more because you have no physical evidence."

"One of the greater axioms of law." Ava hit me. The Age of Aquarius had been replaced by the Age of Appearance. I didn't have to like it. We entered the mall. Rachel wore new jeans and top from the Gap. The mall crowd was thick with noise, junk food, and bad clothing.

"Josh, you've mastered the role of the good Anglo lawyer."

"Well, I don't want to brag."

"You shouldn't, honey. You did it by watching movies."

"Like the rest of the world." People around the globe pay billions to see the idealized American male win—armed, dangerous, and alone against great odds. Better to be tough than smart. Cowboy culture. If it's a horse, ride it. If it's a fence, jump it. If it hurts, hide it.

"Really?" she asked.

" 'Bond, James Bond,' " I said.

"Women don't buy James Bond anymore. And you've read the studies; women increasingly sway jury verdicts."

"You saying I'm not that good with women jurors?"

She stopped at a railing and looked down. Below, a rap group performed to a packed audience. "You can improve."

This was only partially about trials. "How'd I get you?"

"You didn't. I got you."

We listened to the rap, surrounded by tall, angrily dressed children who had no other place to be. Rachel was almost close to us.

"*Hadrow,* the murder case that Stacy won. Why'd you lose?"

"The jury loved her."

"*That's* where she whips you. I didn't get it until you told me that Stacy shared JurPro data with you at that cozy dinner of yours. She *completely* tried this case before actual trial. Like it was a multigazillion civil case. I didn't think White & August would spend that kind of money in a criminal case. But she did it for *Hadrow* and she's doing it for *Moody.*"

They used actors as witnesses, a stiff junior partner as the DA, and the actual client in a mock court. The "jury" was filmed so neurolinguistic and behavioral consultants could repeatedly review each juror's response. Meanwhile, lawyers completely debriefed the jurors.

What did you like about Ms. August's presentation? What did you dislike? So she had won *Hadrow* the moment voir dire was done. That jury loved her. And I went head-to-head with her in a charm contest, against Shirley Temple and Grace Kelly.

"You could beat other lawyers. Not her."

"You're saying I should start thinking like a woman."

"No. Learn how a woman thinks. Stop functioning like a boxer, going straight in, hitting the opponent with all those punches, driving for a quick knockdown. Go slow."

"I don't know how to work like that."

"Sure you do. It's how you raised your daughter."

After dinner and homework, I knocked on what was now Rachel's bedroom. At first, our knocking surprised Rachel; she wasn't accustomed to the smallest courtesies. Her father ignored her and Mrs. Farr tended to barge in to pound her.

Rachel showed me her new blue suit and shoes.

"Hey, that looks great. Rachel, we got a bad judge. He doesn't like prosecutors and he's going to take it out on you. He's mad at me and my boss and so he's going to try to break your spirit.

There's something wrong with him. Not you. He's a raving bully. Forget him. You just answer my questions, okay?"

She looked small and worried. She knew about bullies.

42.

STACY AUGUST'S JURY

Tuesday

Crime trials draw people like an accident scene. The media had named *Moody* the litmus test case for the November election, attracting a more venal class of onlooker. Everyone watched Stacy, as one would study the culmination of the American dream.

She challenged three jurors for bias. She had gotten one to say the cops were always right, another to say he'd distrust a defendant who didn't testify, even with his right to silence.

Maxwell should have questioned the two to verify the implacability of the bias, but he quickly excused them. One was the engineer who would've been a good foreman for me.

"Mr. Jin claims," said Stacy, "that the District Attorney only prosecutes the guilty. Yet the DA himself has pled Not Guilty to battering the teeth out of a good policeman, showing he has the accuracy in these matters of a donkey with a shotgun."

Many chuckled. Judge Maxwell honked, inspiring laughter.

"Objection," I said. "Mr. Conover's pretty picky about whom he prosecutes, and really, because of the multitudes of the guilty in this county, he has no time to harass the innocent."

A chuckle. Maxwell frowned. "Sit down, Mr. Jin."

"Don't insult the mother alligator," whispered Stacy, "before you've crossed the river." She gently clicked her teeth.

Maxwell excused the juror for cause. Stacy had dumped her three worst jurors without spending a peremptory challenge or appearing to be fickle. I, by contrast, would seem picky.

Juror Number One, a homemaker, believed that the Communist

Party had bought off all lawyers; Maxwell dismissed her for cause. A radio station manager replaced her. African-American, he had been hassled by police, but said he had forgiven them. Stacy had been interviewed by his radio station, but he claimed impartiality.

Eleven parents in the box—a huge number. Stacy was going to keep them. It was child assault, where the defense dismissed parents, but these were on her side. I had prayed for parents out of a thin, largely childless venire, and had gotten them.

A sculptor with her work, Stacy went through the jury, perfecting shape and angle. The twelve glowed. She looked at them and found them pleasing. Because of the influence of her *Vogue* wardrobe, our jury panel was better dressed than it was yesterday.

Stacy had made connections, allowing parents to extol their children. She had promoted talk of quilting, fishing, gardening, vacations, travel, relatives. A juror smiled and she was radiant. One spoke of hardship and she sympathized. These reactions were not artificial; Stacy was an empathizer, an emoter, a shaper. I remembered.

In a trial, you use words to corner and cut off your opponent, where all he can do is bleed. But I was the one feeling ropes on both sides. It was a repeat of *Hadrow*.

The jury not only agreed with Stacy August's view of the world, they wanted to be members of her family and see her on holidays. The State Department could have sent her to Sarajevo and taken all the credit.

"The defense accepts the panel, Your Honor," said Stacy, her face illuminated perfectly by the courtroom lights. Justice was in session, truth was on her side, and all was right in the world.

43.

THE JURY

Wednesday

Judge Fin Maxwell took the bench, smiling at the jury and Stacy. The jury studied me expectantly. I had recorded the jury of seven females, five males, and two reserve jurors, with notes to challenge, excuse or accept. I also noted daughters and divorce.

DISTRICT ATTORNEY—SACRAMENTO COUNTY
Voir Dire Jury Information Sheet v.4
People v. Moody/SACA   J. Maxwell, Dept. 21   7 July   DDA Josh Jin / Stacy August

F=FEMALE M=MALE sp=SPOUSE			
7 females 5 males / 11 parents 3 divorced / 7 Democrats / 4 Republicans / 1 Independent			

9	10	11	12
F Richards	F Carlo	M Richeson	M Hendrix
peds RN	sec'y	equip opertr	roofer
Divorced	Divorced	sp: UPS driver	sp: store clerk
dtr 12	sons 5, 7, 10	son 13	sons 16, 23
Republican	Democrat	Independent	Republican
MOTHER*†	MOTHER†	FATHER	FATHER
OK	PEREMPTRY	OK	OK

5	6	7	8
F Sobol	F Wolstoncroft	F Takahashi	M Bukust
Legis aide	homemaker	store clerk	truck driver
sp: lawyer	sp: engineer	sp: CPA	Divorced
son 14	dtr 8	dtr 6 son 2	sons 2, 4, 7, 9
Democrat	Democrat	Democrat	Republican
MOTHER	MOTHER*	MOTHER*	FATHER†
OK	OK	CHALLENGE	CHALLENGE

1	2	3	4
M Clayton	M Goin	F Burda	F Becerril
rad stn mgr	meter man	pic framer	dental tech
sp: minister	Single	sp: artist	Divorced
sons 4, 8, 9	0 kids	dtr 9	dtr 7
Democrat	Republican	Democrat	Democrat
FATHER	0 KIDS	MOTHER*	MOTHER†*
QUEST'BLE	PEREMPTRY	OK	OK

[RESERVE JURORS]			
13	14		
M Machida	F Ford		
firefighter	teacher		
sp: broker	sp: dental tech		
son 20	dtr 26		
Republican	Democrat		
FATHER	MOTHER*		
OK	OK	*HAS A DAUGHTER / † DIVORCED	

I had to build leadership, unity, and accountability and dump those who disliked kids and cops. DAs tend to sound clinical. Criminal defense lawyers tend to sound oily, but Stacy had established a compatability with the panel that exceeded my skills. She had already won the talent, congeniality, and swimsuit competitions before I had a chance to sing.

Seven women seated. Ava wanted me to think like a woman. I needed the jury to be a team. I had studied the mass of uncalled panelists and saw little compassion and less interest. It was an unusually bad group. The few parents in the panel were already in the jury box.

I was better off with the people already impaneled. Josh Jin, former homicide detective, would coldly cull the box, cutting out the usual suspects. Josh Jin, advisee of Ava Pascal, would ask them to agree to fundamental human values, and be rather warm about it.

I had never done this before: I would keep them all. I began with closed-ended group questions, the reverse of the norm. Using the norm, Stacy August had beaten me like a drum.

I stood in front and spoke, making eye contact. I was firm and pleasant. More formal. She had charmed; I would be the steady teacher, the guide. Spencer Tracy. Jimmy Stewart.

"Sometimes it's hard to know if someone is lying. Isn't that true?" A few restrained nods. "But is there anyone here who could *never* tell a lie from the truth?" No one wanted to stand out; no hands. "Okay. Could you believe something happened if only *one* person told you?"

Nods. "Of course. Happens every day. The waiter says, 'The special is fresh mountain trout.' We believe him, without asking a second party." Signs of affirmation. "The judge read to you the definition of 'beyond a reasonable doubt.' You heard Ms. August discuss *her* defini—"

"Objection," said Stacy. "DA is arguing."

"Sustained," said Maxwell. "Ask a *question*, Mr. Jin."

"Do you understand," I said to the box, "that all I have to do is prove my case to the *exclusion* of reasonable doubt? That's different than going *above* reasonable doubt."

Stone faces. The judge had made them afraid to react. "Would you agree that testimony is imperfect? Why? We're not machines. Isn't it true that we tend to remember *meanings* more than exact words. Everyone here agree with that?"

Two nods—Becerril and Burda. "Picture this guy, looking at the sky. He says, 'Hey, it looks like rain.' You look up and see dark clouds, so you nod. It *does* look like rain.

"Another man, on another day, looks up. He says the *same* thing—'Looks like rain.' You look, but it's a clear blue sky, like Lake Tahoe in August. And you wonder: Why the heck did he say that? Later, you see his car. It's packed with new umbrellas." I smiled. "And you nod.

"You don't know this man. But you know he has a motive to lie. Ladies and gentlemen, you won't hold it against me, a simple government lawyer, going up against the famous Stacy August, if I ask you to decide if someone's lying, will you?" I smiled.

A few head shakes: No, I won't.

"Good. Because that's what this case is about. Will anyone *resent* me for showing that someone's lying to us?" I waited. Five, six shakes of the head. Seven.

"Will anyone resent me for showing a person has a *motive* to lie?" Nine shakes. No agreement from Clayton, Juror One, a potential foreman. Or Richeson, equipment operator.

Again, I smiled. "Ladies and gentlemen, isn't it true that outside the court, you *can* decide who's lying? Isn't it true that we decide *every day* who's telling the truth, and who isn't?"

Agreement. Clayton, pursing lips. Richeson, inscrutable.

"It's no different here. Here, you have the same judgment you have outside. We ask many things of you, but not that you leave your knowledge at the door. If anyone did, please pick it up at the break, because we'll have good use for it later."

Tougher questions involved responsibility. I had eleven parents and three divorced jurors with nineteen children, one being a twelve-year-old girl—nearly Rachel's age. We were not in the era of great parenting. I needed the jurors to be open to Rachel's pain and isolation, without their experiencing guilt about imperfect relationships with their own children.

"Anyone who can't offer a child the same *courtesy*, the same *consideration,* that you'd extend to an adult?"

No negative reactions. It hadn't seemed possible, but Stacy's presence was fading.

"You'll meet the alleged victim in this case. She is a child who has suffered a trauma—"

"Objection, Your Honor," said Stacy, standing, Rittenhouse gazing at her. "Not proven."

I looked at Judge Maxwell. "Neither of us has proven anything, yet, Your Honor. I'm still in voir dire. The Evidence Code establishes pretty clearly that proof comes *after* jury selection."

"Sustained," he said. "Keep to the facts, Mr. Jin."

"Your Honor, there are no facts to keep to. Not yet."

"Mr. Jin, you're abusing my patience. Proceed."

I let Hitchcock's shadow of doubt cross my face. "Ladies and gentlemen, the victim is young and understandably nervous. She'll have a lot of trouble talking to you about this. She'll have to use a microphone in order for you to hear her. Anyone who'd resent a child for her reluctance to talk freely about being sexually assaulted?" No one. They were jelling.

I told them that Rachel was nine when her mom died. That Rachel kept her mother's memory alive by talking to her.

"Cowboys," referring to Sacramento's Wild West roots, "talk to cows and horses and even to themselves when they're alone on the high range. Anyone here going to hold it against Rachel for conversing with her deceased mother, in this old frontier way?"

Takahashi, Richards, Wolstoncroft, Becerril, and Burda—who had daughters—shook heads. Two jurors looked past me at Dierdre Farr in a tight red blouse and short black skirt.

I smiled and looked down. "Ladies and gentlemen, can we admit, according to our solemn oaths, that we sometimes *resent* teenagers?"

A stirring. Grins. "You know, we were all teens once, but now we're older. If you ever avoided eye contact with a teen, or tried to avoid a pack of them, or disliked their nutsy music and bad, baggy clothes hanging around their ankles, their earrings and nose rings and juvenile smoking, raise your hand. Come on, now," I said pleasantly, raising mine. "You took an oath."

Nothing but awkward stirrings. "Ms. Richards, you're a ped RN. Ms. Becerril, you're a dental tech. Ms. Takahashi, you work in a store. You three mean to tell me that you've never resented a surly teen who, at some point in your life, made your work difficult?"

Richards's hand went up with almost comical speed. So did the hands of the other two. Then Clayton's went up. The rest followed. "Thank you." I lowered mine. So did they.

We hunt for cause to eliminate adverse jurors. But because the remaining panel was unpromising, I was trying to build team. Instead of attacking weaknesses, I focused on strengths and commonalities. I asked if kids were more likely to lie in court than adults.

"Gee," said Mrs. Wolstoncroft. "I think children might be *more* honest."

"I'm sorry," I said. "Could you repeat that?" I did that for the male jurors.

I asked the men individually, "Can you think of a reason not to report a crime?

"What if it was a sexual assault?

"What if you were thirteen years old and your mom had died and you weren't getting along with your stepmother, and this happened?"

The answers were encouraging. Men don't like to talk about

personal matters in public. Then, "Can you convict someone of a crime based solely on the word of one witness?

"What if that witness is a child?

"What if she's a teenager?

"What if the crime is a sex crime?" Now I faced the fact that I had no expert witness to testify about rape trauma syndrome. I had to be careful.

"Could you believe a child who is raped might think the attack was *her* fault, because she couldn't stop or defeat the rapist?"

"Objection," said Stacy. "This type of sentiment has been eliminated from this trial."

"It's not a 'sentiment,' Your Honor. It's a fact."

"Mr. Jin," said Maxwell, "cease and desist. Now you're testifying."

I nodded. "Can you believe that a child who is raped might be reluctant to report—"

"Mr. Jin!" shouted the judge.

"I withdraw the question. Now, everyone's understandably uncomfortable talking about sex. Is there anyone here for whom the discomfort would be so great, you couldn't *think or reason*?" A question designed to elicit twelve noes. Head-shaking.

I was getting good answers from a fair jury. I saw Maxwell adjusting his gavel, pens, papers, paper clips, perhaps to throw at me. Time to get out of Dodge.

"You took an oath. To tell the truth. To do your job." I focused on them.

"Ladies and gentlemen, you are under oath. Now, if I do my job, and convince you, to the exclusion of all reasonable doubt, that Mr. Moody committed the crimes charged against Rachel Farr, can each and every one of you do your job, and hold the defendant accountable for his acts? You do that by voting and declaring him guilty. Not because he is a good man or a bad one, but because *he did it*. Mr. Clayton, sir, if I do my part, can you do that?"

"Yes," said Mr. Clayton.

"Mr. Goin?" He said, yes. I continued through the box, individually asking each juror.

"Thank you. Anyone here who, because of the nature of the

crimes charged against the defendant"—I pointed at him—"or because of stress of work or personal issues, can't give this case your *total and focused attention*? The attention which the People will demand of you?"

A small sea wave of shaking heads. Somewhere, not so deeply hidden in each of us, is the desire to be a community. To share a garden hose with a stranger who has a fire. It is the true, life fuel of the jury system. They were as ready as they could be.

"Your Honor, the People accept the panel and the reserves."

The ominousness of that statement settled over the courtroom.

The jurors were surprised that no one had been dismissed, each expecting to be the next to go for some private reason, to get chopped out of the group by the Chinese DA. With various emotions, but heavy on pride, they looked at each other.

Carlo, Burda, and Sobol seemed amazed. The mantle of responsibility settled on these common strangers. Jurors who weather voir dire feel like Olympic finalists, survivors on a valuable team. They are the chosen, and something important happens in the heart.

I hoped these fourteen felt it.

The juror who got the most glances of peers was Mr. Clayton, Juror One. The two reserve jurors were almost ignored by the rest; they were outside the box, in diminished status.

Mrs. Aldo, the needlepointing court-watcher, was frowning in disapproval at my voir dire, making me worry. Was it because she had expected more fireworks? Or was it because I had made a huge mistake in keeping the panel? What had she seen that I hadn't?

For the next week, the jury would be a unit. Later, they would decide the fates of two people and impact an election. For some, it would be high drama. For others, a nuisance in overscheduled lives. For all, it would be a unique call to their intellect and their integrity.

I sat. Stacy wore a slight, ironic grin.

Ms. Walker, her JurPro consultant, shook hands with Stacy. Phillips Rittenhouse had the look of a Cheshire after a good meal.

I had excused no one, violating a cardinal rule of voir dire. I could imagine the press asking questions, raising doubts. Perhaps Geneva and Tommy Conover were happy.

I didn't care. It was noon and I had hope. Hope that these twelve people would be decent to Rachel. If they treated her like a human being, I could convict Chico Moody.

I took a breath as the judge excused the forty people in the audience and swore the jury. Liz Heck passed a juror badge to each, asking the jurors to always wear them in court.

I had not cried. I reviewed my opening statement. Masses of packed, pterodactyl-sized butterflies making barrel rolls and figure eights in my innards, a cluster of emotions battling for cerebral attention and blood. God, I'm in trial. It had been a long time.

I was light-headed, nauseous, and jittery. I needed coffee, three nights' sleep, a boxing opponent who'd let me spar him, a deep massage, and a cold shower, all at the same time.

"Ladies and gentlemen of the jury," said Judge Maxwell. "It is noon. We will take two hours for lunch." It meant he had a lot of backlogged work on other cases. He reminded them of the standard admonitions. "We begin Opening Statements at two. Court is adjourned."

Isaac Krakow, crisp and precise, stopped me in the hall. He whispered, "They're saying you kept the original panel. That true? Josh, are you okay? Hey, buddy, do you know what the hell you're doing?"

44.

OPENING STATEMENT

The court audience was Dierdre Farr, Mrs. Aldo, her friend Mrs. Afreem, two Asian press reporters, and two major print reporters, who sat far apart in bitter rivalry.

I had declined interviews. Stacy August and Judge Maxwell did not.

An easel stood near the witness stand. Liz Heck blushed with her customary anxiety as the judge said that the prosecution and the defense could now deliver opening statements.

Someone entered the court and was approaching. François Giggin. He slid a coffee mug to me with an encouraging smile.

"I don't permit coffee in here!" roared Judge Maxwell. François jerked, spilling the coffee on my files, trousers, and shoes. It smelled fresh and felt very hot.

"Oh, man!" cried François through gritted teeth, trying to mop it up with tissues.

"It's okay, François, thanks." I winked. He winced, rolled his eyes, and left.

"If we're quite ready? Thank you, Mr. Jin. As I was saying, opening statements are summaries of what the lawyers think the evidence in this case will show. They are not evidence." He read the Information—the charge sheet—I had filed on Moody. Most of the jurors shifted as the child sexual assault counts were read. Juror Two, Goin, the bachelor meter man, was expressionless. Three winced: Sobol, Richards, and Becerril. Sobol was a legislative aide—a job that required a poker face. RN Richards had seen infants and children die, and Becerril, the dental tech, worked inside angry mouths. I finished drying my papers.

"People wish to make opening statement?" asked Maxwell.

In opening statement, the DA explains the game and reveals his hand. There can be no surprises for the jury in his case; nothing is hidden. Anticipated prosecution weaknesses are openly confessed before the defense can suggest that the DA was hiding something.

It was my first chance to press the defense against the ropes by asking the jury to examine the critical weaknesses in the coming defense case. The weaknesses were always there, because the defendant could be depended upon to be guilty. Even if the DA was wet.

"We do, Your Honor. We've had our morning coffee, and are ready." A few nervous grins. With "we," I was trying to create a plurality, a minority man seeking community. I used to come out to deliver a flurry of hard points, speaking hard and fast so they wouldn't have a chance to reflect on how different I might be. Ava wanted me to go slow.

I centered myself between jurors Burda and Becerril in the first row and Richards and Carlo in the back. I was better when I smiled and modulated my voice, playing with the bass. Touching Rachel's photo in my pocket, I softened my face and spoke conversationally, as if it were normal to have stained trousers and smell like a Starbucks café.

"May it please the Court. Ladies and gentlemen of the jury. On the first day of February, Rachel Farr, a thirteen-year-old, visited a friend named Chico. Chico was leaving on a trip. He needed someone to take care of his dog. Rachel was to spend the night at his place to feed and walk Spango the spaniel, for twenty bucks. Rachel loved Spango and would do it for free.

"It was six o'clock on a Saturday night. The temperature that night was an unseasonably warm fifty-three degrees and clouds moved across a quarter moon. A soft warm breeze from the south rustled the branches of young sycamores. Rachel was on time, using the Timex watch Chico had given her for Christmas. The door was open and she went in."

The jurors were listening. Sobol and Richards took notes.

" 'Hey, sweetheart,' Chico called from the kitchen.

"Rachel sang back, 'Hi, Chico!'

"Chico appeared in a suit. Rachel was in cords and a sweatshirt, ready to munch on some nachos, embarrassed because she was underdressed, staring at the handsome Chico in a tie and a suit. He normally wore jeans, boots, and tee shirts.

"What followed had nothing to do with friendship or a girl taking care of a cute dog.

"What followed was gruesome torture. Unimaginable torture—made unimaginable by the fact that the victim was a trusting child and the assailant had been her friend."

Clayton and Richards leaned forward. Wolstoncroft and Burda, mothers of girls, winced and leaned away from the words, no longer breathing.

"The evidence will show that Rachel began seventh grade as

a quiet, healthy, academically below-average student. She ate regularly. She had a small number of friends.

"You will learn that her mother died when Rachel was nine. That she lived with her father and stepmother, and that her home was neither supportive nor particularly loving. That she had, and has, a distant and hostile relationship with her father."

I looked at the mothers. I ignored Dierdre Farr.

"The evidence will show that this fall, Rachel Farr was befriended by a man. A man *twenty-six years older* than she.

"This man entertained Rachel in his home. He entertained other girls—always teenage girls—most of whom were runaways." I stopped to let the words sink in.

"He offered these kids MTV, music, snacks, Spango the spaniel, a home, a place to hang out. This, during and after school hours.

"You will hear testimony that he treated Rachel Farr as a special friend. He helped her with homework. Her grades, her relationships with teachers and classmates, improved. He called her 'Rache.' She called him 'Chico.'

" 'Chico' is the defendant, Karl Francis Moody, who sits before you." I pointed to get them in the habit, so they could point at him, later, in verdict, and proclaim: Guilty. I stepped back to show that he was neither good nor safe.

Some of the male jurors—Bukust, Richeson, Hendrix, and Clayton—were looking hard at him. They were the fathers.

I opened hands. "This is largely uncontested. The defense and the prosecution agree, in the main, with these facts.

"The evidence will prove, not beyond all doubts, but to the exclusion of all *reasonable* doubt, that Chico Moody sexually assaulted the child Rachel Farr."

I told them what he did, causing pain to cross their faces. I had to pause.

"Her story," I said, "of course, is not uncontested. You will hear a totally different account from the defense.

"I have little physical evidence. There are no scientific reports or lab work. You will learn that Rachel Farr neither sought nor even *accepted* help from nurses, ER staff, doctors, police, or counselors.

"So what, you ask, did she *do* about being raped? Ladies and gentlemen, she did what children do. She wept. She became withdrawn, isolated, hypervigilant, regressed in behavior—acting in the manner of an even younger child. She stopped eating and she couldn't sleep. She bathed obsessively, scrubbing her skin again and again. Her speaking abilities dropped; she had lost her voice." I raised an index finger.

"This case is what is known as a 'one-on-one.' One person's word, against another's.

"Imagine, if you will—against all your fears—that someone known to you hurts your daughter, bruising her, making her limp and cry in the night. And that someone *denies* the act.

"Because you didn't see it personally, would you say to your daughter, 'Well, honey, let's drop it. It's just your word against his. It's a one-on-one.' Of course you wouldn't. You'd look at the two people. You'd ask questions.

"You would figure out what happened. This is no different. Rachel Farr will tell you that she was attacked by Karl Francis Moody.

"And the defense will deny it. The defense will say Rachel is lying." I moved toward Mr. Clayton, a foreman candidate.

"Ladies and gentlemen, I want you to watch very carefully how the defense explains why Rachel Farr would lie about being raped." I faced Stacy August as I spoke.

"Just like you, I'm going to be riveted to everything the defense counsel says—and everything the defense counsel doesn't say. I'm going to be *extremely* interested in hearing Ms. August's explanation for Rachel's testimony. Why?

"Because if Rachel Farr has a motive to lie, then Chico Moody could be innocent." DAs don't speak of innocence very often. Being not guilty does not mean one is innocent; it means only that the prosecution could not prove the defendant guilty beyond a reasonable doubt.

Jurors Clayton, Becerril, Sobol, Takahashi, Bukust, and Richeson glanced at Stacy.

"This isn't a scientific case. There's little physical evidence of the crimes charged. What you will see is the most convincing, the most vital, the most vivid evidence in our world.

"That evidence, ladies and gentlemen, is Rachel Farr herself. As you watch and hear her testify, ask yourselves: Is she speaking from *conviction*? Do her quiet words ring true?

"Or does truth only come from adult voices?"

"Objection, Your Honor," said Stacy. "Counsel's arguing."

"Sustained," said Judge Maxwell. "Straight and narrow, Mr. Jin. This is not the time for argument." I had been arguing. I took a breath.

"I apologize, Your Honor. You will meet Rachel Farr and hear evidence about her schoolwork and evidence about the extraordinary changes that occurred in the late fall.

"Ladies and gentlemen, this is a moral evidence case with direct and circumstantial evidence. Don't be deceived by the media, which tends to knock 'circumstantial evidence' as if it were something flimsy or unreliable. The truth is quite different.

"The judge will later define 'circumstantial evidence' and tell you that circumstantial evidence is as good as direct. It is our good friend in deciding the truth of something."

"Objection," said Stacy.

"For quoting California Jury Instructions?" I said.

"Sustained," said Maxwell incorrectly.

All I had left were facial expressions. I saved them. "Here's what's interesting. Although Ms. August and I are on different sides, the evidence we both present, both mine and hers, will *prove* that Moody did the crimes charged."

"Objection, Your Honor," said Stacy. "DA is arguing."

"Sustained," said Judge Maxwell.

"You will," I said, "also hear evidence about motive, even though I am not required by law to prove motive. Members of the jury. This case is about *motive*.

"It's about circumstantial evidence. This case will be decided by your ability to tell the difference between lies and truth. And your *convictions* about what is right and what is wrong.

"Each of you assured me you'd be considerate and attentive to a teenage witness, a girl who will fear speaking in this room of strangers, who will fear what you think of her.

"The judge, Ms. August, and I are counting on your word. We should fear nothing—nothing but the truth *not* getting out.

"This child, Rachel Farr, should not, a few days from now, fear entering this court and speaking. I have no fear, because this court has your promise.

"The evidence you are about to hear will prove that Chico Moody sexually assaulted the child, Rachel Farr." I looked at the fourteen of them. "Ms. August will now have a chance to address you. The People thank you for your attention."

The jury had listened. I had not broken down. There were no bad signs. They were becoming a unit.

Stacy August moved to center stage under modern circular ceiling lights that highlighted her elegance, her smooth movements. She touched the railing of the jury box, an intimate courtroom move I normally would not attempt until the latter half of the trial. The box is a private space belonging to the jury, and only a Stacy August could enter it so easily. Her hands were those of the Pietà, dancing on the wood, adding tactility to her compelling voice.

"May it please the Court. Ladies and gentlemen. I confess. I *love* listening to Mr. Jin's great voice." She made a fist and pumped it a little. "He has an authority to his diction, a rightness about his presence." She was arguing. So had I. She looked at the women.

"Luckily, it will take a great deal more than a man's deep voice to decide this case. What will decide it? Your good judgment, your common sense, your ability to tell right from wrong. All your life experience is here in this courtroom." Her voice rang clearly in my ears.

"Mr. Jin said that you will see 'little physical evidence.' He advances the notion of charity. What he meant was, you will see *no physical evidence.*" She leaned forward and almost whispered, "All you will hear is a lost, confused, and dishonest girl's accusation."

"Objection, Your Honor," I said, standing. "Counsel is arguing the victim is not to be believed, and she hasn't even been sworn yet. Counsel isn't arguing *her* case. She's arguing *mine.* And frankly, I don't like how she's doing it."

"Well, no harm in that, Mr. Jin," the judge said. "Sit."

Stacy looked at me. So did most of the jurors.

"Ladies and gentlemen," she continued, "this is a place for truth, for truth-telling and truth-knowing. Yet you will hear lies. Lies which will sicken you and fill you with doubts about what is true and what is not.

"I am going to say very little right now. Mr. Jin spoke longer because he has a small case. I need say nothing at all; this case is exclusively his burden. But the truth will not come from the weakness of the prosecution's evidence. The strength of the defense will say it all.

"What can you expect to see and hear in this trial? You will see righteous anger from the defense. You will hear undeniable truth from the defense.

"You will meet Mr. Karl Moody and have a chance to judge his truthfulness against that of the so-called victim and judge who is the true victim in this case."

My heart lifted: Moody was going to testify. We had a chance.

"Under the laws dictated by the Constitution of the United States, Mr. Moody sits before you as a perfectly innocent man. This is the cornerstone of American law. If you had the *slightest* inclination to believe the DA's insinuations, and now sit here, in this court, harboring a sentiment that Mr. Moody might be guilty, you must dispel that thought this instant, or leave.

"Under those same laws, the defense need not utter *one word* against the accusations of the prosecution." She pointed at me.

"The DA has to prove everything—*every thing*—beyond— *beyond*—a reasonable doubt. But you will feel no truth, no resonating sense that his artful bag of tricks represents reality. Not reality as you and I know it." She was arguing. The jury was listening. I let it go.

"You will hear truth. It will come from the defense. It will come from an innocent man."

She stood tall and lovely, the goddess of justice with her beauty and anger and a cadence that mesmerized, and I regretted for a moment not being on her side.

"When you *feel* and *grasp* that truth, and know its weight and texture, you will *acquit* Mr. Moody and feel anger—anger at his false accuser." She pointed at the door through which Rachel would walk. Stacy's voice rang in the courtroom. Mrs. Aldo had put down her needlepoint and the reporters weren't breathing. My pulse was up.

The jury stirred, aroused, motivated. She straightened. "The DA is under pressure to convict an innocent man because of an oncoming election—"

"Objection! Your Honor, that's intolerable—"

"Overruled and sit down, Mr. Jin," said Judge Maxwell.

"But you and I," said Stacy, "are far above politics. We have a calling to identify truth, to be utterly intolerant of those who would promote false accusations. Those who would spin lies. Those who would use us for political purposes. Do not blame Mr. Jin. This is not about blame. This is about doing your sacred duty—by quickly and firmly acquitting an innocent man.

"You are the chosen. My client and I depend upon you. Upon your wisdom. An innocent man has been brought before you. Remember that. Never forget that."

In the hush, she sat. Phillips Rittenhouse was a face on Rushmore, noble and posed for photo ops, flattered to be next to a woman who could throw verbal thunderbolts that left scorched air and ozone and who sowed reasonable doubts like an International Harvester.

"Thank you, Ms. August. The People may call their first witness." Maxwell smiled at me.

45.

KIMBERLEY HONG

"The People call Ms. Kimberley Hong."

As Ava had suggested, she wore a mid-knee navy suit with short heels. I saw her through Anglo eyes: if Hong testified about DNA or serology, the jury would believe her with ease. But they'd distrust her as a counselor, as an English wordsmith. They'd suspect an Eastern collusion. Questioning Asian witnesses had normally worked to my benefit. With a Chinese counselor in a child rape case in which the victim was an Anglo girl, it would not.

Liz Heck said, "Raise your right hand. Do you solemnly swear the testimony you are about to give shall be the truth, the whole truth, and nothing but the truth, so help you God?"

"I do."

"Please state your full name and spell your last name."

"Kimberley Yuan Chun Hong. H-O-N-G."

Ms. Hong sat. I asked the warm-ups. She worked for the Sacramento Unified School District as a counselor at Rio Junior High in the Broadway, Chinatown. She had worked there for eight years. She knew Rachel Farr. Rachel was a seventh grader at Rio. I questioned Hong as she glanced at Karl Francis Moody, ready to send him a bad-luck, go-to-hell, Chinese look.

"At the first grading period, Rachel was only marginal with a high-D average." She was calm and professional.

"Ms. Hong, to the best of your knowledge, did Rachel have a close relationship with any teacher in Rio Junior High?"

"Quite the opposite. Several of us tried, but she was not interested. We also tried to connect with her parents, her stepmother, to no avail." She gave a hard, hostile glance at

Dierdre Farr, confirming for the jury the identity of Rachel's stepmother.

"Is it your job, Ms. Hong, to assist students like Rachel?"

"Yes, it is."

"Is it your job to assess why a student such as Rachel has academic difficulties?"

"Yes, certainly."

"If you formed an opinion about Rachel, please share it."

"Objection," said Stacy. "Calls for an expert opinion."

"An opinion, Your Honor, which the witness—"

"Sustained," said Maxwell. "Move on, Mr. Jin."

"Please describe," I said, "Rachel's physical appearance in the beginning of the year."

"Objection, Your Honor," said Stacy. "Irrelevant."

"This," I said, "goes to the heart of the People's case. The victim's condition before the events of February are highly relevant since they show her status before the attack."

"Sustained," the judge said. "Let's proceed, Mr. Jin."

"Your Honor, permission to approach the bench," I said.

"Denied. Proceed."

The law did not matter and Maxwell was going to slam my case with every evidentiary motion that came his way. I smiled to relax Ms. Hong.

"Was Rachel in school from February one through eleven?"

"No. She was absent. Her absence was brought to my attention by the attendance clerk and the principal, Mr. Engeln."

"Did you see her on February the twelfth?"

"Yes, I did."

"What time of day was that?"

"It was a Wednesday, late first period, around eight-thirty. Rachel's English teacher sent Rachel to my office."

"How did Rachel Farr appear to you?"

"Oh, I was very shocked. She looked terrible, a mess, hair untended. Her eyes were blackened." She gestured to her face. "You know, from hitting."

"Objection," said Stacy. "Speculation by the witness."

"Sustained," the judge said.

I nodded. I had asked Ms. Hong not to guess about the cause of Rachel's injuries.

"Ms. Hong, what else did you observe?"

She twisted in the chair. "Rachel's face was cut. On her temples. Her cheek. Her chin. She limped badly." The stress of testifying was impairing Kimberley Hong's eloquence. "Her English teacher said she had been crying—"

"Objection," said Stacy quickly. "Hearsay."

"It is not hearsay," I said. "The question does not go to the truth of the matter asserted. It only goes to reflect the state of mind of this witness. It doesn't mean Rachel was crying."

"Sustained," said Maxwell. "Jury will disregard this witness's last remark."

"Please describe Rachel's affect."

Kimberley took a deep breath, scared, not for herself, but for me and for her student. I was afraid she would try harder.

"It's okay, Ms. Hong. Just tell us what you remember."

"Rachel cried constantly. She had trouble not crying. She cried so much, I cried." She blinked to contain tears. I said with my eyes: Be strong for Rachel. Ms. Hong shuddered.

"Ms. Hong, what, if anything, did Rachel tell you?"

"Rachel said nothing. Nothing at all."

I approached the counsel table. "Your Honor, I have a poster with fifteen photos, previously shown to the defense. Permission to have it marked as People's One for identification."

Maxwell looked at Stacy, who nodded that she had seen it.

"Very well."

I took it to the clerk. Liz Heck labeled it with an evidence exhibit sticker, Exhibit 1.

"Ms. Hong," I said, placing the poster on the easel so it was visible to her, the jury, the judge, and opposing counsel. "I show you what has been marked as People's One for identification. Please tell the court what this is."

"It's a poster with pictures I took of Rachel Farr, at school, from May second until June sixth. She is standing in the schoolyard, holding a newspaper that shows the day's date. I used a Polaroid. On the bottom margin, I wrote her weight that day."

"Please examine the handwriting on the bottom and tell us whose handwriting it is."

"It's mine. With my chop."

"Please explain what a chop is."

"It is a Chinese stamp, a seal, of my name, made by pressing a carved, red-inked stone block on paper. It is a unique mark, a personal imprint. Like a signature."

My next question would draw an objection.

Instead of facing Hong, I approached the box and looked at the jury. "Ms. Hong, how much did Rachel weigh on May second?"

"Objection," said Stacy. She saw that some of the jurors—Clayton, Goin—the whole first row and half of the second—everyone but Carlo, Juror Ten—were frowning at her. They wanted to hear the witness's answer.

"I withdraw the objection, Your Honor," said Stacy. No lawyer was clearer about whom to please in trial. Many lawyers play to imaginary appellate judges and absent law professors, to the observing press or a family member in the gallery. Some strive for points against the opposing lawyer. Stacy was focused on the jury, the decision-makers, the verdict-holders.

I looked at Mr. Clayton, Juror One. "Ms. Hong, you may answer my question. How much did she weigh on May second?"

Kimberley Hong looked at the May 2 photo. "On May two, Rachel Farr weighed one hundred and eleven pounds."

"How much did she weigh on June 13?"

"One hundred and one."

"You are saying she lost ten pounds in six weeks?"

"Yes."

"Please estimate, for the jury, Rachel Farr's weight in the beginning of this school year."

"Objection," said Stacy. "That was ruled irrelevant."

"Only her condition, Your Honor. Not her weight."

I saw Clayton's eyes. I think the jury wanted the answer. Stacy didn't. Maxwell was caught. "Hm," he said.

"Answer the question, Ms. Hong," I said.

"Objection!" cried Stacy.

"A hundred and twenty to a hundred twenty-five pounds," said Ms. Hong quickly.

"Objection!" said Stacy. "Move that the last response be stricken from the record and the jury instructed to disregard it."

"Sustained," said Finley Maxwell. "Members of the jury, you will disregard the last answer. Reporter, strike it."

Rebecca Coggins nodded, crossing out the last answer.

"Mr. Jin," the judge said, "you risk a mistrial here!"

The words startled the jury, who cancelled their expressions, looking at me and giving me a tactical opening. Stacy could only guess if they wanted an answer. Eyes on the jury and Mrs. Burda, the picture-framer, the mother of a nine-year-old daughter.

"Ms. Hong, how much does Rachel weigh now?"

"Objection, irrelevant," said Stacy.

"Sustained."

"Ms. Hong, did you ever see Rachel actually *eat* a lunch, after missing those seven days of school in February?"

"Objection," said Stacy without standing. "Irrelevant."

"Sustained," the judge said.

Mrs. Burda looked at Judge Maxwell. I looked at Mrs. Wolstoncroft, mother of an eight-year-old girl. "In the beginning of the school year, did you ever see Rachel eat lunch?"

"Objection, irrelevant." Stacy.

"Sustained." Maxwell.

"Did you ever see Rachel with friends—"

"Objection, irrelevant," said Stacy clearly and without regret.

"Sustained." Maxwell.

Mrs. Wolstoncroft frowned. I kept my eyes on her. "Your Honor, the People, in opening statement, said the jury would learn about the victim's condition at the beginning of the school year but that changes would occur. There was no objection. You and the defense deemed it then relevant. Nothing is more probative than the victim's physical condition prior to the trauma, to be compared to her status afterwards. Now that I'm securing sworn testimony—"

"Enough, Mr. Jin. Move on."

"Your Honor, you're not allowing the People to present its case. The case which this court said I could."

"That's enough, Mr. Jin! Stifle yourself this moment!"

Kimberley Hong's face was red. Why are they doing this?

I turned. Softly, "Ms. Hong, after seeing Rachel's physical condition on the morning of February twelve—bruising, cuts, limping—and her emotional state, what did you do?"

"I took her to the Medical Center ER."

"Did Rachel go willingly?"

"Not really. She didn't want to. I think she was afraid."

"Objection, speculative."

"Sustained."

I nodded. "In seven years of counseling at Rio Junior High, how many times have you taken a child to an emergency room?"

"Only once. Rachel Farr."

"Thank you, Ms. Hong, let's quit while we're ahead."

"I don't find that very amusing, Mr. Jin," the judge said.

"Nor I, Your Honor." To Ms. Hong: "I have no further questions. Ms. Hong, the defense now has a turn to talk to you." I sat. I saw, in the back of the courtroom, Geneva de Hoyas.

"Ms. Hong," said Stacy August from the table, "what percentage of Rio's student body is at academic risk?"

"Approximately five percent."

"Compared to most schools, is that low or high?"

"Very low."

"What percentage of that five percent are Asian students?"

"Maybe half."

"And the other half, Ms. Hong? What ethnicity are they?"

"Mostly Caucasian."

"Isn't it a fact, Ms. Hong, that white students are the minority at Rio?"

I knew where she was headed. We would have to afford it.

"Yes."

"Do Asian students pick on whites?"

"Yes, although—"

Stacy stood. "Was Rachel particularly accepted by Asians?"

Kimberley Hong licked her lips. "No, but really, no—"

"Do fights ever occur in your school?"

"Yes."

"Do any of these fights involve females?"

"Some."

"Isn't it a fact that handguns have been found at Rio?"

"Yes, but—"

"Ms. Hong, are you an expert in emergency medicine?"

"No."

"So, you couldn't tell *what* injuries Rachel had, if any, or *when* the injuries occurred, or *how* they occurred, much less *who* inflicted them?" A compound question. I didn't object.

"No."

"Ms. Hong, I couldn't help but observe how you looked at Mr. Moody, the defendant, while you were answering Mr. Jin's questions. Do you not like the defendant?"

"No, I do not."

"Based on your *personal knowledge—that which you have personally observed*—what has Mr. Moody done to Rachel?"

She licked her lips. "Nothing," she said softly.

"But you've made up your mind quite irreversibly, haven't you? No further questions."

"Redirect, Mr. Jin?" asked Maxwell.

"Yes, Your Honor. Ms. Hong, you were cut off from answering, 'Do Asian students pick on whites?' What's the whole answer?"

"We had two incidents last year. This year, none. It's not a problem. The violence is not in Rio. It is in the streets, in the Broadway. The gangs are not in school—they're on the street. They gang-bang full-time. They don't come to class and they are not allowed on campus."

"To your knowledge, did Rachel ever associate with gangs?"

"Objection, beyond the scope of direct."

"Your Honor, defense tried to link Rachel Farr to violence."

"Sustained," said Maxwell. "Move on, Counselor."

"Rachel Farr ever involved in a fight or with guns?"

"Absolutely not."

"Ms. Hong, are you aware of the state's mandatory child abuse reporting statute?"

"Yes. If we see injured students, we have to report it. We have to do something."

"Thank you, Ms. Hong. I have no further questions."

"Re-cross, Ms. August? Miss, you may stand down." Maxwell ogled Hong as she stood. Some women jurors noticed.

Hong, clutching a red good-luck purse, took a step, then stood tall. "Someone hurt Rachel very badly! They *meant* to hurt her! She's a good girl who needs kindness! Not this! She's a good girl, not a gang-banger!"

"Good Lord, contempt!" bellowed Maxwell. "You are outrageous and you are fined five hundred dollars for disrupting the order of this court. Bailiff, escort her instantly to payment."

I stood near Ms. Hong, who shook with anger. "My fault, Your Honor, for failing to instruct the witness regarding court conduct. The contempt is mine, not hers."

"Good, Mr. Jin, I find *you* in contempt as well. A thousand dollars or a night in jail." A deal; a penny more and the contempt would be reported to the disciplinary arm of the State Bar of California, which licensed all lawyers. "Choose."

If I paid a grand, I'd look like a fat-cat lawyer. I earned a fourth of Stacy's salary. "A night in jail, Your Honor." The jury looked at me with something approaching admiration. Stacy saw it.

"Your Honor," she said, "I am moved to ask for clemency for my distinguished opponent. He was only trying."

"And for Ms. Hong," I added. "Because she was as well."

Maxwell steamed until he saw the print reporters in the back. "Miss Hong," he said, "because of the generosity of the defense, you are excused with a warning." Then, I think, he remembered that Miss Hong could vote. "The court appreciates your time. Mr. Jin, we approach the noon hour. Court will recess until one-thirty. Jurors, no discussion of the case and no fraternizing with the lawyers or witnesses." He gaveled and we stood.

I was supposed to be composed, but I felt like punching out a judge. I imagined what he'd be like when Rachel took the stand.

"I hate these people," hissed Ms. Hong. "How can you work with them?"

46.

THE SANER

Killian Boyce was a nurse practitioner SANER, Sexual Assault Nurse Examiner, at UCD Medical Center. Medium height, brown hair, an athletic stride. She wore a pearl blouse, a long earth-toned skirt, a necklace, and light makeup on a strong, open, angular freckled face that had seen too much sun. I jostled past the press to her. "Can we do lunch?" I asked.

We went to China Moon Café by the Confucius Temple, where a square block of Asian businesses are framed by curving, hot, green Chinese roofs and gray, squat stone temple lion dogs with imperial postures and ferocious snarls.

She had tomato beef. I had vegetarian *chow fun* and medicinal green tea. "We have Maxwell. He's turned rogue, anti-child, and anti-DA."

"How bad is it?" She put down her chopsticks.

"As bad as anything you've seen outside of ER. We just have to bash on. I wanted to warn you about Maxwell, but this isn't about him. It's about us. I'm not going to let him get to me, and you're just going to tell the truth, calmly, competently. Watch out for Stacy August. She's good. Be strong and patient. No anger. Show Maxwell how his court ought to be run."

I did not have to establish Boyce as an expert witness; Finley Maxwell and Stacy, to save time, had accepted the stipulation that she was one. An expert witness can be asked leading questions on direct exam. An expert witness can render opinions on hypothetical situations. I could ask the questions that were not permitted with Ms. Hong. Juries highly respect experts. But I would miss Dr. Karenga, the expert on rape trauma syndrome.

Killian Boyce was an experienced forensic expert. She calmly focused on me and ignored Karl Moody's heavy dark eyes, the judge's hostility, and Stacy August's wardrobe.

"I remember her vividly. Rachel was one of the most frightened girls I have ever seen."

"What did that mean to you, clinically?" I asked.

"That something terrible had happened to her, which complicates the interventions. It was critical to assure the patient that she was safe. But this girl never relaxed. Never trusted."

"What else did you notice at the outset?"

"Cuts, bruises, and trauma were approximately a week to ten days old. Shock was still in progress. This suggested a 'blitz' rape—sudden, overwhelming physical violence that accompanies the sexual attack or attacks, causing profound and long-term emotional trauma."

"What is the protocol for examining someone like Rachel?"

"Get her into seclusion. Explain that we needed to do a general physical exam to collect evidence in case she wanted to pursue her assailant in court. I said it would be uncomfortable, but she'd be safe and I'd be gentle. I asked if she wanted her parents or a relative present. Rachel wouldn't even shake her head."

Dierdre Farr, in an aisle seat, crossed her legs and looked at her nails.

"Please tell the jury what you then did."

"I asked Rachel what happened. She didn't say anything. I tried simple questions. 'Are you okay? Where does it hurt? Do you know what time it is?' She was really shut down."

"At the same time, were you observing her?"

"I always do. May I refer to my chart notes?" Killian Boyce explained her records. Stacy had no objection. Boyce refreshed her memory, then: "I observed a pronounced limp suggesting strain of the lower erector spinae—low back muscles—and quadricep adductors—the muscles of the inner thigh, and the frontal hip flexors. Those are muscles you don't want to pull. Those injuries are consistent with resistance to rape. I observed contusions and cuts on her face consistent with being struck, a week to ten days before."

"That would've put it around the first of February?"

"Yes."

"Did these injuries appear to have occurred at the same time or at different times?"

"They appeared to have occurred at the same time."

"Ms. Boyce, what do rape victims usually tell you?"

"The facts," said Killian Boyce. "What. Where, when, who. What orifices were penetrated or attempted for entry. Whether he ejaculated. If evidence was thrown away or clothes changed. Bathing, cleaning, since the assault. Other injuries, bleeding, pain. Threats, weapons, restraints. I take a full gynecologic, menstrual, and sexual experience history, up to the moment she came to the Med Center." She spoke clinically. The jury did not stir.

"I usually photograph the clothing. I asked Rachel, 'When did this happen?' She gave no response. I kept trying, using different dates, but she never answered. I asked, 'Were you wearing these clothes? Have you anything from that day with you, now?'

"At least, then, she shook her head. I took no photos. Did no labeling."

"Did you ask her about bathing since the attack?"

"Objection." Stacy. "No foundation there was an attack."

"Immaterial, Your Honor," I said. "Ms. Boyce is explaining a procedure that occurs, unfortunately, thousands of times every day in this country. Under the defense's fanciful objection, no prosecutor could bring in any evidence in any court."

"Rephrase your question, Mr. Jin," said Maxwell.

"Ms. Boyce, did you ask Rachel about bathing?"

"I asked if she had bathed since the attack. She nodded. Then she nodded again. I asked if she had scrubbed herself. She nodded, long and slow."

"What did this mean to you?"

"It meant Rachel had bathed hard, two or more times, and that given the passage of time, there was no evidentiary value in taking oral or anal swabs. Or fingernail scrapings or clippings, in case she had scratched her assailant. Or combing her pubic hair for the attacker's pubic hair or clothing fiber. Or scanning her body and genitalia with a Woods lamp. She had washed the evidence away."

"Objection, Your Honor." Stacy. "Presuming there *was* evidence, when it seems very clear that we have no idea."

"Sustained." Maxwell was getting his lines down.

"Did you," I asked, "look at her skin at this point?"

"Yes. I saw ample signs of hard, repetitive, abrasive cleansing that's typical of females after they've been raped. I also saw hints of residual bruising."

I waited for the objection. Silence. "What did you do next?"

"I tried to conduct a pelvic examination."

"Why?"

"Rachel's injuries and affect—her demeanor—the weeping, the distrust, the failure to respond. The closing of her legs, the pronounced limping, the pattern of muscular trauma, the shock, the anxiety, depression, disorganized thinking, were consistent with post-traumatic stress disorder. I believed that she had been beaten and sexually attacked. SANERS can *smell* trouble in patients. And I smelled it in her. Rape victims have a sad odor that comes—"

"Objection." Stacy. "We're in Disneyland now."

"Your Honor," I said, "it is well established that professionals in many fields utilize the sense of smell as an indicator of status—a highway patrolman who smells alcohol on the breath of a weaving driver. An MD who smells acidosis in a patient. An oncology nurse who smells cancer in necrotic tissue. A juror who smells a lie coming from a witness. And this is not Disneyland. It's *Friday the Thirteenth*. Ms. Boyce is a trauma care professional with twenty years' experience with thousands of hurting and needy patients."

"It is unscientific, Your Honor," said Stacy.

"Sustained," said Maxwell.

"Ms. Boyce, what is a colposcope?" I would now use her name to open each question in an effort to establish a missing rhythm.

"A high-tech, fiber-optic exam camera capable of finding minute tears in the vagina."

"Ms. Boyce, in a conventional rape victim of Rachel's age and experience, what would a colposcope detect?"

"I would expect to find hymenal irregularity, meaning the vagina was traumatized. I would expect to see persistent clefts in the posterior location of the vagina, which is consistent with forcible penetration. I would then take blood for type, Rh, pregnancy, syphilis, gonorrhea, chlamydia. I would recommend an AIDS test."

"Ms. Boyce, did you conduct a pelvic exam of Rachel Farr?"

"No, I did not."

"Why is that?"

"Rachel reacted very badly when I showed the colposcope. I was explaining its use, and she broke down and tried to leave the exam room."

"What emotions did you observe in her at that time?"

"Fear. Deep, clutching fear."

Boyce testified that for that reason, she couldn't conduct a rectal exam or get a blood sample. Rachel refused an antibiotics prescription for STD prophylaxis to prevent sexually transmitted diseases. Boyce said it was common for rape victims to behave traumatically.

Stacy objected to the last answer and it was stricken.

"Ms. Boyce, how many rape exams have you conducted?"

"Approximately a thousand."

"Estimate how many times, in your experience, a child rape victim refused the colposcope because of pain or fear."

A shrug. "Twenty times."

"So, Ms. Boyce, it happens?"

"Yes, sir, it sure does."

"Ms. Boyce, are you trained in observing patient affect—the demeanor, the presentation, the appearance of patients?"

"Yes. Patient affect is an indicator of condition."

"Ms. Boyce, have you been trained in observing the affect of juvenile rape victims?"

"Yes, sir, I have. I took initial course work for my degree. And I have taken continuing professional education courses that have taught that."

"Ms. Boyce, was there anything in the affect of Rachel Farr that was *inconsistent* with her having been raped?"

"Objection, speculation." Phillips Rittenhouse, a different voice, pitched the interruption, fast and high in voice. The jury turned to look at him instead of focusing on the witness.

"Opinion is allowed from an expert witness," I said.

"You haven't established," said Maxwell, "any expert here."

"Your Honor," I said, "the parties stipulated that Ms. Boyce was an expert, with your concurrence, this morning."

"Ms. August, do you recall me *signing* a stipulation?"

He hadn't signed it. He had only said he would. She shook her head.

"Request permission," I said, "to voir dire and establish Ms. Boyce's foundation as an expert witness."

"Little late, now, Counselor. Denied," said Maxwell.

I fought the impulse to call him a fraud. I had to set the example for my witness.

Calmly, "Ms. Boyce, did you treat Rachel as if she had been raped?"

"Yes, because everything I know told me she had been."

"Thank you, Ms. Boyce. No further questions."

Stacy August studied Killian Boyce for a moment. "Ms. Boyce, did you author an article on sexual assault nurse examining in *American Journal of Nursing*, volume ninety-seven?"

"Yes, ma'am."

I pulled the article. I had no idea where Stacy was headed.

"In this article, Ms. Boyce, you covered a lot of topics. But isn't it true that not *one* involved false rape claims?"

"I have—"

"Answer the question, please. Yes or no."

"Objection," I said, standing. "Counsel isn't even allowing the witness to answer before she corrects her for not answering."

"I daresay you're not helping matters, Mr. Jin. Sit down. The witness will answer."

Stacy August slowly left the table, approaching the witness.

"That is correct," said Boyce. "Our operative problem is

the thousands of women and girls and infants who are being raped. Our problem is not false claims."

"But you wrote nothing about a false claim? Or fraud on a hospital? About a misguided teen making a false rape claim and maintaining it by refusing a pelvic exam? Nothing—"

"Objection, Your Honor," I said. "Compound question."

"I'll allow it, overruled," said Maxwell.

"No, no, no," said Boyce. "To each of those questions."

Stacy held clasped hands at elbow level. "The injuries for which Rachel refused your treatment—were they serious?"

"I couldn't be certain because she never undressed."

" 'Couldn't be certain because she never undressed.' Ms. Boyce, isn't it true that you have *no idea* how Rachel got those bruises?"

"Quite the contrary, ma'am. I have a very good idea."

"But you said you couldn't be certain."

"It's true, I'm not certain."

"She could have fallen down stairs?" Brilliant: domestic violence caused Rachel's injuries. Not Moody; it was her parents.

"No. Her facial bruising and obvious internal injuries were inconsistent with a fall."

"You say this without her having undressed?"

"Her face wasn't clothed. I saw her limp."

"A limp could be faked. But you stated you didn't see her injuries."

"Objection, argumenta—"

"Sit down, Mr. Jin," the judge said. "Witness will answer."

"Argumentative." I sat. Maxwell glared at me.

"I saw *some* of her injuries. They were consistent with—"

"Ms. Boyce, have you *ever* testified for the defense?"

"No, ma'am."

Stacy took three, four steps toward the witness. "But am I to understand that you hold yourself out to be objective?"

"Objection, Your Honor, argumentative," I said.

"Overruled. Interesting question. Witness may answer."

"Interesting or not, Your Honor, priests don't testify against their penitents, drug dealers don't invite cops to their weddings, and SANERs don't testify against their patients."

"Overruled and sit," the judge said.

"I'm objective about my patients and their care. I am not on the district attorney's side. I am on Rachel's. I was responsible for not being able to do a pelvic. She was just a child and I—"

"Did Rachel's hysteria frustrate you from doing your job?"

"She was hardly hysterical."

"She showed emotional control?"

"Yes."

"Which suggests, if you will, no trauma, correct?"

"Not correct. I—"

"Have you ever seen someone mimicking a rape victim?"

"Yes, I have."

"How can you tell a real victim from a fake?"

"Patient affect, emotional state, physical condition, reaction to examination, quality of responsiveness. Our business is patients."

"How many times has a fake victim act tricked you?"

"As far as I know, never."

"But if you had been tricked, you wouldn't know, would you?"

"Ma'am, I think I could tell."

"Ms. Boyce, I wonder how. Could Rachel have mimicked the affect of a rape victim?"

"Objection, Your Honor," I said. "Calls for speculation."

"Overruled," said Maxwell. "Witness may answer."

"It's possible, but not likely," said Boyce.

"But you have *no idea* if she was telling the truth."

"I didn't say that." Color in Boyce's cheeks.

"On the contrary," said Stacy August, "I think you did."

"Objection," I said. "Counsel's twisting witness's words."

"Overruled."

"Ms. Boyce," said Stacy, "what was Rachel's sexual history?"

The question beyond the scope of direct and argumentative. If I objected, I'd imply that the victim had been sexually active—which was irrelevant. Nonvirgins were equally entitled to protection of the law. And I would be overruled. If I didn't object, it'd have the same effect, but I'd be rolling over for an unfair court. He was letting a child be slurred because he was a turd.

"I didn't get her history," said Ms. Boyce.

"In your opinion, was Rachel Farr a virgin?"

"I object, Your Honor. That's as useful to this case as asking if there were anything which suggested she had been a gambler in Monaco. It's irrelevant and prejudicial to a child."

"Overruled."

"Was she?" asked Stacy.

"I have no way of knowing."

"Let me sum up. Isn't it true you *saw* not *one* iota of retainable physical evidence that Rachel Farr was raped? Yes or no."

Ms. Boyce sighed. "Yes."

"Isn't it true that she never said *a single* word about a rape or a sexual assault, or even a sexual *touching*? Yes or no."

"She didn't say a single word about anything."

"Exactly. Isn't it true that Rachel Farr could have had sexual relations with the entire United States Navy, and you would have no way of knowing?"

"That is not true."

Judge Finley Maxwell appeared to be watching, but his mind was dozing. Moody was watching Stacy work the SANER. He loved it. The jury watched Stacy and Boyce.

"Ms. Boyce, you saw a girl who had been scratched, who refused to make a statement or allow an exam, and you concluded, from this, that she had been raped? Yes or no."

"Yes. Absolutely."

"Oh, '*absolutely*'? 'Absolutely'? I offer a hypothetical—"

"Your Honor," I said, "you and I know very well that Ms. Boyce is a *de facto* expert. In my copy of the Evidence Code, only *experts* can answer hypotheticals. A few minutes ago, you ruled that Ms. Boyce was NOT an expert for the People. So obviously you *cannot* rule now that she's an expert for the defense. Under your ruling, the defense can't have it both ways."

Maxwell said, "I'll let her answer this one hypothetical. Overruled."

Using discipline, I closed my gaping jaw. I let the jury see that the trial was not proceeding according to Hoyle. Or Blackstone. Or the law. I nodded grimly and sat. The office was filled with stories of legendarily bad judges and astoundingly foul rulings. Now I had one I could tell. But we were paid to be purveyors of hope. I would be hopeful.

Stacy said, "Ms. Boyce, a female patient arrives in ER with her mother with bite marks on her face, and says she's been raped—"

Maxwell was falling asleep. "Objection, Your Honor," I said. "Unclear in this hypothetical, for the expert witness, if the mother has bite marks or the daughter."

Maxwell jerked, eyeballs rolling. "Overruled." No English accent. The jury noticed.

"This hypothetical girl," said Stacy, "is examined by colposcope. You find hymenal irregularities, anterior vaginal clefts, semen, and pubic hairs, not hers, and a man's DNA under her fingernails. How do you *feel* then, Ms. Boyce, about rape, if not *'absolutely'* certain?"

"I feel—"

"I'm sure you do. No further questions." Stacy walked away.

"Redirect," I said. Maxwell nodded.

"Ms. Boyce, with no physical evidence, how'd you figure Rachel to be a rape victim?"

"Objection," said Stacy. "Asked and answered."

"Your Honor, I asked this question on direct. Defense tried to impeach the answer during cross. I am now rehabilitating."

"Rephrase it, Mr. Jin."

"Ms. Boyce, what diagnosis did you make of Rachel Farr on February the twelfth?"

"She had been raped and beaten in a physically violent, traumatic blitz attack. At least."

"On a scale of one to ten, with ten being absolute certainty, what's your confidence in that diagnosis?"

"Eight point five," she said.

"Thank you. No further questions."

Stacy stood. "Re-cross, Your Honor? Ms. Boyce, your 'diagnosis' of Rachel Farr—was it based on a physical exam?"

"No."

"So your *opinions* regarding Rachel Farr's clinical condition in February are based on mere deduction?"

She paused. "Yes."

Stacy nodded at the bench. She was done.

"Further direct," I said. I wanted Boyce to state the high reliability of a nursing opinion based on observation.

Maxwell announced, "It is time to recess for the day. I think this witness has been sufficiently harried by the legal system. Witness may stand down. Jurors, I remind you of admonitions about silence on this case, and no socializing with the lawyers."

We stood.

François handed me a piece of paper. I moved my water glass back from the edge.

I was hoping for word on Moody's mystery alibi witness. The paper was an invoice from Obstain Private Investigations, charging me for the unsuccessful search for John Quick, Moody's alibi.

47.

NEXT WITNESS

Thursday

I was trying to prove Ava's theme that Rachel Farr had lost more than weight—she had lost everything. Health. Grades. Relationships. School. Friends. Appetite, meals, nutrition.

I called six of Rachel's teachers, junior high and elementary school, to index the strength of her relationships, but Stacy's objections kept half of their data out of evidence.

I noted the number of contacts with Rachel, by month, on a flip chart visible to the court, creating a graph.

Rachel's four friends testified from those years. They spoke of her shyness and her privacy in sharing personal feelings, prior to February. About her lunch and eating habits. Her small circle of strong acquaintances. Their testimony became small red dots on charts.

To energize the jury and hold its attention, I moved the witnesses in and out of the stand quickly.

Small things were happening: jurors acknowledged each other during breaks. Learned each other's names. Looked at each other during testimony. Took notes. Goin started to doze and Clayton nudged him. Richards cried and Carlo passed a Kleenex. The three women I had questioned as a group— Takahashi, Richards, and Becerril—were becoming a mini-community. As were Burda, Sobol, and Wolstoncroft, Jurors Three, Five, and Six, seated to my right in the first row. The three divorced jurors, Eight, Nine, and Ten, were curiously seated together.

Judge Maxwell liked a four-thirty quitting time. He shut me down at four.

Rachel would be tomorrow's first witness. The thought made my guts weak. I reminded myself that questioning her in Rag's Gym was not so hard. Neither was putting her on the stand in a relatively empty prelim courtroom. Asking her questions in front of a jury would constrict most adults and terrify her. And that would precede Fin Maxwell and Stacy August sticking their pitchforks in her. One more time, Rachel.

One more time, Sum. Just one more surgery. Do it for Daddy.

"Court is recessed until nine a.m. tomorrow." We stood.

"You look perturbed," said Stacy as we filed our papers.

"In two days, you've made fifty objections in bad faith. Smut-raked a child's sexual history. Failed to set the record straight with the Boyce stipulation. Fabricated objections to the testimony of teachers and students. Good days for the law, fortifying my faith in our system."

"I'm fighting for a man's life," she said. "Maybe I owe you one."

"You can't trade ethical points like they were mutual funds. 'I got away with something this time, so I'll let you get away with something next time.' If the public heard it, our popularity would plummet from the bottom."

Stacy closed her briefcase and handed it to Phillips Rittenhouse. She leaned forward, her face close to mine, almost crossing her eyes as she looked in mine. "Joshua, you forget what side has the evidence. And I think you would hate happiness if it kissed your sweet rear."

"I'll tell you what happiness is," I said. "Happiness is a conviction on all counts and full-force consecutive sentencing on upper terms on child molesters. Fin Maxwell and your client can kiss my sweet rear."

48.

RUNAWAY

Ava's voice spoke to me from voice mail.

"Josh, Ava. It's three-thirty. I'm on I-80 at West Sac. I dropped Rachel at Rio for school. She wasn't there at three and Kimberley Hong says she missed all classes. I'll be home in fifteen minutes to see if she's there. I'll call. Hope nothing's wrong with Rachel. Bye." A beep.

"Josh, Rachel's not here. She took everything—toiletries, clothes, and Miss Piggy. She left the blue trial dress and shoes. No note. I think she kept the house key and probably has about five bucks. I'm checking the bus station. It's four-fifteen. Call me on my cellular." Beep.

"No luck downtown. The Sac bus runs every half hour. My guess is she's in Sac. I'm driving your Porsche. I'll meet you at Intake. Wait for me or call me. It's four forty-six. Bye."

I called Ava as she pulled into downtown. I got François. He groaned, his young voice high and to the left. "Boss, it's that old Latin axiom of the law: 'E Pluribus Screwed.' "

"François, kids run to their friends. Check with Kimberley Hong, the Rio counselor. Find Rachel's buddies—Serena Wong, Mary Lee, Belinda Howell, and Art Chen. Wong and

Lee are in band. Chen's a soccer player, a goalie. If no luck, get Obstain and find her."

The jury had been impaneled in the presence of the defendant, so criminal jeopardy had been established. If I didn't make my case, now, before this jury, it'd be dismissed with prejudice and there could never be another jury trial. A second jury trial would be double jeopardy—a condition not allowed in American law. Once again, it was now or never.

Where was she? No cavalry—the DA chief of investigations had been informed that I was Typhoid Jack. Geneva would have a hoot and the cops didn't like us anymore. I called Wilma Debbin in police SACA. She was in court. I left a message.

"Wilma, this is Josh Jin. It's Thursday, four-fifty p.m. My victim in *Moody* is now a runaway. Please put her on the wire: Rachel Farr, thirteen. Five-one and a half. Hundred and ten pounds. Shoulder-length brown hair. Hold her and anyone with her as material witnesses." I gave the clothing description. "She's first witness, nine a.m. Department 49. My fear is, someone spooked her, she ran, and someone's snatched her. Forget politics—her life could be up for grabs. It's an emergency and she needs help. If you can't find her, you and Pico are my next witnesses in her place. I'm in Maxwell's court, getting hosed. Thanks." I left my number.

I called Victim-Witness and subpoenaed Wilma Debbin and/or Pico Larry for Department 49, *Moody,* by one-thirty tomorrow to testify. With the books missing, and their anger against our office, there had been no point to calling them. Now, I would have to use them to kill court time while we looked for Rachel. It was no way to run a well-orchestrated jury trial. It was judicial CPR.

I was usefully rubbing my face when someone knocked.

Jan Yanehiro, a San Francisco TV journalist.

"Hi, Josh. How about a short interview?"

I shook my head.

"Off the record?" she asked.

I nodded. "I have two minutes. Hardly worth your long drive up here."

"Have you lost your victim?" she asked. "I heard it go out on the police radio."

There were no secrets, only rumors, in the courthouse. "And I have to find her."

"Josh, we haven't really spoken since you fund-raised for Conover, four years ago. You know the case has drawn attention in San Francisco because you're Asian. Asian-Americans are looking at you as a role model. How much pressure does that add to your job?"

"Nothing, compared to not having a victim to testify."

She smiled. "Any advice for Asian-American kids interested in doing trial work?"

"Believe in what you do. Do it ethically. Serve your victims. Never give up."

"Media's saying this case will decide the DA election. Why do you think that's true?"

"Because the press says so. How are the kids?"

"They're good, Josh, thanks. Call me when you have some time." We shook.

Ava shut the door and offered me a bunch of bioflavonoid-rich red grapes and a bottle of cold filtered water. I ate the grapes and emptied the bottle. I thanked her.

"I like living in limbo," she said. "I can cook for three people, go out on dates with a silent, grumpy curfew from my ex-husband and feel sick because we've lost another girl."

I sighed. "I can't help it if none of the people you date are worthy of you."

"You can change things if you want," she said. "Where do you think Rachel is? And don't tell me, somewhere with nachos, Fruitopias, video games, a cute dog, and MTV."

"I asked her once to think of a kind and safe place. A place where she could talk to us. She said a park. She said, 'families. kids. playground. people. fruit stands. a park.' "

"Farmer's Market," said Ava. "Of course. I think she likes it there. If she likes anything." She looked at her watch. "I have to be home anyway, in case she comes back."

"Thanks, Ava."

"I like it when you say my name. Maybe I'll cook up some veggie stir-fry. For three."

"Good. Call me if you find her. I'll do the same."

"Where are you going?"

"West Sac. Bilinski said it's a runaway haven."

Ava shuddered. "The Chickenhawk Nation. Good luck. I hope you don't find her there. Hurry, Josh. Don't let Harry drive." She didn't kiss me good-bye.

49.

WEST SAC

I called Harry Bilinski, recently released from the VA. He was listening to Dr. Laura, a principles-based radio adviser on life. I liked her. Most defendants didn't. He had the volume so high I could see Dr. Laura's tonsils.

"How are you doing?" I asked. "Can you turn that up? I can almost hear you."

He turned it down. "Jin, I'm so happy I could pass a big brick."

"That's pretty happy. Harry, tell me how you really are. Then I need your help."

"Who the fuck cares how I am?"

"I do."

"Which is why you only call when you fucking need something."

"Does it count if I was thinking about you?"

"Shit, Jin, you're sucking up like a politician."

I shook my head. "You really know how to hurt a guy. How are you doing, really?"

Pause. "I'm doin' better. I'm in a group. We talk."

"That's good, Harry."

"Yeah?" He laughed bitterly. "IA's after my ass cuz I shot a Ch—sorry, an Oriental, and you're glad. Here's how I grade out your communication, Counselor: *F* for bullshit."

"You said it was a justified shoot. The kid was armed, and you used to be a good cop. I count on that. And not your spelling abilities."

"Well, fuck, the good cop went south when the dream shit took over." He coughed. "Jin, I told the guys in the group. I woke up one morning and couldn't fucking move. Stuck to the sheets like an old stain, not one fuckin' funny left in the world. Aw, ferget it. Don't matter."

"And you didn't go get help."

"Aw, fuck you! Did YOU get help when you started cryin' like a baby in court and committin' whole-ass, second-degree political suicide in front a Conover?"

I thought. "No, I didn't. I guess you're right."

"You're damn right, I'm right. Enough patty-cake. What the fuck's happening with *Moody* and how's the girl?"

"I got Judge Maxwell, who's so ticked at Conover and so desperate for votes that he's nuking us. It's unbelievable. Rachel skipped. I need help finding her by nine a.m. tomorrow."

"What about Capri?"

"De Hoyas officially pulled her off. No help there."

"Tell me you at least still got Giggin, the Boy Wonder."

"I got him. Sort of. He's also helping on a SACA computer sting."

"And now you want me to strap my gun on and help."

"I want help. No guns. You up to speed with the runaway traffic in West Sac?"

"The Pope know 'Ave Maria'? Start Giggin with the truck stops on the south side of Jefferson Boulevard. Have him head west. Only a few runaways go there. You start at the Exult and work down motel row. I'll meet you at the Paradise Motor Lodge."

"The Exult?" He gave me the address.

I called David Obstain, who'd charge less for not having to search West Sac.

The pink-stuccoed Exultation Motel made the heady claim of being Sacramento's foremost adult hotel with water beds, wall and ceiling mirrors, and a fine array of adult movies.

I flashed crisp bills and Rachel's sad Med Center photo while François Giggin did the same on the other side of Jefferson Boulevard. Barreling eighteen-wheelers roared, throwing gravel. Truckers stopped at diners to eat chicken-fried steak and picante Valley chili.

"You're a cop," said the manager flatly. Thin shoulders poked like a wire hanger in a moth-eaten gray cardigan that covered a faded floral aloha shirt. The air conditioner was busted, it was eighty degrees in the office, and he looked bloodless. He ignored the classical music, which created an aura of elegance for an operation that sold dirtbag sex by the minute.

"I'm a DA, looking for a lost girl."

"That's what they always say, ain't it?"

"Look at my honest face and tell me I'm lying."

He shrugged. "You're lying."

"Am not." I flashed the photo.

"Nah, she's not here. I wouldn't let a kid hook here."

"I said, she's a runaway. She's the last kid in the whole world who'd ever hook. No lick on you if she's here."

"That's what they always say, ain't it?"

"I don't know if they do or not. But if it turns out she's here—"

"Yeah, yeah, I know. You'll beat the crap outa me and throw me through the wall, rip out my Coke machine, and shut me down."

I frowned. "Do I look like someone who'd do that?"

He looked suddenly tired. "That's why I said it."

"Would you believe I *used* to be a cop, and really good at zapping sarcastic pimps?"

"No, I wouldn't. And you *are* a cop. Who's way too interested in that girl. It's why your style's off. She ain't here."

"Where would you suggest I look?"

"Try Orlop's Bed and Nook. Or Paradise Motor Lodge."

I left my card. "Nice talking to you."

"That's what they always say, ain't it."

I left. Movement in the dark. I turned, fast.

"Scare you?" asked Bilinski.

I held my heart and tried to swallow. "No."

"You need a gun. Jin, I'm packing—but don't go ape and hit me with a writ. Billy McManus was a senior sergeant with a good nose, right? But after Tommy Conover beat him up on the church steps, he was shot dead by a freakin' chickenhawk.

"Now we're in the Hawk Nation. Don't ask me to help you and then fucking disarm me. It'd be okay if I was still zippy in the head or if pervs didn't shoot cops. But they do, and now I talk to strange guys about my fucking feelings. So I'm lots better."

"Harry, I can't even tell you how angry I'm going to be if you shoot me or François."

"Goddamnit, Jin, I was in Chinatown! What am I gonna shoot, Puerto Ricans? If I was in Rio Linda I'd be shootin' hillbillies."

"You know I had to go to law school to argue that well?"

He snapped his fingers. "Gimme her picture. Want a gun?"

"No. We're going to be around children."

He spit out his gum. "Counselor, you need a men's group, bad."

No one on duty at the Paradise Motor Lodge, a red-faced strip of moldering bungalows with wheezing, rattling window air conditioners, paper-thin walls, cracked windows, and heavy, stiff drapes. Twenty units in a U shape. Most were occupied. Music by Kafka. Cars were vintage but not worth collecting.

Women cried or argued. A baby screamed. TVs blared. Beery men yelled boorishly. Harry surveyed quickly, smiling, rubbing his hands together. "Jin, you want the girl? Or a good arrest and a good search by the book? I assume, the girl, am I right?"

I nodded. "I want the girl." Some lawyer I was.

He took a crowbar from his trunk. "Back me up. Anyone runs, she's yours." He went to Unit One and knocked without his badge.

"Who is it?" came a man's voice.

"Manager," said Harry. "Gas leak. Open up."

The door opened. Harry went in with the crowbar. He came out, leaving an unhappy couple. And so it went, awakening tired truck drivers and bruised women and sleepy kids on the run. One of the women attacked him and I pulled her off with a wristlock before Harry shot her. I was holding the woman when a car screeched out of the motel parking lot.

Bilinski and I sprinted into the lot. The car was gone. The door to Unit Fifteen slammed and the lights went out. Harry cracked the lock and pulled his cannon as the door swung inward on canted hinges. I touched the empty space on my hip as we went in, crouching.

"Put it down. Now," said Harry as I turned on the lights.

A balding, goggle-eyed man dropped a gun. I picked it up with a pen through the trigger guard and slipped it in a plastic baggie. I closed the door but we could still hear all the radio stations that were bouncing off each other in the parking lot. Maybe we heard them better.

"Good evening," said Harry. "Detective Bilinski." He checked the bathroom. "How's tricks tonight, and who're you, sir?" I put on surgical gloves.

The room was littered with child porn magazines, female child clothing, and low-grade potato chips. Signs of another man and a girl. I checked the kid clothes—too big for Rachel.

Bilinski began combing the man's pockets and wallet, then held up the driver's license, comparing it to the trembling man. "Hello, William Chapin," said Bilinski. He spread the wallet's contents on the dresser. I saw something on the floor and lifted it with tweezers: a plastic membership card for the Adult Video Club. I showed it to Bilinski.

"John Orse. The guy who just booked with the girl in the car, right? Forgot his Adult Video Club card." Bilinski arrayed Mr. Chapin's credit cards and license, pulled a camera and took pictures of them. "Sir, time for you to get outa bed."

Chapin stood, holding a thin, torn sheet. On the dresser, I looked carefully at John Orse's plastic rental card, a name and fingerprints we couldn't legally use or legally pursue.

"Mr. Chapin, see her before?" I showed Rachel's photo.

Chapin shook his head, panting.

"She's all we want. We're not after you. Look carefully. You've seen her, it helps you."

"Yeah. Tell us and you get a candy bar and a red balloon," said Bilinski.

Mr. Chapin shook his head, his eyes pulled to the bed.

I followed the gaze and picked up a fresh Polaroid photo of a tall, overweight girl, maybe fourteen years old. I put it in a baggie and gave it to Harry.

"How'd you find this kid?" asked Harry, holding up the photo. The girl was naked and stunned, lying on a bed. This rumpled bed, here in the Paradise.

The man shrugged. Harry put the photo in his breast pocket.

"Mr. Chapin," said Harry. "I don't like people who take pictures of little girls without their clothes on. This room's lousy with your liquid crud. You're, like, real uncooperative, and that puts a BIG fucking strain on my diplomacy, which frankly ain't my strength."

Chapin looked at me with hope.

"Don't look at me. I despise you."

"You bastards can't do anything to me," said Chapin viciously. "I got rights."

Harry hit Mr. Chapin with a high right, knocking him over the bed to crash into the nightstand. "Oof," said Chapin. The neighbor pounded tiredly on the wall.

"Me, I don't despise you," said Harry. "I like you 'cause you're such an asshole, it's a pleasure to hit you. And you should know better than to piss off someone who's nuts."

"I bought the photo," said Chapin, moaning. We couldn't prosecute him because of our flagrantly illegal search. Tonight, free creep passes, with police brutality thrown in, gratis.

"What's the girl's name?" I asked.

"I don't recall."

"Think harder," said Harry, "or I'll rip your dick off."

Personally, I'd rather tear off lips.

Harry searched the room. "What's the girl's name, again?"

"I don't recall," said Chapin.

"Where do we find Mr. Orse?" I asked.

"I don't recall," we all said in unison.

"Okay, it's been real, and now we're going," said Harry.

"Hey!" yelled Mr. Chapin. "Where you going with my keys and pants!"

"I don't recall," said Harry. "So fuck you very much."

The man stupidly said, "Hey!"

"I'm sorry, Mr. Chapin," said Harry. "What part of 'Fuck You' didn't you get?"

In the lot, Harry slipped the keys in a Baggie to protect prints, then tried the auto door key until it fit a blue Econovan. So John Orse, fast flight expert, had taken the girl in unknown wheels to an unknown destination. I bared my teeth.

"You can't do this," said Mr. Chapin, half dressed and stumbling backward as Harry re-entered his once-private motel room. "Dammit, I'll sue your goddamned badge!"

Bilinski smiled broadly. "That's what *I'm* talkin' about!" He showed him the badge number. "Mr. Chapin, what kind a car does Mr. Orse have? Whisper it and you're not a snitch."

Mr. Chapin violently shook his head. Harry was perturbed; a subject feared something else more than him. I called DMV for a printout on John Orse. He didn't exist.

"What's Orse's REAL name?" No answer. Harry pushed Chapin on the bed and sat opposite him as Chapin squirmed and whined, covering his bruised head.

"Shaddup. I ain't gonna hit you. Sit quiet so I can nail your face." Like Harry, I never forgot a person I had interrogated. Chapin's thick flop sweat imprinted the image in police memory. I sat next to Harry and also eyeballed Chapin, who bit his lip as we memorized him.

"Okay," said Harry, standing. "Look funny at a girl and I catch you? I'll rip off your unit and fold it in your wallet so it'll still be close to home. Think I'm kidding, asshole?"

I shook my head. Outside, I shook it again. "Bilinski, working with you is like having a hallucinogenic flashback to the Spanish Inquisition. You make me want to join the ACLU."

"I am not surprised," said Harry. "Damn lawyers. That was a bad guy in there!"

I pointed at the tattered American flag on the pole.

"Yeah, yeah, fuck you," he said, face in pain.

We continued down motel row. Every half hour, we connected with François, who had experienced no luck. We reached Denny's at the end of Jefferson. If we kept going, we'd be in Davis. Midnight, no Rachel, stale Camel smoke and unremarkable coffee.

"What happened" said Harry, "at Fred and Gary's River City?"

"I didn't do Fred and Gary's," I said.

Bilinski almost broke his coffee cup rushing out.

The night manager was huge, dense, and broad. An old brown leather vest over a bare and mean-smelling chest the size of Iowa. Fifteen dark hairs were swept optimistically across a bald pate and a short forehead that resembled a vertical cliff in Yosemite. He was six-three and would be six-five if he abandoned his crouching bear stance to stand straight. Drop him in an Olympic pool and the water would empty. The hair he could have used above his eyebrows sprouted from ears, back, and nose. Hard hands. No donuts. No mints.

"Hi there," said Bilinski, locking the door behind François and turning off the illuminated *VACANCY* sign. He passed Rachel's photo to the manager, whose brows dipped near his lips. He was trying to put together Bilinski's mass; a quiet six-one Chinese in a suit; and a small, soft-bodied, nose-geared sidekick with Tevas and earrings who kept banging into things.

Harry pointed at Rachel's photo. "Mr. Manager, that's my kid. She's just thirteen." He slapped a crisp Ben Franklin hundred on the counter. "Your reward if you locate her. She woulda showed up sometime today." We watched the eyes.

He had seen Rachel. He started to lie.

"No, peabrain," said Harry. "Don't even think about it."

The manager frowned. He stepped out from the counter, brass knuckles on his right hand, ready to take us. "Like bleeding, ya fat bastard?" A thick, deep, simple voice.

I hooked him in the gut and he grunted politely. I shuffled to his right and put another hook into the hard skull, then went left, landing another to the jaw to invite a change in altitude. To help, Harry punted into the groin and caved in the man's right knee with a sickening snap. Out of grunts, the brute hit the floor, shaking the walls and rattling windows and blinds.

"No," I said. "But thanks for asking."

Harry scooped his bill and someone unlocked the door. A small, lean man with a bullet-shaped head, his forgettable features casual, genetic afterthoughts. He hefted a baseball bat with the confidence that comes from knowing the power alleys, batting .290 on away games, and being married for years to the owner's daughter.

"Here's a fun guy," said Harry. "Listen, Mr. Stupid. Don't never pick a fight with an ugly man. He got nothin' to lose."

There was a long pause. "Callin' me ugly?" asked Mr. Stupid, frowning afterwards.

"You idiot," said Harry. "*I'm* the ugly one! And it ain't real bright to pick a fight with a cop *and* a DA who used to fight gorillas in a ring for money." Facing violence, Bilinski hadn't killed anyone. His howitzer was still snug in the shoulder holster. I was happy, so I smiled.

"Who's 'at?" Mr. Stupid pointed at François.

"A doctor," said Harry. "To surgically extract that bat from your ear if you don't drop it. Hey, but don't sweat him and don't sweat me. SWEAT HIM!" Harry pointed at me. "He's a goddamn grinnin' Mongolian! Fucking Mongols are the BIGGEST SHITEATERS IN THE WORLD! They suck blood and they don't do six things! They don't fuck around!"

The huge manager groaned, struggling to find his feet, one of which twitched. Bald Mr. Stupid tightened his batting grip, heavy eyes flitting quickly between Harry and me.

"Mister, drop it." It was François, his finger pointing through his jacket at the batter.

Mr. Stupid nodded slowly, then swung hard at François, who squeaked as I punched Mr. Stupid in the head and Harry kicked him deep in the groin. Mr. Stupid, now following our advice, dropped the bat. Harry lifted him bodily and dropped him in a full-floor felony stop. He was cuffing him with some enthusiasm when the immense manager struggled to rise to all fours. I tapped the manager's hand until his shiny brass knuckles rattled on the dirty floor.

"Asshole," snarled Harry to François. "Don't screw around when were havin' fun."

"Sorry," said François, grimacing at the two men with spectacular groin injuries.

Harry lifted the manager and dropped him on the counter, the empty mint bowl exploding. "Let's you and me talk," suggested Harry. "WHERE THE FUCK'S THE GIRL!"

The manager was unresponsive while Mr. Stupid groaned pitifully as he gripped his privates. Eventually, he managed to shake his head. His legs quivered and he was analyzing the floor as if it were the Rosetta stone. He tried twice to get out, "Uhhh. Dunno."

"Not asking you," said Harry. "Asking *you.*" He lifted the manager's jaw, but there was no focus in the rolling brown eyes until pain sizzled through him from down below.

"Oh, my fucking balls," hissed the manager. "Oh, my goddamn busted knee . . . fucking leg. Uh, my fuckin' head. Damn teeth. Fucked-up mouth. Oh my dick." Out of adjectives, he remembered to moan like a lonely moose in spring. He would be of no help.

"See this girl?" I asked Mr. Stupid, flat on the ground. I showed him Rachel's photo.

Mr. Stupid tried to peer carefully. He nodded. He recognized her. Fighting nausea, he said she was last seen hitchhiking on I-80 East.

"Thank you," said François, taking a breath, "very much."

"You know her," said Harry to the whimpering, eyeball-rolling manager.

"He tried to hire her," said Mr. Stupid. "She runned off. Oh. My. Nuts."

"How long ago?" I asked.

He tried to shrug but pain made him bleary. "Hour. Two. Fuck, you kick hard."

"Wasn't me. I closed your eye. What kind of vehicle?" I asked.

One of Mr. Stupid's eyes—the working one—expanded. The question was too hard.

"Thanks," said Harry, warmly patting the manager's face and

letting go. The man toppled and crashed loudly, reshaking the room and raising dust. Moans. "Oh, fuck, my knee! Ah, Jesus, I need a doctor!" He was nasal. I didn't hit his nose; it was from the fall.

Harry's ambition to be fired could launch some spectacular lawsuits in which I would be an automatic co-defendant with one plea option: Extremely Guilty.

"All cops are not like this." I lifted him.

"That's right. Some aren't as nice as me," said Harry.

"Think you can uncuff me?" groaned Mr. Stupid.

"Say 'pretty please,' " said Harry. Mr. Stupid moved his lips. "Too slow," said Harry. "Listen up, scumbags. You're under arrest for assaulting a police officer and a DA and a law intern. Now tell me true, sweethearts, why all this fucking muscle for some runaway girls?"

The manager fell back, unconscious, his face scrunched. Mr. Stupid was thinking but had no idea. Harry called for medical transportation, put a bulletin out on Rachel, and said DA Jin in a Porsche would be going like a bat out of hell up I-80. "Let him go. He's after a missing two-eighty-eight victim in a case that's in trial." Harry waited with his prisoners.

François and I drove north on the Interstate with Harry's red emergency dash light and two of his industrial-strength police flashlights, pushing the Boxter above a hundred and ten. I could have done more but it would've been wrong.

We looked for Rachel on the road and in the cars we passed. The engine thrummed smoothly, the exhaust a steady, throaty roar.

"I do okay back there?" asked François. "Harry was pretty pissed at me."

"You did fine. But forget everything. It's not how we operate. Bad sign." I shook my head. "I liked hitting those pimps. I'm sorry. Bad example." The lane dividers had been recently painted and the moon was behind silver-tinged clouds. Near midnight, traffic was light.

I tried not to be panicked about Rachel. I failed.

"So, boss, think I can have a gun?"

"François, guns are trouble. A small piece is no good. A

nine-millimeter or a Glock unbalances you, makes you sweat. You have to clean them and qualify every year. . . ."

I slowed in the mountain town of Auburn, a speed trap with saloons, antique shops, and cops with radar. A kid on the road—a girl—two hundred meters away in my lights, her thumb out and looking cold. Fear in her eyes as she recognized the car. Rachel turned and began running into the dark, trying to run out of the headlight beams.

50.

A GUARDIAN

Friday

Someone small trying to shake me. I thought it was Summer, years ago, and awoke to see Rachel's small face, eyes crusted and puffy with unhappiness.

"Good morning, honey," I mumbled thickly. "How are you?"

"i'm sorry," she said. It was five-thirty.

I looked in her eyes. "Well, I'm glad to see you." She looked in mine, giving me that glance into a child's void, then looked away. I rose from my Intake desk and stretched.

There was a message from Krakow on my voice mail. The web sting was stalemated; they couldn't get past the pedophile gate-keeper's password requirements. The sting had new tactics: follow runaways. The FBI was investigating the overseas connection while local detectives were at the bus and railway stations, the adult bookstores, theaters, and seedy motels. It was too much territory with too few cops chasing transients who lived in cars, jumped the freights, and pimped children for airfare to distant locales.

I asked Rachel, "How about a hot chocolate?" Her blue trial dress was on a hanger, the shoes beneath it. I took them.

The river was quiet, glowing gold from the false dawn and rows of halogen bank lights. The owls had retired and starlings were soft black silhouettes against twinkling water.

The Pilothouse Restaurant on the *Delta Queen* riverboat hotel was open. Lobbyists worked better in darkness.

"this is cool," she said, sipping hot chocolate.

We watched the water shimmer, dancing with the early morning sun.

"you brought your daughter here, didn't you."

I pointed with my nose. "That was her favorite spot. She liked being close to the kitchen. It was the Chinese in her." Sum used to sit like Rachel, elbows on the table, blowing on the chocolate, liking the steam in her face, warming her eyelashes on a cool morning.

Rachel looked where I was looking. Then she edged the salt and pepper shakers away and played with the small packets of artificial sweeteners, shuffling them, making the sound of a Chinese girl's slippers on a dark Shanghai rug.

"Momma said kids need guardians. someone who'll be there if they're sick. someone they can talk to when everything's shitty. sorry. when it's bad. you know who my guardian is?"

I wondered if it was Miss Piggy. "Ms. Hong?" I asked.

"Mr. Chow, the church janitor." Rachel looked up at me. "a very cool guy. looks at me with real soft eyes. grown-ups don't look at you. they don't like you. they act like you're dirty, dripping AIDS cooties. they see you coming and, like, cross the street. or they look away." She turned toward the river. "oughta be a place where old people smile at kids."

"There're a few places like that. Some homes. Some churches. But not enough of them."

She made a face. "Chico used to talk like that. i'll take you to Rome. . . . i'll take you to see something real cool. men talk big like that."

"DAs, to do the job, have to be unemotional. But I hate him for what he did to you." I sat closer. "You're stronger than Chico. It's because you care for people. For your mom. For Belinda Howell, who'd be his next victim if you hadn't stepped up. But if you shut down and *never* trust again, he wins. But if you're good to others, *you* win. Because you're stronger. And that's it. You control that, the most important part. He hurt you, but he couldn't take your soul."

Her eyes were closed, almost dreamily. Perhaps she had heard nothing. Or heard and thought it was crap. She put her head on the table, atop crossed arms. "you hate me, Mr. Jin?"

It was a sad question. I lifted my hand to touch her. I stopped. "No."

She looked up. "you did at first," she whispered.

"It hurt to look at you. You reminded me of her. It wasn't hate. It was fear."

Machinery hummed. The drawbridge raised for a smart cargo vessel named *Maggie Mae*. It was loaded with tons of sugar beets and its wake slapped the hull of the *Delta Queen*, rocking us gently. I liked the motion, its randomness, its youthfulness. Rachel watched me.

"One day," I said, "I heard her voice. Summer's voice."

"you mean, after she was dead? like I hear my momma?"

"I was at the lake. She said, 'If you're patient, Daddy, Rachel will talk to you.' If Summer were still alive, she'd want to be your friend." I swallowed. "She'd be a good friend."

Rachel nodded. She looked away. "but you think i stink on the stand. like, be honest."

I smiled. "You're not as good as you could be."

She nodded. "cuz a my voice."

"And because you're afraid of hurting Chico."

Shivering, she sat up and put her hands under her legs. "i know. 'i'm not hurting Chico. Chico hurt himself.' but that's bull." She freed a hand to brush hair from her face. "feels like i'm hitting him. i'm not frosted at him. i wanted to say that. he couldn't help what he did."

"It's true we're not doing this out of anger. We're doing it for justice. For the right thing. Rachel, just tell the truth. We have a good jury and a bad judge. Take the oath and just talk to me. It's *my* job to sweat the judge. Now. Talk to me about the defense counsel."

"she'll ask lots of questions. she'll say i whored. that i lie.

that i talk to my dead momma. she'll ask a hundred questions about what he did. i don't have to be perfect. just tell the truth."

I touched her hand for an instant. "Rachel, you've already gone through hell and come back. What's coming is nothing."

She licked her lips. They were dry. I felt like applying Chap Stick to them, as if she were Summer and Sum were eight, a good year, no surgeries and she could play catch for hours.

"i don't want to do it." Pause. "i get nightmares. words. like, his voice."

To come this close. I could not force her. "I don't blame you."

"i hate this. i can't tell you how much. it makes me so, like, *extreme*." She looked out the window again, biting her lip until it bled. The sun came up brilliantly, making the world painfully bright, turning the American river crimson and Asian and far away. She closed her eyes.

"Rachel, how'd Moody threaten you?"

She shook her head, her hair flying. She began crying. She mouthed the words: don't make me.

"I won't, Rachel," I said. "It'll be your choice."

"but you make me do things . . ."

A shiver up my spine.

Ava said that Summer was living for me. "She wanted to die last year. She had a real bad year, holding on for you because you couldn't let her go. When I sent you out of the room, before that last, damned surgery, I told her it was okay, that she didn't have to try anymore, for us, that she could use the anesthesia to follow the light that she had seen so many times.

"I told her she could go to God. I lied! I said, 'Daddy knows, and he doesn't want you in pain anymore, so go, honey. You know Daddy. He just can't say the words to you.'

"Josh, it's like you've became Kwah, your stepfather, demanding kowtows from children—even after they're dead. You're acting like the one man you didn't want to be!"

Moody had made Rachel do things she didn't want to do. I leaned back. I had made Summer live longer than she wanted. I was her father, and I had silently asked her to endure pain, for me.

And prosecutors must do the right thing. I closed my eyes.

The right thing was to fight.

Rachel should not whimper away from her assailant.

That was the theme.

"Rachel, whatever happens, I'll be someone you can talk to. Someone who'll help. If I can." I don't know if she heard me. She was crying hard, her shoulders shaking, the pain in her belly becoming mine.

"i can't! i can't!"

"I hear you, Rachel, I hear you."

"don't make me do this! ah, shit, Mr. Jin, just let me go! please!"

I couldn't carry her pain. I closed my eyes.

Dear God, I said silently, help us. God, help us.

51.

RACHEL FARR

"Mr. Jin," said Jan Yanehiro the reporter, "the Asian press is terming this as David versus Goliath—with you in the role of the boy with a sling. Is that you? Are you David?"

"No. The girl is. The focus should be on the courage of a child who's doing this to protect other children, to make them safe from men who victimize kids. I just work here."

Stacy Antoinette August read the discovery I had delivered her, stating that Rachel Farr had run and been found in Auburn, and that she had asked to be allowed to not testify.

The court was cold. Stacy wore gray, Moody wore white, and Maxwell wore black. Dierdre Farr was dressed like a successful hooker. I wore blue and stood, facing the judge.

I sent a Chinese message: You can screw with me, but do not mess with my victim. You lock me up, and Krakow takes the case. If you throw two DAs in the clink for prosecuting a child rapist, you'll lose reelection in November by a biblical landslide.

Be nice, and no one gets hurt.

Maxwell saw I was staring at him. "Yes, Mr. Jin?"

"Your Honor," I said, "I'm about to call a child witness, who, with your permission, will enter this court with all the protection available under law, guaranteed by you, personally."

"No speeches, Mr. Jin. Proceed."

"No speech, Your Honor. I'm stating legal expectation of judicial performance."

I looked at him for a while. He glared back until he blinked.

"Thank you very much, sir," I said. "People call Miss Rachel Farr."

Bailiff Goss opened the door. Rachel entered. My heart stopped.

She wore the blue suit and matching shoes. She looked lovely and tired and more filled out. I met her. We slowly walked down the aisle. I could feel her wild trembling. I smiled at her.

Liz Heck administered the oath. Rachel took it, her arm twitching. I was standing near and could hardly hear her "i do." I felt the jury's eyes on Rachel Farr, measuring her.

She took the stand slowly. Quivering, eyes flat, waiting for the blow.

"Permission to approach?" I asked. He nodded. I smiled at Rachel and moved the mike closer to her, the metal neck groaning as if in pain. Do the toughest part first, while she was amped by adrenaline with the high readiness for psychic pain.

"Good morning, Rachel. Do you know Karl 'Chico' Moody?"

She nodded. I kept my eyes softly on her. "yes." Her voice, in the mike, came out.

"Rachel, look around. If you see him, please point at him."

She flinched. Eyes averted from the jury, she pointed hesitantly at Moody.

When her finger steadied, I said clearly, "Let the record

reflect that the witness, Rachel Farr, has pointed out the defendant, Mr. Karl 'Chico' Moody."

"Record will so reflect," said Maxwell flatly.

I stood where Rachel wanted me, to her left. Mrs. Aldo, the Knothole Kid courtroom watcher, had passed the word that today was the big trial day. The audience held the familiar assortment of the retired, the disabled, mothers of murdered children, high school dropouts thinking about legal careers, and old, retired soldiers quietly enduring ancient wounds.

Stacy August appreciated the audience for the discomfort it caused the key government witness. The jury, the judge, and the audience made me nervous.

Rachel's stomach probably felt like an overcrowded aviary.

"Take a breath," I whispered. She nodded, then breathed.

Rachel was a child. The jury had to understand that. I asked Rachel if she understood what an "oath" meant. She did.

"it's bad to tell a lie. but this is like a promise to God."

"Rachel, you believe in God?"

"i do." I believed her.

I began by revealing our weaknesses before Stacy raised them on cross. Jurors can dislike the government, but they expect DAs to be ethical. They absolutely hate us if we're not. No such expectation is placed on the defense. I had credibility to protect. I took a breath. This was what we had worked for. To bring her testimony before a good jury. I looked at them, reminding them, letting the light of their power, their decision-making, touch her. I whispered to her, "Remember, this is where we've always wanted to be. Let's use the chance."

Rachel nodded nervously. I asked the questions. She said that after Momma died, her dad hit her more. Her stepma, Dierdre Farr, kicked her a lot. They didn't hit or kick her the end of January or early February "because i was hardly at home no more."

"Did your father's blows ever leave bruises or cuts?"

"yes."

"Where on your body, Rachel?"

"my back."

"Did your stepmother's blows ever leave bruises or cuts?"

Rachel turned her body away from Dierdre Farr.

"yes. on my legs. she likes to kick my legs. she hits my head but it doesn't leave marks. it doesn't hurt all that much. the bruises and cuts i got in February, i didn't get them at home."

Rachel whispered that she had lived with me and Ava before trial. That we had reviewed her preliminary hearing testimony that she had given earlier in Judge Hays's court. That I had asked her the questions that I intended to ask her today.

"Rachel, did you and I get along when we first met?"

There was no objection.

"no," she said.

"Whatever your feelings are for me, would those feelings cause you to lie during testimony?"

"no."

She said she ran away yesterday because she didn't want to testify, and because she didn't want to think about this anymore and she didn't want to face Chico Moody.

My questions took Rachel from home life to the music and snacks at Moody's. The four months of her own hanging out with Chico. The dog, MTV, the homework, the gifts.

There was no mention of marijuana; Maxwell had dismissed those counts, and raising them could bring a mistrial by clouding Moody's legally presumed innocence with uncharged misconduct of drug use. Her earlier lie, denying its use, was obviated by Stacy's inability to raise the issue without implicating her client for providing marijuana to a minor.

Her amplified voice was an electrical whisper with a tinge of the unreal and a hush of the ominous, a nightmare's echo, a Munich cabaret on a crystal night. Rachel sat in the witness stand, eyes unnaturally large and rimmed in dark circles, focused on me as if I were a Svengali. Her hands were under her legs; now she was holding on by willpower.

She went to Chico's with a bag to spend the night. Chico was going on a trip and she would take care of Spango the spaniel for twenty bucks. She wanted to do it for free.

The door was open and she went in. It was six o'clock in the evening, Saturday, February the first. The moon was small and the wind was warm and Rachel was on time, using the Timex watch Chico had given her. They greeted each other. He was in a suit. She felt underdressed. Spango was nowhere to be seen.

Rachel described dinner, her small voice dropping. Les Goss, the bailiff, upped the volume. The court was silent. Mrs. Aldo had put down her needlepoint. The news reporters took notes. We were close. "Near the end of the meal, Rachel, how did you feel?"

Her intake of breath was audible in every corner of the court. She said, "i was real sleepy. i conked out."

"Rachel, please tell the jury what awakened you."

"i felt this pain inside me. . . ." And she told the story.

Stacy occasionally objected, always stopping before the jury tired of her interference with Rachel's hushed, otherworldly testimony. The repeated attacks. Rachel crying to Chico, begging him to stop. "please, Chico, stop!" Most women jurors dabbed their eyes.

I avoided looking at Maxwell, who was twisting, glancing at Stacy for an objection he could sustain, for a wrench he could throw at the little girl with shock-expanded eyes and the horrible lies. I realized that Maxwell actually disbelieved Rachel. He didn't trust kids, and suddenly I had an insight into the wholesomeness of Fin Maxwell's childhood.

Stacy knew the jury would now deeply resent objections.

The testimony had returned Rachel to Moody's house and into the room of her nightmares. Her mind accepted to an astonishing degree what had happened to her that first weekend in February.

"i asked him, 'why, Chico, why?' " and she began crying. Unable to continue, she sobbed. Her voice had bought her what she had wanted—personal space from adults, her crying loud and grating. I twisted the mike away as Les Goss switched it off. I turned my back to the jury, afraid I would cry in the wash of such agony from a young girl. I breathed. Rachel blew her nose and fought for breath and control. She looked up, worried about me.

I aimed the mike at her and Goss turned on the power. After a small whine of feedback, I resumed questioning. We had a rhythm and worked well.

When she had testified to thirteen of the fourteen 288 counts on the record, she covered her mouth. I gave her the airsickness bag in my coat, turning off the mike, and shielding her while she filled it. Bailiff Goss took the bag. I thanked him.

She looked smaller, younger, painfully brittle, as if her innards were of tissue.

Moody was glaring at her. Time to do it.

I moved out of his line of sight, looking at him as if I were lining up the front blade sight of an automatic while I fully exposed Rachel to his gaze. The jury followed my stare and saw his face. She was trembling, her tummy quaking, while his eyes narrowed and glowed.

"Your Honor," I said, "People request a short recess."

Maxwell was going to deny it, so Stacy joined me to win compassion points.

"Defense concurs, Your Honor." We got a ten-minute recess. I wished Capri were here, but Rebecca Coggins, the tireless court reporter, escorted Rachel to the rest room. Rachel's eyes were tightly shut, and a shade of her old limp trailed her small steps.

Ten minutes later, Rachel was ready. Gingerly, she resumed the stand. I smiled at her and kept asking the simple question. "Rachel, what happened next?"

And she answered.

She talked about the choking and the beating. I did not allow her to say that the choking felt like murder. She described how Chico tried to comfort her and then drove her home. How she apologized because she threw up in his car.

"Did you actually throw up?"

She nodded.

"Or did you dry-heave?"

"Objection," said Stacy, "leading."

"Child witness, Your Honor," I said.

"Sustained," said Maxwell. "Behave, Mr. Jin."

It was okay. There was no instruction to disregard her answer. When the defense argued that the DA failed to search Moody's car for vomit, they'd remember she dry-heaved.

"Rachel, why did you see Ms. Kimberley Hong, the school counselor?"

"my English teacher looked at me and then she sent me to her."

"Did you tell Ms. Hong what had happened to you?"

"no."

"Why didn't you tell her, or report Chico to the police?"

She looked away. I knew her answer: she was afraid and ashamed and he scared her and she couldn't tell her parents and it was all her fault and it was Chico. . . .

"Chico was my friend . . . my gentle man . . . my friend." Her words were clear and loud and bounced against the corners of the court. This was no TV drama; the audience was silent, without Hollywood courtroom hubbub. Her pained words stopped common breath.

"Rachel, was he like a father to you, a good father?" I asked.

"Objection, leading," said Stacy.

"Sustained," the judge said.

She nodded: he was my father. She blew her nose.

"Besides your momma," I said, "who, in your life, have you loved more than Chico Moody?"

The voice of a child, foreign and alone in the high-ceilinged court. "nobody at all."

"Rachel, how do you feel about Chico Moody now?"

"Objection, Your Honor," said Stacy softly. "Irrelevant."

"The victim's feelings about the defendant reflect on whether he attacked her. The case turns on their relationship. Her credibility now gets its test."

The jury wanted to know, but Maxwell looked at the little girl in his witness stand and followed his politics.

"A child witness's perceptions, Mr. Jin? I think not. Sustained."

"Permission to approach the bench and cite authority," I said.

"Denied. Proceed, Mr. Jin." He looked at his watch. So did Mr. Clayton.

I focused on my victim. "Rachel, does Chico Moody look any different today than he did when he attacked you? Please, look at him."

Clutching Miss Piggy, Rachel scrunched her eyes tightly shut. She didn't open them again until, in response to my questions, she finished describing his last attacks on her.

It was eleven forty-eight in the morning. On her strength, we had gotten the evidence in before the noon recess. She was looking at me and at my chest, perspiring and sad.

"Rachel Farr, on behalf of the People of the State of California, thank you. You're very brave. As I told you, Ms. August is going to ask you some questions, very respectfully."

I winked at Rachel. Her facial muscles strained, as if to keep her head from imploding. Her small shoulders rose stiffly as they had the first day I saw her in Kimberley Hong's office. They said: I can't run away, so I'll cover my ears.

I sat slowly, as if an elastic cord connected me to her, making sitting difficult. I realized that I had locked my knees.

"Miss Farr," said Stacy, "what did you do at six in the evening on January the twenty-sixth of this year?"

Rachel was trying to puff herself up against Stacy August.

"Objection, Your Honor," I said without rising. "Relevance."

"Overruled. Witness may answer."

"I don't know." Her voice, almost normal, seemed outsized in the courtroom.

"Interesting, how you've recovered your voice, all of—"

"Objection, Your Honor, argumentative."

"Overruled, Mr. Jin. Proceed, Ms. August."

"How about Saturday, February the eighth, this year?"

"I don't know."

"Rachel, how many times did deputy DAs Gonzo Marx and Josh Jin, and Catherine Capri, a DA investigator, and Police Department Detectives Wilma Debbin and Pico Larry, ask you about the events of Saturday, February the first, this year?"

"I don't know."

"Please estimate for us."

"lots of times."

"Oh, and where now, your voice?"

"Objection—"

"Contain yourself, Mr. Jin," said Judge Maxwell. "Nothing

wrong with a little advocacy. This is, after all, if I'm not mistaken, a jury trial of two parties. The defense can play, too."

"But it's not a TV show called *Badger the Child Witness*, either." I sat.

"lots of times," repeated Rachel.

"Your Honor," said Stacy, "that was unresponsive."

"Witness'll answer the question," snapped Maxwell.

Rachel wrung her hands. I barely heard, "i don't know."

"Did you say that Mr. Moody handcuffed your wrists and ankles and spread your arms and legs?"

"yes."

"Rachel, hold up your wrists. Show the court the terrible abrasions, the awful, deep cuts, from struggling to break free."

"Objection, irrelevant! Counsel knows a child victim of rape need not demonstrate resistance, and the attacks occurred nearly half a year ago." My stomach fell; I had forgotten to ask Killian Boyce, the SANER, about the missing wrist abrasions.

"It goes to her credibility, Your Honor," said Stacy. "She testified she was cuffed. Wrist abrasions would be highly corroborative in a case utterly devoid of physical evidence."

"Your Honor, I repeat, the attack occurred—"

"You mean, sir, the *alleged* attack."

"Your Honor, the alleged attack occurred on the first of February, six months ago. It is the prosecution's point that the scars that remain are psychic. Judge, you could've boxed Evander Holyfield in February and nary a scratch would show today. It's simply not probative."

"Hold your wrists up, young lady," said Maxwell in a cutting voice that made all stare.

Rachel, leaning away from Maxwell, held up her unmarred wrists.

"You remember any marks on your wrists in February?" asked Stacy.

Rachel nodded. "yes." I motioned for her to drop them, and she did.

"Rachel, isn't it a fact that you became sexually active at the age of twelve with a boy named Owen—"

"Objection!" I cried. "That's irrelevant to a child assault.

Under the law, a child is incapable of consent! Rachel Farr could be Mata Hari, but her virginity prior to February the first is as irrelevant as the price of brussels sprouts, and counsel for the defense has now gone past badgering to break the law that protects children from abuse in court."

"Your Honor, this is unbelievable!" cried Stacy August. "Mr. Jin uses the victim's sad background to beg tears and sympathy, but isn't willing to accept the natural downsides to such an existence! Such as early sexual promiscuity!"

"Lower your voices," said Finley Maxwell, coloring.

I stood and spoke slowly. "If you allow this question of a child witness, Your Honor, it will constitute a direct breach of your duties and I'll fight you to the Judicial Council and back. Judge, it's not worth it. Sustain my objection."

"Approach the bench," demanded Maxwell.

"Nice, Josh," said Stacy. "Threatening the judge in open court. Prosecution has no real right of appeal. And you don't have the political moxie to make public statements that sound like electioneering. Only defendants can do that. Not DAs. Now, say you're sorry to the bench."

Maxwell was waiting.

"What's your ruling, Judge?" I asked.

"I," said Finley Maxwell, "want this damn trial to end." It meant he, a fickle beast, was no longer intrigued by watching Stacy on stage and had golf balls to hit and votes to influence.

"Your Honor, I have every right," said Stacy, "to explore the victim's sexual history as a means of impeaching her."

"Not true. She," I said, "didn't claim she was a virgin and she has statutory insulation."

"Christ," said Maxwell, "overruled. Mr. Jin, I will not look kindly on further frivolous objections. Understand?" We returned to our stations. "Restate your question, Ms. August."

"When did you become sexually active, Rachel?" asked Stacy.

"that night. at Chico's."

Stacy nodded. I could now expect a parade of dishonest punks who would impeach Rachel by claiming they had slept with her and called her sweetheart.

"Your father, Rachel, struck you in November, last year?"

"probably. i don't remember."

"How many times did your stepmother kick you in December?"

Rachel tried to think.

"Isn't it a fact that you can't *exactly* recall whether your father hit you in late January or early February?"

"Objection," I said, standing. "Counsel's not allowing the witness to answer. And she's badgering a child in your court in violation of the statutes implaced to protect children."

"Overruled, Mr. Jin! Now you sit!"

Rachel was breathing in short bursts. My anger could not be helping her, but I couldn't allow Stacy to break her on the stand.

"i don't think—"

"You don't 'think'?"

"Objection," I said slowly. "Argumentative, interruptive, inappropriate, unprobative, unfair, and unprofessional."

"Overruled," snarled Maxwell.

"Rachel," said Stacy, "did your father strike you in late January and early February?"

"no. i don't think so." Rachel was shrinking from Stacy August while trying to lean away from the judge. I sat down before I distracted her.

"Isn't it a fact you had a special relationship with Karl?"

"yes. i think so." Her small chest rose and fell.

"A *very* special friendship?"

"i think so." She closed her eyes, shoulders up, waiting for something bad.

"Isn't it a fact that you became *insanely* jealous when he helped a girl named Belinda Howell with *her* homework?"

She blinked. "no."

"Isn't it a fact you told a classmate that if anyone came between you and Chico, you'd kill her and make Karl Moody sorry?"

"No!"

"There's your voice, again. So all others are liars?"

"no."

Stacy pitched rapid queries on the sequence of events, unnerving Rachel without inducing a contradiction. I objected periodically to break her rhythm.

"Isn't it true that you talk to your mother at night, but she died over four years ago?"

"yeah."

"Isn't it a fact that you were flirting with some Vietnamese gang members when they beat you and gang-raped you and threatened you with death if you reported it?"

"NOO!" Rachel's face contorted and I slammed the counsel table, making Stacy, Maxwell, Rachel, and most of the jurors jump.

"Objection, Your Honor! EC 765b prohibits the badgering of a child witness. We're all officers of the court, responsible for what's happening here. Ms. August, stop this NOW!"

"Don't you DARE address counsel directly!" cried Judge Maxwell. "You will direct all objections to the *bench* and *never* break that fourth wall by addressing opposing counsel! I find you in contempt, Mr. Jin. A thousand dollars. Sit."

I remained standing. "I was wrong, and I apologize to Ms. August and to the bench. Ms. August has to swing away for her client—that's her job. You and I, Judge, we have to protect this child. That's *our* job."

The cumulative tension of trial and memory and the pain of argument made Rachel emit a tiny sob. She hid her face, her small body racked with sobs.

"Two thousand," said Maxwell.

I locked on his eyes until he looked away. "Jin, sit."

"I will the moment you agree to protect this child witness."

Judge Maxwell glared at me. "Proceed, Ms. August."

"Your Honor, the People demand a response."

"Three thousand." I remained standing as Stacy faced Rachel.

"What if," said Stacy, "those gang members came to court? What then?"

Silence. Later, "i want to leave."

"You," snapped Maxwell at Rachel, "volunteered for this. Now, young lady, behave!"

Rachel put her head down, her small back shuddering.

I spoke softly. "That was unnecessary, Your Honor. She

didn't volunteer. She was brought by judicial process via a mandating subpoena."

"You may resume, Ms. August," the judge said.

"A recess, Your Honor," I said, still standing.

"Mr. Jin, that's five thousand dollars."

Bailiff Goss stood uneasily, looking at Maxwell and at me.

Liz Heck held a handkerchief to her bright crimson face. I acted as if he had granted the recess. "Thank you very much, Your Honor. I appreciate it. Permission to approach."

I quickly offered Rachel my hand. She took it, small fingers clamping onto mine with almost feral ferocity. I escorted her out of the witness stand.

"By God, you stop!" cried Maxwell. I heard him rise and lift his gavel. If he ordered the bailiff to stop me, I was still getting Rachel away from him. I had to be prepared for his seeking my disbarment. I thought the record was on my side. It didn't matter.

"The media's here," I whispered to Stacy on the way out.

She nodded. "It's okay, Your Honor," trying to salvage the judge. She could score a hundred legal points on Rachel, but lose ground with the jury—the only scorekeepers that counted. And turn from a media darling to its dunce. "I have no further questions."

"I don't care!" shouted Maxwell. "This is—is intolerable! Six thousand dollars and you're in jail until you apologize!"

"Your Honor, he's a DA," said Bailiff Goss softly, sliding a fresh cup of coffee across the bench to the judge. Maxwell jerked to face his bailiff.

I walked Rachel to Ava's office. Ava embraced her, but Rachel's arms hung lifeless.

Returning minutes later, I found the court still in session, the witness stand empty, the jurors still in place.

"Your Honor," I said as if nothing had happened, "move to admit People's One through Ten for identification into evidence."

Maxwell had a prepared speech. "You have a lot of umbrage, Mr. Jin—"

"Objection, Your Honor," said Stacy. "These charts are highly anecdotal and hardly scientific. They're gibberish." Her eyes said: don't fight this battle with the DA. Not now.

Maxwell nodded, cheeks red. "Sustained," he said, smiling. "They're out."

The jury craned to look at them a last time. The bailiff was in no hurry to remove them. My case-in-chief was completed. Rachel had given her everything and I might be applying to the police department in the lower San Joaquin Valley for a slot in traffic enforcement.

I made a fist. "The People rest," I said.

52.

KARL MOODY

Early afternoon. Ice-cream sales soared as the Capital slowed. The infamous Valley heat infiltrated the shade and made the air and the lungs heavy. I missed the thunderstorms.

Rachel sat in Ava's office, eyes vacant, breathing shallowly, cheeks flushed. I sat close.

"Rachel, you were *fantastic*. You are incredibly brave and strong. Thank you." My words sounded hollow. I took her small, cold, limp hand and shook it. I put both hands on hers and sat with her. It seemed that Rachel no longer had a pulse.

She could stay here while the trial went on.

The defense would open its case-in-chief. We would meet John Quick, but the most promising fact was that Chico Moody was going to testify. Rachel's testimony had made his appearance tactically necessary. Chico was my chance to win one for Rachel.

I would let him talk, all he wanted, and pray he revealed himself. Most cons do.

Court reconvened. Rebecca Coggins nodded, ready to record all words. Stacy August turned in her chair toward me. A sphinx.

She was dressed in an understated soft cream-colored suit. She stood and faced her client, as if everyone should focus on the man. She would limit his time on the stand. Each answer in direct exam exposed him to my later questions on cross.

"Your Honor, the defense calls Karl Francis Moody."

Mr. Moody took the stand after swearing to tell the truth, the whole truth, and nothing but the truth, so help him God.

He stated his name and spelled it. He easily pushed aside the mike. He wore a new dark gray suit. The knotted tie made him stretch his neck and grimace, a habit I had learned to suppress. His ponytail was gone. He looked good, square, composed, confident, lightly tanned, rested, and ready.

Stacy asked him if he understood that he was charged with fourteen felonies and two misdemeanors and that he had a constitutional right to remain silent. He said he did, and that he waived his right to silence. He understood that only the DA had to put on evidence and prove something; he could sit back and watch. Stacy joined in the waiver of his right to silence.

"Mr. Moody," said Stacy easily from the table, "what do you do for a living?"

"Ma'am, I'm disabled. I got my neck broke in an accident, some years back. It weren't my fault, so I got some money for it. I look squared away, but my neck and back got no strength. Not proud a that particularly, but there it is." The woodcutter's voice. You could smell morning coffee in the pines and see wood chips at the base of a tall, shadow-casting sequoia.

"Sir, this is a very personal question."

Moody sat straighter and hitched his neck.

"Your disability, Mr. Moody, does that have any effect on your sex life?"

"Uh, yes, ma'am. Can't really . . . have sex. The back, it's all tore up. That's what's kinda, you know, silly about all this."

Two or three men shifted in the jury box. I took notes.

"Mr. Moody, do you know Rachel Farr?"

"Yes, ma'am, I surely do." He looked sad.

"Tell us how you met her."

"Well, last year, I opened up my house to youth. Let them hang out. Play music." He smiled. "Not *my* kind of music, but they liked it. It gave me company. Later, I come to realize they're hungry, so I started gettin' 'em snacks." Traces of the Virginia Baywater accent, a charming, soothing pattern of rounded words suggesting sunlight in soft, mossy glens.

"This girl got in trouble with a bunch of Namese toughs, out in front of the house. I was already lettin' kids in. It was easy to rescue the girl. The girl, she was Rachel."

"Did she appear to *know* these tough kids?"

"Oh, yes, ma'am. They knew her. They knew her real good."

I would explore that with him on cross.

"Sir, you heard Rachel testify that she only saw girls at your house. Did you ever allow boys in?"

"All the time. Lotta girls come for 'em."

"Mr. Moody, let's go back to January of this year. Describe your relationship with Rachel Farr at that time."

"I'd say it was super. She was an easy kid to get along with. Her mom had died a few years back. Her father was a jerk. Her stepmother's a *real* jerk." Moody shifted his shoulders and eye-balled Dierdre Farr. The jury looked at her as one. "She liked to whup on her—"

"On Rachel?"

"Yes, ma'am! Bruised her, cut her skin, all the damn time. I'm not gonna brag, but it's crazy. I *saved* her from her own family! They were dangerous to her." The responsible rescuer.

Stacy approached the jury box.

The men—Clayton, Goin, Bukust, Richeson, and Hendrix—sat taller or adjusted the angle of their heads to their necks. "Mr. Moody, how did you *feel* about her?"

"Ma'am, I'd have to say, I loved her. Like a daughter." The compassionate father.

"Why do you think that is?"

He shrugged. "She's a pretty girl. And she's smart, real smart. There was this day. I just looked at her and said to myself, what a waste if she don't use the brains God gave her. I started kickin' her booty to get her to the books. See, I never done that. Me, I was a lazy cuss. Should've, I guess. But Rachel, she could."

He was giving overlong answers, but they worked for me. In every word lay some opportunity to plant Rachel's flag. I took verbatim notes, watching him, studying him.

Moody spoke at length about the time, energy, and resources he poured into Rachel's homework. The committed and patient tutor.

"It was that, I think. Workin' together with our heads, and we just grew close." He wiped his forearm across his face and he blinked. "Never had kids. If I did, I figure I'd feel toward 'em the way I feel toward Rachel."

"You have identified some of her features that you admired. What were some aspects of her that you did not admire as much?"

He was silent, as if he did not want to answer. "Mr. Moody?"

"She had trouble with fibs. She'd say, I'm not hanging with the Namese gang-bangers, but she did. They sorta fascinated her. I guess it was the danger of it."

"What do you mean by 'Namese'?"

"Vietnamese, ma'am. They're all bad gang people."

"Objection, Your Honor," I said from my seat, as much to break the flow of Moody's smooth testimony. "No foundation that the Vietnamese are all bad gang people."

"Yes," said Judge Maxwell, looking at the Asian print reporters in the back, "I will sustain." Like Conover and every other candidate, he needed the Asian vote. "The jury will disregard that last remark by the witness." Rebecca Coggins wiped it out.

"Mr. Moody," said Stacy, "did Rachel Farr visit you on Saturday, February the first of this year?"

He shook his head. "Ma'am, she surely did not."

"Or any part of that weekend?"

"No, ma'am."

"How can you be certain that she did not visit you?"

"Ma'am, February one's my birthday. Celebrate it every year with my pal, Johnny Quick. At the Old Spaghetti Factory on Folsom Boulevard in Rancho Cordova." Warm smile. The convivial comrade we couldn't find. Bilinski was still looking for John Quick.

I quickly checked Moody's rap sheet.

"Do you recall when you were there, on February one?"

"I'd guess about six-thirty to eleven p.m."

"And what did you do after dinner?"

"Johnny and me, we went barhopping. Keyhole Lounge, Rudy's Hideaway, the Rusty Duck. We closed the Aviation Club Bar on El Camino. Ended up at his place. Didn't wake up 'til noon, Sunday, and was worthless as duck crap 'til Monday. I guess I got knee-walkin' drunk."

I scribbled: *Find the bartenders*. I turned. François held up the OK sign: he'd do it.

"Mr. Moody, do you recall giving a statement to Detective Pico Larry of the Sacramento Police Department?"

"Yes, ma'am."

"Why didn't you tell him what you and Mr. Quick did on your birthday?"

"Ma'am, I couldn't hardly believe what I was hearing from the detective. Rachel, accusing *me* of hurting her." He inhaled. "Rape. Unbelievable, know what I mean? Rachel!"

"Why was it unbelievable that she would accuse you?"

He blew out air. "We were friends. Ma'am, I could no more hurt Rachel than jump over the moon. See, I would've *killed* anyone who tried to do anything bad to her. I was like her guardian. No way could I even *think* about anything like that. A little girl like Rachel."

Stacy took a breath; she had tested the waters and found me acquiescent. Now, for some real trashy questions.

"Mr. Moody, you didn't know Rachel that long, but why do you think she's accused you of assaulting her?"

"I think she got hurt by those Namese toughs and if she tells who did it, they're gonna kill her and her family and maybe she thinks, even me." He wiped his face, eyes in a squint.

"She didn't accuse nobody of *nuthin'*. But the teachers and nurses and cops and the DA got to her and pushed her, scared her down to her socks. I think they *convinced* her, with the election and all, that if she didn't name someone, *she'd* be in trouble. See, ma'am, she named the one guy she could trust not to get riled. Not even enough to throw a hissy fit."

"You aren't upset at her, Mr. Moody?" Concerned.

"I'm facin' life in prison with a child molest tag, and all I can do is wish she'd tell the truth. Ma'am, I got a life, but she's younger and got more years. I ain't done much with mine." The forgiving patriarch.

"Mr. Moody, what basic values describe your life?"

He cleared his throat, tugged at his collar, stretched his neck. "Tell the truth. Live and let live. Care for the kids, for tomorrow is theirs. No cussin', or you're not righteous."

Stacy gazed respectfully at her client, knowing the jury was now looking at the sturdy defendant. "What would you say, Mr. Moody, to Rachel, if you could?"

I converted my grimace into a faint smile. This wasn't evidence. It was Barbara Walters doing a celebrity interview of a child raper.

"I'd say, Rache, I forgive you, girl. You did what you thought you had to do. You thought you could rely on me to bail you outa trouble." He looked at the jury. "Well, Rache, you got yourself in a fix, but I'm good to go. I'm your gentle man. This what you want? Okay, then."

"Thank you, Mr. Moody." She had gotten what she wanted: a brief, low-profile, limited exposure statement by a man who didn't seem capable of attacking a little girl. Something to counter the powerful presence of Rachel Farr. Something that resembled reasonable doubt on two legs.

"Your witness," said Stacy. Passing, she discreetly slipped me a piece of paper.

The courtroom door opened and Geneva de Hoyas entered. I stood, prepared to argue, however hopelessly, if she moved to dismiss my case. Our eyes locked as she stood, the jury watching her, each second raising problems for the People's case. Geneva looked at Moody and sat. I unfolded the note.

Baby, he didn't do it.

53.

CROSS-EXAM

Geneva was a fighter, so I smiled at her as I stood at center stage. Moody took deep breaths, flexed his neck, eyes narrowing. He was ready. I smiled. No flurry of punches, no crowding of blows. Just two guys chatting. I put my hands behind my back.

"Mr. Moody," I said, "how are you at remembering names?"

"Pretty good," he said.

"You opened your house to youth. Please name some of them."

"There was Heather, Linda Jean, Gloria Bee, Julie, Wanda, Courtney Sue, Annie M., Pia, Tamara, Cynda, Roz, Jo. And, of course, Rachel."

"Thank you." I was blocking his eye contact with Stacy, but somehow, behind my back, she, or Rittenhouse, prompted him.

"And, uh, Jim and John. Uh, Bill. Jim."

I looked at him. "Yes. Of course. How are you with names of people you've just met?"

"The bailiff, he's Les Goss. Court clerk, she's Liz Heck. Your intern over there, the little fella with the earrings and the little fairy sandals. He's François Giggin."

"How are you at remembering physical descriptions?"

"You, you're six-one, one eighty-five or -six and you got a bad left ring finger, don't curl up the right way. Mr. Clayton over there in the jury box in the number one spot, he's six-two, two hundred, and I'd guess he got a bad left wheel, probably from sports." He stopped. Stacy had sent him the signal.

"Mr. Moody, how are you at remembering dates?"

"I'm pretty good." Shrug. "Actually, I'm REAL good."

"Let's test you, then. Mr. Moody, when were you born?"

"Yeah, that's a tough one. Well, I celebrate my birthday on February the first."

"Mr. Moody," I repeated pleasantly, "when were you born?"

"Objection, Your Honor," said Stacy. "Asked and answered."

"Your Honor," I said. "I sure as heck asked, but I wasn't answered. I asked for date of birth. He told me date of party."

Maxwell frowned, intrigued. "Overruled. Witness will answer."

I smiled at him. "Mr. Moody, when were you born?"

"February first," he said.

I had hoped he would be stupid. At the table, I opened a file. "I have in my possession a certified copy of Department of Motor Vehicles California Driver's License Number 589902 in the name of Karl Francis Moody on Tulip Lane, Sacramento, California. I show it to the defense." It was a conventional part of a felony trial file. Stacy August and Phillips Rittenhouse zeroed in on the date of birth. No reaction.

"Your Honor, permission to have this marked as People's Eleven for identification."

Maxwell nodded. Liz Heck attached the numbered exhibit sticker.

"Permission to approach the witness," I said.

I stopped three feet from Karl Francis Moody. "Mr. Moody, I show you what has been marked as People's Eleven for identification and ask you what it is." I offered it. He took it.

"Copy a my driver's license."

"Please note date of birth and read it aloud for the court."

"It's wrong." He looked at me. "Okay, February eleven."

I moved the mike toward him. "I'm sorry, Mr. Moody. Did you say, February *eleven*?"

He nodded. "Let the record reflect," I said, "that the witness nodded his head in the affirmative. Permission for counsel to approach the bench," I said to the judge.

Maxwell nodded. Stacy joined me and the court reporter followed.

I passed Maxwell a sheet. "Your Honor," I said so Moody could hear me but the jury couldn't, "that's Moody's CDC"—

California Department of Corrections—"certified rap sheet. Date of birth is reported as eleven February. I have five booking sheets from three counties. All show the same—eleven February. I have a noncertified letter from Social Security with a date of birth of eleven February. I'm going to impeach this witness with these documents. I propose to refer to his prison record as a 'state tax record' so as not to prejudice the jury against an ex-con." I looked at Stacy. If she objected, I could bring state officials into court to prove the record. Or try to. Stacy couldn't ask for a recess now without making Moody look worse.

"I'm sure my client," she said for Moody, "will clear this up." Stacy returned to her seat. I approached Moody and held his rap sheet against my chest so the jury could not see it.

"Mr. Moody, I show you a certified copy of your California tax record. Ask you to please read the date of birth, aloud."

"February eleven."

"Mr. Moody, I now show you a Social Security benefits letter for your account, dated twelve March of this year. What date of birth is reflected there, as being yours?"

"February eleven."

I closed the file.

"February eleven. But you *celebrate* on February the first."

"Yes, sir, I surely do."

"When I asked you for your birth date, you didn't say 'February eleven,' did you?"

"That's right, cuz I celebrate it different. On the first." A smile. "Sir, that's what counts."

"Mr. Moody, how'd you get disabled?"

"A logging accident, north country, winter. Chains broke on a semi and I took a logroll on my back. Crushed my vertebrae— five-C, six-C—that's in the neck. And one-L, two-L, and three-L. They're in the low back. Those were the killers. Lucky I wasn't paralyzed."

I nodded at him. "That must have hurt." He nodded back. "Sir, how exactly did these spinal injuries disable you?"

"Lots of pain." He scrunched his face. "Constant. I used to have a real high voice, now it's lower, but it comes at a price.

Constant sore throats. Come from a traumatized pharynx. Bad gut. Pain in the legs. And the part I said—you know—no sex."

"From the moment of that accident on, to today?"

"Yes, sir."

"Mr. Moody, did you have to do a lot of painful therapy for these extensive and life-changing injuries?"

"Yes, sir, I sure did. In a way, I still do."

I asked him to describe them in detail. He did. The jury stirred impatiently. Maxwell dozed. I wrote: *check out Moody's back therapies*.

"What was the date of that logging accident, Mr. Moody? If you can remember."

He licked his lips.

"Objection, Your Honor," said Stacy. "Irrelevant and beyond the scope of direct." She cited two cases as authority.

"Ms. August," I said, "opened the door. The witness stated on direct that he was disabled in an accident, and on cross, that he was good with dates. Dates are relevant to this case, because the defendant's alibi is that, on the dates of the attacks, he wasn't home." I cited the two cases Stacy used, *Gallego* and *Coles*. They supported my position.

"I am familiar with them," said Maxwell, smiling at Stacy. "I don't agree with your interpretation. Objection by the defense is sustained."

Moody twisted his neck from side to side. "Early, or mid-November, 'eighty-four."

"You didn't have to answer that," the judge said.

"Please advise my client to follow your direction, Your Honor," said Stacy, on her feet, looking at Moody, who ignored her. He didn't like having others in control.

"You don't remember the exact date?" I asked.

"Objection," said Stacy. "Irrelevant."

Moody was angry and spoke before Maxwell could open his mouth. "I got hurt pretty bad that day! My mind got all fogged up from the pain and the pain meds and the friggin' doctors doing me as they do. Hey, man, I was pretty messed up."

"Isn't it a fact that you claim to remember dates well?"

"Objection, Your Honor," said Stacy. "Argumentative."

"Sustained," said Maxwell. "Slow down, Mr. Jin, or I'll stop you cold."

I held up my hands, offering no conflict. I lowered them. "Would it surprise you to learn that the accident in which you suffered these life-changing injuries occurred on the twenty-sixth day of October, nineteen eighty-five, one year *after* the date you just testified to, under oath?"

"Your Honor," said Stacy, "this avenue has been closed to the DA, but he keeps driving down it. Now, he's speeding and trying to pick up hitchhikers."

"His answer's on the record, Your Honor," I said.

"Counsel will come to chambers, now."

I stood aside as Stacy coolly passed me. She sat placidly in a winged red leather chair. I sat in the one next to her, unavoidably aware of the old gravities between us.

"God," hissed Judge Maxwell, "you've done THAT for the last time! I'm declaring a mistrial! This jury's history! Your girl can go through this, all over again! How do you like that?"

"I'm telling," I said.

"Oh, who?" He struggled to control his breathing.

I leaned toward him. "Papers, television news, the radio, and the Asian press. There's a scandal in this courthouse. I figure my boss started it by battering Billy McManus and by unethically refusing to apologize. But you're taking his bad leadership and turning it into science fiction. We have a child victim. We have an Evidence Code and a Penal Code and you treat them like *Mein Kampf*. To get rid of Conover, you're willing to burn a little kid who got raped. You display the same judicial integrity utilized by the courts of the Third Reich."

Maxwell threw up his arms. "God, that's blasphemy! Infamous slander!"

"Sue me."

"Jesus, this is extortion, bloody blackmail, threatening me like this in the presence of other counsel!" He pointed at Stacy. "You heard him!"

"Not blackmail, Judge. It is notice. I'm not giving you a Condition Subsequent, that if you declare a mistrial, I'm telling the press. I'm telling, period. You *don't* declare a mistrial, I tell.

You declare one, I can't wait to rearrest Moody—in your court, in front of the press—and take him in front of another jury and a *real* judge." I made myself slow down.

"You know what? Your Honor, I *demand* a mistrial. There is no way on earth the People can gain a fair forum with you on the bench. You're an abomination to all judges and to the robe you stole from Central Casting when no one was looking."

Stacy touched my arm, her hand staying. "Don't do this, Josh."

"I'd listen if I were you, Counselor," hissed Maxwell.

"I've heard plenty. My victim's heard too much. Let's go back on the record so you can flush the jury. We're wasting time." I stood and looked at my watch. "Can you imagine how strong Rachel Farr's voice will be when she has judicial protection? By God!"

I picked up his phone and called Capri, praying she was back from court.

The secretary picked up. "Capri's in court, Josh."

"Capri," I said clearly, "this is Jin. Come to Department 49 right now, and rearrest Moody for fourteen two-eighty-eights, attempted murder, and furnishing to a minor. We got what we wanted—Maxwell's declaring a mistrial. We're getting a new court."

"No," snapped Maxwell. "We'll keep this jury. No mistrial. Mister, you'd best reconsider—"

"Cancel that, Capri," I said, and hung up. Someone was touching me.

"Josh," breathed Stacy, removing her hand, wondering at my recklessness. DAs do not challenge the competence of sitting judges without violating the dignity of the entire judicial system. I could take down Finley Maxwell, but only if I were willing to destroy myself.

"It's not our job to expose judicial iniquity," she whispered. "That's up to the Judicial Council. And the voters."

Maxwell knew his best defense against my charges would be a rock-solid *Moody* trial record. He rubbed his face. For the first time, I felt a tinge of sympathy for him. It passed.

* * *

"Mr. Moody," I said, "you testified that the doctors 'did' you 'the way they do.' What did you mean by that?"

He motioned with his left hand. "You know. They screw with you. They know your back's killin' you, but they stick the needles and they're slow with the painkillers and they have that long-nose way of lookin' down on your ass. On you. *That's* why I wanted Rachel to do her books. So those types wouldn't treat her like they treat me." He squirmed, his back hurting him.

"You have legitimate anger about unsympathetic doctors."

"Yes, sir, I'd say I surely do."

"Mr. Moody, when Pico Larry searched your home, wasn't he a little like those unsympathetic doctors?"

"He did think he was cock a the walk. Yes, sir, he was quite full of himself, he was."

"A little angry, Mr. Moody, legitimately angry, at a little roosterlike man rousting your house, going through your study, your underwear drawer?"

Moody looked at the jury, nodding. "Who wouldn't get a *little* hacked off over that. Little squirt left a mess everywhere."

"A little anger, perhaps," I said with a smile, "for lawyers?"

He smiled back. "Who doesn't?" The reserve jurors tentatively smiled.

"But no anger, Mr. Moody," I said softly, "for a kid who lies about you. Who says you did unspeakable things to her."

"Objection, Your Honor," said Stacy, "argumentative."

A pause. "Rephrase that, please, Mr. Jin," said Maxwell.

"Mr. Moody, Rachel's put you in more trouble than you've ever seen before in your life. You're not angry at her?"

He shook his head. "No, sir. I'm not."

I came closer. "Mr. Moody, your principles are, 'Tell the truth. Live and let live. Care for the kids, for tomorrow is theirs. No cussing, or you're not righteous.' Correct?"

He nodded solemnly, one eye narrowed. "That's right."

"But Rachel's lying through her teeth, right?"

"She surely is. Sad but true." He shook his head, mystified.

"She's violating one of your life principles, right?"

He thought about it. "Yes, sir, she is."

"Those Vietnamese toughs, what life principle of yours were *they* violating?"

He licked his lips. " 'Live and let live.' And, 'Care for the kids, for tomorrow is theirs.' "

"So they violated *two* principles, and you got hacked off?"

"Yes, sir, I confess I did."

"You said you'd even kill those guys, if necessary to protect those principles, correct?"

"Well, I don't really mean *kill*. But I'd make a stand." He coughed. "For her."

"Mr. Moody. How are you at telling the truth?"

"Objection, Your Honor, vague, argumentative, disputatious, and, as posed, irrelevant."

"Sustained," said Maxwell appropriately, clearing his throat.

I wanted Moody to answer fast. Quickly: "Mr. Moody, in the last ten years have you ever cheated on your income taxes?"

"No, sir."

"Mr. Moody, in the last ten years have you misrepresented the value of your home to a real estate appraiser?"

"No sir." He was already in rhythm with me.

"Mr. Moody, in the last ten years, have you ever lied?"

"No, sir."

I let that sink in. "Ten years, and not one lie. Mr. Moody, you know anyone else in the world who's as honest as you?"

"Objection, Your Honor, argumentative."

"Your Honor, the witness has made a remarkable statement, worth ample exploration."

"Sustained," said Maxwell. "You're about through the ice, Mr. Jin."

I looked at the jury. "You loved Rachel like a daughter. What does that mean, sir?"

He fidgeted, his voice lower. "I watch out for her. I'm there for her. Help her with science projects. Do the math with her, the words, the damn vocabulary flash cards. Drive her places."

"You make sure," I asked, "that no harm comes to her?"

He nodded. "Sir?" I asked.

"Yeah, that's right. No harm. No harm to Rachel."

"Mr. Moody, according to your principles, whom should a man love more? His wife, his father, or his daughter?"

I could feel Stacy toying with an objection.

"Daughter," he said.

"For you, sir, it's the highest level of love there is?"

"Yes, sir, it is," he said softly.

"Mr. Moody, your body's hurt, but can you admit that you *look* like a man who's physically fit, like a man of action?"

"Well, pain or not, I'm still a man."

"What does that mean, sir?"

"It means," he said slowly, "that I get around. I can break up a gang of Namese. Scare 'em off. Maybe I couldn't fight 'em all. But I *look* like I could." He smiled, his charm warming.

"Mr. Moody, did you love Rachel Farr, as a daughter, on the first day of February this year, while you were partying?"

"Yes, sir, I sure did."

"Do you think she loved you as a father that day?"

He nodded. "I do."

"Mr. Moody, why didn't you invite the girl you loved like a daughter, and who loved you, to your birthday dinner?"

"Uh, she said she was, like, busy. And it ain't right, her bein' around drink."

"Mr. Moody, who'd she love more than you?"

"I don't know. Her parents."

"But you stated under oath that her parents were 'jerks' who abused her, cut her, bruised her. You saved her from them."

"Okay, you ever hear of abusive relationships, huh? Where a kid gets whupped but she still loves 'em, anyway?"

"Yes, sir," I said, "I have. Is that who Rachel is?"

"Well, now, I can't really say."

"Fair enough. Mr. Moody, you described your relationship as being as father to daughter—the highest love in your world—yet you're telling us you 'can't say' who she is?"

"Didn't say that. You're twistin' my words, Mr. DA."

"Argumentative, Your Honor," said Stacy.

"Sustained. Continue," said Maxwell, tapping a pen.

I backed off. "Mr. Moody, how dangerous were those Namese toughs? The ones you say raped and beat Rachel."

"Plenty dangerous. Damn, they're hard boys."

"Mr. Moody, was Rachel capable of defending herself against a gang of Vietnamese—like the Vhanh Gang or Saigon Dragons?"

"Don't hardly think so. Why I wanted her to stay away."

"Mr. Moody, how badly did you want her to stay away?"

He nodded like he was rolling a cigarette. "Plenty."

"Were the Namese toughs more dangerous than, say, drugs?"

"Big time."

"More dangerous than drinking and driving?"

"You bet."

"Think back to February the first. In your mind, was *anything* more dangerous to Rachel than these Namese toughs?"

"No. Hell, you know that." He smiled with his teeth. "You being an Oriental and all."

I smiled back. "Mr. Moody, would your mere presence be adequate to protect Rachel from the Saigon Dragons?"

He nodded, squaring shoulders. "Yes, sir."

"You knew Rachel was still running with the Namese toughs?"

"Yes."

"Were they the ones you rescued her from?"

"Yeah, they were."

"Describe them. Like you described me. Like you described Mr. Clayton of the jury."

He licked his lips and shifted. "All them Orientals, they look alike to me. That's why I haven't chased them down. All I know is they're short and skinny and armed and dangerous."

"Knowing that the Namese toughs were the *most dangerous* thing in Rachel's world, you let her run with them?"

"I didn't *let* her. Her choice. Seems she sees something in Oriental people I sure don't."

"Would she have run with them on Saturday night, February one, if you had stayed home? Or if you had taken her to dinner?"

A pause. "Probably not. I don't claim to be perfect. And I feel plenty guilty about it, that night, partying late."

"Who are you angry at for what happened to Rachel?"

"Angry at? Me, I guess. Yeah, me."

"Objection," said Stacy, "irrelevant."

"He's already answered," I said.

"And I want it stricken from the record," said Stacy.

"Answer will be stricken," said Maxwell.

"I want to understand this, Mr. Moody. Rachel, the girl you love as a daughter, was tied up, beaten, and sexually assaulted *fourteen* times, and the person you're angry at is . . . *you*."

"Objection! Asked improperly once. Twice is ridiculous."

"Sustained."

"No, that's okay," said Moody. "I shoulda protected her better."

"How angry are you?" I barked.

"REAL ANGRY!" he yelled.

Softly. "But you're not angry at the Namese toughs."

He coughed. "Well, sure, I am."

"I can see that," I said.

"Objection, Your Honor!" cried Stacy. "Baiting the witness."

"Mr. Jin, quell yourself."

"I withdraw the observation," I said. "Mr. Moody, you stated that on the celebration of your birthday—ten days before your date of birth—you closed the Aviation Club Bar. Was that at approximately two a.m., Sunday, February two?"

"Yeah, thereabouts. I confess, I was a little soaked."

"Out of all the bars in town, how'd you pick it?"

"They got real nice people there. Not like here." He smiled.

"Mr. Moody, you had been there before?"

"Sure, plenty of times."

"You heard Rachel's testimony about becoming sleepy and passing out, after dinner on the evening of February first, and waking up to a stabbing pain, many hours later?"

"I heard."

"Isn't it *possible* that Rachel's assailant could have had dinner with her, left her when she fell asleep, then returned, after two in the morning of February second, to rape her?"

"Objection," said Stacy. "Irrelevant. It's *possible* the moon will fall on us in the next minute, but it isn't very likely!"

Some smiled. Hendrix, the roofer, looked at the ceiling.

"If the moon fell out of its orbit toward earth," I said, "its gravity would suck up our oceans and cities—and our courtroom ceiling and us—first—long before hitting the planet."

More smiles as almost everyone looked up.

"I want to hear this. Overruled," said Maxwell.

I tried to keep my feet. The judge was becoming curious about the case that was raging in his own court.

"I don't remember the question," said Moody, grinning until he saw Stacy's expression. He went convict-flat.

I repeated it: Couldn't someone have had dinner with her and then attacked her after closing the bars Saturday night?

"No," he said. "Don't see how."

"Why is that?" I asked.

"He'd be too drunk."

"What if this man only drank soft drinks?"

"Well, he wouldn't do that."

"Why not?"

"He just wouldn't." Moody looked at Stacy August. "Now, I have an alibi, sir," he blurted.

I let his words bounce around the court for a while.

"Mr. Moody, that doesn't answer my question. Why wouldn't the man who raped Rachel Farr drink soda pops or soft drinks?"

"I don't like soda pop!" He colored. "And I figure no other man does, either!"

Someone stumbled loudly on the courtroom aisle. Clearing his guilty throat, François put a note on the counsel table. I read it. "Mr. Moody, what's the name of the bartender at Rudy's Hideaway?"

"Beats me." A big smile.

"It's Rudy. How about at the Keyhole?"

He looked at the note in my hand and cleared his throat. "Joe Keyhole?" He smiled and winked. "Hey, I have no idea."

"The Rusty Duck?"

"No, sir."

"This is easy. The barkeep at the Aviation Club Bar, with real nice people. The bar you've been to plenty of times and closed on your birthday like you do every year with your best pal, Johnny Quick. What's the barkeep's name, Mr. Moody?"

He shrugged with a modest smile. "Man, I was pretty drunk."

"What's his name?"

"I don't rightly know."

"You love Rachel Farr right now, Mr. Moody, as a father?"

"Yes, sir, I sure do."

"Love her like a father when she testified against you?"

"A father's love don't change with the weather."

"Sir, see Mrs. Heck, court clerk, sitting to your left?"

"Yes."

"Sir, if Mrs. Heck testifies to your facial reactions during Rachel's testimony, will she say you beamed at Rachel with fatherly love?"

Moody looked at Liz Heck, who recoiled. Her cheeks colored a bright red. She lowered and covered her face. Moody looked at the bailiff.

"She don't know what's in my heart," said Moody through clenched teeth.

"Unresponsive," I said. "Judge, I request the witness be directed to answer."

"Yeah, okay! So I wasn't so happy! Jesus Christ, who would be?"

"Objection," said Stacy. "Counsel's provoking the witness."

"Sustained," said Judge Maxwell. "Back away, Mr. Jin."

"How unhappy?" I asked, low and hard to the ribs, through my teeth.

"Pretty freakin' unhappy!"

"HOW UNHAPPY, MR. MOODY?" The harsh, barking voice of a prison bull, smacking him in the center of his face, calling up his readily available surface adrenaline.

"DAMN unhappy! Bitch forgot who I was!"

I turned away to preserve the moment, knowing that Stacy August wanted the moon to fall. My heart was pounding. I gestured as if to speak, to keep him from opening his mouth.

I put the note in my breast pocket and took the DMV record

to Liz Heck's table. "Move to admit People's Eleven, the DMV record, into evidence, Your Honor."

No objection. "Thanks, Liz," I whispered. "Sorry to embarrass you. Please forgive me." She nodded, gulping, still redfaced. I couldn't see Geneva de Hoyas's face. It was lowered.

"No further questions of this witness," I said. There was another note from Stacy waiting for me at the counsel table.

54.

JOHN QUICK

I dropped my Trial Manual on top of the note and sat as Stacy repaired the damage with a flawless exercise in witness rehabilitation. It explained away his damaging responses, made light of my gains, and reestablished the beaming confidence of her client.

Moody apologized for having a big head about dates. He developed the habit while trying to impress Rachel Farr about his knowledge of school and history. Works with kids, doesn't work with grown-ups, he said. Dang, ma'am, I'm sorry. That was pretty dumb of me.

I celebrate my birthday on February one cuz it's easier to remember than the eleventh. Not a smart man. If I was smart, I'd never let kids use my place. Or use me as a fall guy.

It's true, I confess, he said, I don't like Mr. Jin. Reminds me of the Namese toughs. Man scares me. He's big and tricky and it looks like he's gonna haul off and hit me with some kung-fu karate chops. He has all the words and that college education and that badge and I was angry at him and it slipped out against poor Rachel.

Ma'am, I'm so sorry. I confess, I'm tryin' real hard to maintain, but truth is, I'm scared blind.

I ignored Moody rather than re-cross him. He was a liar and I had surprised him once. I couldn't do it twice without risking a reversal of fortune. I had made the points I could. Would the jury remember them? They could be footprints in the sand, washed away by Stacy's rehab on redirect. I looked at the jury. They were smart. They would remember.

An assistant public defender entered the court with a sealed envelope. She handed it to Stacy, who glanced at it and gave it to Moody, who read it, then whispered in Stacy's ear.

Stacy asked for a ten-minute recess.

The jury was happy to stretch and use the rest rooms.

Moody requested a latrine break. David Obstain motioned from the door. We found a relatively quiet corner near the end of the court hallway, flanked by an arguing couple, an angry bail bondsman, and a wailing baby. Obstain handed me a large envelope.

"Good news or a big bill?" I asked.

"Jin, we reinterviewed Rachel's classmates. Got no change in weather. Girl's not known as a liar and she don't have a case a round heels, neither. So she don't sleep around or pass out oral sex like a lotta them girls. She's shy. Has a rep of bein' weak, sickly, and whiny."

"I can live with that. Thanks, Mr. Obstain."

We shook.

When it was time to resume, neither Moody nor Stacy August was present. The courtroom stirred with impatience. Moody was the first to return, followed by his counsel.

Stacy had a small habit of touching her collarbone when nervous. She was pressing on it. She called to the stand Dr. Priscilla Anna Jost, a renowned criminalist and former employee of the FBI Crime Lab. Jost had participated in the shattering revelation that the world-renowned federal evidence analysis center was troubled by falling standards in quality control and personnel management. Last year she had done great damage to the prosecution in a federal explosives trial. The U.S. Attorney's Office had provided me with the trial transcript.

I had two questions I could pose to her without great risk and about three hundred that would only hurt. Dr. Jost was tall and composed, her eyes deep and observant.

She testified that a nurse's observations in a rape case, without accompanying biochemical analysis, were less probative, of lesser forensic value, than good, solid lab work.

On cross, I got Ms. Jost to acknowledge that there was nothing forensically defective in prosecuting without the standard array of physical evidence.

"It simply makes the prosecution's job harder," she said.

"I can appreciate that," I said, smiling. "But it should make yours easier. Ms. Jost, do you generally trust the clinical proficiency and scientific professionalism of SANERs?"

"Yes, sir, I do."

"With a high degree of professional trust?"

"A very high degree, sir. They're well educated, well trained and self-managed."

On redirect, Stacy August asked her to relate the importance of *volume* of scientific evidence in rendering a finding or a conclusion.

"Volume is critical in assessing credibility. The more data, the more sure I am."

On re-cross, I asked if the standard of scientific inquiry exceeded the law's criminal standard of beyond a reasonable doubt. She said it did. I had no further questions, and she was excused. Stacy was quietly speaking to Moody. He angrily shook his head.

Stacy asked for permission to speak to the judge in chambers. Maxwell readily agreed and we retired, leaving the jury and the court in place.

Stacy stood in front of his desk. "Your Honor," she said, "I ask the court to allow me to withdraw from employment in this case under Rule three dash seven-hundred-bee-two, California Rules of Professional Conduct. *In re Hickey,* fifty Cal. App. third, five-seventy-one." Rule 3-700 (B)(2) permitted relief because the client was knowingly pressing a conduct that would result in a violation of the code. Fin Maxwell found his copy of the Rules.

"Page thirteen-cee," said Stacy, sitting, eyes fixed to the front as he read. Stacy crossed her legs, her mid-knee hem rising. I moved away from her.

"Josh, this is ex parte," she said without looking at me. A meeting by only one party with the judge. "I am going to be compelled to reveal attorney-client confidences."

I asked, "Are you withdrawing your firm as well?"

"Yes."

Phillips Rittenhouse would not take over. There would be a significant delay to allow another counsel to be substituted and to become familiar with the case. He or she would move for a mistrial, which Maxwell would instantly grant. And Rachel would have to testify again.

I sat in the courtroom, rehearsing closing argument, just in case the trial resumed. I avoided contact with others, closing my eyes as I reviewed my major points and mentally restated the key passages. The jury fidgeted. Rittenhouse amended trial scripts.

"Sir?" asked Juror Clayton of me.

"Mr. Clayton," I said, "I'm sorry, sir, but you can't ask me anything." I motioned to Les Goss. "You can put any question you want to the bailiff, okay?"

"Mr. Bailiff," said Clayton, "can we stretch?"

Half an hour passed while jurors quietly discussed the weather. Two jail deputies in brown uniforms appeared and escorted Moody into chambers.

An hour later, Moody was brought back to the counsel table. I was instructed to rejoin Maxwell and Stacy August in chambers.

"Mr. Moody," said Judge Maxwell, "has conceded several points to counsel and court. Ms. August will not withdraw. The witness John Quick will not be called. Nor will other witnesses. Witnesses whom you no doubt anticipated to enter court and impeach your victim."

I nodded.

"Josh," said Stacy, "you are not to comment on the absent Mr. Quick." Perfect composure. Beneath it, a well-managed, abject misery I had seen once before.

"Under what theory?" I looked at Maxwell. It would be the

most natural trial tactic to carefully exploit the fact that the defense had advertised a named alibi witness but had failed to produce him at trial. It would be a Chinese banquet, awaiting the dinner bell.

"Under the theory that you can't," the judge said.

"Cite the authority, Judge." I looked at Stacy. "You going along with this?"

"It's not my decision. It's the Court's."

"That's a cop-out," I said.

She drew herself up. "I would be ill advised to argue against my client's interest. And what are you complaining about? I tried to withdraw and here I am."

"You should've dumped this case," said the judge.

"You have no standing to address prosecutorial discretion," I said. "Not in this case."

"Heavy slander, my boy," said Finley Maxwell, coloring. "Not to be quickly forgotten. What are you going to do?"

"I'm going to convict Moody despite you. Let's go back on the record." I left.

Judge Maxwell and Stacy resumed their seats. The jurors were ready.

"It is late Friday afternoon," said Maxwell. "Court is recessed until nine a.m. Monday." He repeated his admonitions.

We stood as the jury departed. They were resembling us—hiding their thoughts, their questions, and their doubts under neutral expressions. Some looked at Moody with somberness. Others pointedly ignored him.

I thought: Good signs.

"You are so crazy," said Stacy softly. She was writing notes in her tabbed trial log. Rittenhouse turned toward her and she gestured him away.

"Not without effort, and not without help." I stowed my files and books, leaving the note, imagining its contents, the scent of her in my mind.

55.

CLOSING ARGUMENT

Monday

I liked Mondays. The sun was kind, coffee was strong, insults were amusing, broken furniture had been repaired, and police error was not without comedy.

I was on the Yolo Causeway in thick traffic with the radio off, trying to avoid spilling cappuccino on my closing-argument suit with a high-contrast tie. The case was about honesty and lies, a man and a girl. It wasn't about Summer. But who would the jury believe?

"Ladies and gentlemen of the jury," said Judge Maxwell, "you have heard the evidence. The lawyers will now argue. What they say is not evidence. The prosecutor, then Ms. August, will deliver closing arguments. Then the DA, because he carries the burden of proof, has a rebuttal, a final chance to argue his case. I will then instruct you in the law and charge you with the case. You will retire to pick a foreman and deliberate. Mr. Jin?"

I stood before the jury. For the first time, I crossed the invisible border and touched the rail, joining their space. I looked at them.

"May it please the Court. Ladies and gentlemen of the jury. Thank you for your attention to this case. I said last week that the evidence of both the prosecution and the defense will prove that Moody did the crimes charged. I spoke the truth."

I held the rail as if I were gripping them. They were awake, focused, and ready. I made eye contact with each person.

"I said this case was about motive and circumstantial evidence. That it will be decided by your hard thinking and by your ability to tell the difference between lies and truth.

"It will be decided by your *convictions* about what is right and what is wrong." Clayton and Goin nodded. I turned to face Karl Moody.

"Ladies and gentlemen, the door was open and Rachel went in. It was six in the evening, Saturday, February the first. It was warm and clouds moved across a quarter moon, pushed by warm southerly winds. Rachel was on time, using the Timex watch Chico had given her for Christmas."

I looked at Moody. " 'Hey, sweetheart,' Chico called from the kitchen.

" 'Hi, Chico!' Rachel sang back.

"Chico appeared in a suit. Rachel was in cords and a sweat-shirt, ready for nachos. She was embarrassed because she was underdressed, staring at the handsome Chico in a tie and a suit. You know these facts.

"They rang true in your minds. They hold a spot in your hearts." I faced the jury. "You know what followed. Hideous torture, made unimaginable—*unimaginable*—by the fact that the victim was a trusting child, being savagely attacked by the man she loved."

I had placed seven empty easels on the floor of the court.

"I ask you now to use your memory.

"Picture some charts based on the testimony of teachers and students at Rio Junior High, under oath." I focused on Sobol, Richards, Clayton, and Goin, people who used graphs. I pointed at the first blank easel.

"Grades. Rachel was a good student until fourth grade, when her mother died. Rachel flunked and remained at a D for fifth and sixth grades. In the late fall of seventh grade, her marks rise dramatically to A's. Something wonderful had happened to her. What was that?

"Chico Moody was tutoring her. Helping her with vocabu-lary, history, math."

I pointed at the easels. "Everything in Rachel's life improved. Relationships with classmates. Relationships with teachers. Nutrition. Attentiveness in class . . .

"But in mid-February, something happens. She begins to fail." I held the pointer vertically, pointing straight down. I retraced the imaginary graph of grades. A drop at mother's death. A rise for Moody's tutoring. A sudden plummet this February.

I narrated the fall of the other imaginary curves. Attendance. Teacher contacts. Contacts with friends. Not eating lunch. Crying in class. The jury watched as if something were there—the drop, the rise, the plummet. Stacy watched me. I kept my eyes away from her.

I pointed into space, four years back on an absent flip chart.

"Here died Debbie Farr, wife of Ray, mother of Rachel. And a bright student with all Excellents became a marginal pupil who ended up failing the fourth grade. We all understand that. What happens to a child when her mother dies? A mother to whom she still speaks. And her father proves to be uncaring—"

"Objection, Your Honor," said Stacy. "Not established by the evidence."

"Your Honor, counsel didn't allow me to finish. I submit that it's more than fair to say that a man who permits the beating of his daughter, who lets a school counselor take his daughter to ER, who doesn't go to the hospital, and who doesn't come to court for his daughter's testimony, is someone who does not care. And, Your Honor, this is argument."

"And too much of it, Mr. Jin. Move on," the judge said.

I nodded. "Rachel then got a stepmother, who beat her. And her grades worsened.

"What do kids do when they are unloved? What do *any of us do* when we are uncared for? We look for love, for acceptance, somewhere."

Moody, for the first time, was frowning at me.

"Enter Karl Francis 'Chico' Moody, who gave her a place to hang out." The jurors looked at him. He rubbed his face.

"Later, he tutored her, helped improve her grades. He helped improve her *life*." I pointed at the many imaginary upswings.

"Then, February. The absence from school. The end of her doing homework. The plunge of her grades. The end of her meals. Sudden disassociation from teachers, friends. A huge, horrible, gut-pained, downward spike of hot tears."

I moved to the seventh easel and a flip chart lined with vertical and horizontal axes. On the vertical was printed LOVE above the horizontal axis and HATE below it. On the horizontal axis were printed SEPTEMBER, DECEMBER, FEBRUARY, and JULY.

I marked the dots. September, Rachel didn't like Moody at first. Then thought him cool, moving from DISLIKE to LIKE. He singled her out for study, and she began to care for him. The wonderful Christmas, the exchange of gifts. The rising ramp.

February one, a vertical drop, a right-angle dive. No more visits. No more Spango. No more Chico. "Rachel did not say how she now feels about Mr. Moody. But you all saw her face. Her bodily reactions. Those, perhaps, speak more loudly than any words.

"What caused this change, this incredible, dramatic drop from trust and love to what you saw in this court? Fear. Loathing. Trembling. Disgust? I will tell you what: Violent rape. Forced sodomy. Forced oral copulation. Beating. Choking. Abuse. Unspeakable spiritual pain, all from a man in a position of trust to a vulnerable and isolated child.

"There are no lab reports. So how do we measure anguish? *Nothing* could speak to us with greater eloquence, with greater force, with greater conviction, than a child's broken heart." I looked at Bukust, who had four kids he seldom saw. "The People have no physical evidence.

"But what have you seen and heard and witnessed? A child's crushed voice." Clayton, whose wife was a pastor. "A child's lost innocence." Richards, the nurse.

"A child's broken trust." Carlo, raising three sons alone.

"A child's loss of both parents. A mother, to death. A father, to his insufferable indifference. Then, like a miracle, comes a new father figure, bringing hope.

"But that new father figure turns out to be a child raper, a savage molester, a blitzer of children." Richeson, Hendrix, Takahashi, who had lost parents.

"A child goes from love and trust to revulsion and hate, where the very idea of that person causes the stomach to rebel." Clayton, Bukust, Richeson, Hendrix, fathers.

"What makes something like that happen?" Sobol, Becerril, moms.

"You know the answer. We all know it. And there is only

one." I looked at Wolstoncroft, a mother with a very soft heart who might have trouble convicting. "Or four answers."

I drove my fist into my left palm four times, the impacts echoing. "Rape. Sodomy. Forced oral copulation. Beating." I dropped my arms, then raised my palms.

"Ladies and gentlemen, ask yourselves: Does it make sense that Rachel would *lie* about being beaten, raped, sodomized, and subjected to forced oral copulation? You have heard from her teachers that Rachel is not a person with a powerful imagination.

"These were *unimaginable* crimes. You have heard that Rachel is a very private person who fears being the focus of attention. Think of what this trial cost her.

"You saw her testify. You *know* where she learned about the offenses which were committed against her. She learned them by being savagely attacked by a man whom she thought loved her, but, in fact, cared not at all for her. Except as a thing.

"Think back to when you were thirteen. Imagine if you made a mistake and went into the wrong neighborhood, and a Vietnamese gang subjected you to unspeakable crimes. Would you blame the person you loved most? Ladies and gentlemen, you wouldn't. You wouldn't falsely accuse a person who had given you his time, attention, help, and care.

"You saw Rachel. She's wounded and small of voice. But she's a fighter. A brave kid who came into this intimidating court, filled with adult strangers, and took the oath to God, testified in front of the man who tortured her, and endured his lawyer's intense cross-examination and the hostility of the court itself." I had to take a breath.

"Is this a kid who's afraid of a gang? When you think of what was done to her—when you recall her testimony that she *asked God to kill her and cursed God for not doing so*—does it make sense that she wouldn't seek justice by going after the gang?

"The defense would have you believe that DAs and cops and nurses forced this girl to lie against Mr. Moody. So a gang of raping thugs could go free. Does *that* make sense? If we had *that* much power, why not use it to go after the gangs? Do you really think that an ER nurse would look at Rachel and say, 'Oh, let's not prosecute the gangs for this! Let's blame an innocent man! And just to make it interesting, let's make it the man the little girl loves.'

"You saw in the counselors, teachers, and nurse, the thing that connects us as people: Compassion. Integrity. Caring. There's no global conspiracy. You saw everyday people serving as a community of care for a wounded child.

"Ms. August told you in her opening statement that there was no physical evidence in this case. But there is. Her name is Rachel Farr. And despite and because of what she has suffered, she remains, to us, precious, cherished, priceless.

"Ms. August said that you will see anger and truth from the defense. When you felt and grasped that truth, you would acquit Mr. Moody, and, I quote, 'feel anger at his false accuser.'

"I have to tell you: I hope you *did* experience anger and truth from the defense. Mr. Moody is as believable as a State Fair carnie at the Expo asking you to toss a dime at a jar. It *almost* looks like you could drop that coin in. Don't fall for it. The dime is a lie. It won't fit most jars, he doesn't have that magic coin, and the jar isn't even there.

"See, to win, the defense has to turn the facts around. Nurses are the bad people. Child molesters are angels.

"Those are lies. But we'll let the defense explain it. I want you to listen *very* carefully to Ms. August when she argues. See how she explains what happened to the Vietnamese gangsters Moody said raped Rachel. And the witnesses who saw Rachel hang out with the gangs. The witnesses who could even *identify* a gang. And where are the witnesses in the bars who saw Moody on the night of February one and the early morning hours of Sunday, February two, as he openly drank his way across the county? Where are the waitresses, waiters, servers, and fellow diners from the Old Spaghetti Factory who sang 'Happy Birthday' to Chico Moody?

"This is a man who lies about his birthday. He lied about being good with dates. He explained his lies by blaming Rachel. It was Rachel's fault. And he explained that he wasn't really angry at Rachel when he called her a terrible, an unacceptable, name, right here, under oath, in open court.

"There's more. It was *my* fault that he lied. Mr. Moody doesn't like the Chinese prosecutor, says I scared him. So he blames the child victim and calls *her* names."

Moody looked at the jury, nervous. I shook my head. "You know, maybe it *is* our fault that criminals kill and rapists rape. But I don't think so. I think it's theirs.

"Who is Karl Moody? He's a lonely, isolated man. He may have the odd friend, but you heard him. He opened his house to youth. Kids. Children nearly thirty years younger than he. He fed them and entertained them. Got them teen junk food, hip-hop music, a cute dog, and juvenile tattoos—things that speak to youthful interests, not adult tastes. Body rings, MTV, afternoon popcorn. It's possible he has the social skills of a less mature man. He pals with kids. Teenagers. Maybe that's okay.

"He was attracted to Rachel. How did he describe her for his lawyer? His first words—'She's a pretty girl.' The reporter, Mrs. Coggins, can read it back for you if you wish.

"Did he regard her as his daughter? Probably yes, to some degree. But he never lost sight of the fact that she was pretty. That's important, because what he did to Rachel Farr on the evening of Saturday, February the first, was dictated by *his* needs, not hers.

"He sat up here and testified under oath to you that he'd be the fall guy for Rachel. He'd take fourteen false sexual assault felony charges. He said that if she wanted to hurt him, he was her gentle man. The truth is the exact opposite.

"He wanted sex with Rachel, but he knew she was thirteen and wouldn't want that. So he knocked her out with something. When she was asleep, he savaged her, then soothed her, attacked her, calmed her. Raped her. Comforted her. 'Go with the flow, Rache,' using the shadows of her former trust to bandage his savage attacks.

"To get away with it, he planned it carefully. And he counted on *her love for him*. Her need for him, to give him pleasure and, later, to give him sanctuary from the consequences of his terrible, hideous acts. It was close, ladies and gentlemen. It almost worked.

"If Kimberley Hong had not been *absolutely insistent* about taking a battered and bruised, underperforming student to the Med Center, we never would have known. Why?

"Because her parents weren't going to report it. And neither was Rachel herself.

"The defense says Rachel is lying. Does that make sense? If you're going to tell a big lie, you have to *say something*. If you want to stick an innocent guy for a rape, you have to tell someone that he did something to you. You know what? You'd *scream* it from the housetops. But Rachel said nothing for months. When asked by the school, by the hospital, by the police, and by the DA, she said *nothing*.

"Mr. Moody claims that teachers, nurses, cops, and DAs—the so-called bad guys—told Rachel that if she didn't name someone, *she'd* be in trouble. Because of an election!" I shook my head. "Old vegetables in a frying pan have given better explanations than that.

"The prosecution charges Karl Moody with fourteen felonies committed against an innocent female child. But I will never accuse Mr. Moody of being a good liar.

"Ladies and gentlemen, he's proven, beyond a reasonable doubt and to the exclusion of all reasonable doubt, that he's a *wretched* liar, a *terrible* liar. He's done to the truth what the captain of the *Titanic* did for seamanship.

"Members of the jury, who has the motive to lie? Rachel? Rachel gets nothing out of lying except the reputation of being a raped girl, an utterly undesirable condition.

"What does *Moody* get by lying? His *life*. His *freedom*. His *everything*.

"Rachel is doing the right thing, no matter how painful. For Moody, it's getting away with raping a child, no matter how shameless.

"Who's more believable? A teenaged girl who is in the most self-conscious stage of her life who, in telling the truth, shames herself before total strangers and all who know her by admitting that terrible, unspeakable things were done to her? What will be said at school about Rachel? How will she be regarded by the other students and the faculty? She could be the best student, the best athlete, the kindest friend, the most generous tutor—it won't matter.

"Forever more, she'll be That Girl Who Got Raped. This'll be whispered behind her back—and said to her face—for the rest of her adolescence and much of her adulthood. Who wants that? No one! This is no great prize to be won. Who's kidding who? That kind of attention is something she tried with *all* her youthful might—to *avoid*.

"Her rape was a terrible truth to carry—but a truth to be told—at great personal cost.

"Or, ladies and gentlemen, do you prefer to believe a man who says he loves Rachel like a daughter, but calls her— pardon his word—a 'bitch'?

"You told me, under oath, you could hold the defendant accountable for his acts. Not because he is a good man or a bad one, but because *he did it*.

"Do you wish to know what a guilty man looks like? How he walks, talks, carries, and explains himself? How he dresses and speaks under a godly oath in front of a sworn jury?

"You have seen him. He is right here, seated among us." I approached Chico Moody. Phillips Rittenhouse tensed. Stacy August remained perfectly composed. My voice was raw.

"It isn't difficult to identify truth." I stood in front of the defendant, looking at him without anger.

"It isn't difficult to find falsehood." I pointed at Moody's face. "It's not hard to say, I don't believe you; I believe you lied to us, and I find you guilty as charged."

Pointing, I looked at the jury. "Under oath, you, as a jury, said you could do it. Of course you can. The People expect you to do your duty. Do not shirk it."

Stacy August slowly stood in the center of the courtroom floor and delivered a short, perfunctory argument, excellent in diction and powerful in language. I quietly sucked on a Ricola to restore my voice while I listened, mesmerized, to hers.

"Ladies and gentlemen. You have heard the evidence. I cannot more powerfully warn you against the hazards of relying upon a child witness to determine the outcome of this case. We distrust children for a reason. That reason is impeccably clear in this case.

"Children lack the maturity to know truth. They are too easily confused, too quickly distracted, too hormonally charged to know the true state of reality."

It was too early for me to object.

"Mr. Jin has suggested that my client is not telling the truth. I ask you to remember Mr. Moody's words and judge them. I have heard voices like Mr. Moody's before. They belong to men of character, of integrity, of reliability. Men like him settled the West, cleared homesteads, defended the range, supported others, joined in the common defense.

"Mr. Jin," she said, using a tone that suggested I was a toxic polluter, "made much of Mr. Moody's birthday." She looked at me with pity. "Is this the stuff of which verdicts are made?

"Are you to decide this case based on the date of a birthday party? No, of course not. You're better than that." A pause. "Smarter than that. You know I speak the truth.

"Let's look, for a moment, at the prosecution's case. It's based on a girl's *extremely* stale claim that a man who cares for children abused her. Attacked her. Savaged her.

"This *stale claim* was fortified by some charts." Stacy crossed her arms as she hitched her head toward the empty sheets. "Grades. Attendance. Teachers. Friends. Lunches." She shook her head. "We know what teenagers are about. Inconsistency. Confusion. Dishonesty—"

"Objection, Your Honor. There's been no evidence of those qualities by *any* teenagers in this court, much less the victim in this case."

"Overruled. Mr. Jin, I dislike interruptions of closing argument. Please restrain yourself in the future."

I sat. Stacy walked by the easels, eyes on the jury. "You heard what a case such as this *should* have as a foundation in physical evidence. Mr. Jin, here, says his victim is the physical evidence. That is nonsense. It is the *prosecutor* who offers you a carnie trick.

"We live in the scientific age. We have computerized DNA and blood serum analysis. Scientific semen analysis. Automated latent fingerprint and DNA comparison analysis. Skin and dermatological analysis. Microscopic fiber analysis. Woods lamps. Electronic voice analyzers and light detectors." She paraded past them, holding their attention, her face turned to them, the general reviewing her troops, her physical presence drawing and holding them.

"*That's* evidence, ladies and gentlemen." She held her hands as if measuring a fish. "Not," moving her hands dismissively at the blank easels, "that." She leaned on the rail and faced me, causing fourteen sets of eyes to settle on my face. "We should expect more of our prosecutors than manipulative and vague, inexact little ink dots of teenage behavior in our crowded, dangerous classrooms. We *demand* more if he is to claim he 'did his job,' and produced evidence that exceeded reasonable doubt.

"I will tell you what disturbs me. There is nothing *but* reasonable doubts in this courtroom, but Mr. Jin presents himself as if he had removed them. Worse, Mr. Jin *exaggerates* the fears of the victim while making light of those of my client. Mr. Moody stated that Mr. Jin worried him. Mr. Jin rattled him. Mr. Jin *intimidated* him.

"Do you believe him? Or, if you had *this* DA," pointing at me, facing me, eyes incandescent, "pursuing *you*, working out his devils on *you*, with the vast, virtually unlimited powers of the State and the entire District Attorney's Office at his disposal, would you also be worried? Rattled? Intimidated? You felt it. Mr. Jin imposed his physical presence on my client. I tell you now that such bullying does not constitute the operation of law. It is the low, mean maneuvering of a common street thug, the tactics of gangsters. You know I speak the truth.

"Who here is David and who is Goliath? Indeed!

"But I am not here to reproach my opposing counsel. I am here to remind you of the presumption of innocence of my client. I am here to remind you that with all of Mr. Jin's energetic efforts to present a case, my client's innocence remains intact. And I am here to inform you that the prosecutor has been forced by the unavoidable weaknesses of his case to resort to tricks and empty graphs. To illusions of strength. To posturing, to bullying."

She paused to smile, almost inwardly. "It's true that lawyers are conditioned to *win*.

"We learned this in law school. You know, if I were the district attorney, I'd want Mr. Jin on my side. And he is trying. It's his job. I do not blame him. Nor should you."

She looked at them kindly. "But none of this is evidence worthy of conviction.

"Remember. The defense need do *nothing*. Absolutely nothing. The prosecution carries the totality of the burden of proof. It must prove, *beyond* a reasonable doubt, that Mr. Moody did each of the acts with which he is charged. BEYOND a reasonable doubt.

"Mr. Jin has not even come close. He is a good speaker. But how much better he would be were he arguing a strong and worthy case, rich in evidence, supported by science, helped by logic, based on a victim who cried out her outrage! How grateful I am that he is not!

"Ladies and gentlemen, we know a good case. The victim cries, weeps, and *screams* her violation! She does not whisper to a jury, half a year after the crime—but cries *instantly*! A fresh complaint is a credible complaint. A stale cry for help carries no conviction, no persuasion. It raises doubts because it is subject to manipulation, imagination, creation, rehearsal, embellishment, subterfuge, cinematic enhancement, rewriting.

"Ladies and gentlemen, we know a good case. The victim reports the crime and cooperates with the nurses. Physical evidence is obtained. A police search is conducted. Clothing, DNA, PGMs, blood, semen, hair, fingerprints are found. Now the DA has a worthy case—a victim's fresh statement and forensic evidence." Stacy held her hands easily.

"And even then, convictions do not come easily. This is because the Constitution of the United States of America requires the prosecution to hurdle a very high standard of proof.

"Ladies and gentlemen, this is not a good case. All the DA has offered you is a deep voice, a birthday party, imaginary graphs, and an unhappy teenager." A slight beseeching angle of her back. "For this, we vote to convict?" She straightened and took a deep breath. "I think not. You *know* not." Her words rang in the court.

"Mr. Jin has a chance to argue with you again. This is my last statement to you. There is much at stake here.

"We asked you to do many things as a juror. We take your precious time. Your attention. Your knowledge of life. We did not ask you to abandon your common sense. Is Mr. Moody guilty of naïveté, of overtrust? I think so. But guilty of child sexual assault? Not possibly.

"Not possibly. Please. Do not mistake the prosecution's argument for evidence. The evidence in this case would not threaten to overturn a thimble, or raise an eyebrow, or budge Lady Justice's proud scales." She leaned on the rail. "You know I speak the truth."

She frowned, charging them with her will. "Do not be fooled by sparkling advocacy when you have heard no evidence. Ladies and gentlemen, doubt rings so loudly in our minds that this place seems to be the nave of the great cathedral of Notre Dame.

"You have but one choice in this matter: you *must* return verdicts of not guilty. Why? Because there is nothing *but* reasonable doubt regarding Rachel Farr's whispered little statement. There is nothing *but* reasonable doubt regarding who beat her. The girl has *two* battering parents! She attends school in Chinatown—filled with danger and guns and gangs. And she admits to being under the influence of some sort of narcotic.

"This girl has suffered much loss. We sympathize with her, and that is generous and that is right. We need not believe her fabrications, for that would be unwise and unjust. The Constitution of the United States was written for this case. Something terrible happened to Rachel Farr, but the defendant is presumed innocent. You have heard nothing to shake that presumption. He sits before you, innocent and trusting in your judgment.

"Against him, in the scales of justice, sits a false and stale claim. Ladies and gentlemen of this esteemed jury, you are obligated by the facts of this case to reject that claim.

"What is doubt? Doubt is the angel of conscience. It sits in your mind, and in your heart, and when it is triggered, a small light is illuminated on an internal dashboard. A warning light, telling you something." She shook her head. "There was no evidence. No proof. The light of doubt that went on before this trial began yet glows brightly in your consciences. . . . Follow your conscience. Do the correct thing. Vote not guilty for each count. And do it now."

Stacy bowed slightly and with elegance, returned to her seat.

I had the burden of proof and therefore, a final chance to address the jury with the last argument, the Rebuttal. I took a shallow breath, relieved that my voice was strong and resonant. "I have three brief messages for you.

"One. Children can speak truth. It's one of their skills. Adults see things as they ought to be; kids see things as they are. This all boils down to a girl's word against a man's.

"When my daughter was four, she already knew to hold my hand when crossing the street and to stay close to me in the park. Once, I asked if she had brushed her teeth. She smiled, showing colorful hints of Froot Loops cereal she had finished only minutes before.

" 'Yes, Daddy,' she said." My voice broke. I looked down for a few moments. Thinly, I said, "Children's lies are called 'fibs' because they're transparent and trivial. Webster's Dictionary says that 'fib' is probably a shortening of 'fable.' A fable is a fictitious narrative, a legendary story designed to enforce a useful truth. But a fib is a child's lie.

"Children, bless them, can't tell good lies. They tell immature ones. My daughter told a fib. Why? Because she didn't want to brush her teeth. She wanted to go to the park now.

"A seventh grader says, 'Mom, I did my homework,' but when you look, it's obviously not done. A fib. Why? To avoid homework, to get to the tube or the game.

"Rachel, embarrassed and ashamed, told you that Chico Moody raped her. If this is a lie, where's the transparency? Where's the Froot Loops stain? The undone homework? Where's the motive—the thing she gets to do, or receive, as a benefit of the lie?

"She lied so she could be shamed? What benefit does she enjoy by becoming physically ill through the memory of rape? There is no added value in fabricating a rape. She's shy and quiet, and this place, ladies and gentlemen, makes her stomach hurt. This place is not her stage. It's her hell. But she has a conscience, and she has courage.

"As do you.

"My second point. Ms. August said we know what a good case is. She's wrong. There are *no* good child sexual assault cases. But this case shares one commonality with other child rape cases with scientific evidence: the harming of a child. Harm you can see and believe.

"My final point. Ms. August said I have suggested her client was not being truthful." My voice returned. "She does me a disservice. I suggest nothing of the sort." My eyes on them.

"I say that the defendant, Karl Francis Moody, is a rapist and a fraud, but I repeat myself." I pointed at Moody. "I don't suggest he is slow to the truth. Mr. Moody is a patent, arrogant, in-your-face, deep-dyed, sheep-dipped, stone-cold, remorseless, unconscionable, unforgivable liar, a cowardly raper of children by night and a bold liar by day." Quieter.

"I ask you to remember your oath and to do your duty. Be not reluctant. Embrace it willingly, with care and with moral courage." I gripped the jury railing with both hands.

"Remember where we came from. Beneath tall and noble shade trees, soccer games are played and softballs are knocked through amateur infields and children shake hands after all is done. Year in and year out, teachers teach again and again, and care. Parents do the thousands of small, endless duties of raising children. This is our world. In it, there is justice.

"We feel it every time our children take breath. Now, you twelve and you two backup jurors hold justice in your hands, in your hearts. Do not be distracted. Be not discouraged.

"A man hurt a child. The child deserves justice. *Give her that justice.*" I pointed again at Moody. "Do not shrink from this duty." After a moment, I released the railing.

Stacy, Judge Maxwell, and I had reviewed CALJIC, the California Jury Instructions, including Stacy's and my independently fashioned instructions. Maxwell had accepted all of Stacy's and two of mine. Now, he read them, giving the law and explaining the thirty-two verdict forms. All twelve jurors would have to agree for them to be signed by the foreman or fore-woman. I was happy to see some of the jurors still taking notes. He said they would not be sequestered, and that they would deliberate until lunch, and then again until four-thirty.

He instructed them to retire and select one of their number to be foreman/woman, who would then preside over their deliberations. We stood respectfully as the jury exited.

"Not bad," said Stacy, smiling at me over her shoulder as she went to face the press.

The media was almost interested in me. Rittenhouse hoped a reporter would spot him. "Mr. Jin, a fine argument," said a reporter. "I've never seen a judge so biased. Why's that?"

"I can't comment on that."

"But you agree that Judge Maxwell was actively opposed to the prosecution?"

I sat next to Mrs. Aldo, the curious octogenarian, and her friend, Mrs. Afreem.

"You had some fire today, young man," said Mrs. Aldo.

"I hope that's good. Who's the lucky recipient for that?" I asked.

"Lynnie, my great-granddaughter." She held it up unsteadily. A brown doe in white snow with red holly. She coughed deep in her chest once, twice.

"It's beautiful. Are you okay, ma'am?" She nodded. "What's the verdict?"

She gathered her breath. "Young man, even without any evidence, I think you're going to convict him. Mrs. Afreem agrees with me." Mrs. Afreem nodded in confirmation.

"But Mr. Moody's not as bad a man as you think."

56.

VERDICT

Wednesday

François Giggin struggled through the door with his empty felony box. It was the third day of deliberations and life for everyone but Rachel and me had resumed normalcy—she and I, for the moment, had no other cases. I sat, reworking the trial, wondering if I had given the jury enough to convict. Worrying that I had not. I was no different now than when I began in felonies. Lawyers did eternal postmortems on their trials, playing endless what-ifs.

"Horse walks into a bar," said François. "Bartender says, 'Hey, why the long face?' "

The phone rang. The jury was back.

François called Bilinski, Capri, and David Obstain. I called Ava. She'd pick up Rachel and Kimberley Hong at summer school.

The court could deliver verdicts without the victim present, but it couldn't without the attorneys of record. I delayed arrival in Department 49, waiting for Rachel. We would take the outcome together, as a team. I looked at my watch.

Moody had to be moved from lockup, suited, transported to court. We had half an hour.

I waited by the fourth-floor elevators. It was easier to greet colleagues; I had done a trial, whatever the result, and was again part of the brotherhood, the sisterhood, my wounds and abrupt demotion parts of a storied past. The word had gone out that Jin had not cried, so the litmus test case was not an automatic loser. I heard the talk: before you know it, he'll be after Tanya Churchill to recover his bureau and his investigators and his old parking space.

316

Capri appeared. She smiled and hugged me. "You did good."

"Don't know that," I said. "Not yet." A receiving line. Harry Bilinski and François Giggin were next. Capri shook hands with both, Ms. Perfect offering an olive branch to the Backshooter.

"You're going to make me sentimental," I said.

"Exactly," said Harry, "what we fucking need from you."

David Obstain emerged and handed me an envelope. "Discount."

"Thanks. It's the only way I'd know." The trial had been expensive—almost a night in jail, five thousand in contempt fines, Obstain's PI fees, and maybe my job and my law license.

Four more elevators emptied. We clustered to one side and from the back came Ava, Kimberley Hong, and Rachel Farr in clean black jeans and a white shirt.

"They're back too early to acquit," whispered Ava in my ear, her breath making me sigh.

That's what I'd say if it weren't bad luck to say it. I shook with Ms. Hong, her hand shivering with excitement. I placed an arm around Rachel, smiling as she accepted.

"It's *ji hui*, bad luck, to look at the jury with hope. Just say a prayer." Summer, maven of families, would have enjoyed this moment, her parents marching into court with a lonely child.

Down the aisle. Bailiff Goss put a chair next to me for Harry. Rachel, Ava, and Capri were in the back to avoid the assembly of reporters and the austere Geneva de Hoyas, still in black, seated with two bureau chiefs, including the lean Tanya Churchill. Other deputies were sprinkled in small felony team groupings, lending moral support and fearing an acquittal as a harbinger of Sethman Jergen's inauguration. I shook hands with most. François sat behind me, in case he was needed. Obstain sat alone, studying the jury.

The jurors entered in file to fill the box. I didn't study their faces. It wasn't good luck.

Stacy wore somber gray. Rittenhouse tightened his tie. Moody wore blue.

"May we stipulate," said Judge Maxwell, "that all jurors are present and seated?"

"So stipulated, Your Honor," I said.

"Yes, Your Honor," said Stacy, who was studying the jury, looking at faces. Only one, Wolstoncroft, made eye contact.

"The record will reflect that alternates are present, defendant is personally present, and counsel are present. Will the forewoman please stand and answer, either yes or no?"

Ms. Sobol, Juror Five, the legislative aide, rose.

She was the mother of a fourteen-year-old, married to a lawyer. Clayton, the man I thought would be foreman, had traded seats with her. Ms. Sobol said, "Yes."

"Will you please declare your verdict by handing the verdict forms to the bailiff, who will hand them to me for examination?"

Les Goss took the verdict forms from Forewoman Sobol and handed them to Maxwell, who, without emotion, silently read them. Liz Heck waited by the bench, waving a Kleenex in front of her bright-red face. Fin Maxwell handed the verdicts to her.

"Madame Clerk, please read the verdicts to the jury, and ask if the verdicts as read are theirs. Defendant and counsel, rise."

Rittenhouse. Stacy, then Moody. We adjusted our jackets. I had been through this hundreds of times. But the heart always pounded as breathing accelerated and the blood became thick and heavy, its pulsing audible. The desire to look at the jury became irresistible.

I kept my eyes on the flag, almost light-headed. The jury was going to tell us if Moody was free to rape girls. Or if he was to die of old age, or at the end of a con's bloody shank, in state prison. If Rachel was to be redeemed. Or not. Liz Heck, face beet-red above a pale-green dress with a narrow belt, took a deep breath and turned to the first verdict form.

"In the Superior Court of the State of California," she said unsteadily, "in and for the County of Sacramento, People of the State of California versus Karl Francis Moody, Case Number 983422, Department 49. Verdict, Count One:

"We, the jury in the above-entitled case find the defendant, Karl Francis Moody, guilty of the crime of violation of Section 288(b), of the Penal Code of the State of California, sexual assault on a child as charged in Count One of the Information. Dated July twenty-one. G. Sobol, Forewoman." I exhaled.

This was court and not television; there was neither an excited chorus of exclamations nor a rush to telephones. Only hushed silence in which mice could be heard.

Bilinski squeezed my neck with a meaty paw. I took a breath.

"Ladies and gentlemen," the judge said slowly, flatly, "is this your verdict?"

"Yes," said the jury, as one. I seldom turned to look at the victim or the victim's survivors, but I turned to look at Rachel.

Her face was down in her hands, Ava holding her, crying, nodding at me. Geneva de Hoyas left, the bureau chiefs in tow. Whatever happened to the other charges, it was a victory.

I didn't understand why Geneva had stomped out. This conviction would make Conover look good. He'd garner all the Chinatown votes he could want. It could give him victory.

Liz Heck read the second count. "Guilty of the crime. . . ."

And so it went for the remaining felony counts and the two misdemeanor batteries, guilty one, guilty all. A clean sweep. A silk purse had been stitched from a sow's ear. I knew Professor Sachs would be pleased; I shouldn't have won this case.

When the verdicts were read, the judge asked if Stacy or I wanted the jury polled—asking each juror aloud if he or she agreed. Had Stacy seen one wavering juror during the reading of the verdict, she would have answered in the affirmative. Polling can shake a borderline guilty vote into a not guilty, creating a hung jury from an apparent verdict.

"No," said Stacy in a soft voice. I concurred.

"The Court," said Maxwell flatly, "declares the verdicts to be complete and directs the clerk to record them."

"So recorded," said Liz Heck, color draining from her face.

The judge referred the case to the Probation Department for a presentencing report and set the date for imposition of judgment and sentence two weeks later, on August 4.

Stacy requested an appeal bond to free Moody pending the results of an appeal. Judge Maxwell looked at the assembled press and knew, politically, that he could not grant it.

"Motion is denied. Defendant is remanded to the custody of the sheriff." Judge Finley Maxwell's accent shifted again across the cliffs of Dover. Moody would not look at anyone.

"Ladies and gentlemen, your services in this case are now completed. Will you kindly remove your badges. I thank you on behalf of the People of the State of California. You may now speak about the case, if you wish. You are all invited into my chambers—we cannot talk about the case, but I can answer general questions about the law.

"You may speak to the attorneys if you wish. I have directed the bailiff to only permit press questions in the hall. You are not obligated to speak to the attorneys. It is your individual choice. You are now excused from further attendance on this case."

Ava and Capri were still holding Rachel. Two deputy sheriffs watched warily as Les Goss cuffed Chico Moody. I'd see Moody again in two weeks for sentencing. Stacy August was speaking urgently to him. He kept shaking his head, then turned his back.

"Get me outa here, Bailiff," he said. "Now."

I sat. I lacked the energy to stack papers. My hands and arms were numb, as if I had been boxing a heavyweight for a month.

"Congratulations, Joshua," said Stacy.

I nodded. She had been handicapped at the end and was still beautiful. "Maybe someday you'll tell me what happened."

"Someday, my dear," she said, "I'll think of this trial again and I'll bite a dog."

I looked up and she was gone. Rittenhouse was gathering his books.

I faced the jury. They were waiting for me.

The forewoman and I shook. "Thank you very much," I said. The forewoman's eyes were moist and I turned around and silently cried.

"Jesus, Jin," said Bilinski, quickly turning away.

I shook their hands. Some touched me, some wept. Goin, Burda, Becerril, Wolstoncroft, Takahashi, Bukust, Richards, Carlo, Richeson, Hendrix. A jury I'd never forget. Machida and Ford, the alternates, had remained on call. I thanked them, too.

"If you ever think that the system doesn't work, remember this. Remember each other. How you trusted, believed, and worked. I can't tell you how proud I am of you. Or how proud I am to have worked with you."

Unified by a single week of work, they were reluctant to leave. People touched me, looking for words. "You cared for her," said Mrs. Takahashi. They parted as Rachel approached, her head slightly lowered under the weight of so many adult eyes. Almost Chinese. I offered my hands.

Rachel squeezed them. "you stopped him," she whispered.

"No, Rachel, you did."

Isaac Krakow and other deputies shook my hand. So did Bilinski. François Giggin could not stop smiling. Capri hit me, then hugged me, smiling.

"Don't even think about it," said Obstain. We shook.

And Ava was in my arms. I resisted the impulse to swing her around the courtroom. She leaned back and opened a hand to Rachel, who, head down, embraced us as people began applauding.

Ava looked at me as if all things were possible.

57.

NEW EVIDENCE

I gave interviews to Jan Yanehiro for the Bay Area news and local media, including the *Davis Enterprise*. I thought people should know a teenager had triumphed against high odds.

Ava and I took Rachel to Noodle Express in Davis, where she ordered frequently and well. "How do you feel?" I asked.

"Like another Smoothie."

The office held a ceremony and granted me the Silk Purse Award. My name was engraved on an old, cheap, garish plaque, adorned with a pink purse and a pig, joining others who had produced convictions from sow's ear cases. I held the plaque for a while.

"Speech! Speech!" cried staff, lawyers, and investigators.

High tribute—no one else would ask an attorney for more words. I said the award was won by the guts of a kid who had lost hope. All she needed was someone to help—a courageous school counselor, a conscientious ER rape nurse, four good cops named Wilma Debbin, Pico Larry, Katherine Capri, and Harry Bilinski, François Giggin the law intern, and a great DA's office, none of whom gave up on a silent girl. I told them that they were great.

"Put back the pictures of your kids. It's enough that we lost Summer. Let me enjoy your children. We all need to see their pictures, and hear about them."

Ava and I were seated in Ray and Dierdre Farr's cold and cluttered living room. It was early evening. The verdict had resolved Chico Moody's case; it had not fixed our marriage. We were trying to discuss Rachel's future while she was with Capri, killing root beer floats.

Mrs. Farr was enthusiastically in favor of Rachel staying with us for the foreseeable future, despite the fact that it was not an option. Ava and I, for all our progress and civility, were not reconciled. It was my fault that all things were not proving possible. But Ava and I agreed that Rachel should not be in this house.

Mr. Farr searched for words. His wife snapped open a plastic Hefty garbage sack and entered Rachel's room.

Ray removed his smoke. "Maybe we can wait on this."

"Where's her damn backpack?" came her voice from the back. "Bitch lost it."

"Damn if I know," he muttered.

Mrs. Farr returned, the sack half full. "I need to move this. Mind, for a sec?" She brushed back her hair. We stood.

Mrs. Farr grunted as she pushed back the sofa. It was heavy but she was motivated. I helped. On the unfaded and newly exposed rug were a backpack, pencils, a pen, an old TV schedule, and Lucky Charms candy wrappers covered with thick, heavy gray dust kittens.

"Damn, I knew it. You can have it, too." She kicked it distastefully. Dust flew.

"This is the one she lost?" I asked, waving away the dust.

Mrs. Farr nodded.

"How'd it end up under the sofa?"

"I don't know. Long time ago. It was after she was gone for two or three days and came back looking like death warmed over and she gave me lip and I kicked it. Hurt my foot."

"Last month?"

"Oh, hell no. Way back. January." She snapped her fingers at me. "Back when she had all this trouble. You know. *Your* shit. The legal variety."

"Mrs. Farr, since you threw it there, how many times have you, or anyone else, pulled that backpack from under the sofa?"

"I swear I forgot it was there. Ain't been touched since I-don't-know-when." She returned to Rachel's room with another Hefty bag. Ray struggled off the couch and joined his wife and shut the door. They were arguing.

Ray didn't want Rachel going to a Chink family. I appreciated Mrs. Farr's standing up for the theory of tolerance, even if it was for the most venal of reasons.

I was staring at the bag. Rachel wore cords and a pink sweatshirt when she went to Moody's on February 1. A pink Nike sweatshirt. Using a knife to avoid leaving prints, I hooked the zipper and pulled, releasing strong, stale odors. Using a pen, I gently inspected. Cords. Dirty pink sweatshirt with a Nike black swoosh. Stiff, soiled underpants. Bra. Hairbrush, hair her color. A bent photo of Rachel with an old spaniel. Spango, the dog to bond with. "You can't have her," said Ray. He was almost crying.

"How about another family?" asked Ava. "A white family."

"That'd be fine," said Mrs. Farr. "Right, Ray? Ray! Hel-lo! She's a pain in the ass, Ray. She drives me nuts, Ray. She doesn't belong here, Ray! Goddamnit, be a man, for once!"

"okay." He was looking at his shoes. "she's my daughter," he added, perhaps more for his exultant wife than for the quiet couple in his living room.

"I have to take this backpack," I said.

"okay," he said, sniffing.

"May we keep Rachel until the other family is found?" asked Ava. "The medical releases and power of attorney still work."

"Sure," said Mrs. Farr. She was disgusted with her husband, who still looked as if the answers were on the floor. We quickly stepped outside and closed the door.

"You cheap bastard," said Mrs. Farr. "Why don't you move out, too?"

"What color were the panties that you wore the night Chico attacked you?" asked Ava.

We were at the dinner table. "white, with flowers. they're all the same." Her voice had grown small again.

"Honey, what color was your bra?"

"white."

I knew the answer. "Where," I asked, "were the panties when he raped you?"

She was pale, closing her eyes, her sad hand movements suggesting the unpracticed steps of a newborn foal. "i still had them on. he pulled them, you know, over. so he could. . . ."

I asked a public defender friend to be a witness. If it hadn't been the election, I'd have asked a cop. When he arrived, I presented the backpack. "Please look at this. Don't touch."

Rachel was wondering why the stranger was here. "where'd you get this?"

"It was under your living room sofa."

I put a paper clip on the pack zipper. I pulled it and shifted the clothes with a letter opener. She looked in, gulped. "My clothes . . . that night." She shut her eyes, shivering.

"I'm sorry, Rachel," I said.

I personally delivered the backpack to the County Crime Lab and observed the chain of custody. The criminalists could harvest fibers, semen, DNA, pubic and head hairs.

I told Stacy August. She agreed to the taking of blood and hair samples from Karl Moody, who had nothing to lose. A male RN drew Moody's blood and took hair samples at the County jail dispensary while Harry and I watched carefully, ensuring they were his. We delivered the specimen package to the lab.

I was drafting the sentencing memo on *Moody* when Tom Baker came in and closed the door. Tom was director of the County Crime Lab.

"We have a situation," he said, putting a report on my desk.

I read it, then reread it. I appreciated his diplomatic assessment of disaster. The results had been double-tested and then sent to an independent lab. They were irreversibly solid.

"Anything you can tell me," I asked, "that's good?"

"Sorry. A tiny suggestion of tampering. Appears the clothes were thrown into a domestic garbage can, and then retrieved. It's not significant, since it doesn't explain away the results. The stain patterns are consistent with sexual assault, not debris osmosis.

"Josh, you shouldn't get something like this in the mail. Only the deputy lab director, the criminalist, and I know about this. We'll keep it that way until you tell us different."

I thanked him. He left. I stared at the report.

Another rapist was out there. Rachel was uncovered. I drove, fast, to summer school at Rio Junior High. Watching her, I called Ava. "The evidence we found in Rachel's clothing?"

"Yes," she said.

"It doesn't match Moody."

Intake of breath. "God."

I gave her the details.

Moody was O-positive and a non-secretor.

The semen in Rachel's panties was A-negative from a serum secretor—a male whose semen contained blood platelet secretions. It wasn't his blood. Nor was Moody's DNA in the semen. I read out the Ladder and K562 Control lines in the DNA printout, knowing that Ava was visualizing the fatal variances in the black DNA, pellet-shaped dot patterns.

The DNA in the panties, the known, did not come from the test sample belonging to the defendant—Karl Francis Moody.

"It means Moody," said Ava, "didn't rape Rachel. Someone else did. Or she was gang-raped. I assume no CODIS match?"

"No." We had the assailant's DNA. Unlike having fingerprints, having DNA didn't mean we had a name. The Combined

DNA Index System—CODIS—had too few specimens to be a good suspect-identification instrument. We had millions of fingerprints but few DNA records. We had two irrefutable forensic pieces of evidence and no ID. Only the scientific certainty that Moody hadn't left semen in her.

"What," I said, "if she was wrong and wasn't wearing panties when she was attacked—"

"And a person smeared them with someone else's semen in a pattern consistent with rape? And planted the backpack for us? Who could've predicted we'd be in the Farr house, asking to move Rachel out? Causing Dierdre Farr to remember the backpack? Rachel was wearing those panties when she was raped. She always said that." She frowned. "Josh, why didn't Wilma Debbin or Pico Larry find that backpack?"

"It was a stale-rape dump without a victim complaint. Mrs. Farr didn't cooperate. This case wasn't supposed to go to trial. Okay, what if Moody raped Rachel frontally with a condom. Or didn't ejaculate. The second guy, the A-negative secretor, then attacked her from behind. That'd be consistent with the evidence. With the right side beating pattern, front and back."

"But even if it's true, Rachel couldn't describe this other man. It was dark and she was tied down, restrained. Attacked from behind."

Unspoken was the chance that Rachel was lying. But she had no motive to falsely accuse Moody of rape. More to the point, I believed her.

I couldn't imagine reopening her wounds. But I had to tell her. We were moments from having it become front-page news: DA CONVICTS INNOCENT MAN OF CHILD RAPE, CONOVER BAFFLED.

Rachel came out of class, smiling, expecting a pleasant surprise. A lake trip? A Baskin-Robbins double-dipper and an order of large fries?

"Hey, Rachel," I said.

"Hi." She smiled softly at me.

We sat under the old, hundred-foot elms in the schoolyard where we had spent the spring, apart from each other, near the empty basketball courts. I looked in her eyes, feeling like a killer. "I'm going to give you some hard information. It won't be easy to hear."

She shut her eyes, her small brows furrowed with sadly well-practiced muscles, getting ready for something bad. okay, she said soundlessly.

"The Crime Lab checked out your clothes from the back-pack. They found semen. Rachel, it didn't come from Chico Moody. That doesn't mean Chico didn't rape you. It means that there was another man who also did. But the other man who left physical evidence, who left the semen, wasn't Chico."

A questioning gasp. She opened her eyes.

"Another man raped you. Rachel, I want you to go back in your memory again. To when you saw a man's face."

She was quivering without tears, eyes open, pupils absent.

"I know you have nightmares. But please do it anyway."

Panting, eyes jumping, the fear returning, anger brewing. "for you."

"No. For you. You should know."

She pushed away from me and walked, stopping near the spot where we had stood under the spectacular thunderstorm, soaked by the downpour.

"Did you ever see Chico's face?"

Shake of the head. "i heard him. it was for sure his voice."

"While you were being attacked?"

She thought about it, shrugged, and walked away. She picked up a twig and broke it.

"Or only afterwards?"

She was breaking the twig into smaller and smaller pieces, saving the debris. I waited. She said, maybe only after-wards. We listened to the sounds of traffic. She emptied her hand, found another twig and broke it, repeating the pattern. Snap, snap, snap.

I apologized. I said she had to be with an adult until we found the other man.

Rachel walked slowly to the car, as if each step reawakened a former injury, like an old woman who has lost her children, clutching the small pieces of broken wood.

That night Rachel did not appear for dinner or for evening

ice cream and cookies. Nor for breakfast the next morning. I listened at her door for sounds of life, fighting nausea, fearing death. From inside came a sound. Snap, snap, snap.

"Hello, Josh," said Geneva de Hoyas. "What's up?"

"The lab report on Moody exonerates him. I still think he raped her. But if he did, he didn't leave semen. Someone else—a complete John Doe—did." I gave her the report.

Geneva was an experienced trial lawyer and remained motionless amidst surprise. She was also chief deputy, concerned preeminently with politics and image. She read the report and asked the rational political question. "Who knows this?"

"Tom Baker, his deputy, the criminalist, you, me, victim. Ava."

"Let's keep it that way. Is there any good news?"

"I'm dismissing. I'll ask Maxwell for an 1181.8, new evidence trial, so I can dismiss I-E." Insufficient Evidence.

"Which," she said slowly, "is all I ever asked of you."

"You asked me to break the rules."

"Don't push it, Josh. You can't complain—I didn't override your discretion. I came to your court twice with the specific intent to dismiss it." She exhaled. "But I didn't."

"Why'd you want me to dump *Moody*?"

Senior male attorneys plop street shoes on desks, toy with fountain pens, scratch their heads, and adjust personal equipment. It seemed to me that women executives had none of these innate rights, behaving with impeccable Seven Sisters decorum.

Geneva crossed her hands. "Tommy asked me to get rid of that case. I asked him why. He said, 'Just for once, I want someone around here to do what I ask! Do it, Geneva.' "

"And you did it."

"I'm a lot more cooperative than you. Of course, with this case, Son of Sam looks more cooperative than you. But I still busted Tom's nuts. Because I didn't dismiss it for you."

"Why'd he give that order?"

She scratched her neck. Male habits were contagious. "I

think Thomas has some connection to Moody. I don't know what."

It was a huge admission. "What's your guess. A former case?"

"No idea. It's an ignorance I'm actively cultivating."

"That's not like you. You hinted we'd get Moody some other way. What way?"

"No way. It was something to throw at a charging animal. To slow you down."

"Why didn't you just tell me that? Instead of lying?"

"Let's just say I wasn't totally disclosive."

I exhaled. "Now you talk like Tommy."

"If I talked like him, I'd tell you to get out." She had given me some information and admitted lying. "You know, the press won't be kind. You'll have to hold a conference alone."

"It's all right. I'm not running for anything."

"You're still tilting at windmills. That's something."

"I could use your help. The windmills keep moving."

She shook her head. "If I get the boss's connection to Moody, I'll share it. You won't use it against him."

"I'm the guy who turned against Jay Wendell Nobis, the DA who hired him."

"You won't do that twice. Not for Seth Jergen. I'll bet on that."

Rachel slowly withdrew from us, and primarily me, spending days with Ava and evenings with Jodie or with music in her closed room. I noticed that she had folded her new wardrobe and put it in her new backpack, and slept with it close to her pillow. Miss Piggy had been dropped in a corner, forgotten.

58.

GONZO

"Mr. Jin," said a reporter, "District Attorney Conover said he tried to persuade you to dismiss *Moody*, but you persistently refused. Is that true?"

"Yes, it is. The DA's judgment was a lot better than mine."

"You've gotten job offers from the defense bar and a book offer. What will you do?"

"My job. I have a lot of work. A lot of repairs. Later I'll reassess."

"Mr. Jin, you've virtually destroyed a man's reputation. We hear you apologized."

"I was convinced he did the crime. I did." Moody had given me a flat con's stare.

"How do you feel about Seth Jergen's jump in the polls?"

"This case was about an innocent girl being raped. Not politics."

"Are you trying to adopt the victim in this case?"

"No."

"If you did, wouldn't that be a conflict of interest?"

"I applaud any adult working for the benefit of *any* kid. It's in our common interests to care for all our children. I think all our problems today stem from our failing to do that."

"Would you work for Mr. Jergen if he becomes DA?"

"We have a great DA's office. But we're not a personality cult. We work for the People. Our client is this community. We work for the law." I stepped away.

"Have you found the real rapist yet?"

"How do you sleep at night, Mr. Jin?"

"Do you think, in view of the O. J. Simpson case and Judge Ito, that Asian-Americans are poorly suited to trial work?"

"You're being investigated by State Bar Discipline for threatening Judge Maxwell. He said you're a violent man with an ugly temper, that maybe you're punch-drunk from your years in the ring. Do you think you'll be disbarred? Or should be? Or just suspended from practice?"

Joe Pelletier was on the second floor of the courthouse. He was the assistant public defender who opposed Gonzo Marx in the first *Moody* prelim. I asked him what had happened.

"It was weird," said Pelletier. "It's like the judge *wanted* Gonzo to fail. He harassed the hell out of him. He's the one who urged Gonzo to yell at the girl to spark her to talk. So Gonzo yelled, and the judge says, 'Do that again at your peril!' "

"Crap, what the fuck do *you* want?" asked Gonzo Marx. A dark shirt with a light, off-center tie made him look like a junior Mafia lawyer. His shoes were on the floor and his feet were on the desk. His desk was very neat, which was unlike him.

I closed the door and leaned on it for strength. "Gonzo, I convicted an innocent man. There's a torture rapist still on the street and I got a victim who can't sleep at night."

He thought about that. "Your worries don't have anything to do with your damaged rep."

"That too," I said.

"Okay," he said. "Fair enough. You got a minute."

"Think back. To Intake. There was no victim statement and no physical evidence, but it gets filed anyway. Think about case assignment. There were only *two* deputies in the office who should never have gotten a SACA case. You and me. And we *both* get it."

He took his feet off the desk.

"Then Geneva unethically orders me to dump it. Then Geneva makes you my co-counsel, but you had an openly bad relationship with Rachel. Not to mention that we don't have co-counsels in SACA cases." They were only used in death penalty prosecutions.

"And everyone," said Gonzo, nodding, "knew you were screwy after your daughter died and shouldn't get a kid case. Geneva said you needed help. From me! What B.S."

"There's more," I said, "judicial interference. On day of trial, Judge Thackery Niles tells me to dump the case—"

Gonzo sat up. "For what reason?"

"He's been pushing me toward the bench. He said this case would hurt my chances of appointment. But I don't want the job."

Gonzo stood. "That's what he said to me."

Gonzo being pushed onto the bench, also by Niles. I started taking notes. "When?"

"In the *Moody* prelim. Called me to a sidebar. 'Bucko,' he said, 'dump this. Want to be a judge, scrape this off your boot.' Hell, it was Niles who *told* me to yell at the little girl. So I did and then he rebukes me! Hell, I thought I was going nuts.

"Then I get Capri and Krakow jumping down my throat for being an asshole with the kid. I was going to tell them that Niles made me do it, but that's exactly the kind of lame shit I'm *always* saying." Shrug. "Wasn't like that case lost me a lot of friends and influence."

I looked at his vertical file tray. Most felony deputies toted about seventy cases—an immense caseload, twice what it should be and a third more than it was fifteen years ago. Gonzo had five thin cases. Geneva was hiding him until November. Then: Turn in your badge.

Unless Sethman Jergen won.

"Gonzo, we're both almost out of work. You got the time. Help me figure this out."

He paced, checking out pretty women on the street. He turned. "Who filed *Moody* in Intake? Who did Intake before you?"

"Masuda," I said. "It went from him to SACA. SACA to you."

He shook his head. "Masuda's a good DA. You know, first time I saw the *Moody* file was the morning of the prelim? I mean, you can do that with some cases. But not SACA." He picked up the file, checking dates on its face. "April eleven. I took that case and that weird little kid—sorry, I know you think she's cool—to court—stone cold. No prep. Fucking doomed to fail."

"I didn't know that." I drew circles and arrows on Gonzo's flip chart:

1 Det. Wilma Debbin arrests Moody....> [angry at DA ofc]	→	2 <u>MOODY</u> goes to Masuda/Intake....> [per Debbin]	→	3 Masuda sends <u>MOODY</u> to SACA [why'd he file it?]
		←		
4 SACA gives <u>MOODY</u> to Gonzo late....> [why and who?]	→	5 J. Niles nukes weak case...........> [anger at Gonzo?]	→	6 de Hoyas has <u>MOODY</u> go to Jin [dump/Chinatown case]
		←		
7 Jin convicts wrong guy..............> [surprise?]	→	8 Conover loses election................> [likely outcome]	→	9 Seth Jergen wins election [likely outcome] ✗

"Yeah. It was Geneva," said Gonzo. "No, come on! She has access to everything. She could make sure *Moody* went to SACA instead of back to the cops for further investigation. She could have lifted the case and dropped it on my desk the morning of the prelim. A SACA case requires rapport between the DA and the kid victim, right? I hadn't even met the damn kid, and she was a dead clam. And a chief deputy, as smart as her, could disappear those books out of Evidence." He shook his head. "Fuck. That doesn't make sense. Forget it."

"It adds up." I told Gonzo that Geneva thought there was some connection between Tom Conover and Karl Moody.

"Jesus. You gonna try to find out what that connection was?"

"No. We are. Gonzo, you take Conover. I'll cover Moody." I looked at him. "I've always wondered. You like being called 'Gonzo'?"

He shrugged. "My given name's Ardent."

I needed ex-con data. The resident expert on ex-cons was

Reverend Joel Frost. His number was disconnected. The phone company no longer had an account and he had vacated his last address. His neighbors had no idea who he was or even that he was gone.

At Fanny Ann's, Miss Gothic, in black fingerless lace gloves and a black bra, said that St. Joel hadn't been around for weeks. "Hey, what are you, Mexican or Chinese?"

I talked to Seventh Step workers who, like Joel, advocated for ex-cons. They heard that St. Joel had returned to Minnesota.

Joel Frost's marriage license revealed an ex-wife in El Dorado County. She wasn't happy to talk to me.

"That's my past, and my past's not part of me. My new husband won't take kindly to your pressuring me about this and you're not a DA here."

"I'm sorry, but I'm worried about Joel. He hung with a tough crowd."

She blew out air. "He brought ex-con perverts home. They were all pigs."

Her voice made me say, "Talk of the town was that you liked one of them."

There was a silence. "What are you saying?"

"Joel said you had an affair with that ex-con."

"Oh, Jesus H. Christ! That's real likely." She hung up.

Joel had attended the San Francisco Theological Institute. I called them.

No Joel Frost had ever attended.

59.

STACY

Stacy August had intended to call John Quick to the stand to alibi for the defense. Quick was to testify that Moody was with him all night. But there had been no John Quick.

Instead, there had been her attempt to withdraw because Moody planned an illegal course of action, followed by Stacy's conduct of her case with atypical restraint.

The black Double Quarter tower absorbed the searing hot sun. Surrounded by watch-checking attorneys and wallet-touching plaintiffs, I welcomed the cool glass and chrome elevator ride to White & August. I was bearing a boxed and beribboned gift.

"Hello, Josh," said Stacy August. A snug white suit, shorter than mid-knee, with heels. She came close enough to bite me, settling for a kiss on the cheek, a hand on my chest.

"Thanks for seeing me." I followed and sat in my appointed place.

She sat close, looked at the gift and crossed her legs. "Looking for a party?"

"I want you to help me find John Quick."

She recoiled slightly. "Well, that's ridiculous. That's privileged information protected under the broad reach of attorney-client confidences. I couldn't possibly reveal that."

"You might give me hints." I smiled.

"Why flirt with an ethical violation if a hint had the same result as a direct breach of a client's secrets? You were a homicide detective. An alchemist turning hints into admissible evidence. Handle this one, Josh, on your own, without me."

"Something happened in your case-in-chief. It changed you

and it's the key to my case. Give me a hint, so obscure I'd miss it. We both know you're smarter than I am."

She didn't argue. "Why on earth would I do that?" she asked.

"I have a victim and no one in custody and we both like doing the right thing."

"Oh. And we're officers of the court in pursuit of justice— that 'right thing' that we haven't much seen in practice?"

"Ballentine's Law Dictionary couldn't have said it better."

"Funny, isn't it, how we do the same work, but I get less media abuse, and am better paid? It appears the axiom applies. Better to be overpaid than to be right."

"You don't believe that. You put in twice my hours. They own you. Golden handcuffs."

"Pshaw. And they don't own you?"

I laughed. "I'm about to be fired. Maxwell's trying to disbar me."

"The State Bar's not interested in hurting you. You were outrageous. Not unethical."

"I appreciate that. Look, before you definitively turn me down on John Quick, let me bribe you." I opened the box and removed tinfoil-wrapped takeout from China Moon.

"Peasant dishes," I said. "The best." Stacy and I used to eat there at midnight.

She inhaled. "I remember."

I served them on her dining table. We took a few bites. I canted my ear at the music.

Handel's "Arrival of the Queen of Sheba." My crude wooden chopsticks scraped the paper plate. Outside, birds flew silently. The professional building was quiet, making money.

She put down her chopsticks. "Are you happy, Josh?"

"I am content. It is better than where I was. How about you?"

"Yes. I am." Her eyes traversed me. "You and Ava reconciling?"

"Not yet. I'm trying."

She sat back. "Will we always know each other?"

"I don't know that one. What happens when you tire of litigation?"

"I'll get a yacht, hire a Chinese chef, and sail around the world, diving in every deep lagoon, reading the great books, and eating a lot of fresh lobster in black-bean sauce."

It sounded good. From the box, I gave her the present. She unwrapped it. "How quaint. Its meaning?" She extracted a bright crystal ball.

"I've looked into the depths of that globe and have seen the future. You will find a smart, strong, and humorous man."

She smiled gloriously.

"You probably haven't met him yet. You'll work entirely too hard, but you'll be very happy with him on that boat."

She looked down for a while. I looked out her window.

"I can't have children, not now," she said. The light played in the crystal in her marbled office. "I waited too long. And you don't want kids. We'd be perfect. I'd let you have your male adventures, chasing all the bad guys you want. You'd let me have my highprofile trials."

I said nothing. She took a breath, shook her hair, and dropped the ball in its box. "You're a fool. An idiot." She smoothed her skirt and stood.

"I've heard that."

At the door she said very slowly, "And that is a horse of a very different color." She leaned on me. I inhaled her. Her arms were soft. The kiss was soft and distant and then she was clutching me, breathing in my ear, whispering.

"I never want to see you again. Ever. Zero contact, forever."

She pulled away. I looked in her eyes and she looked down, crossing her arms. "Go. Have a nice life. Plague other women. Protect your victims and chase your crooks. Lock them all up and beat up the other ones. Now be a good boy and say, 'Goodbye, Stacy.' "

I touched her cheek. She leaned into my hand, her jaw flexed, eyelashes blinking.

"Good-bye, Stacy."

60.

A MYSTERY

Steve Masuda, a senior deputy with a beautiful family and a black belt in karate, looked at the *Moody* case file. Most of us knew each other's handwriting.

"Those are my initials, Josh. But not by my hand." He put down the file, waiting.

"Check your calendar for March 3 and tell me who visited Intake."

He checked it. "Geneva de Hoyas. She was here." He looked at the file. "The same day that case got sent to SACA with my fake initials. Want to tell me what's going on?"

I smiled ruefully. "No, I don't."

SACA's secretary reviewed the logs. *Moody* was one of a thousand cases approved for prelim this year. She found the *Moody* entry on the daily SACA log for March 3.

"That means," she said, "someone slipped *Moody*, an unworked case—heck, an *unfiled* case—into our prelim calendar. That someone pulled it out, holding it out of circulation, in cold storage somewhere, for *five* weeks. And then handed it off, unprepped, to Gonzo—good God, Gonzo—on the day of the prelim?" She shook her head. "And Gonzo would just do it, wouldn't he? Without a friend to talk to or a supe who'd listen. Poor guy. Is this phantom someone in the office? Please tell me it's not. And tell me it's not going to happen again."

"I think the person's in-house. I think it was a one-time thing."

She looked around and almost peered under her desk. "Find him, Josh."

* * *

We were at the dining room table. Rachel glanced at the sheet of paper.

"You have," I said, "a choice of helping, or, if you'd rather, helping."

"Nice choice, Josh," said Ava. "What's for dinner?"

"Pizza, salad, and chocolate ice cream. Soon."

Rachel was hypoglycemic and short-tempered in a bad year. She looked down. "i don't want to and you can't make me."

"That's true. I can't. But this meeting's about you."

"what're you going to do if i don't? send me back?"

I nodded.

"That's not fair!" The trial had matured her, but the discovery that Moody was not her assailant had stunted her, her young soul and voice a yo-yo on a frayed string.

"Life's a curiosity. But it always gives you another day. And maybe that's more than fair." The oven timer dinged. I served the pizza and the tossed salad. "It's really good pizza."

Rachel looked away. "oh, who're you, the big mack daddy of, of pizzas?"

"That's him, honey," said Ava.

Rachel rested her head on her arms, tired and sad. She took a breath and burst into tears. Ava put her arms around her. I waited a few minutes.

"Okay," I said. "Let's connect the dots. There's an unknown rapist out there. On your sheet are listed eight subjects."

1. **VICTOR PETTY/MR. BUTTFACE** (kidnapped Tiffany Prue)
2. **JOHN QUICK** (Moody's nonexistent alibi, known to Stacy August)
3. **WAYNE FLUTE** (pedophile who tried to deal Moody, but died)
4. **JOHN ORSE** (pedophile who fled the motel with a girl, leaving a video card)
5. **6 RUNAWAYS FROM MOODY'S CRIB** (all disappeared same day)
6. **THOMAS CONOVER** (ordered Geneva de Hoyas to dump *Moody*)

7. **MRS. ALDO** (jury watcher who observed *Moody* trial and knows something)
8. **COPS** (got FLUTE's statement just before he died, but wouldn't share it)

"The good news," I said, "is that we have help. The bad news is that it's Gonzo Marx. He's trying to redeem himself. I say we let him."

Ava raised her eyebrows and fluttered her lips. Rachel violently shook her head.

"Okay, that's unanimous. Gonzo'll check out Mr. Conover. Rachel, would you sit down with a cop ID artist and describe Moody's runaways? Let's find them, and John Quick."

I started with Buttface's lawyer. Victor Petty would give us a statement in return for full immunity. No way and no deal.

"Forget it," said the cop who had transported Wayne Flute to ER. There he had expired from the bullet holes put in his body by the dying Sergeant Billy McManus. "You get Conover to kiss my ass on the courtroom steps, I'll think about it."

I looked at the cop and knew he was bluffing—there had been no statement. The cop didn't care what Flute had to say—he just wanted Flute to check permanently out of the net. What Flute had done for the cop was gargle out most of his life in the cruiser while he got lost on the way to the ER. It was a dead end.

I had checked Chico Moody's phone records in the search for John Quick. I rechecked. Moody had no credit card; besides being a factually Not Guilty ex-con, he was barely an American. I re-questioned his Chinese neighbors on Tulip. I called his deceased parents' neighbors in Virginia. We crawled the bars he claimed to have visited. Nothing.

61.

CATHOLIC SERVICES

In the guest room, I thought of Ava in our bed, alone, a floor above. An image of slipping under the covers. Perhaps I was like Stepfather Kwah. We were drawn to bright, beautiful women and solitudes, wide social spaces and bad times. But I had been a good father. Only for Summer. Her heart condition demanded that I stretch myself. And Rachel?

I imagined sailing blue waters, diving for lobster. Stacy. I had said to her, "I want you to help me find John Quick." What had she said?

"That is a horse of very different color." Horse.

John Orse.

I bolted up. The perv who fled the Paradise before Bilinski and I entered the unit. He had left an Adult Video Club card, a buddy, porno Polaroids with possible prints, and a .38.

John Orse was John Quick. Orse had split the Paradise Motel with a fourteen-year-old and had never been found. He snatched girls. I punched the phone number as fast as I could.

"Catholic Social Services, Home for Girls," said the staffer named Bette Maddock. The one who wore Lands' End ensembles. I identified myself. "How is Tiffany Prue?"

"Tiffany Prue packed and left with a policeman, a detective, just a few hours ago."

"Did you ask for ID?"

"Mr. Jin, please! I follow the SOP—I copied his driver's license and badge number. Yes, I'll fax you the copies. What's your number?"

I told her. "How did Tiffany act with this man?" I asked.

"We wouldn't have let her go if we had seen a problem. Sir, is there a problem?"

"Yes. Watch over your other girls. No one else gets released."

I said to Ava through the bedroom door, "Someone snatched Tiffany Prue. I think it was John Orse. Orse is John Quick, Moody's alibi. He's a kid snatcher. Get dressed, get the gun, and take Rachel to the bed and breakfast on University. I'm calling Capri for backup. I think we've stepped on the anthill. They're taking out the girls, starting with Tiffany."

"As in *killing* them?" asked Ava, opening the door. She wore a purple nightgown designed for practicality. Design failure.

"We have to presume it. These guys are facing a million years in state prison. I always liked that nightgown."

The phone rang—the fax from the Home. The sheet rolled out. The badge was 719—Sergeant Billy McManus's old number. The driver's license belonged to a Charles Devereaux. I knew the face and the man. He had a candy-apple-red Impala convertible, a bad neck, and a dog named Spango. Corrections knew him as Karl Francis Moody.

I called for a statewide alert, starting on Tulip Lane.

It was three a.m. and the lights were on. Harry O. Bilinski came to the door with a half-eaten Ho Ho and a trail of crumbs. Behind him, *Pulp Fiction* played on a VCR. On the floor was a disassembled 7.62mm M-14 adapted for deer hunting. He had been cleaning it.

"You ought to try carrots, PBS, and paint ball gunnery," I said.

"Thanks," he said warmly. "Fuck you."

Bilinski feared death. To stay alive, he'd kill anything. "Harry, where'd you put John Orse's Adult Video Club card? You found it on the dresser at the Paradise Motor Lodge."

He took a bite, thinking. "In the Evidence Room. Not your squirrelly one. Ours." He swallowed. "But I think I forgot to run prints on it."

I awakened the Crime Lab duty officer. I asked for a fingerprinter to run a plastic card on AFIS, the Automated Fingerprint ID System. The duty officer said nothing would make him happier and asked how Tommy Conover was doing. I said fine, and thanks for asking.

I called the Night Watch Commander to retrieve the video card.

He called me back. "It's not there, Mr. Jin."

Intelligently, I said, "What do you mean, it's not there?"

"Log shows you gave it to us. Envelope was in the bin, but the evidence bag's empty. I'm checking into it. Mr. Jin, this isn't payback for Billy McManus. It's righteously gone."

I told Harry to find his photos of the video card. He rummaged through piles of pants. In a pocket was his camera.

I reawakened the Lab duty officer to develop photos.

"I like your style, Mr. Jin. Convict the wrong guy and wake me up twice."

"I owe you breakfast."

"You owe me squat. See you there."

The Adult Video Club was at 731 Greenhaven. Harry drove there while the sleep-deprived criminalist found prints on the blown-up photos of the card. He entered them into AFIS.

Harry returned unhappy. "Greenhaven's bullshit. The place burned down years ago."

"Got it," said the criminalist, printing the results from the computer. AFIS connected the prints to a John Runner Orse, on 731 Greenhaven. The Adult Video Club address.

"Shit," concluded Bilinski. Redundant loop.

In the CLETS room—California Law Enforcement Teletype System—the tech typed in our man. Teletypes had been replaced by networked minicomputers, but cops have an Irish sentimentality, and the CLETS name survived against technological advances.

ORSE, JOHN RUNNER DOB: UNKNOWN DOB/SSN/CDL/NAC 731 GREENHAVEN, SACRAMENTO CA 95855 RECORD PURGED DL572

Unknown date of birth, Social Security number, California driver's license, and no hits in the National Agency Check. "DL" stood for delete local; 572 was witness protection.

"Fuck you," said Bilinski, flipping a middle finger at the screen. "We got a real bad guy here, getting protection from Upstairs. All these computers and bureaucrats can bite me."

"No, it's a bug," said the tech. "We got stealthed. Stop cussing. It means a major-league creep decoder, a game addict bug-tester, spooge-spinning microserf slipped into our hard drive, knew gate, the code, burned the password and the file address. Hey, he whacked us good. He snatched the data and zeroed out the file and his entry trail."

"Can't we still audit something?" I asked. "There a bug-proof housekeeping program that logs all the Protection Program entries?" The Tech was already working that.

PROGRAM ERROR X999

Every time the tech retried, the screen repeated itself.

"This guy's good," he said. "I think he's a badge. Big badge. Way on the inside."

I knew a big badge. "Okay. The gods owe us. Next lucky break's ours."

"Oh, yeah, Mr. Jin," said Harry, "I'll be sure to fucking hold my breath for that."

62.

REVELATION

Gonzo passed me photocopies of a campaign fund account.

In bright yellow highlight were six $3,000 checks written on a Wells Fargo account to the Reelect Thomas Conover Campaign.

Each was signed by Karl Francis Moody of Tulip Lane.

Moody had written checks to Conover, who at the time was guaranteed reelection. It was like a street insurance policy, crude and unenforceable. But now, because of Moody, Conover was due to lose. If Moody had $500K to pay Stacy, he also had $18K for the DA race.

"I think," said Gonzo, "that Geneva horsed around on the *Moody* file and your evidence. She did it so you and I'd tube the case. So a child molester's campaign contributions wouldn't become public. Hell, she'd prosecute Moody after the election. What a fucking hoot."

"I'm struggling not to laugh." I hated politics.

Tanya Churchill, the lean careerist who ran my former bureau, had been eavesdropping. "Oh, really, Josh? You hate politics. Then tell me how you got the bureau."

"My sense of humor. Congratulations on your promotion. You being good?"

"I'm actually not bad at management."

"Management's not hard. Leadership is."

"Um-hm. Josh, I just came from the Board of Supes. Guess whose name, under an obscure election law, has been added to the ballot as candidate for DA?"

"Tanya, please. Don't tell me you're running."

"You flatter me. No. Your old friend Jay Wendell Nobis."

The former district attorney, who had asked me a legal ethics question before hiring me. He had handed me my badge. And I had helped Tom Conover unseat him.

The Highway Patrol had stopped a candy-apple-red Impala with California plates on I-80 near Kyburz, on the way to Lake Tahoe. Tiffany Prue was unharmed and would be returned to the Home for Girls. Moody would be in Sac County Jail by three p.m.

Capri interviewed Tiffany. She, raped by her father; impregnated by a stranger; punked, cut, and photographed by Victor Petty/Mr. Buttface at Fred and Gary's River City Lounge; and taken from the Home for Girls by Chico Moody, had nothing to say. She was a little tired of cops, nuns, DAs, and pedophiles.

François had made no progress with Moody's runaways.

Victor Petty, the pedophile who had kidnapped Tiffany Prue from the bus stop, the man she had fled naked into downtown traffic, was represented by the Public Defender. He redeclined an interview, and we had nothing to offer a chickenhawk. We were stuck.

I showed Rachel how to look up her own name in the national search program and left her with Ava. I punched up the day's docket of horrors.

Judge Janice Hayes had a multiple 187, murder.

I went to her court, passing a gaggle of bald, shirtless, tattooed teens in chains and sagging pants. I smiled and said hi, drawing a collective recoil and a shy wave. We checked each other out and I waved again. One smiled and said, "Hey."

I'd have to try this in Chinatown, treating teenagers as if they were human.

I felt an ownership of the court, a connection to strangers and familiar court personnel. Here, people came when summoned, took oaths when asked, listened as directed, and deliberated as expected. The Founding Fathers had to be happy. Here, woe came to be measured. Commanding verdicts were issued by common citizens. There was always error, because humans were everywhere you looked, but justice was tangible.

Mrs. Aldo was at the railing in Judge Hayes's court, seated next to her friend, Mrs. Idora Afreem. She had no needlepoint. Her head wobbled. Summer should've lived to this age.

A Major Crimes deputy DA was doing direct exam on the coroner. Charts showed entry and exit wounds for three people.

The jury glanced at me as I sat next to Mrs. Aldo. I gave her a note and a pen: "Can we talk?" I had drawn two boxes, *Yes* and *No*. She checked Yes.

In the hall, she said in a high vibrato, "Mr. Jin. I was wondering when you'd get around to me. Buy me a spot of tea in the Plaza coffee shop, like you used to. You're a nice young man. Of course I'll tell you what I know."

Matt Cox, the buffed Plaza proprietor, smiled warmly as he served Constant Comment for Mrs. Aldo and Chinese green tea for me. The Plaza catered to process servers, DAs, private detectives, criminalists, court clerks, cops, public defenders, and reporters. To me, it was a place of exaggerated professional overkill, but to Mrs. Aldo, this was a hive of busy workers who spun the seductive honey she savored in her late years.

It was cool in the shop. She warmed thin, trembling, liver-spotted fingers on the teacup, adding sugar. She sniffed my tea and nodded.

"Mr. Jin, it was during the defense's case-in-chief. A young public defender came in and gave Stacy August a note. It was a note for Mr. Moody. Do you remember?"

I nodded.

"Stacy August asked for a ten-minute recess. Am I right?"

"Yes, exactly."

"Mr. Jin, what did Mr. Moody do during the break?"

"He used the rest room."

"Yes, sir. And someone was waiting for him behind the clerk's office. You were watching the court reporter take Rachel Farr to the girl's room. Very sweet, sir, how you did that. As if she were your daughter. I don't have to ask you if you have children because I can see you do. And lucky children they are." She smiled slyly. "But you missed the action."

"Who'd Moody meet?"

She grinned, liking the game. "Someone who gave him yet another note. And spoke to him, rather conspiratorially, I would say. Mr. Moody's body shielded the other person. Oh, but Mr. Jin, I saw that person. My eyes are still quite good, thank heavens. I see everything!

"But how poor Mr. Moody's shoulders dropped when he read that second note! You could see he was a victim of something, as well. The criminal, caught in another web. Of his doing or someone else's. Oh, yes, I'd bet crumpets on that."

She sipped loudly and smiled at the café's patrons. Her eyes were a shallow brown, her brain bright and acute, her body aging as I watched. "I knew I should say something to you. You know, my dear Mr. Jin, in the old days, you would've talked to me after court every day. But I read about you. You became a big shot. And then you broke my heart. You had cried in trial. I was so sad to see that. Was it drugs? Everyone uses them nowadays. None of my business, of course." She restirred her tea, frowning at the dissipating steam.

"Mrs. Aldo, you're killing me. Who was it?"

She sipped her tea gaily, looking at me from the corner of a wise and twinkling eye.

"What's going on with you and Stacy August?" She poked my arm. "Eh?"

63.

COUNTY JAIL

Moody looked more believable in bright yellow prison utilities with the SACRAMENTO COUNTY PRISONER logo than he did in a five-hundred-dollar Brooks Brothers suit. He was tired and gray. Nocturnal jail noises please some convicts, but not all. It was dark and cool.

I liked jail. It was where the bad guys were supposed to be.

"We're taping," said Capri, setting up the recorders.

"Mr. Moody," I said, "you have the right to remain—"

"I'm waivin' my damn right to a lawyer, and to silence." A new, gravelly voice.

"You don't want Stacy or Rittenhouse, or another lawyer?"

"No." Wrists manacled, he rubbed his face with both hands. His hair was growing back for a ponytail. He stank of bad sinks. It was a new jail, but here, it quickly didn't matter. "No more goddamn lawyers." He stretched his wrist manacles. "Fuck all of you." Awkwardly he signed the waiver form. I took the pen. I wasn't worried, but you never know.

Behind us sat three labeled evidence sacks with everything taken from him and his car when he was stopped on I-80 by CHP. It had been inventoried but not yet analyzed.

"I know it's the law," said Moody, nodding. "You can't plea-bargain a child sex assault. But I didn't hurt the Prue girl. You gotta groove to that or I shut up right now."

"I understand that," I said. "You took Tiffany Prue, but you didn't hurt her."

His lips, a bitter rosebud, talking to the cops. He coughed. "Shit. Well, here's the whole string. Giving you the leadership." Hands through his hair. "Wayne Flute. Good ole Wayne.

"Wayne was the man. He started the Ionian Society." Wayne Flute, the chickenhawk who killed Sergeant McManus, bled in a cop car, and died in ER trying to deal Moody to us.

Moody looked at Capri. "See, the Ionian Society's the local NAMBLA chapter."

Capri exhaled. The National Man-Boy Love Association, the child molesters' guild.

"But," said Moody, "Ionians includes NAMGLA. National Man-Girl Love Association."

The Man-Boy Love Association declared pedophilia as cool. Small kidnapped boys weren't "victims"—they were "lovers." Pedophiles weren't perverts—they were lovers, too. Children were tortured for "romance." NAMBLA was the hot acid test of the U.S. Constitution.

Man-Girl would do the same honors for little girls that NAMBLA did for little boys, based on the presumption that children enjoyed fatal, satanic torture. Man-girl. "Man-ghhh."

That's what Flute was trying to say before he died in surgery after McManus blew holes in him. That Moody was a Man-Girl Love guy.

"Flute," said Moody, "was a business guy. He had an MBA. Knew marketing. Worked with the HMOs and hostile takeovers. Man knew how to make money. But he didn't know law."

Capri's eyes were luminescent with heat, her breath uneven, her chest moving under disciplined control. She wrote: *FLUTE: THE BRAINS, MADE MONEY FROM KID RAPE.*

Moody leaned back, the chains complaining. "You don't agree with me on this one; I know it, like, turns your stomach, but there ain't nothin' sweeter than the love of a little girl. I'm not talkin' about sex. I'm talkin' love. Innocent love. These girls don't mess with your head or trip on you. They're fuckin' pure. They naturally love older men. They look to men for comfort and safety. Fathers. And most people, they look at teenage girls, and *hate* 'em. It's a fact."

"NAMBLA's about sex," said Capri as my stomach turned.

"Sure it is. But I'm no damn NAMBLA man. I *hate* dudes who do little kids. Especially the ones who do boys. But I like girls. Not for sex, but just for their company. They pick me up." He looked at his hands. "Ain't like women, who fuck big-time with your head. I meant what I said about Rachel." He frowned. "She was nice to have around. As a friend."

Capri and I kept nice expressions. "And your job with NAMBLA?"

"I'll get there. Wayne Flute, he told the pervs to get wise and use the Internet. A way to find kids who wanted us. Just businessmen doin' a service. Then he got legal advice from a smart lawyer. *Adopt* the kids overseas, then bring 'em home and sell 'em.

"Flute said, stand tall, go armed. 'Chickenhawks' is what the cops call you. Flute said, 'You're thunderbirds, proud of what you do.' If a girl goes south on you, stab the bitch in the eyes a hundred times and she can't ID you. Hey, I wasn't one of them, but I dug his rap. He swore he'd shoot dead the next cop who hassled him. And, man, he did." Moody smiled grimly.

Capri's jaw clenched below a neutral face.

"But Flute gettin' blowed away slowed us down. Then Orse took over. Orse's a computer geek, a hacker. Fool lives in cyberspace. Not cool with money but smart. Bastard's got major brains." Moody pointed with both hands. "Helluva lot smarter than you two."

Capri wrote: *ORSE, BRIGHT, COMPUTER HACKER. MICROSERF.*

"Now John Orse, he was different. Flute, he did time. Me, I did time. Victor Petty, he did *lots* of time. But John Orse, he was *real* afraid of lock-up." He shook his head. "Psycho-afraid. It's all he talked about. So Orse recruits a lawyer into the Ionians, just to keep his own ass outa the joint." He snickered. "Orse sure sweated endin' up in stir." He looked back and forth.

"Flute was NAMBLA. Man-Boy. John Orse likes boys and girls. Man-Boy-Girl."

"So the pervs were uniting," said Capri.

"Yeah, they were. Join our chat room, pay up big, get a boy *or* a girl to call your own."

"But," said Capri, "there was a hassle between the girl pervs and the boy pervs. About who gets more time on the web page. Whether the kids coming out are mostly boys or girls."

Moody nodded, leaning forward, face heavily shadowed. "You got that right."

I asked, "What was Victor Petty's job?" Mr. Buttface.

"Transit. Picked up adopted kids in Southeast Asia, Latin America, Russia, old East Germany. Moved 'em around when the cops came. Made deliveries to clients. Shit, he was good at it cuz he knows drugs. Knocks those girls out. He's the best."

"That how you raised Stacy August's legal fees?" asked Capri. "Selling kids?"

"Oh, hell no. That's Seth Jergen's cash. I mean, some of his money was from us, so maybe it looped around, but most of it's meth and horse. You didn't know that?" He laughed. "Everyone on the Ionian gateway knows that. Jergen's their Roman emperor, too high up to know what's happenin'. We call him 'Caligula,' but I don't think he's into the shit himself. When he's DA, it's the Roman Empire, baby. Perversions 'R Us. He'll shut down SACA. His fund-raising sure shot up after Conover fucked up that cop. Fuckin' cop who blew away Flute."

Geneva de Hoyas had accelerated an unprepped *Moody* case so it'd die before the November election. Seth Jergen funded Moody's defense to make sure it would live, having no clue he was obliquely supporting a coven of electronically empowered pedophiles. And Geneva would refile *Moody* after the election, regardless of who won. But it was still wrong.

"Your job," I said, "was to house the kids until Victor Petty, aka Mr. Buttface, delivered them to the customers?"

"You called him 'Buttface'? That's good. Yeah, but I only scooped locals. Plumped 'em up. Some Ionians pay more for white boys and girls, but like I said, I don't do boys. Ionians use the boys and it was like them, as kids, getting punked all over again. By their daddies."

Capri and I were quiet for a while.

"Who's John Quick?" I asked.

He sat back, clanking. "Who you think it is?"

"John Orse. The hacker who took over after Flute died. The one afraid of the joint."

A small head hitch: It was. "Know what's funny?"

I said I didn't. Something squeaked behind me. Capri unhooked her automatic.

Moody alerted, then relaxed when he saw we had heard it, too. Capri went to check. "John Orse wasn't gonna be *my* alibi. I was gonna be *his*." He squirmed. "Is that funnier 'n shit? Hell of it was, we *were* righteously together that night. I gotta use the latrine."

I escorted him into the rest room.

"So, Mr. DA, you like your dandy little job?" asked Moody.

"Yeah, I do."

"So you like fucking with people," he said, his back to me.

"I like protecting the community from bad guys."

He snorted. "Bullshit."

"As opposed to, say, your job. The rape of children."

"Fuckin' lawyers," he said, shaking his head. "You are such assholes."

"Yeah, we're bastards. Putting away kid rapers. What were we thinking?"

In the hall, Capri was waiting, handgun up.

Moody backed up. "Christ, you think I'd jump *him*?"

"I think," said Capri, "that we got a bad actor on the inside, and that you're in danger of being killed by the Ionians. I think that's why you're talking. I didn't find anything."

We were seated, the tape turning, Capri ready.

"They segregate us," said Moody, "in county, just like Corrections. Sex offenders, they're on Six West." He hitched his head upstairs. "Where they keep *me*. And right fucking next to me is Victor Petty." He laughed. "Buttface. I says, 'What the fuck *you* doin' here?'

"Bastard shines me on. Meals, exercise, TV room, at night

after Lights Out—no contact. Ignores me like I'm a dead man. My first hint I didn't have no alibi witness no more. I was a fuckin' outcast. The night before John Orse was gonna come to court and alibi me and say he was John Quick who was with me the night Rachel got it—the Ionian messenger visits me in jail. Says John Orse had been popped and was on the run. That true?"

"Orse was on the run. He had a kid in a West Sac motel. But he got away and took her with him. We didn't bust him and we haven't found him or the girl yet."

"What a putz," said Moody. "What a jerk-off. Fuckin' idiot." Moody sat up.

"What happened next?" I asked.

"So I said, 'John Orse is standin' up for me, right? He's comin' to court tomorrow, right?' Messenger gives me this look and I knew I was screwed with a rope around my neck."

"They want you to kill Rachel, don't they?" asked Capri.

He exhaled. "Yeah, they want her snuffed. Afterwards, I figured they'll do me."

"Who's 'they'?" asked Capri.

"John Orse. And Victor Petty. One a the guys in the yard said Orse put a contract out on me. He was gonna off me in jail! So I punched a bull." A guard. "I'm in Iso now." Isolation.

Reluctantly I made a note: *protect Moody from Orse.* I asked, "You were supposed to kill Tiffany Prue before she testified against Victor Petty?"

"I was gonna let her go. They took my dog. Spango's old and needs a walk every day and good food. Not fucking table scraps. They're killin' him by accident now, I know it."

"Mr. Moody," I said, "who raped Rachel?"

"I gonna get a break here?" he asked.

"I don't think so," I said. "Who was it?"

His shoulders slumped. He played with a hangnail. A shake of his head. His eyes narrowed. "Ah, hell. You saw him. In the transit corridor, checkin' you out."

The man Mrs. Aldo had seen.

Judge Thackery Niles. I considered the possibility. His interference in the case.

"You're not serious," said Capri, looking at me. "He's law-and-order."

Moody nodded. "That's what *I* said. Niles was the lawyer John Orse brought into the Ionians for legal insurance. But Thack Niles, man, he wanted to take over after Flute got blowed away by that cop. But he was the new guy and his job was just strictly keepin' us outa the joint. Niles, he didn't like the NAMBLAs, the guys who did little boys. Not that I blame 'im."

"What happened that night?" asked Capri.

Moody was breathing hard. Time passed. There was no sunlight, but shadows deepened. We waited like good cops, motionless, the friends of slow time. He spoke.

"Rachel was due to be shipped. Orse got ten grand for her cuz she was clean. But I just, I just couldn't let her go. That's when they took Spango." He threw up two hopeless hands, an eye closed. "I dropped roafie-R-2 and some Versed on Rachel. Knocked her out cold. Supposed to zap memory. Orse and Thack Niles came. I begged 'em to not send her.

"I had on a suit, to look good, and had good beer out, too, so they'd listen. But to them, I was just a fuckin' ex-con, a mule for their kids. Judge Niles checked her out. He said, 'Moody, you're right. She's too good for us to give away.' We moved her and he strapped her down with his velvet cuffs and opened his pants like it was a piss break on a con labor detail.

"And they did her themselves, takin' turns. Right in front of me. I couldn't leave—I was afraid they'd snuff her. It was like they was doin' it to me. . . ."

Mealtime. The jail distantly clanked like a chained beast. Capri adjusted her gun.

"Niles, now, he used condoms. Orse, he didn't. You gotta believe me, I never did no sex thing with Rachel. I just cried along with her. I felt sick to my stomach. I kept trying to clean her up, and to keep them from bein' too hard on her. I tried to stop Orse from hitting her. When Orse was chokin' her, I hauled him off. He was high on speed. He pro'bly don't even remember.

"Judge Niles, he knew all about sex cases, SACA cases. He

washed her, combed out her hair, put her head in Listerine, douched her with chemicals, scraped and cut and cleaned her nails, threw away her clothes, treated her cuts, searched for hairs and fibers. Had me keep washing her off 'til my hands got all puffy." He looked at Capri's gun.

"I knew if I turned them in, I'd end up in Folsom Lake with my car around my neck. And they still had Spango, with him on heartworm pills. You probably think I'm pretty lame, lettin' them take a girl to save my ole dog." Pipes hummed in the interrogation room.

"Look, they paid me and I did my job. All I ever asked 'em was one favor. Rachel. And they do her like that." His eyes glinted. "I was torqued, big-time. I dug her clothes outa the trash. Put 'em in her backpack. A crazy thing. I didn't care if she busted 'em all. I didn't even *think* she'd accuse *me* of doin' it to her. I knew I broke her heart. That was bad enough. Damn, I was dumb about the whole thing." His Baywater "aboot" was growing stronger.

"And that thing I said out loud, to the jury and the papers and the whole fuckin' world? Shit, man, I really *can't* have sex. Kills my back somethin' fierce. After what happened to Rachel, I don't even *think* about it no more."

"Where did the sexual assaults occur?" I asked.

"House next door. The other Victorian." I forgot to check it out. "When she conked, I carried her there. It was dark. It belongs to the Ionian Society. Got the computers there."

He had delivered her to the demons, freighting her to their torture chamber.

"What's the Ionian gateway address code?" asked Capri.

He told us. We wrote it down. François would be happy. Capri already was.

"Where are the girls, Chico?" I asked.

"There's a list. In the briefcase, in the evidence bags." They were nearby.

Capri recovered a list of victims and users that crossed state lines and social and professional borders. She showed it to me. Not all were cons and infamous pedophiles. Some were notorious politicians.

"The girls okay?" asked Capri carefully.

He shrugged. "They don't have a real long life span, know what I mean? I mean, they grow up into witnesses."

Capri closed her eyes. Mine were wide open. "What does Stacy know?" I asked.

"Jackshit. In comes a public defender, gives Stacy August a note. It's for me from Thack Niles. He's gonna come see me during a latrine break. I asked August to get a recess.

"Niles is waiting in the transit hallway of Maxwell's court. He says John Orse ain't coming. Says you—the DA—can't cross-examine worth rabbit shit and I got nothin' to fear.

"I said the DA just drilled me a new butt and did he notice that I was walkin' funny? Niles told John Orse and me that you was weak as dogshit as a lawyer. No offense."

"None taken."

"He said, instead of hasslin' me, you'd break down and cry. Cuz a some death-in-the-family thing. Yeah, like I wish. You lit me up good. Hell, I didn't care. Hearin' Rachel talk about what happened was like I *did* do it to her. I was hurtin'. I told Stacy August the truth. I was there that night when two guys, so-called buddies a mine, did her again and again. She says, 'You mean, Rachel's not lying?' Then she asks if the Namese punks who ganged her were for real." He shrugged. "It was stupid. Shoulda kept my trap shut. I told her we bought 'em.

"*That* busted her chops. I mean, that I was workin' for a chickenhawk group and she didn't know shit. It torqued her big. That lady, she got a temper on *her*." His eyebrows arched. "Then she got weird on me and refused to call 'em to the stand. Somewhat tubed my case." He sniffed. "She argued okay, but way short, and the bitch didn't use our good witnesses." He sniffed. "Aw hell, I wouldn't a believed 'em, either. Fuckin' Oriental gang punks."

Stacy August, the good lawyer, had held the line.

"Stacy knew that Jergen paid your attorney fees?" I asked.

"Man, this whole gig was about politics. She's some big Democrat, and Conover's a Republican. She said when Conover lost, you'd have to go be a *real* lawyer. She was gonna whip your butt in this trial, make you change jobs and write bad checks." Moody swore, then shook his head. "Fuck. Better if you *had* been a real lawyer."

I asked, "Why'd you want Jergen to be DA?"

"Hell, I didn't give a shit. Man, I could sure see Judge Maxwell had a hard-on for Conover. He sure busted your balls, didn't he?" A laugh. "Ah, Jergen's an idiot. Had no idea what this case was really about." A shrug. "Guy doesn't give a shit. He'll make a perfect DA."

"You ever *see* Jergen pay for your legal fees?"

"Fool gave me the money orders, personal. I got photocopies of 'em in the bags."

Capri found them and put them in evidence bags. They looked good. With them, we could smear Seth Jergen. The glory of politics.

Capri asked, "You grabbed Tiffany Prue to get arrested?"

"And I'm safer in jail. Safer for Tiffany that I got her outa town. You liked getting her back, didn't you? I mean, it meant something to you. Her bein' pregnant and all."

"Yes," said Capri. "It meant a lot."

"I mean you," said Moody.

"Yeah," I said. Moody smiled, long and slow, looking at me with hope, seeing himself on the outside in a red convertible on a long green road, ancient oaks rustling in a summer wind, a young girl on his arm and his old, well-fed dog sniffing the warm breeze.

"And John Orse is John Quick," I said.

A pause. "Um-hm. Orse, he's a genius. Man buries computer records, cranks out IDs. Moves through a computer like a ghost, deleting shit and erasing his trail. Man's too much."

"Who's Orse, Mr. Moody?" I asked.

Big grin. "Now, I *thought* you didn't know! You gonna give me something for it?"

"No, " I said.

His jaw tightened. "You're a real pisser, aren't you? Okay, hotshot. You find 'im."

"Come on," said Capri.

"No, let's go," I said, standing and starting to leave.

"Aw, what the hell. Orse is St. Joel. The good Reverend Joel

Frost, patron saint of ex-cons. Man's addicted to sex with girls. Due back from Thailand Monday with a new shipment a goods. Vietnamese kids. Lao, Thai. They'll be hungry and ready to follow orders."

The room chilled. Joel Frost, fraudulent pastor. A pedophile? "You have proof?"

"Got a video of him doin' a kid. In my stuff."

Capri found a tape labeled *Joel and Lia*. "Who's your Perv Network messenger?" she asked. "Save us some time." She popped the tape in a backup minicam and pushed *Play*.

"I already saved you years." He liked guessing games. "Someone who was in court every day. Digs money and hates kids, long as she gets a new house out of it."

"Mrs. Dierdre Farr," I said. She hadn't been in court to watch her stepdaughter; she was working for the Ionian Society.

"It's real clear," said Capri, "where her soul's going after the party." She turned off the videotape. "It's Joel Frost, all right. Chico, did they want to kill Rachel that night?"

"Yeah, they did. But I told Orse—Joel—that we'd be caught for murder, her blood all over us. You'd be proud a me—I was arguin' like a damn lawyer. They backed off. They gave me her life. But now they want her dead and they got my dog." He lowered his voice.

"I helped you big, man. I gave you the whole damn string. I want your help now. Okay? A little grease for that slide back to hard time. I need some help, here. I want some psych time and then parole. Man, I can't go back to the Q." San Quentin. "Listen, man, I *loved* Rachel. I still do. Listen, I even told her that. Hey, the girl didn't get hurt that bad. They didn't cut her insides or anything, or cut her stuff, like they do some a them before they kill 'em. And I cleaned her up." Moody leaned forward. "So, man, you gonna give me some help?"

I took Capri's gun and placed it on the table close to him. Capri started to move it back. I stopped her. I unlocked Moody's cuffs and let them drop to the concrete floor.

"I'll help you," I said, "to full-force consecutive life terms. You got kids to trust you and you set them up for torture. You 'plumped' them like calves in a slaughterhouse and shipped them to be cut to death by pervs." I moved the gun toward him and he jerked his hand away.

"You let two pervs rip apart a girl, right in front of you. A girl who loved you like her father. While she was crying out for help. You were supposed to protect her."

I went around the desk. Moody stood, knocking over his chair as he backed up.

"Jin," whispered Capri, standing, "don't."

I was inches from his face. "You were supposed to *protect* Rachel. Whatever it took, whatever the cost. Talking the creeps out of murder—good for you—but you were just sweating your own skin. You knew they'd snuff her later." The room was red, he hadn't gone for the gun, and I wanted him to swing on me, to help me ease my pains, my illness.

"Stopping them from raping her—that was your chance to be a man. Stuffing her clothes in the backpack—that was a puny shot to make sure *you* didn't get convicted."

"Jin!" Capri's voice, sounding far away.

"Come on, Chico," I said, "haven't you always wanted to knock out a DA?" I nodded hopefully. "Or shoot him?" I backed up, opening up the gun. "Hey, man, this is your last chance. You're going to the SHU in the Q. You're going to die in stir. Have some fun now."

Moody abruptly turned his head away, arms at his face, eyes scrunched shut.

"Josh, don't," hissed Capri. "Think of Summer!" And I did. The red dissipated around a frightened man who stank sourly like a trapped animal. Like Rachel. I took a deep breath. I forced myself back. Capri recovered her gun, glaring at me.

Moody was panting. He faced me, his body still contorted into the corner. "Fuck you! You goddamned screw! Fuckin' dickhead lawyer! I give you all this help—"

"You should've helped the girls."

"Man, now that ain't fair! I deserve some help, here!"

"I'll take care of your dog. But you're going down."

"You asshole! You dirty bitch! I got shit I could drop on you! On your fuckin' office! How about that, you fuck! You want some a that? I'll GIVE you some a that! It's political shit!"

"I don't care about politics. You care about the SHU at the Q?"

"Fuck you, you goddamned fucking dickhead! You screw you jerk you stupid fuckhead!"

"Hey, Chico, 'No cussing, or you're not a righteous man,' " I quoted.

Moody sagged, arms dropping, panting wetly, eyes glazed and far away, not in distance but in memory, all his lost chances accumulating now for a final accounting, for prison math, for bad, slow-moving days being hunted by angry bulls and quick red punks.

Capri brushed curls from a wet forehead. "Jin? Those names he called you? Ditto for me."

64.

POLITICS

The autumn air was thin and soft. It accented the scents of oo-long tea and hot *dim sum*, Chinese high tea tidbits of encased shrimp and pork, taro-wrapped glutinous rice, foil-wrapped chicken, and sweet buns holding small surprises that were kind to the heart.

Metal chair legs scraped sourly in the Asian Community Center's meeting hall as twelve suited men and women turned from the long table, fanning themselves with Asian news-papers. Bodyguards in cheap suits downed their playing cards. Bright porcelain teapots marched in a wavering line down the table. An old box fan vibrated in the corner, swirling cigarette smoke and doing less good than in May, when I was here to atone for our mistreatment of Rachel Farr.

Kimberley Hong greeted me, her hair tall and dramatic. We shook and she kissed me on the cheek, a kind sister. In the guest chair sat Sethman Jergen in a road-rumpled tan suit, tall, sallow, and angular. He worked a runny red nose with a gray handkerchief. He blinked in the light. He had been drinking. I should have worn a party hat.

I bowed. "*Neh ho ma.* With permission, I will speak. Hello, Seth."

"Jin *singsong*," said Ms. Hong, "this is your home, where you are always welcome."

"Should I leave?" asked Seth.

"Stick around," I said. "I'm going to talk about you."

"I thought you didn't like politics," said Ms. Hong.

"I discovered it's better than not having a voice at all. I'm here to talk about Superior Court Judge Finley Maxwell. Next month he faces election. I believe he is an immoral judge. To get votes, he allowed a child to get abused in his courtroom. So I commit myself to supporting those who run against him. Judges, like us, must honor all persons. They must respect those who need their protection. They must be rich in *ren*, in human regard. Judge Maxwell is in this way a poor man." I named the candidate for whom I was going to vote.

"Next month you also elect the DA. Mr. Jergen promises you more cops to fight Asian gangs, to protect your businesses, correct?" Heads nodded. "He offers cops for votes. Let me ask you this question: Will the gangs die because of more cops?"

A few nodded. Most didn't. Elders, highly relational, looked at each other, waiting.

"Aren't gangs a disease of the heart, and not the skin? We Chinese families own our children, always. If our children are not moral, isn't it our fault? Am I right, sir?"

Mr. Chew, a highly regarded patriarch who never wagered, said "Yes, Jin."

"They are *our* youth, who need *guanxi*, face, with *us*. Not cops. And not the DA. It's our problem to solve. Guns and prisons will not cure what ails us. We have to go back to our roots and be the excellent parents. Fathers must show merit to sons, every day. Gangs are filled with children of overworking, absent parents. That's *our* problem to fix. It won't be easy.

"The district attorney can't allocate police resources. They are not his to give; they belong to the chief of police. Therefore, Mr. Jergen can't deliver on his promise.

"In November, you should vote for a man of *ren*, of humane feelings. If that man is Mr. Jergen, then vote for him. But you should elect a district attorney for his honorable nature. Not for your ability to extract favors from him. Someone who has already done the job."

"Who?" asked Ms. Hong. "Jay W. Nobis? Not Thomas Conover!"

"I would pick someone who never forgets who the bad guys are. Someone who will protect all neighborhoods. That specifically means not voting for Mr. Jergen."

"Fine, Josh," said Sethman. "Vote for a guy who beats the crap out of a cop."

"That'll be a disqualifier for a lot of voters. But I'd vote for someone who takes responsibility for *all* people, not just the twelve of you, and not just for Chinatown. That is the same reason why you should vote against Judge Maxwell."

"Jin-ah," said Mrs. Jin kindly, my restaurant-owning friend on the council. "The *gwailo* not like us, but you say, treat them like brother. We not take care of ourself, who will? You know saying. 'You cannot straddle two boats with one foot.' "

"Jin *taitai*, I know another. *'Ji wang bu jiu.'* The Master K'ung Fu-tzu said: We must forgive what was done in the past." Master K'ung was known in the West as Confucius.

"Like you forgive criminals, defendants, and bad guys?" asked Seth.

He had me there. I was not forgiving toward the cons I knew. I could hear BaBa saying that I couldn't influence anyone toward a moral position totally foreign to myself. "Good point. I should forgive the bad men I've known." I had placed thousands of them in confinement.

Later, facing him in the abandoned hall, I gave him photocopies of the money orders which had paid Stacy August for Moody's defense. Money illegally drawn from the Elect Jergen fund. The carbons could've gone to the Fair Political Practices Commission for formal investigation, but, coming from me, it would appear to be an attempt at an ugly smear.

"They're the only copies we have," I said. "You know what? You're one of the bad men I've known. I forgive you."

He looked at them. "Josh, you could kill me with these."

"I'm not real fond of homicide. I think you already killed yourself with your major life decisions. If those are what it takes for you to lose, I'd rather you won."

65.

THANKSGIVING

"I'm not going to wait forever," said Ava. I was carving the turkey. Rachel knew Ava wasn't talking about food. So did Capri, whom Ava had engaged in a lively debate about the death penalty. I admired both of them for being able to argue without animosity.

My mother sniffed the cranberry sauce. Every Thanksgiving, she wondered why a heavy, semisolid colloid was called a sauce.

"Why this call 'sauce'?" she asked, poking it. "Too hard!" She rolled up the sleeves of her favorite rose sweater. Her philosophic inquiries gave me pleasure.

"Tradition," I said.

"Ay, that what you always say, every year." She pinched me.

Mr. Chow, the custodian from the Chinese Methodist Church, also prodded his cranberry sauce with a fork. "Ah-ha," he said inconclusively.

There was a crash of crockery on the kitchen's unforgiving tile floor. I heard an "Oops." François Giggin reassured us with his call, "It's just the gravy! I'll clean it up!" A slip of wet heels, a small cry, and a bright, continuous smashing of plates. Ava motioned for Ma and Mr. Chow to remain seated as she went to help, but they both followed her; it was each one's job.

Capri turned to Rachel and asked how she was doing with friends.

I knew the answer: Not well. "Fine," said Rachel.

Bilinski put his chin in his hands and watched me carve.

"He too slow," said Kwah, my stepfather.

"Damn, you *are* slow," agreed Harry.

"For you, Harry," I said, "bones."

Eventually the plates were passed around. Ma lit the candles. Later tonight, she would cook the turkey carcass into *juk*, the savory rice soup that was the best part of American Thanksgivings. Ma said a prayer in Chinese.

"Dear God, thank you for getting my son out of trouble with the State Bar policemen, and for canceling the embarrassing, shameful fines against him. Help my impossible son keep his job and his most beautiful wife. Don't let all these big Americans eat all the food. Hold close my dead granddaughter, little precious Summer. Amen."

"Amen," said the table.

Capri whispered to me, "I didn't catch all of that."

"She thanked God," I whispered back, "for the fellowship of this table and for our honored guests." Ava smiled.

We were passing pumpkin pie and a Chinese Eight Happiness red bean dessert and Harry's voice was booming and François was giggling when Rachel softly asked if Ava and I would be her guardians. It was for our ears, but everyone heard. She was asking in public to increase the chances of the right answer.

"not, you know, legal-like. but, you know. for real."

"Yes," we said.

"promise?" Rachel whispered.

"Promise," we said, looking only at her, having no idea of our own future. Rachel smiled with tight lips, surveying us with a hot, earnest gaze, seeking truth. Ava beamed love and Rachel closed her eyes, almost in pain.

Ma hugged her. "Sweet girl," she said. "Sweet, sweet girl. I think I keep you, okay?" She hugged until Rachel said yes.

"You weren't happy, were you?" asked Ava. Everyone had left and I had cleaned the kitchen. Ava and I were on the upper-level overlook. Below us, in the great room, sat Rachel, curled up, watching Disney's *Beauty and the Beast*, unaware we were above her.

"I was happy," I said. "Ma really enjoyed it. Kwah didn't start a fight. Harry didn't shoot anyone and the food was great. It was good to have the Wrecking Crew join us. Thanks for the banquet, for all the work." I put my arm around her.

"What about us, Josh? I've waited for you to soften. What's going to happen to *us*?"

I carried Rachel to her bed and covered her. I sat in Summer's bedroom chair, looking out the window at the night sky, listening to her uneven breathing, purposefully not looking at the box of Summer's memorabilia. Rachel was avoiding conversation, as if words might hurt. Now she stirred, perhaps wanting to speak to her momma, perhaps because she wished to be alone. I spoke softly.

"You're very brave, Rachel. I think life's about only one thing: people caring about us. You haven't had much of that since your mother died. What you've done without it is remarkable. You are so strong. But now, I figure, you got two things pulling on you.

"One says you should take chances, do things on impulse, follow your feelings, and get hurt. The other wants you to be smart and let people care for you." I smoothed the blanket, touching the silk of its border that Summer had always liked. Rachel's eyelashes blinked wetly. "Sweet dreams, honey."

66

THE WOMAN IN RED

Isaac Krakow, Diane Richardson, Patti Kelly, and I were eating a late lunch at A Shot of Class. I looked out the window at the steps of the great gray eminence of the Cathedral of the Holy Sacrament, massive and unmoving. I paid the bill and said I wanted to be alone.

My heels echoed inside the cool, dark, and medieval sanctuary, a home for Old World monks and modern moles, the bright sun filtering in brilliantly hued shards through tall glassworks. Worshippers were dotted in singleton patterns through the long, hard military ranks of dark hardwood pews. Bright, flickering votive candles lined the west wall.

I used to pray fervently to God for Summer's life in every church I passed. Now I was a round peg in a right-angled place. I sat on a hard, unforgiving bench, letting memories and random thoughts play. A dramatically obese man sat near me, creaking the old wood. He wore a faded brown suit over small rounded shoulders and an immensely bloated waist.

The man Tommy Conover punched the night of the Incident was overweight. Tom had been at A Shot of Class. Tommy's favorite hangout.

Back then, on a Friday, he'd be drinking with pretty women. Women with good chests, long pasts, and bad luck. When he drank, he became romantic and combative. To impress a woman while his judgment was impaired by martinis, he'd eagerly rescue a damsel in distress on the mall. I hurried to the Department.

Thomas Andrew Conover III's arrest report, filed by Sergeant Billy McManus's partner, was in Non-File records. In the report's witness boxes were the Woman in Red, the Obese Man, and the Screaming Damsel, whose cries were loud enough to be heard by drinkers in the café and Sergeant Billy McManus inside his cruiser.

Their names: Cherie Kerr, Kimmie Brooke, and Jeffrey Samuels. A business owner, a software engineer, and a music teacher. In the midst of prosecution, large Mr. Samuels had abruptly refused to prosecute Conover for bashing the daylights out of him. His attorney had written the chief of police, threatening an embarrassing civil action if the cops did not stop pressuring his client to press charges. The file had been quietly closed.

I called up full NACs, National Agency Checks. All three had Bay Area domiciles and none had criminal records. I checked with River City dental surgeons. No luck. I tried Bay Area dental surgeons and also struck out. I tried face and neck surgeons in both regions.

"Sure, I remember Mr. Samuels. We were in surgery all morning," said the cutter. "A mandibular fracture. His injuries would've been a lot worse, but get this—he was wearing a boxer's mouthpiece when he got mugged! Like he knew it was coming! Samuels is huge, but the mugger knew how to knock out a guy. It was like a professional blow."

The IRS was a help; each of the three parties of the Incident had gotten W-2s from the same organization: the American Conservatory Theater in San Francisco. Kerr, Brooke, and Samuels—Red Dress, Screaming Damsel, and Obese Man— were part-time actors.

Cherie Kerr came into the world via the Children's Hospital in Columbus, Ohio, as Cherie Belle Shannon DiPietro, marrying a Mr. Kerr. Now in her thirties, she was a producer, an actress, a speech coach, and the author of a memoir and books on humor, drama, and public speaking.

Her parents had died in a car crash when she was very young.

When she was four, she had been adopted by a young, childless couple in California. Her adoptive father was a new lawyer, working as a deputy district attorney.

His name was Jay Wendell Nobis.

67

PAYBACK

The office was redone in bright antique white. I had stood here in the dark while Tommy Conover struggled with bad PR, a mediocre crossword puzzle, and a six-letter word that began with d. Brittle autumn sunlight gleamed on the silver coffee service. The DA was at his desk.

"Hello, Mr. Jin. A fine morning. The heat's abated and wind's softened. How are you?"

"Couldn't be better. Mr. District Attorney, I apologize for my disloyalty."

Mr. Nobis opened his cigar box, inhaling. "Ironic, isn't it? You took the high moral ground with Tommy Conover, urging him to apologize for battering a cop. But you never apologized to me for supporting Tommy against my incumbency. You cost me Chinatown."

"Proving that the Greeks weren't the only ones to explore irony."

"And you're too smart to think an apology will get your bureau back. So I accept." He shut the box. "And now I apologize to you. Josh, I was hurt when many good deputies turned against me, four years ago. I was surprised how much it hurt that *you* turned with them. You were just starting out, but I thought we had a special understanding. You and I know that people can do inappropriate things when their feelings are hurt. Like not intervening when Fin Maxwell turned on you. I could've helped. I felt sorry for you as you dangled in the breeze."

"And pleasure, when you set up Tom Conover on the mall."

A hint of a curled brow. "Do you wish to explain that?"

"I remember that night. There was a warm night wind. Your daughter, Cherie, went to A Shot of Class in a hot red dress, and Tommy was holding court for drinkers of the grape.

"Cherie's drama buddy, Kimmie Brooke, in a short white dress, gave a classic Wes Craven scream on the mall. Jeff Samuels, a big guy not likely to get hurt, a fellow actor, yelled at Kimmie. Kimmie kept screaming. It was a recipe for a Conover castastrophe."

I opened Jay Wendell's cigar box and removed a cigar.

"Tommy went onto the mall and broke Mr. Samuels's jaw—but no teeth—he was wearing a mouthpiece, prepared for what he thought would be the worst. Cherie didn't have to call the cops—they, by happenstance, were already there. And the election was settled when Sergeant McManus showed up, and Tom belted him without saying he was sorry.

"I know Tom met your daughter, but I guess it was well before she went to college. I guess she grew up a lot, and he didn't recognize her."

His eyes twinkled, proud of his thespian girl.

"Mr. Nobis, what you did was wrong, but it wasn't illegal. It was immoral, but it was also almost funny. A political hoot, a payback. I owed you a debt. You collected. My convicting a then—apparently—innocent Chico Moody gave you the election. And it didn't help when Moody issued a jailhouse statement that he had given campaign money to Conover."

Mr. Nobis sat back. "And you got what you wanted. Judge Finley Maxwell." The former Judge Maxwell was now a struggling personal injury lawyer in the High Sierras, hanging out in emergency rooms and warming his soul for a hot space in the hereafter.

A glance at his watch. "Mr. Jin, allow me to join you for Moody's sentencing. The press will be there and I feel the obligation to take immediate public credit for your good work."

I smiled. "I'd be honored. Next week, join me for Joel Frost and Thackery Niles. I think they'll get upper terms." Judge Niles was being sentenced in Alameda County; Capital judges had been recused—excused for conflict—because Niles was a fellow jurist, a colleague.

Mr. Nobis adjusted his tie. He was older and more sedate, resembling his dark, solid, cherrywood furniture. He fit his office, this place, its gravity, its heavy work.

"Josh, I hear you're very good with kids. I have a downtown trial slot in SACA for you."

He took the cigar from my hand and slipped it in my pocket. "Welcome home."

Epilogue

Families filed into the Davis Community Church for Christmas Eve services. Smaller children held hands with older siblings as the combined adult and children's choirs sang carols that penetrated the church walls to thinly fill the night air.

A month ago, Rachel left. There was no note.

I posted mass bulletins for a runaway teen and put her name into the National Missing Children's Center computer. Harry Bilinski and I searched for her, flushing West Sac and chasing Greyhounds to San Francisco, Chico, Eureka, Reno, Portland, Seattle, Toronto. I needed to know that she was all right, so we focused on the worst places. Harry enjoyed rousting chickenhawks, but not being able to find her was making him sick. He took most of his concerns out on me as North America sprawled ominously and fruitlessly in all directions.

In the United States and Canada, six hundred thousand kids were in the six-billion-dollar-a-year child sex industry, perishing before they died. From Victoria, I phoned Dr. Teo Sandoval, the shrink at the Med Center who had offered me therapy. "Why'd she leave?" I asked.

"I would guess, fear of abandonment."

"By *us*?" I asked.

"I'm afraid so. Children who are conditioned to it expect it. They work for it, even when they're accepted. I think she left before you could reject her, not knowing you wouldn't."

I was quiet for a while. "Might she come back?"

"Unlikely. But you might frequent her favorite haunts. Sometimes they come back."

When Harry and I returned, Ava was gone. She had left a note.

Josh. Want a last chance? Call before Christmas. Ava.

Every weekend I came to the Farmer's Market, Rachel's favorite spot. Now, across the vacant field, in the church, the congregation sang "Silver Bells," and I was engulfed by a warm wave of *ren*, human feeling. Jodie and Spango, Moody's dog, looked at me expectantly from hopelessly intertwined leashes.

The high winter moon was full and bright. According to legend, it was there that *yin*, the spirit of girls and women and of emotion itself, was born. The night was silent and still. There was no wind. Clouds seemed to softly embrace and kiss a placid moon.

It was not up to me if I was to be a father. I already was and had never ceased being. First Summer, and then Rachel, had seen to that. In the wake of her sad flight from the blow we would never deliver, I saw how Rachel Farr had healed me, grown me, fortified me. You were sent to save me, more than I was here to help you. Thanks, I said. Now come home.

A final pass around the park, the dogs pulling as if they had never been here before.

They curled up in their soft beds. I was in Rachel's room, looking at the small chest that had been Summer's. I pulled it from the closet and set it on the bed. Inside, among the dress-up clothes, the horse collection, and poetry journals, were her frayed pink blankie and her favorite stuffed toy giraffe from infancy. I touched them, held them, smelled them, clutched them for the games she never finished, the seasons she never saw, the romance she never knew. I exhaled her disappointment for knowing that her once-warm father had become a distant man, frightened by the things that had sustained her.

Showering, remembering my daughter, I recalled her mother.

Her face, her body, her scent. Her skin was of the sea, an instrument of song, a beautiful lyre of endless chords, lost and distant over an unachievable horizon. I thought of Harry Bilinski and Rachel Farr, and I leaned against the shower wall, not wishing to be so alone.

I was flanked by polite drivers aware of the majesty of the evening. Sacramento was alight with brilliant decorations, its majestic towering shade trees draped in twinkling lights.

A parking place presented itself. Ava's apartment window was framed in small white Tivoli lights. Cars and bright music—a party. Her door held an immense wreath, suitable for a fair-sized family. I stood, listening to the music and the murmur of the crowd. I left and drove away. I stopped. I made a U-turn. A couple walking their dog huddled closer to each other.

I knocked, vibrating the wreath.

The door opened and she drew in air, sharply.

Her eyes were bright, guarded, wonderful, deep.

"Hi," I said honestly.

A slight frown. "I'm sorry. I thought you knew. I only see married men."

"That's okay. I'm married. And I love my wife, and all her children." I looked in her eyes. "I love you. I know you have a party going, but I was wondering if you'd join me at church?"

She took a breath in a manner I knew. She smiled deeply in the light of a cloudless Chinese moon. She touched my face so gently I may have only imagined it. Perhaps I cried.

I remember her words. I always will. "Honey, I'd love to."

And my arms were around her, her always-cool nose in my warm neck. I thought of an old saying of my people. *Chi de ku zhong ku fang zhi tian shang tian.*

After suffering, one knows happiness.

**Don't miss these thrilling novels
by Gus Lee:**

HONOR AND DUTY

"MASTERFUL."—AMY TAN

Kai Ting knows what it means to become an American and lose all that is Chinese. It happened to his father, a former officer in Chiang Kai-shek's army who never came to terms with his new life in the United States. Now, as a West Point cadet in the 1960s, Kai has a golden chance both to retain his heritage and to become undeniably, gloriously American.

But the Point has dangerous preconceptions about Asians, especially as the war in Vietnam escalates. Kai walks on a razor's edge . . . and falls into the dark pit of a cheating scandal. Suddenly he must learn a new tribal behavior, a new etiquette. And his very survival depends on learning it fast. . . .

"SUPERB."—*Chicago Tribune*

HONOR AND DUTY
by Gus Lee

**Published by The Ballantine Publishing Group.
Available in your local bookstore.**

TIGER'S TAIL

"REMARKABLE."—*Philadelphia Inquirer*

A career officer trained at West Point. The number-one son of a hardworking Chinese family. A soldier still tormented by his tour of duty in Vietnam. Jackson Kan is a man caught in the middle of clashing worlds. Now Kan is bound for Asia once again, this time to the volatile demilitarized zone between North and South Korea. His objective is to track down a missing American investigator, also his closest friend. But in fact Kan has no idea of the enormity—and the danger—of the mission that awaits him.

"IRRESISTIBLE."
—*San Francisco Examiner & Chronicle*

TIGER'S TAIL
by Gus Lee

Published by The Ballantine Publishing Group.
Available in your local bookstore.